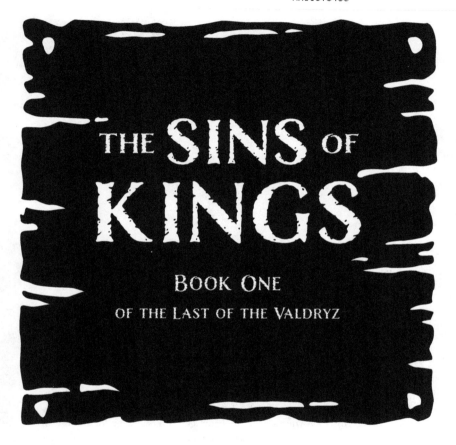

THE SINS OF KINGS

BOOK ONE
OF THE LAST OF THE VALDRYZ

By Daniel Thomas Valente

BARRENTE
PUBLISHING

This is a work of fiction. Names, characters, places, and incidents either are the product of the author's imagination or are used fictitiously. Any resemblance to actual persons, living or dead, events, or locales is entirely coincidental.

THE SINS OF KINGS: BOOK ONE OF THE LAST OF THE VALDRYZ

Book design by Alejandro Colucci
Map by Leon Richter

Copyright © 2023 by Daniel Thomas Valente

All rights reserved. No part of this book may be reproduced or used in any manner without written permission of the copyright owner except for the use of quotations in a book review. For more information, address: d.thomas.valente@gmail.com.

A Barrente Publishing Book
Published by Barrente Publishing

First paperback edition October 24th, 2023

ISBN: 979-8-9886475-1-5 (paperback)
ISBN: 979-8-9886475-2-2 (hardback)
ISBN: 979-8-9886475-0-8 (ebook)

For Claudia

*Without your love and patience,
none of this would be possible*

I'll be in the garage

Acknowledgements

If they say it takes a village to raise a child, I have found it takes the Wide-World to raise a novel. I would like to thank, first and foremost, every single person who took a chance by reading this book. A self-published author is as close to a struggling punk or metal band that the literary world has. My most sincere gratitude is extended to those who might tell a friend about this story, or take the time to leave a review on any website that will allow one. It sounds incredibly self-serving to say, but you, the reader, are the Samwise Gamgee to an author's Frodo…and we all know who the real hero is.

I must also give a colossal thank you to my editor, Britta Jensen. As much as I hated changing anything about my *perfect* story, it would not be what it is without your stern—yet kind—advice. To my proofreader, Rachel Carter, thank you for every tweak and nudge you either added or removed. I would be remiss if I did not thank the following: Jonathan Oliver, your advice was without equal. Deborah Murrell, you helped me see things that may have otherwise been clouded. Katherine D. Graham, you gave Darrin legs when he needed it the most. Lastly, I owe a debt of gratitude to my Beta Readers: Silvia Villalobos, Patrick Sweet, Bettina Luna, Ricbre, Matthew, Joanna Alana at Kindled Quill, and Mario G. at booksarelife.

Contents

Chapter One: Darrin
The Eyes of the Forest 1

Chapter Two: Edlen
The Executioner's Lament 17

Chapter Three: Rhen
The Giant and the Pedagogue 39

Chapter Four: Aldir
The Iron Woman 55

Chapter Five: Everly
Before the Tournament 76

Chapter Six: Darrin
The Great Wheel 91

Chapter Seven: Edlen
Lost and Afraid 110

Chapter Eight: Aldir
The Hall of Glory 130

Chapter Nine: Everly
The Timid Wolf 155

Chapter Ten: Rhen
The Dark Journey   166

Chapter Eleven: Darrin
The Primacy's Chamber   175

Chapter Twelve: Edlen
The Voice Underground   188

Chapter Thirteen: Everly
The Missing Giant   200

Chapter Fourteen: Aldir
Gods and Demons   213

Chapter Fifteen: Rhen
The Cage Opens   227

Chapter Sixteen: Darrin
The Morning Run   237

Chapter Seventeen: Aldir
The Sins of Kings   241

Chapter Eighteen: Darrin
The Mermaid's Kiss   257

Chapter Nineteen: Everly
The Glory of Youth   270

Chapter Twenty: Aldir
The Rising Tide   275

Chapter Twenty-One: Darrin
The Greathouse of Straten   288

Chapter Twenty-Two: Rhen
The King you are Meant to Be   302

Chapter Twenty-Three: Everly
After Death   309

Chapter Twenty-Four: Edlen
The Girl in the Walls   312

Chapter Twenty-Five: Darrin
The Empty Fortress   328

Chapter Twenty-Six: Edlen
The Blank Page   337

Chapter Twenty-Seven: Everly
The Queen   345

Chapter Twenty-Eight: Darrin
The Two Rovers   360

Chapter Twenty-Nine: Rhen
The Coursleess Sea   371

Chapter Thirty: Aldir
The Third is for Truth   379

Chapter Thirty-One: Darrin
The Akkuladine   402

Twenty Years Prior   421

CHAPTER

DARRIN

The Eyes of the Forest

Two severed legs stood upright in their boots. At least that was what Darrin Cantlay thought he saw.

"Come! Look at this!" Darrin called back to his two companions. He squinted, his amber eyes narrowing in an attempt to focus on the strange sight. Sweat dripped from his mop of curly black hair down his tawny forehead. He sighed.

Without waiting for their response, he dismounted from his piebald charger and strode towards a fallen oak that barred their path. The ground, still slick with mud from last week's storm, proved a danger of its own. Though he wore heavy black boots, his feet nearly slid out from underneath him, and had he not caught himself just in time, he would have slammed into the forest floor.

He steadied himself, hoping his fellow rovers hadn't noticed his lack of footing. *Bart would never let me live that down*, he thought. The last thing he wanted was for that lowborn arse to have anything *else* to tease him over.

More cautious than before, Darrin reached the fallen oak and peered over the top of it. *Still too far away*. He would have to climb over the massive tree in order to be certain the severed legs weren't some trick of the forest.

His mother had told him stories of Nauringale Forest when he was a child; tales of wild beasts hunting lost travelers, shadowy figures changing once well-known paths, and blood-thirsty monsters feasting on unsuspecting victims. He had never believed her, though. Well…maybe he half believed her.

As Darrin leaned against the oak awaiting the others, the day was turning to dusk. He glanced at the bruised pink sky and wondered if he shouldn't have heeded his mother's words more carefully. He glanced nervously over his shoulder.

Haron Ridgefront, Chief Rover of the Eyes of the Forest, cantered slowly upon a dappled-grey destrier almost the same color as his hair. His rough-hewn face may have once been called pale, but the years he'd spent patrolling the forest had turned it near as tan as Darrin's. "Probably more *huge* bear tracks," he snorted in his gruff northern accent.

"Can't be a blood drinker's bracer," added Bart, who was trailing behind his chief; the pimples on his ruddy face were close to bursting. "Tinny found one of those two days ago." He removed a weather-beaten glove and scratched at his cheek with dirty hands.

Darrin bristled at being called *Tinny*. Bad enough that the other Eyes had taken to calling him *Tin Horse* after he naively boasted to his instructor of his wish to be the next Iron Horse, but Bart—that foul smelling son of a tanner—had no right to refer to him as *Tinny*.

"It's neither." Darrin gnashed his teeth. *And if you call me Tinny again, I'll show you my iron.* He clenched the sword hanging from his belt. *Then we will see if I am a Tin Horse.*

"Ain't but a fallen tree, lad," said Haron, his bristly gray eyebrows arched in concern. "Will is gonna 'ave a right bugger a' this mess when his woodcutters come through." He leapt off his horse, his travel-stained leather boots sloshing in the mud. He took two steps and placed a gloved hand on Darrin's shoulder. "Aye, it's big. But a lordling like you should 'ave no trouble jumping it."

Darrin stared back, exasperated. Blood rushed to his cheeks, turning his light-brown skin scarlet. Haron never missed a chance to insult his noble birth, as though being born to the lord of Redrun somehow deprived him of having any sense. But Darrin knew he'd spotted something peculiar, and regardless of his companion's mockery, he hoped they might take him seriously if he proved his use. Their commendation was needed if he wished to rise in the ranks.

He had joined the Eyes of the Forest three months ago—two days after his eighteenth birthday. Now, as he stood behind the fallen oak, he wondered if he should have listened to his father and attended lessons at the Lyceum instead of defying him to become a rover.

Damn you, Father! he thought. *You were right; I am no warrior.*

"Further down." Darrin attempted to steady his hand as he pointed at the severed legs. "Past the bloody tree! Do you see it?"

He watched Haron shade his eyes from the setting sun. Bart joined them, but before he could utter one of his lowborn jests, Haron silenced him.

"Keep quiet. I think Cantlay may 'ave found something."

Until then, Darrin had never heard Haron say a kind word about him. He smiled for the first time since leaving Elmfort.

This was his *staining* after all—his first mission after

taking the Oath of the Eyes. It was during this patrol that he was expected to depart Elmfort in a clean, beige uniform and return covered in the colors of the forest. Rovers wore these stains as a badge of honor. Haron was so stained it was impossible to believe his clothes had ever once been clean.

Darrin's gaze flicked back to the legs sticking upright in the middle of the glade like two small tree stumps. "You see those?" he asked.

"Aye," answered Haron.

Gods! It's not a trick of the forest. Darrin didn't know if he should be excited or appalled.

Haron's baleful brown eyes narrowed, and he placed his hand on the hilt of his dagger. "Best get yer blade ready, boy. You was the one to find them. Time's right you earn your *eyes.*"

"You mean…closer?" Darrin asked, the skin at the back of his neck tightening.

"No!" snapped Bart. "Run back to the Oak Gate and tell us what you see from there."

"Shut that flytrap 'o yours, Bart!" Haron said. "Pay no mind to 'im, Cantlay. He's a twat an' he knows it too." He glared at Bart then turned to Darrin. "Now, time ya go an' see if that ain't what we think it is."

Nauringale Forest was the largest in Onyris. The Pedagogues of the Lyceum in Rose Isle estimated it to be seventy-five thousand square leagues, but in that moment, the forest seemed to condense into a claustrophobic mass of roots and branches that almost appeared to be reaching out for Darrin with their grasping tendrils.

He knew this was his lot, though, and he hoped this single event might prove to his companions that he was not a child who played at being the famous knight, Sir Matthew Dorne, the Iron Horse. He was not a Tin Horse.

He scrambled over the oak, his slender frame sliding over the slick moss, then moved carefully to what he was now certain were a pair of severed legs.

Darrin heard Bart snicker, safe behind the fallen tree. "Brave soul, that one is. I can hear me mum's voice right now: 'That's why we don't climb trees, Barty, broken arms and scratched knees.'"

Darrin glanced back in time to catch Haron rapping Bart over the head. He stifled a laugh and crept forward. When he finally reached the legs, he stooped down and let out a choked gasp. His stomach roiled, hot sick lurched up his throat, and he vomited.

My first staining, he thought, *and it's my own sick.*

"Gods!" said Haron, jumping over the oak as if it were merely a branch. He reached Darrin and pulled him to his feet. "Get it together, lad."

Darrin looked up at his chief and noted how the stoic face of the older man had dimmed. He thought he saw a hint of fear creep along the creases near his eyes.

Two legs, hewn at the knee and still in their boots, stood upright. No blood on the ground and no blood on the severed limbs.

Where's the body? Darrin surveyed the glade but saw nothing else. It seemed to him that the forest grew silent, and he thought he heard Haron mumble a quiet prayer.

"What is it, Harry?" asked Bart, still standing behind the oak.

"Best come see for yourself," Haron answered.

"Safer back here." Bart ran his fingers through his stringy red hair. "Me mum says she wants me home for dinner."

"Your mum's been dead for three years," said Haron. "Now get your arse over 'ere!"

"I guess I will be seeing you tonight, Mum," murmured Bart as he attempted to climb the tree. Halfway over, his muddy boots slid on the wet moss and he fell to the ground with a thud.

And you call me a fool? Darrin smirked.

"Get up, ya twit," said Haron. "You've an eye for this sort." He lifted one of the severed legs, staring at the intricate pattern stitched into the leather.

Bart shambled towards them, covered in mud. "Hand over that foot!" But his smile disappeared as he stared at the boot.

They're both afraid… Maybe there is something more to this?

"It's the Wheel, Harry," whispered Bart. "The Great Wheel…ya see it? This is a Graymere's boot." He pointed at a detailed etching of a giant wheel with many spokes, all bleeding into trails that ended in stars, suns, and moons.

"A Graymere?" asked Darrin as he eyed the supple leather and tried to find an answer for why one of the royal family's legs would be in the middle of the forest.

"Aye, I think it might be. But these legs is new dead," Bart said. "Old dead is all pale and blue—or maybe yellow, like Harry's armpits."

Haron scowled. "His Grace and the prince were 'ere only a fortnight ago. Came to watch your batch receive their honors." He looked at Darrin then back to Bart. "'Ow new is this dead, Barty?"

Darrin recognized the soft grin that pulled at the corners of Bart's lips; it was the same smile he wore when Haron praised him earlier. Bart was the son of a tanner, and his years apprenticing for his father gave him insight into the colors and textures of skin.

"By color alone," Bart started, "I'd say one day cut—not over two at most. Look at this..."

But Darrin did not want to look anymore. He felt the hot sick rise in his throat again. *How can they look at this carnage so dispassionately? Is Bart enjoying this?*

Bart pulled the boot away from the leg. "This ain't an old man's leg, mind you." He pressed his gloved finger deep into the dead flesh. "It ain't all speckled and saggy yet. This ain't the king's legs. It belongs to a man thirty to forty years old. My guess is the prince."

Prince Odain? Darrin recalled an adage his father was fond of reciting. *Scratch a king and you will lose your head. Kill a king...and you will wear his crown.* He grew quiet, wondering if this was a declaration of war they had stumbled upon.

Bart glanced at the others and laughed. "Belonged to, I mean. This poor bugger ain't walking this off. And these boots—" He rubbed the leather almost tenderly. "These are castle quality. No tanner outside of Rothspire can do this... 'cept maybe me dad."

"Who'd be fool enough to kill a Graymere?" asked Haron as he stared at the stump.

A name came to Darrin, and before he could stop himself, he blurted out, "The Voress Ní?"

The Voress Ní were a rumor. A hushed name he remembered from his mother's stories. According to her, they were a mysterious organization of councilors, lords, and criminals referred to as the *Shadow Kings*—when referred to at all.

Bart and Haron both laughed.

"Aye, and maybe Naught itself cut this poor bastard's leg

off with the Blade of Darkness," said Bart, his beady eyes taunting Darrin.

Haron smirked but cuffed Bart's ear. "Don't go saying that name aloud, ya fool." Ten more creases seemed to materialize on his already-leathery face.

"My father says the Voress Ní are still active," started Darrin. "They rule over the Vines in secret, operating in the shadows of the lands by the Redwater Sea." He knew the others wouldn't believe him, but that didn't make his theory untrue.

"And your father is a middling lord of a bankrupt and decrepit holdfast." Haron's face grew stern. "*Lord Phillip Cantlay* says what he must to excuse his debts to His Grace."

Angered, Darrin glared at his chief but held his tongue. There was nothing he could say if he still wished to be a rover after today.

"Aye, but I hold you to no account for your father's folly, my lad." Haron softened and ruffled Darrin's hair. "Mine was a gambler and a drunk. Suppose we should both be glad we're rovers now."

Darrin shrugged from his chief's touch.

Hearing his father's name aloud reminded him of their awful parting. He had walked away from the lordship of Redrun, renouncing any future claim to the lands he once called home. His heart ached at the memory, though more from his mother's tears than his father's angry words.

Darrin pushed the thought aside and stared at the legs. "Do we take them back to Hadley?"

"The captain is back at Elmfort, boy, fifty miles away." Haron pulled off his grass-stained cloak. "There's an outpost not five leagues away to the south where we can get ourselves some fresh horses and a hot meal…and maybe some cold ale. We'll 'ave one of their boys ride back out to Elmfort with these. Let Hadley and the stewards suss this out."

We were the ones to find them, so shouldn't we see this through? Darrin knew better than to question his chief again, but if the legs belonged to the Prince of Onyris, perhaps it wouldn't be wise to entrust them to strangers. "Haron, maybe we should—"

"Listen to your chief?" Haron scowled at Darrin then motioned to Bart. "Get our mounts round that tree, Barty. It's getting dark, and I want to put as much mud between us and this accursed place as possible."

Just then Darrin realized something none of them had caught earlier. "Mud! Why are there no footprints in the mud? How did we not notice this?" he shouted, no longer worried about Haron's rebukes. He took slow deliberate steps, inspecting the ground.

"He's lost his wits," said Bart. "Damned fool."

"You're the only fool I see," said Haron. "Cantlay is an Eye for certain."

"There are no prints." Darrin felt more astonished than worried. "We've been riding through mud since we set out, but there's not a print here other than ours."

Haron nodded.

"You said, one, maybe two days since these legs were cut, is that right, Bart?" asked Darrin.

"Could be three," said Bart.

"Not more than a week, though?" asked Darrin. "Can you be certain?"

"Well…not a chance it's over a week." Bart studied the boots. "Now, I'm not me father—he could tell ya down to the hour." His thin lips sagged into a frown. "I'm not as good as him, but I can say these ain't been here over four, five days at the most."

From one day to five, thought Darrin. *But still...the storm was only seven days past.*

"Where are the prints?" Darrin asked. "There are none leading up to this place, and none leading away. If these were put here five days ago, there'd still be prints in the mud. Men leave prints. But…"

"What if a hawk—" Bart wiped at the oily strands of red hair that fell over his eyes— "dropped 'em from its beak?"

"These'd be half a stone each at the least," said Haron, his crooked nose twitching. "There ain't no bloody bird flying round with fourteen pounds of flesh in all the Wide-World." He draped his cloak around the legs and lifted them up.

"Haron is right," said Darrin. "*Someone* placed them here."

But why? Why had someone placed a Graymere's severed feet here? Or why would someone want us to believe they're a Graymere's? Maybe the Voress Ní are sending a message? "We need to alert the king."

"Best get going, and now," commanded Haron. "The sun is almost gone; I don't want us here come nightfall."

"Just a few more minutes," Darrin urged, forgetting his rank.

"That's an order, boy! You got eyes but no brains." Haron's face twisted into a veil of rage. "I'm Chief Rover, not you. And I say we leave. Now!"

"Aye!" As discouraged as Darrin was to end his investigation, Haron's anger terrified him more. He snapped out of his thoughts and repeated his compliance.

Bart struggled round the oak with their horses. The animals had caught wind of something that set them at unease, and they grew fey as they approached Haron holding the severed legs.

"Steady now, steady," said Bart as he yanked at their bridles. "I don't think they're loving this stretch of road."

"Me neither." Haron leapt atop his charger. "Now, mount up!"

Beyond the path came a crashing noise that exploded from behind the fallen tree. A murder of crows screamed into the dusk. The rovers jerked their heads at the loud crack of heavy branches.

Haron Ridgefront turned quickly on his destrier, steel bared. "Ride, you fools! Ride like death!" His voice boomed like a war horn.

Darrin's charger bolted before he could mount. He struggled to run alongside it, one hand clutching tight to the pommel, his lungs searing with every breath he took. He could not do this for long. His heart would burst, his arm would break, or he might fall, trampled under heavy hooves.

Gods! Save me! He managed to get his foot into a stirrup, and with all of his remaining strength, he pulled himself up into the saddle just in time to look behind him.

A bear reared up, standing at least twelve feet tall. Its teeth were daggers, its eyes glowing black and red.

He knew he should have listened to his mother's tales. Had he not been atop his horse, he would have stood frozen in fear. *I'm going to die on my first roving...*

Wet with blood and mud, the creature roared. The sound was the most terrifying thing Darrin had ever heard. Worried his ears might bleed, he released his reins and covered them.

Haron turned his horse and whirled upon the beast—his blade glinting in the moonlight. But just as he approached it, five gruesome claws slammed into his chest and hurled him to the forest floor.

"Haron!" shouted Darrin. He didn't know what to do, but his charger neighed wildly and raced off into the forest.

The bear moved like a black leopard as it turned from Haron and darted towards Bart. Slower than Darrin to mount his red warhorse, Bart screamed.

The bear roared again and charged.

Bart pulled tight on his reins, spinning so quickly that Darrin was certain the destrier's legs would break, but they didn't. He took off like a bowshot into the thick cover of pine trees.

The heavy thudding of the bear's paws in the mud grew closer to Darrin, but he dared not look behind him. If he were to survive this, he must keep his wits about him.

Haron must be dead, he thought. *If his neck didn't snap then for a certainty his legs shattered.* Darrin pushed his horse forward. *And now Bart is gone too.*

Low-hanging branches slapped against Darrin's face, leaving bloody welts and lashes, the pain a mere annoyance. The sound of his horse's hooves stamped out all other noise.

Haron said there was a village five leagues from here. He ducked his head and held tight to his galloping charger. *Can I make it that far? Not at this pace. My horse will collapse if I keep at this run.*

He chanced a quick glance behind him. The bear was nowhere to be seen. The sound of its footfalls had vanished. *Did it give up?*

He slowed to a canter and scanned the forest. Night had fallen during the chase and he had to squint in order to see anything. His senses sharpened slightly, and when he could finally think straight, one singular thought filled his mind. *Haron!*

He stopped riding and took a breath. *I must go back for him.* A single line of the Oath of the Eyes came to him: *Rovers do not leave their own to die in the forest.* He would not have it said that Darrin Cantlay broke his word...even if it meant his death.

He turned to the side of the path and rode a few yards into the overgrowth, taking a cautious sip from his water skin but stopping himself from drinking any more than absolutely necessary. *I must save some for Haron.*

A soft voice came from the edge of the forest.

"Tinny?"

Darrin gazed into the dark overgrowth, certain he recognized the voice. "Bart?" he answered quietly. "Bart, where are you?"

"Oi! Sweet Gods!" Bart rode out from the cover of the woods. "What in the name of All was that?"

Relief washed over him. Bart was alive. He never thought he'd be happy to hear that voice again. "How?" was all Darrin could ask.

"Gave it the slip, Tinny. It looked glad enough to 'ave you!" said Bart as he neared him, but Darrin noted the terror behind the jest.

They rode together, branches crowded over their heads as the forest grew closer and thicker. Away from the path now, it was as though they'd wandered into a world of suffocating darkness. Darrin walked his horse carefully over a twisted root that sprang from the ground like greedy fingers.

"Haron..." Darrin's voice was a rasp.

"Aye...he's dead, ain't he?" asked Bart. "Or at least, will be dead."

"Aye." Darrin shuddered. "But a rover does not leave the fallen. We have to go back."

"Back?" exclaimed Bart. "There ain't no back now, Tinny. That thing! It's still out there. Me mum ain't ever told stories of a beast like that!"

"Your mum isn't a rover, though, is she? Is she stained like old Haron?"

"She's stained, alright. But no, she ain't like Harry." Bart hung his head.

"He might still be alive…"

"Did ya see that thing?" asked Bart.

"I'm going back for him." Darrin reached for the sword at his belt. *The Iron Horse would never turn aside from a companion.*

"Aye, and maybe I ride for that outpost ole Harry mentioned," said Bart. "I'd rather 'ave a meal than be one."

Darrin stared at Bart. Darkness shaded his face, but his eyes burned with disgust. "You can go where you like, but a rover who abandons his companion is no rover of the Eyes of the Forest." With that, he turned around and made his way back to the path.

"And a rover ain't a warrior…" Darrin heard Bart mumble as he disappeared into the forest.

Darrin neared the spot where the bear had attacked them. He tightened his fists and took a sharp breath. "Haron," he whispered. His charger's footfalls were the only response.

"Cantlay…" a muffled curse answered.

"Haron?"

In front of the giant oak that blocked the path lay Haron's horse, crumpled and broken, its neck snapped.

Darrin dismounted, tying off his charger. "Haron? I've come back for you."

Where is the old bastard?

"You're a bigger fool than Bart," said Haron, his voice no more than a gasp. "I told you to ride."

"The Eyes do not leave a companion behind."

"Stout-hearted fool," Haron spat.

Darrin crawled over the oak to find his chief slumped against the tree, blood dripping from his mouth.

Gods! Darrin bent down and placed his hand on Haron's shoulder. "Here, let me help you up. I'll take you back to Elmfort."

Haron laughed, and as he did more blood spewed down his chin. "I'm done for, Cantlay. Leave me, save your skin."

Haron's legs were a tangled mess. One had bent almost completely behind him and the other was shattered—bone protruding from the shin. His left arm dangled from the shoulder; blood pooled around him.

"I cannot leave you to be this beast's dinner," said Darrin.

"It'll come back," Haron murmured. "And best it have only one Eye to feast on...not two."

"Three Eyes!" Bart rode forward from the forest, sitting nervously upon his steed, and looked down at them. "A three-eyed meal is one for legend."

A figure cloaked in brown and green approached them, birthed from the forest itself. Its voice was a soft hum—the sound of wind in the reeds—and hollow, yet musical. "The beast shall trouble you no more. Come with me! Your trials are at an end."

The rovers stared up in fright. The sudden appearance of another presence made Darrin step back. He tried to speak, but his voice turned dry in his throat. Unable to make out the shape of the figure, he squinted.

A man towered over them. Eight feet tall—but no, it had

shrunk into a bent old hermit who stood no taller than a child.

It vanished, but its soft voice—the passing of a whisper—rustled through the leaves like wind.

"This way…"

CHAPTER

EDLEN

The Executioner's Lament

EDLEN GRAYMERE SPUN a small astrolabe between her fingers absentmindedly as she gazed out of her grandfather's window. Far below the tower lay the tourney field. She stared down, imagining the ringing sounds of steel on steel, the thunderous footfalls of warhorses and the shouts of mail-clad knights.

One day I'll be down there, she told herself. *Right in the thick of things.* Her revelry was short-lived, however, as the deliberate coughing of her grandfather reminded her of her lessons.

Forced from her fantasies, she dropped the astrolabe. It shattered on the stone floor with a clang.

"Just missed the bloody rug…" she muttered. *That's my luck, though.* She knelt to pick up the pieces and looked up at her grandfather, ready to apologize.

"Leave it, leave it now." Laustair rose from his high-backed chair, glowering at her.

Shame-faced, Edlen continued to collect the debris, certain her grandfather would devise some unique punishment for this. Her thick, jet-black hair draped her pale face like a raven's wing. Deep-blue eyes, which normally gleamed like summer sun on the Rosewater, shaded over with a mist of gray.

"I told you to leave it!" Laustair stood over her, imposing and stern. He wore long gray robes—stained and blotchy—that housed a world of muted colors within roughly stitched wool. A white beard hung from his face, pulling the skin around his mouth into a disconsolate frown. His eyes, though, held no hint of his untellable age; they flashed brown and gray like burning coal.

"Had you been paying attention to your lecture, you would not have broken an irreplaceable tool, made many hundreds of years before your father cursed me with you." He glared implacably before a wide smile broke his lips.

"Grandfather?" asked Edlen, unsure how to respond. The old man had a tendency to tease her, but to say he was *cursed* with her? Perhaps she had truly offended him. She studied his face then anxiously grabbed at the pieces of the broken mariner's tool, setting them in a neat pile on the floor.

The smile on her grandfather's lips gave way to a hearty laugh. He knelt down to pick up the debris. "It is nothing but a bauble, dear girl. A trinket I purchased in the Great Wheel; it holds no value. And even less now." He laughed again—a warm, contagious laugh.

Edlen smiled, her nervousness transforming into relief. Perhaps there would be no punishment. Still, she rambled an excuse. "I'm sorry, but Old Tulk, the stableman, was bringing horses out for the tournament, and a few have run off." She giggled. "Now he's hobbling after them. Look for yourself."

"Horses run and men chase after them. Men run and other men chase after them. It is a tale as old as all the lives of horses and men," her grandfather said without even a glance to the window.

Edlen stared up at him and tried to riddle out the meaning of his words.

Laustair was her mother's father, and though Edlen's mother died sixteen years ago, just after her birth, her grandfather had been her tutor for as long as she could remember.

It was difficult to tell if a person aged when you spent every day with them, but Edlen believed it near impossible for anyone to be older than her wizened grandfather. Though she loved him dearly, she feared his admonishments. And it seemed to her, she earned more of these chastisements daily.

Laustair placed his hand on Edlen's shoulder. "*Old Ian Tulk* possesses more wisdom in his little finger than some of the king's councilors can claim to have in their entire bodies." His mischievous grin brightened the deep lines on his face.

Edlen returned his smile and figured now would be the best time to ask to be dismissed from her studies. "May we continue our lesson tomorrow?" She eyed him eagerly. "Rhen is fighting in the melee today, and I promised to see him off before it begins."

Rhen was her best friend. And though he was a brocken —a descendant of the giants who walked the Wide-World in the elder days—she thought of him as a brother. They had both recently turned sixteen, but Rhen already stood near ten-feet tall. He would become the sworn Shield of Edlen's cousin, Princess Amara, on his seventeenth birthday.

"Ah..." Laustair peered down at the field. "A mighty warrior he will become one day, but I fear his strength will never match that which I empower you with."

"What strength?" Edlen snapped. The memory of the master-at-arms refusing her request to practice with live steel still gnawed at her. She had no proof, but she knew Laustair had issued that order. "You've yet to place a sword in my hand."

Laustair turned from the window, and Edlen noted his surprise. "You are willful, Edlen. Your tongue is sharp. But the sword you long to wield will never be stronger than the thoughts in your head. A sword does not unlock the mysteries of the mind."

He pointed toward an enormous row of bookcases that stood against the eastern wall of his chamber, the bracelets on his wrist clinking together. "Those tedious tomes you shirk from contain more power than an entire army. There is time ahead of you to slash and parry, but *wisdom* alone outlives such brutish tactics. Those with severed arms find it exceedingly difficult to hold the hearts of men."

"But," asked Edlen, her lips pursed, "is it not the strength of *swords* and the *victories* of heroes that protect our lands?"

"No, my dear," Laustair said and tapped the top of his head. "It is here that protects our realms. Is it the hammer that builds the castle? It is but a tool. A hammer in the hands of a fool might destroy a wall the same as build one." He stood, glanced out the window, then paced the stone chamber. "Intelligence is the means of prosperity. A sword is also but a tool. Corpses of men and women who lifted swords and axes litter the Wide-World. Children your age and younger find their throats slashed because ignorant people wield sharpened blades."

Edlen listened dutifully but wondered if her grandfather was not simply over worried for her safety. She watched as he stepped to the bookcase and studied the faded spines of countless texts crowding his shelves. *I can just as easily die from a papercut too...or boredom, if I'm forced to read one of those.*

Laustair's eyes darted up and down until he reached for an ashen gray, leather-bound script. He pulled it towards him and blew dust from its cover. "A shame," he grumbled.

Gods! That is no book, it's a bloody anchor, thought Edlen. "What is that?" *Why bother asking?* She knew. *It's my punishment.*

"It is a little light reading." Laustair turned and dropped the massive thing on the nearest table. A goblet of water wobbled before falling over when the book landed in a thunderous thud. His piercing gaze caught Edlen. "This is *The Executioner's Lament*. I expect a full report on the merit of its text at our next lesson."

Edlen inspected the cover. What at one time had no doubt been a lustrous black leather had faded into ugly gray. Though torn and frayed, the intricate inlay of a dazzling curved axe still glowed on the cover in mesmerizing mother-of-pearl. The cost of this artwork alone was more than some realms held in their entire vaults.

"It is...large," Edlen said with a hint of sarcasm.

"And irreplaceable, my lady," Laustair answered. "I suggest you treat it with slightly more care than my astrolabe."

At this, Edlen peered at the pile of broken pieces she'd set aside and cursed herself for dropping the silly thing. "But our next lesson is in three days! I won't finish this until I'm as old as you." She stared at him imploringly, her thin nose wrinkling at the thought of reading the ponderous tome.

"Best to get started soon then," Laustair replied, paying no attention to her attempt at pity. "I hold no certainty I will live long enough to see that day." He messed her hair.

"But…the tournament?" cried Edlen.

"You will be witness to many tournaments in your life. Perhaps, you will fight in one or two as well. But our lesson is in *three days* by your own admission, and I expect—"

"A full report on the merit of its text by then," said Edlen in a singsong sort of way.

"I knew you were a quick learner."

Edlen placed the book under her arm and rushed from the chamber. She bounded down the stairs and exited the tower.

Bright-blue sky stretched above Edlen as she stood in the manicured courtyard of her grandfather's tower. She squinted up at his window and noticed him gazing down at her—framed in silhouette—over a hundred feet above.

How does he climb those stairs every day? Edlen thought. *Maybe that's why he's so cranky?* Edlen strode from Laustair's tower and wandered the sprawling castle grounds of Rothspire.

Intersecting streets of worn cobblestone twisted around the miles-wide baileys of the kingdom. The scaffolding, which just yesterday had been removed from one of the older towers in the city square, was now raised against another crumbling structure on the other side of the street. A group of olive-skinned men tugged at the thickest rope Edlen had ever seen as they lifted a load of granite and quartz up to a man shouting in some strange tongue. The castle had been under some form of repair for as long she could remember. When she was a child, she'd paid little attention to the laborers, but as she grew older, she found it peculiar that her home had been crumbling around her since before her birth.

She turned her gaze from the working men and hoisted

the heft of *The Executioner's Lament* under her arm. *Perhaps I should give this to the workers—it's probably heavy enough to fortify their next build.* She smiled at her jest then stole down a narrow road and past a row of shops that led to the tourney grounds.

Smallfolk had erected canvas pavilions of all sizes around the vast field of the tournament ring; the largest of these vibrant tents shone in a brilliant patchwork of red and green, the color of the Graymere family, her family. She grimaced at the reminder of her royal family's pretentiousness but couldn't help admiring the spectacle that was unfolding.

Wagons and handcarts rolled up and down the Trail of Kings, the main thoroughfare of the realm. Some of these were filled with timber for the barriers of the tiltyard while others carried huge casks of mead or wine…or ale, Edlen's favorite.

Today's tournament was in celebration of Rothspire's five-hundred-year reign, as well as her grandfather, King Ulisaren's, seventy-fifth birthday. What extravagance might be in store today? Edlen's mind whirled at the thought. And Rhen, her own nursing-brother, was to compete!

Rhen! I promised to see him before the tournament!

In an instant, Edlen forgot about her lessons. Her only care was to uphold her promise, as she knew the big oaf would be nervous before his first melee. Perhaps a pint or two would help settle his nerves, and it would surely make the tourney more enjoyable for her as well. But she had no intention of attending the festivities as a royal.

A new thought sprang into her mind, and she wished not to waste any more time walking the crowded streets dressed in her family's colors. If she judged her time correctly, she might still have time to throw on a disguise and maybe pull a prank on Rhen.

Edlen ran, feet pounding and chest heaving, past those preparing for today's events, nearly crashing into an old serving lady. She veered out of the way to prevent herself from careening into the old woman.

"Slow your damned feet, child. Where's the bloody fire? You're a bloody Graymere, after all," the old woman shouted after her.

"I'm sorry!" Edlen responded, but she was already at least fifty yards past the grumbling woman. *I'm sure my father will hear about this.*

What she wouldn't give for anonymity. But no! When she went to her lessons with her grandfather, she had to dress like a *Graymere*.

No wonder all my family does is prance about. You can't run in silks.

She couldn't wait to rid herself of these horrid clothes. The fabric clung to her in all the wrong places, and as she sweat through them, she became immediately aware of her femininity. *If all the knights of the realm had to wear these bloody dresses, there would be no wars.* The thought made her laugh, but the chaffing in her thighs gave her pause. She slowed her pace as she approached the imposing stone walls of her family's home.

She pulled at the bunched material riding up her legs and grimaced. Two gigantic wooden doors, intricately carved with the image of the Great Wheel, stood before her. They were too heavy for her to throw open, so instead she yanked at a polished brass handle and slid through the narrow gap.

Dartsuil's Keep, the towering structure in the center of Castle Dartsuil, was named after the first king of Onyris, the man who'd founded Rothspire almost five-hundred years ago. King Dartsuil was Edlen's own blood, and a legend of staggering might and will—if all the stories her father told her were true. But she thought nothing of her sire's history as she ran headlong into the great stone keep. Her only thought was of unburdening herself of Laustair's ridiculous book and then making her way back to Rhen.

A city unto itself—one of interweaving halls and chambers—the keep was a fortress so immense and spread out that, had she not spent her life in its upper apartments, Edlen might lose herself in its labyrinthine design.

Well-versed in every feint of its zigzagging pathways, she believed herself the only one (other than Dartsuil himself) aware of its secret tunnels and hidden ladders.

She ran through an ornate antechamber of gilded moldings, polished wood, and paintings so obscenely large she felt too embarrassed to even look. As she pushed open a pair of gargantuan oak doors banded in iron, she found herself in the Hall of Glory: the huge, stale, eerie throne room of the King of Onyris.

Upon entering the hall, she glanced up at two colossal statues of King Bradain and King Berad the Vicious, her grandfathers who lived nearly two hundred years ago. Barely noting these ageless edifices, Edlen quickly spun underneath a leg of the statue of King Bradain and slipped into a small passage only she knew of.

A stone shield barred the path, but as she knew the secret needed to pass this deterrent, she traced her finger around the indented wheel and stepped into a pitch-black passageway.

Countless iron rungs placed by ancient builders crawled up the stone walls of the keep. Had she not climbed this secret ladder many times, she would never have known of their existence.

But Edlen used this ladder nearly every day and was no

longer fearful of its dizzying height. She tucked *The Executioner's Lament* down the front of her sweat-drenched silks—ensuring the book would not slip—and pressed her belly against the cold rungs.

She climbed quickly and effortlessly.

At thirty rungs, she stared down into the blackness. *Twenty more—you've got this Edlen.* Sweat dripped into her eyes as she glanced up and glimpsed the faint light that framed the secret door leading to the floor of her family's chambers.

She always wondered who originally designed this hidden path. Whether it was there for Dartsuil to escape the ghosts he believed haunted him, or simply a way to sneak whores into an ancient king's bedchambers, Edlen wondered if one of those books in Laustair's room might hold the answer.

He would just make me write an essay on the importance of architecture if I asked him about it. No, she would keep this secret. Besides, this ladder acted as a perfect means of moving about the keep without alerting her father.

The *secret* door, nothing more than a loose stone set into the base of a wall on the eighth story of the keep, was hidden tight against the floor, accessible only by crawling on her stomach.

When she exited, she found herself in an empty stretch of hall between a disused privy and an abandoned row of bedchambers.

Her family's personal guards were the only ones permitted up here, other than herself and her father, Lord Aldir.

Two guards stood sentry, blocking the entrance of both bedchambers. They bowed at her approach.

Both men, hulking figures clad in polished mail and boiled leather, would seem giants to her if she didn't spend most of her days with a ten-foot tall brocken.

Edlen smoothed out her red and green dress, aware of how she must look to the knights. She lowered her voice in a mocking tone.

"Hail," she said, pretending to reach for a sword as though she were one of their rank.

"Hail, my lady." The knights bowed, giving no indication of understanding her jest.

Edlen curtseyed then strode past them as they opened her door. She placed her hand on the tanned cheek of the shorter knight and whispered, "See no one bothers me today...not even my father." Her attempt at seduction was laughable, even to her.

He bowed his head, but Edlen noticed a slight blush fill his bronze face.

Boys are so easy... she thought to herself as she gave a practiced smile.

She slammed the door closed behind her and swept over to a cedar chest at the foot of her bed, giving no more concern for the flustered guard.

Looking down into the chest, a treasure trove of oddments greeted her.

In a jumbled motion, she shuffled broken toy swords and bric-à-brac around to make room for her grandfather's monstrous tome. The moment she was rid of her lesson she stared out her windows.

The sun shone bright outside. Any thought of spending her day behind the pages of this dense book vanished. Instead, she opened the doors of her wardrobe and stared at beautiful silk dresses from Avon Bay, fine garments gifted to her family from some lord in the Blades, and the leather boots of the Graymeres—embroidered with the sigil of the Great Wheel.

She scowled at the extravagance of the clothing. Edlen despised being a Graymere. She felt trapped by her lineage, a prisoner of privilege. Any other person might decide their future for themselves, but her path was ordained, her future foretold. She envied those of low birth. Perhaps she might become a sailor, or merchant, or blacksmith—someone who actually earned their living.

No! Edlen Graymere would be forced to sit in councils! Forced to uphold her family's name. Forced to be a thing she never asked to be.

She closed her eyes then shoved her family's clothes aside.

I may as well attend the tourney with my father's guards and wait for the heralds to sing my name.

She removed the false backing of her wardrobe, and there it was: poorly stitched and weatherworn, the dress of the commoners—her most treasured possession. Without a second thought, she stripped out of the red and green clothes of her family and put on the rough-spun brown tunic, a beaten leather belt, and stained trousers. Her boots, given to her by a blacksmith's son, were ashen gray. A color she noted was quite similar to the cover of Laustair's book.

After dragging a pale green-yellow cloak over herself, she took a moment to admire her reflection in the mirror.

If she hadn't seen herself through her own eyes, she would not have recognized the image in the glass. In no way did she resemble Edlen Graymere, the daughter of the Primacy of the Realm. Her long black hair, bound in a tight ponytail, framed a drawn and masculine face. Any remnant of womanhood had vanished. The foreign smile of a scrapper-boy smirked back at her.

Edlen was reminded of the time she wore a similar garb a few years ago that sent her father into a tizzy. Had she not claimed her name and provided information only he would recollect, she might still be in the Dark Cells of Rothspire.

This costume would suit her perfectly, but she needed to figure out a way to leave her chamber without being noticed.

She contemplated the best route to take to the tournament. There was no way she could leave through her chamber doors, especially dressed like this, without her father being notified.

My guards would not hesitate to tell my father that I went to the tournament dressed as a commoner, would they? No! I will not give them the satisfaction.

Just then, she remembered the rope she kept hidden in her wardrobe. It was nothing more than a crude grappling hook, but she fixed the iron claw into the inside of her windowsill and dropped its length down the outer wall of the keep. It had been sometime since she'd last tried this, but heights no longer frightened her. She would not be in need of rescuing this time.

The memory of clinging to the windowsill and shouting for help flittered through her mind. But she was approaching her seventeenth birthday, and that helpless ten year old girl whose fingers dug into hard stone as she wept uncontrollably seemed like a different person.

She slid down, the cold wind stinging her cheeks and her bare hands burning as she gripped the rough rope. But pain was a small price to pay for an unmarked departure.

THOUSANDS of people cluttered the courtyards and grandstands that surrounded the giant field on the western grounds. Kites of all colors danced above, proudly displaying the sigils of powerful families.

A young girl and her older brother ran past Edlen, the

flag of an Arstring's harp flying behind them. She moved aside quickly to avoid being trampled.

Today was a day of glory. Tournaments were always a welcome day of frivolity and joy, and being able to roam freely, unencumbered by the duties expected of a Graymere, made this day even more exciting.

Edlen tramped gaily from a vendor selling candied dragon eggs to a man who promised a salve that might cure any bruise. Her head swirled with the sights and sounds and smells.

A giant boar spun slowly on a spit outside of one tent—its skin crackling—while a small, brown-skinned woman poured thick sauce over it. The aroma was intoxicating.

She walked closer and asked, "When will this be ready?"

The small woman eyed her up and down, a frown appearing on her face; her dark-purple lips tightened in a grimace. "This be for the king and his lords, ya dirty scrapper. Off with ya now. There's a butcher down the way selling pigs' feet and tripe for the likes of you."

Edlen smiled, gave a courteous nod, and moved on.

Gods, it's working! She thinks I'm a scrapper.

She continued past the delicious scent of cooked onions and peppers, rainbow fish, and her favorite: roasted game hen smothered in herbs, its golden skin crisped to perfection.

The man selling the game hen stood under a sign that stated: *Five-Noles-4-a-leg*!

Edlen searched her pockets and found seven noles, and in her excitement, handed all of her silver coins to the vendor.

The man glared at her.

Edlen understood that he believed she'd stolen the coins from someone, but though he was clearly dubious of the manner in which she'd paid, he took the seven noles from her.

Edlen continued deeper into the throng of people, biting into the perfectly cooked meat, unashamed of the grease that dribbled down her chin.

She pushed through a cluster of men dressed in black and gold doublets and caught the glance of a smiling man. He separated himself from the group and waved at Edlen.

"Boy!" he called.

Edlen turned and noticed the man was dressed differently than the others. She attempted to slink away into the crowd, but the strange man dogged her.

"Boy!" He raised a gloved hand of shimmering silver silk that blended seamlessly into his deep-gray sleeves. A puppeteer's rod, sewn in sable, ran conspicuously down his chest.

"Slow down. May I have a word with you?" The man's voice was pleasant, if not cloying. His dark-gray cloak hung just above a pair of fine leather boots. He smiled, his flat nose and fat lips dragging themselves into a congenial grin that softened the sharp features of his face.

Edlen studied him. His reddish-brown hair came to a widow's peak that dipped severely into a creased forehead. He looked around forty to Edlen. She knew the colors and symbols of every prominent family in Onyris, but this sigil seemed odd. The men he had been with were obviously the Windsongs of Maresport. Everyone in Onyris knew the black and gold of their family, but Edlen had no intention of being dragged into a conversation of courtesies with them. Instead, she apologized, and affected her voice to match the speech of the smallfolk. "I meant no harm."

The man laughed, a disarming sort of laugh, well-practiced yet natural. "I see! And no harm was taken. Are you from Rothspire?"

"Aye, well, not Rothspire, my lord. From Pleasant Hill. Just down the way, off the Great Wheel." Edlen glanced around and pointed in a random direction, having no clue where Pleasant Hill actually was. She hoped the name of that town alone might excuse her from this intrusion. "What can I help you with?"

"I'm looking for someone." The man surveyed the courtyard. "What's your name?"

"My name, my lord?" asked Edlen.

"Yes, your name. I can't just keep calling you boy, can I?" He grinned and extended his hand. "Here, I'll start. My name is Tomm Harken."

"Aye, my lord," said Edlen. "Mine is Rayfield. Harris Rayfield." The name came too quickly to her tongue. Where had she heard it before?

"Well met, Master Rayfield. Perhaps you can assist me." Tomm let go of Edlen's hand. "I'm looking for Edlen Graymere, the king's granddaughter. I'm certain you are aware of her. Funny thing, though. No one here seems to know what the girl looks like, but I hear she's around your age. A youth of fifteen or sixteen? Am I near in my reckoning?"

"Spot on, my lord."

Does he recognize me? Edlen looked around distractedly. "But I've never seen her, myself. Mayhap one of these fine lords or ladies might be more helpful?" She bowed slightly. "Good luck to you, my lord."

"That's the damndest thing, Harris," said Tomm. "These bloody lords and ladies wouldn't know a royal unless their faces were tattooed red and green. Oh yes, they will curtsey and bow for certain, but most of these noble fools are more clueless than a stable hand from Whetfield." He laughed again, but this time it held none of its earlier ease.

"If you don't mind, I hope you might show me around the castle?" he said. "You look like someone who knows their way around. Perhaps we might stumble upon this mysterious lady I seek."

Does he know me? Is this some cruel jest of his? Edlen wondered.

There was not a chance.

Painters came often to Rothspire to make portraits of King Ulisaren and the other Graymeres, but her father never commissioned anything as vain as that for himself or his daughter.

Few people might be able to recognize Edlen by sight, but with how she was dressed today, she'd hoped no one would look too closely.

Who was this man? And why would someone who kept the company of the Windsongs wish to speak with one of the smallfolk—let alone request one to escort him?

"Aye, my lord, it would be my pleasure," said Edlen. *What choice do I have? Most smallfolk would salivate at being asked to accompany a noble.* If she wished to keep up her masquerade, she should act like one of the lowborn, even if that meant assisting one of the Windsong's retinue for a time.

Tomm clapped his hands. "Thank the gods! I have always believed the commonfolk are much more observant of their lands than those who rule them."

He started towards the tourney pavilions. "Let's start with a drink, Master Rayfield. How does that sound?"

Edlen glanced behind them. "What of your company, my lord?"

"They're big boys, Harris, they can entertain themselves.

You need not worry about them. I doubt they'll notice I've left."

They walked through the yard of the upper bailey—an enormous expanse of grass and dirt almost a mile square, surrounded by a curtain wall over two-hundred feet high. Six gigantic drum towers stood sentinel around the perimeter.

Edlen took occasional glances up at the strange man's face, hoping to get a read on him. Every time she did this, though, he would catch her gaze and make a jest about something he noticed. The more he did this, the less she worried. His words set her at ease, and before long she found herself laughing almost giddily at his observations.

His wit was near infectious. Any disquiet she felt earlier gave way to a desire to appear as astute and educated as him.

Soon, they stood under the shadow of the Tower of the Shield, home to Rhen and his father. Tomm surveyed the massive structure then turned to Edlen. "I hear this is where the king houses his giants. Have you ever seen one?"

Every day of my life. "No, my lord. I ain't seen one before, but we hear tales of them down in Pleasant Hill." Edlen quickened her pace, hoping Rhen would not come lumbering out of the tower, calling her name and ruining her farce.

"I've always wanted to meet one." Tomm stopped and gazed at the gargantuan doors. "Maybe a detour is in order. If luck smiles on us, I may catch one of their enormous women bathing." He winked.

"There are no brocken women," said Edlen, as if she were reciting some well-known fact.

Well, at least there had been none in Onyris since the Sundering War—or so the stories went. For all Edlen knew,

Rhen and his father, Rhohl, were the only two brocken left in Onyris.

"Is that correct?" asked Tomm. "Then where do brocken boys come from? Birthed from the mountains, are they?"

"Aye, they must be." Edlen never gave much thought to this. She assumed they came into the world like anyone else. But if there were no brocken women? The idea of birthing a baby that big made her shudder. *That would kill a normal woman.* She pushed the terrifying vision aside and stared at the ground.

"Can I tell you a secret, Harris?" Tomm leaned down, his face taking on a hint of conspiracy.

"Of course, my lord," answered Edlen, flattered to be taken into his confidence.

"Good…very good." He lowered his voice and looked over his shoulder. "If I told you a *brocken* was to compete in today's melee, how might you react?" His eyes darted furtively about the grounds.

Is he talking about Rhen? He must be. She considered his intentions but could not help herself from answering truthfully. "I would double my bet. Ain't no way anyone else would stand a chance to win."

"An incredibly smart bet that would be too," Tomm said. "But, Harris…do you think it's fair for a giant to compete in a tournament designed for men?" His thin eyebrows narrowed.

Edlen stopped herself from responding with complete indignation. She was playing a role and had to remember that most of Onyris looked down on the brocken. Careful not to let her love for Rhen cloud her next words, she paused and scratched her forehead. "The brocken have protected the kings for over two-hundred years; I don't see why they can't fight a few knights with a wooden sword. Anyway, if you ask me, a brocken is a man…bloody tall, but a man, nonetheless."

"I'm glad to hear that." Tomm laughed again as if he were relieved. "I needed to be certain you weren't one of those brocken-hating imbeciles." He rubbed his nose and glanced behind him. "I've heard rumor the poor brocken boy who's meant to compete today will be refused entry. I am of like mind to you, Harris—there should be no distinction between us and them."

Us and them? What do you mean by that? Edlen took a step back, unsure if she trusted the man anymore.

"I told you earlier that I was looking for Edlen Graymere… Well, I fear she might be the only one who can ensure this brocken finds some justice." He pulled a slip of paper from one of his pockets. "This document grants the brocken's place in the melee, but I need one more signature in order to legitimize it. Edlen Graymere's. Her royal autograph is the only thing that can abolish an ancient injustice."

Edlen stared at the parchment, dismayed. If this was not some elaborate ruse of Tomm's, she could come clean and claim her name right now. But was he telling the truth? She needed to find out.

"Can I see that?" she asked, forgetting that most small-folk could not read.

Tomm hesitated to hand over the paper. "I can tell you what it says, if you prefer?"

Edlen realized it might seem strange if she were to read the document, so she only pretended to scrutinize the words. "I'd appreciate it, my lord. Seems a bunch of chicken-scratch to me."

Though she handed the parchment back to Tomm, she'd already read enough to understand this declaration could be used to overturn an old law that refused a brocken's entry into certain tournaments.

He isn't lying. She sighed, glad to know this wasn't a trick. It was time for her to reveal her identity. "My lord, I am—"

"Thirsty? Me too." He rolled up the parchment, slid it back into his pocket, and pointed to a pavilion not far off. "Let's get that drink, eh, Harris? I'll explain everything to you, but where I come from, difficult conversations are best discussed over libations." He put his hand on her shoulder and started towards the ale-tent. "If we're lucky, we might even stumble across Lady Graymere. I hear her and the brocken are rather chummy. They might be sharing a pint before hearing he's not allowed to participate." He winked at her.

Edlen nodded and walked with him, unsure if he had purposefully stopped her from saying who she was, or if he might actually be thirsty.

As they continued on, her worry dissipated. Tomm would tell her everything she needed to know. He wanted to help Rhen, and that was all she could think of now. It didn't matter how or why he wanted to do this. The fact that he cared to seek her out was telling enough of his character.

"My lord, have you come here just to help the brocken?"

Tomm stopped at the entrance of the ale-tent. "That... and other things," he whispered to her as they entered.

The first thing Edlen noticed as she stepped inside was the oppressive heat; a result of too many people in too small a space. She wiped away beads of sweat from her upper lip. This was not like the smaller ale-tents she and Rhen would sneak into after her lessons with Laustair. Those open-aired spaces rarely hosted more than ten to twelve people. Here, she lost count at seventy, though there must have been nearly double that.

Knights, lords, and smallfolk mingled about, pressing into one another as they jostled for position with bedraggled barkeeps. A pungent, wafting aroma of spilled ale and body odor filled her nostrils. She squinted at the scent as though it were actively attacking her senses.

Tomm moved swiftly to the barkeep, sliding past a throng of eager patrons. He gestured for Edlen to follow him. Once they were both seated, he took out twenty noles and handed them over to the frazzled man behind the bar. "Six glasses, my good man."

Six glasses? I'll be on my arse before the tournament starts. Edlen stared at Tomm in disbelief. "That's too many."

Tomm waved off her protest and waited for the drinks.

When the barkeep returned, he placed six pints of ale in front of them. His face almost seemed relieved, as though he'd just marked them off of some internal list he kept in his head.

With one gulp, Tomm downed the drink immediately. "The first is for pleasure." He clinked his empty glass against hers and gestured for her to follow his lead.

Edlen drank the first pint as fast as she could, stopping halfway through to catch her breath.

Tomm grinned and lifted the next glass. "The second is to savor." He took a small sip of ale.

Dizzy from swigging her first drink, Edlen was relieved to see him nursing this one. *This is a strange custom.* She met his smile and held the frothy drink to her lips. "And the third?"

"For truth, Edlen…for truth."

CHAPTER

RHEN

The Giant and the Pedagogue

RHEN PACED THE inside of the large tourney pavilion, his head bent to avoid hitting the wooden frame. He had stopped listening to the little man when he'd said the words, "Forbidden from participating."

This can't be. You're wrong! His dark-brown eyes darted about in an attempt to evade the stern look of Patrick Lindon. "There must be a mistake! I'm almost the Shield of the Princess! I'm of noble birth, Patrick. Surely they can't refuse my entry." His jaw quivered in frustration.

"By ancient decree of His Eminence King Halstone the Third, Lord of Onyris, it states: *'No man of brocken birth may take part in any contest of strength in which four or more challengers of high birth are also participants.'*"

Bugger the old fool, thought Rhen. *Halstone died three hundred years ago. We weren't in service of the kings then.* "But the brocken weren't—"

"Sworn protectors of the crown. I am aware, Rhen. But a king's decree is law…no matter how old." Patrik Lindon was the Adept of Law, a small heavyset man in his fifties with thin wisps of white hair that sprang from atop his red-speckled pate. He stared up at Rhen apologetically. His pale-green eyes, which were always watery, conveyed a look of pure regret.

Rhen stared down, tears welling in his eyes. Though he towered over Patrick and could easily tear him apart, his immense strength would be of no avail in this situation. The Adept of Law was the ultimate word concerning disputes of any measure that were not under the province of the king himself.

"Patrik, please. You are the only one who can help me with this," said Rhen, almost begging. "I have dreamed of this day for five years." Tears rolled down his smooth, dark brown cheeks. "Please, for the friendship you claim to hold with my father, can't you just let me fight?"

"I spent the last two nights researching this. I know how important it is to you, Rhen, but I have scoured the libraries and found no texts precluding you from the law." Patrik bowed. "There will be other tournaments in which you may compete—but today is the king's birthday. We are hosting over forty high lords and their families. Knights from every corner of Onyris are here to compete."

"This is exactly why I should be allowed to participate!" said Rhen. He scratched his cheek. "Let's show them all that the brocken are equal."

"It would be an act of treachery," replied Patrik. "With all the eyes of the Wide-World on you, it is folly to flaunt the law." His voice grew stern. "Not every man in attendance is as stalwart as your family, Rhen. Some lords might see your entry as intentional disrespect."

"Why would my competing be disrespectful?" Rhen grew angry. "What have I done?"

"You? You have done nothing. But your people..." Patrik trailed off.

The adept's confidence clearly waned and his discomfort grew as he said, "Not everyone understands the Graymere's fondness for the brocken."

Now, visibly nervous, the small man continued. "You are a wonderful young man, and certain to become everything your father is, but there are some Southron lords who scorn your nearness to the king."

Nearness, thought Rhen. *Nearness to the king is not being the king.*

"I did not ask to be born, Patrik. I did not ask to be a brocken, nor did I ask to be my father's son. All I ask is to be given a chance to fight. To prove myself."

"I am sorry, Rhen. There's not enough time to have King Ulisaren change this now." Patrik avoided his eyes. "Just or unjust, it must be followed. These are my last words on the matter." He bowed his head and departed.

Rhen shook with anger. The red and green steel he wore clinked and clanged as he raged. He pulled a monstrous sword from its sheath and slashed wildly at the heavy canvas of the pavilion. When his childish outburst no longer satisfied him, he flung his sword to the ground and ripped off his steel gauntlets and vambraces. His dark-brown gambeson, almost the same color as his skin, was drenched in sweat.

Giant folds of lacerated canvas flapped in the wind behind him as he stamped through the grass near the tourney field. It was almost midday; the tournament started in less than an hour.

Knights, dressed in resplendent armor, cluttered the fields. A few dashed from Rhen as he flung his arms madly about, cursing loudly. His wrath was terrible to behold and cowed even the boldest of warriors.

Rhen hated himself for his petulance, but his anger was a tempest he could not weather.

And where is Edlen? His mind turned to his friend. *She promised to meet me before the melee. Damn her! But I'm sure she'll have an excuse…like she always does.*

Rhen glared through his tears. His enormous footfalls brought him to an ale-tent a few hundred yards away. A cluster of knights parted at his approach. He stormed past them without a glance and ducked his head as he entered the tent.

Inside mingled a crowd of people high and low born alike. Fiddlers and drummers pounded out a jaunty rendition of *The Beast and the Beaut*, while a few women danced provocatively around a group of men dressed in amber and scarlet. The music and excitement dimmed as Rhen burst in. A few men from Evermoore took their gaze from the dancing women and eyed him.

He paid little attention to the change of mood, though, having grown accustomed to peoples' muted fear and apprehension—his constant companion. Instead, he walked to the ale-keep, hunched and irritable.

All pavilions were too small for him, and this one was no different.

"Ale! Now!" demanded Rhen.

The ale-keep abandoned his patrons and immediately tended to the command. Most people acquiesced to Rhen's demands, and this bedraggled man was no different. He carried over three immense flagons of ale and placed them in front of the brocken.

"More!" shouted Rhen over the noise of the musicians

who had resumed their frolicking tune. He downed the three flagons in seconds. "More, much more."

Six more flagons appeared.

"The barrel! Give me the barrel."

"My lord," the ale-keep squeaked, "I'll have none for me other guests."

"Do I look as though I care?" he roared.

"My lord, I—"

"You will do as I ask," growled Rhen.

A soft hand fell on his shoulder, and he turned around quick as a serpent. "Get your bloody hands…" But his last words slipped back down his throat faster than the ale.

Edlen Graymere stood there, dressed in dirty brown rough spun and a hideous yellow-green cloak, her hood pulled over her head.

"Perhaps nine is enough for now," said Edlen. "I would like at least one."

Rhen smiled for the first time in what might have been ages. "My lady, I—"

"Harris, my friend," said Edlen, winking. "You are deep in your drink; I do not expect you to remember me, but my name is Harris Rayfield."

"My Lady…Harris…I mean," said Rhen, slowly understanding his friend. *Gods! She even looks like a boy.* "I expected you earlier."

"Ah," started Edlen, "about that." She gestured to the far end of the tent. There sat a strange man dressed in silver gray. "Come sit with us and let our good ale-keep get back to his business."

Rhen's anger subsided and he followed Edlen, doing his best to duck under the inner framework of the tent. As they approached a small table tucked into a corner, he crouched down and smiled nervously at the strange man who awaited them.

"You grant my wishes," said the stranger, looking at Edlen and then back at Rhen. "Allow me to introduce myself." He stood and bowed then stretched his arm out. "My name is Tomm Harken, and I am aware of what vexes you."

The ale was finally going to Rhen's head; his anxiety faded. He grabbed the man's hand and said, "Any friend of Master Rayfield's is a friend of mine."

Tomm said, "It appears our young lady wishes to continue with her farce."

What in the bloody hells does he mean by that? Rhen eyed Tomm with a suspicion that teetered on rage. *Lady Edlen plays no farce. If she wishes I address her as Harris, or Martinn, or Narine, then it is my duty to do so.* "Harris Rayfield is a man of honor; he plays no farce," he said, his eyes flaring.

"Harris Rayfield truly is a man of honor. Just as Niles Craston wrote him in the old fables," said Tomm. "*The Pauper Prince* was my favorite book as a boy. A low-born thief masquerading as the prince; a classic, and one day I hope to read it to my children."

Tomm gave Edlen a knowing nod. "Lady Graymere and I have cleared the air of deceits. But if she prefers her new sobriquet, who am I to judge? Perhaps she only wishes the ale-keep not grovel when a royal is in his midst."

"It is alright, Rhen," said Edlen. "Tomm is a friend. He saw past my ruse immediately, though he let me play it out… for far too long, if truth be told."

Rhen smiled nervously as he watched them laugh at some hidden jest. Disquiet gnawed upon him. *You may call him a friend, but I do not trust him.*

"Do not over-worry, Master Rhen, I am an ally," said

Tomm. "Well, better stated—I am an ally to you and Lady Edlen, but there are those who might believe me a worm in their apple orchard."

"I am more confused now than when I walked in." Rhen grabbed a flagon of ale in an attempt to hide his concern.

"I think I can clear this up," said Edlen. "You received unfortunate news today, did you not?"

Yes. And you were not there to support me. You were not there as you promised you would be. "Yes," was all Rhen managed to say aloud.

"Well, Tomm here was aware you would receive ill information, but he has the means to set it right." Edlen smiled behind her flagon of ale.

Rhen glared at Tomm. "The Adept of Law himself told me. It is too late for any of your schemes, Edlen. The king's word is law."

Tomm leaned in. "And what exactly did Patrik Lindon say to you?"

Rhen was beginning to loathe this man dressed in gray; a coward's colors. Patrik Lindon was a friend of his father for years beyond count. Rhen broke bread with him on numerous occasions. Patrik and his father would discuss laws and statutes into the night as they laughed together.

"He read an ancient decree from one of the Halstones. I can't remember which one though, there are so many."

"'No man of brocken birth may take part in any contest of strength in which four or more challengers of high birth are also participants,'" recited Tomm Harken. "Was that the one?"

Each word was a dagger in Rhen's heart.

"Yes." He hung his head, no longer wishing to be a part of this discussion.

"What if I told you that poor old Patrik Lindon seems to have forgotten his history?" said Tomm, a wry smile spreading across his lips.

"Show him," said Edlen.

"Show me what?" Rhen grew impatient. "Patrik assured me he'd researched this for two days. He is my friend... I believe him."

And I also believe a brocken will never be given the same rights as men.

"Two days he researched this?" asked Tomm, more to the air than to anyone in particular. "It is well I arrived *three* days ago then." With that, Tomm pulled a cracked and yellowed parchment from a hidden pocket in his cloak.

"I believe our fine Adept of Law may have perchance missed this in his studies."

Rhen glanced at the parchment with passing amusement. *Another old text written by another old man.*

"And what does this forbid me from?"

Tomm smirked. "Just the opposite." He unfolded the parchment and read aloud:

"'By decree of His Eminence, King Berad the Second, Lord of Onyris: No man of brocken birth may compete in any contests of strength unless otherwise endorsed by three lords, themselves not engaged either in body or house, of said contest.'"

King Berad the Second, or *King Berad the Bold*, was secretly named *King Berad the Brocken*.

The grandson of King Berad the Vicious, many expected him to continue the actions of his grandfather, but his reign was remembered mostly for the ending of the Sundering War.

The end of the genocide of the brocken.

Rhen was well-versed in this history, but it did not stop

him from feeling perplexed. Endorsements would avail him little now. *What in the bloody hells does that mean? The tourney starts in less than an hour; this may have been useful two days ago.*

He stared at Tomm and then Edlen, both of whom smiled.

"What does this help now? How am I expected to get any signatures? The melee is about to begin."

"Our new friend has already seen to this." Edlen unfurled a roll of fresh parchment on which the wax seals and endorsements of four lords were emblazoned. One of them being the Great Wheel. The signet of family Graymere.

The room spun around Rhen, the thudding rhythm of the drums filling his ears. He stared at Edlen in disbelief. *You did it again. I am not a sickly pup in need of your rescuing. If I wanted your help, I would've asked for it.*

It was then he noticed the eyes of all the people in the tent. How easy it was for him to forget their stares, but today it was as though he could sense seething poison in their gaze.

Patrik Lindon said it plainly enough: He would always be an outsider, he would always be reliant on a king's decree, he would never be one of *them*. Not even with Edlen.

The tent grew hot, and Rhen silently stamped out, bent and humiliated. A young woman stared. He turned toward her and roared, like a beast.

As he left, he passed Patrik. The sight of him filled Rhen with rage. For a brief moment, they glared at one another. Patrik acted as though he were about to say something, but when he saw the hate in Rhen's eyes, thought better of it. They passed each other in silence, Patrik scurrying inside like an old rat.

Outside of the tent, Rhen pushed past the half-drunk knights who cluttered the entrance.

"See you on the field?" a knight dressed in cerulean and cerise mocked.

Rhen's anger was savage when he spun around. He stood almost four feet taller than the lavishly adorned knight. A thousand curses came to his mind, but to his lips came only: "I will kill you." Each word dripped venomously from his mouth.

He did not wait for a response but instead walked slowly and dazedly, retracing his steps back to his pavilion.

When he entered it and stared at the slashed canvas, he fell to his knees and sobbed.

Only moments later, Edlen entered. "What in the bloody hells was that?" she asked before seeing the tears in Rhen's eyes. At once she rushed over and threw her arms around her friend.

"What's wrong? I thought you'd be happy."

Rhen let Edlen hug him. Angry as he was, he desired this embrace.

"You don't understand, do you?" asked Rhen, sobbing. "You never will."

"Understand what?"

"You..." He stopped. *If I can't say this to her, then who can I?* "It is easy for you."

He pushed Edlen away and stood, his eyes red. "It is easy for you, my lady. You can throw on dirty rags and become someone else. You can pull a hood over your head and escape your name. But I am a brocken. I will always be a brocken, and there is no hood I can wear to hide it. I can never escape who I am, Edlen. People stare at me wherever I go—and I always hear their curses. Gods damn them all, but it hurts! It hurts more than you will ever know." He wiped away a tear. "You and your family may love us, but your family are not the only people in the Wide-World. I didn't ask for any of this, Edlen...I didn't ask for it...I didn't..."

Edlen stared at the ground. "I do not know what to say, Rhen." She paused, then walked forward, placing her hand on Rhen's arm.

"I will never say I can understand how you feel. All I can say...is that I love you. You are my brother; your hurts are mine too." She looked up to meet her friend's eyes. "Tell me what I can do, and I will do it."

That is the problem. You believe you can fix my problems, but there is no wizard's wand you can wave to fix this. Your family cannot create a law that makes men regard me as an equal.

Rhen mustered his courage and said, "I do not want you to do anything."

At that moment, the flap of the pavilion opened and Tomm Harken stepped in. "My lord and lady, may I have a word?" His face was solemn; no smirk hid behind his lips.

Rhen glanced up, his anger subsided. The only thing that remained to him was quiet resignation. "Say what you must."

Tomm approached Edlen and whispered in her ear. She sped off like a whipped palfrey.

Alone, Tomm sat on a bench and eyed Rhen for a moment before he spoke. "Anger is a useful tool, my lord."

"I am not a lord!" Rhen felt that same anger stir inside.

"And neither am I," said Tomm. "But it feels good to be called one every now and then. The world is full of men who wish to be lords, or kings, but never have the chance. For most, a spade in their hands and dirt on their face is all they will ever know—and those are the lucky ones. No one has a choice in their birth, Rhen. All the gods give us are the choices we make *after* we are born. Every person in this world has things they are good at and those that they fail at—it is up to us to turn those failures into knowledge. I, for one, am rather good at eavesdropping, but I consistently fail at keeping that to myself." He smirked.

Rhen laughed. It was not a hearty laugh, but it raised his spirits. "Why are you telling me this?"

"Because I believe you and I are very similar, and I refuse to believe anyone like me might be deterred by a bit of unfortunate news."

"How are you anything like me?"

Tomm lowered his voice. "My father was a drunken sot who abandoned my mother and me when I was not but a suckling babe. She was a kind woman, my mother, if memory serves, but she died before my fifth birthday, leaving me at a brothel in Whitecliff.

"I had no choice in any of this, you see, and the people of the Vines don't look kindly on the son of a dead whore who now begs for loose noles at the port."

Rhen studied Tomm, a tinge of pity for the stranger creeping into his heart.

"I saw the way those people gaped at you in the aletent. Trust me, I am familiar with that look." Tomm smiled. "That look is fear, Rhen…nothing more. Oh yes! It may be laced with derision, or self-inflated superiority, but I tell you, Rhen, it is fear. You represent something inside of them they will *never* be able to understand—and everyone fears what they do not understand."

"And what is that?" Rhen asked.

"Ah! Now we get to it." Tomm's voice softened and he leaned in close to Rhen. "It is something you will discover in your own time. It may not be today and may not be for years to come, but when you find it, you will be truly unstoppable.

"Let them stare at you, let them snigger to themselves,

and let the boldest say what they will, but always remember their words are but wooden knives; they might sting, but they will not kill."

Tomm stood. "And as far as Edlen Graymere is concerned…" He placed his gloved hand on Rhen's shoulder. "She wishes only to help. She is young, yes, and slightly misguided in the way she helps, but it is out of love…not fear. And I am here to help as well."

Rhen's eyes narrowed as he glared at Tomm. "And why should I trust you?"

"The sins of kings shall be atoned for," muttered Tomm.

The flap of the pavilion swung open and Edlen entered, leading Patrik Lindon. "Master Lindon, we have something you must see."

Patrik's face reddened even more. The ale was definitely working its way to his head. "My lords, the tournament is about to begin—what nonsense is this?"

At that, Tomm spun from Rhen. "I would call this a reversal of nonsense, Master Lindon." He pulled out the text of King Berad the Second and read it aloud.

After reciting the ancient law, Tomm said, "I find it queer that the *Adept of Law* missed this niggling decree in his research."

"I-I…" Patrik stuttered. "Give that here!"

"Surely," said Tomm, and he handed over the parchment. "Lady Edlen, if you would."

"How did you—" started Patrik. He studied Tomm and asked, "Who are you?"

"My name is Tomm Harken of Maresport. I arrived in this beautiful city three days ago in the retinue of Lord Byron Windsong, nonetheless. I am certain you know of him." He stared at Patrik. "Regardless of my exquisite company, I grew weary from our travels. You see, I have a tendency to become irritable when weariness descends upon me, but alas, I have developed a ritual for when this foul mood arises...I retreat to my books.

"Well, seeing I was now in the capital of Onyris, I was certain your libraries would be of immense interest to me. And Master Lindon—I was not disappointed." Tomm winked at Rhen then eyed Patrik Lindon perniciously. "The most interesting thing happened as I walked through those vast rows of tomes. A magnificently bound book sat open on a table in the farthest corner of the building. Being the curious man I am, I sat in front of this gorgeous volume and began to read. Regardless of the old adage—and though the cover was beyond reproach—the text was ponderous and dull. Ancient laws going back hundreds of years. Not a gripping read, mind you."

Patrik grew uneasy. "This is why Rothspire employs an Adept of Law, Master Harken." He looked to Rhen and then Edlen. "Laws are not a spellbinding study, but they are of vital importance. I would not expect you to understand their value." He forced a laugh.

"Truly," said Tomm. "But after a time of monotonous indulgence, I came across a thing of wonder. A page with a surprisingly fresh fold."

"Old tomes will have folds. This is not a wonder." Patrick grew impatient. "I appreciate your interest in ancient law, but I must be going; I am needed at the opening ceremony."

Rhen stepped back to block the opening of the pavilion and stared Patrik down. "They will wait for you."

What is Tomm getting at?

"Anyway," Tomm started back up again, "when I turned to this page, I was suddenly intrigued by what I read. A decree from King Halstone the Third, rather unambiguous in its wording. *'Brocken are forbidden from participating in tournaments."* He frowned.

"Well, much to my chagrin, I had just ridden over two thousand leagues in the hope of seeing a brocken compete in a tournament. You might understand my devastation. But I am quizzical by nature, so, being who I am, I continued to read, and after only a few more pages into my new favorite book, I found another entry concerning *Tournaments and Participants*. Well…you now hold it in your hands. Are you familiar with it?"

"You tore this from the pages of Dalantis the Wise?" Patrik almost bellowed. "This is sacrilege."

"The book is very heavy," said Tomm. "I did not want to burden you with its weight. Dalantis the Wise will never be confused with Dalantis the Succinct." He grabbed the text back from Patrik's trembling hand.

"Now please explain to us how the Adept of Law missed such an important amendment to such an important law, no more than four pages past the law preventing our friend—" Tomm looked up at Rhen—"from competing today?" He strode towards Patrick, stopping only a breath away. "You are a proselyte of the Pedagogues of Lyceum, are you not?" Tomm licked his lips. "Would they be proud to have an adept as *inept* as you?"

Patrik stared agape and shook with anger. "What would you know of being a proselyte? You are just some jumped-up racketeer. Yes, I am aware of the Windsongs…and their shadows."

Rhen eyed Tomm. *If Patrick does not trust you, why should I?*

Tomm only smiled and removed the glove from his left

hand. A thin, intricate tattoo covered the skin in fine script. Four of his fingers brandished rings of different metals: gold, silver, platinum, and palladium, burned into his flesh. These were the symbolic marks of the pedagogues; the wisest, most venerated teachers in the Wide-World.

The path to becoming a pedagogue was incredibly long and difficult. Most who entered the Lyceum became only proselytes—students—and even that was a widely revered position. There were no castles or lords who did not desire a proselyte in their council.

But a pedagogue was something else entirely.

Patrik Lindon marveled at the sight. His voice caught in his throat. "You must be the youngest pedagogue in over—"

"*Ever*," said Tomm. "Ever, is the word you are searching for."

CHAPTER

ALDIR

The Iron Woman

LIGHT STREAMED INTO *the sacellum through beautifully stained glass; a wonderful array of colors that dazzled the eye. Aldir Graymere, a powerfully built man in his late thirties with long, thick, golden-brown hair, kept a silent vigil under this domed ceiling. He stared up at the painted windows, noting their ornate depictions. Warriors and commoners alike walked along twisting paths, guided by the hand of All—The Creator.*

Above the followers of All was a mosaic of pillowy white clouds set against a blue sky in which twenty radiant stars gleamed. These stars represented the watchful eyes of the Ten—the Gods who shaped Onyris.

Aldir turned his gaze from the dome and clutched the frail elbow of a shrouded figure who lay upon a stone dais. He knelt, his thick, muscular shoulders hunched over the unblinking corpse of his wife, Irymar.

Wrapped in fine silks, she was as beautiful in death as she was in life.

Time stretched on as he stared down. Though he knew he

should not, he pulled back the shroud that covered her face, longing to look upon her once more.

Her lustrous black hair lay in lazy ringlets upon milky-white shoulders and spilled over her pale chest. Clerics from the Temple of Dracoyn had painted her lips red, using their arts to form her lifeless mouth into a smile. Dressed in the same white gown she wore on her wedding day, an intricate lace neckline lay against the top of Irymar's breasts.

Her neck, though, was much more slender than Aldir remembered, like thin parchment laid over bone.

Death has a way of corrupting our memories, he thought to himself. He stroked the outline of her face—just as he'd done every night before they slept.

Tears did not come.

He stared down at a pallid face, the memory of her smile a cold dagger in his heart. He could not bear to see her like this. Tearing his gaze from her, he glanced back at the domed ceiling.

The blue of the sky dimmed, now grayer than he remembered. *Perhaps it is a trick of the light*, he told himself. Instead of twenty stars, the same ones he'd memorized as a child, he counted only twelve—two of them grew dark, almost black.

He looked back at Irymar. Something was wrong. The shroud that covered her had wilted.

He held Irymar's elbow tight. Her skin yellowed somewhat and her features were wrong—distorted.

An icy wind blew through the sacellum and the skin on his neck chilled, gooseflesh covering his arms. The white lace Irymar wore was now aged and tattered, as though dug up after many years buried.

Aldir glanced back at the mosaic. All but two stars vanished. Two black eyes stared down at him, shining eerily dark against a black storm.

The Sins of Kings

The paintings on the stained glass changed. No longer the many-colored portraits of those following the path of All, now black and red warriors were silhouetted in the act of slaughter. Lifeless bodies lay slumped against their feet. The hand of All shriveled, contorted like the claw of some horrible insect.

Aldir's breath caught in his throat. What is happening?

The room shook violently, but only for a heartbeat. It happened so fast, Aldir thought he might have imagined it.

He released Irymar's elbow and stared at her face. It was now a ghastly dirty yellow, the color of old wax. He took a step back and gaped in horror.

The shroud that covered her had burned away, and Irymar lay there, skeletal, decomposing before his eyes. Her black hair was now white and straw-like, thin and dry. Her gown rotted, and a black stain spread from her lap, pooling about her. Small drops fell on the floor beneath the dais and dyed the stone below a deep crimson.

Aldir tried to scream, but his voice choked on his terror.

Irymar's chest rose and dropped. Slight at first, but soon her entire body heaved, as though gasping for air. And then it stopped. She was still.

Still as a corpse.

As though guided by some unseen hand, Aldir reluctantly approached her.

She was now nothing but splintered bone and ragged skin. Flesh sloughed from her face, leaving open gashes where skull protruded through skin. Her cheeks had ripped apart, creating horrid black pits. Her eyes stared back at him like chips of burning onyx. No longer the soulful dark brown he had loved, they were bestial, haunted...and they glared at him.

A horrible retching sound came from her as black-green phlegm guttered from her decaying mouth and dribbled down her chin. Slowly, she moved, sitting up. Her terrible face turned to Aldir, her voice a hissing whisper full of blood and putrescence. Black eyes flamed as her mouth creaked in a rictus smile. Through a gurgle of horror and blood she spat one word... "Somath!"

ALDIR awoke with a start. Midday sun streamed in through the shutters. Sweat beaded on his brow and his underclothes were soaked through. He lay still, too afraid to move.

Somath? Who or what was Somath?

It was the day of King Ulisaren's tournament. Aldir wished he could avoid the entire thing. Though forced awake by the nightmare, he closed his eyes again, hoping to find solace in new dreams. The moment he closed his eyes, the rotting face of Irymar flashed before him. Sleep would not come again.

He dragged himself up and opened the curtains. Sunlight hit him like a flaming brand. He squinted and peered down at his family's kingdom.

Throngs of people had gathered, milling about like thousands of rats. Canvas pavilions of every color had sprung up seemingly overnight and peppered the sprawling green fields of Rothspire. Each one of these garish tents was surrounded by an outcropping of smaller ones. The cobblestone streets were packed with visitors from nearly every realm in Onyris, and though he knew these people would spend all the coin they had today, it would not be enough to replenish the coffers of the crown.

The ledgers he and Yvonne Babbit, the Adept of Accounts, had peered over last night still lay open on his table.

We owe thousands to half the kingdom, and that was before this ridiculous tournament.

Ten-thousand golden crowns for the jousters' purse, five thousand for the melee, and over fifty-thousand silver wheels to be paid out in other costs—all to appease King Ulisaren's appetite for grandeur. They were paying over two-thousand silvers simply to bring singers up from the Applecoast.

This was his father's celebration; it would be no good to try and dissuade him from these extravagances, but the king's indulgences would fall upon Aldir's shoulders. As the Primacy of the Realm, the responsibilities of the crown's debts were his to oversee. His aunt, Teryse Killion, had stepped down from the role eight months ago and he still felt out of his depth with these new duties.

Perhaps I should pay her a visit before meeting my father.

Teryse's malady may have caused her to retire, but she still proved to be a vast wealth of knowledge, and any excuse Aldir could find to forestall being a part of the festivities would be a gift.

He wished, not for the last time, that Irymar was still alive.

Irymar was an amazing buffer for days like this. She understood the *black thought* he suffered from and would always allow him his rest when these days came.

The memory of her smiling at him as she squeezed into an ill-fitting dress—only three-weeks away from giving birth to Edlen—came rushing back to him. That night she had insisted that she be the one to accompany the king to the Autumn Harvest while he spent the evening in bed.

She had gushed upon returning to their chamber, only to inform him that she had single-handedly broken up a heated dispute between Lord Brastor Archwood and the king. He remembered how they had both howled with laughter at her impression of the Lord of Straten.

According to her, she'd stood between the two men and used her full belly to bump into Brastor's prodigious gut. "My lord." She'd blushed. "Have you lost weight? The last time we danced, I don't recall being larger than you."

The two cantankerous men had immediately forgot their argument, and Brastor, flustered with appreciation, had bowed as low as he might and wished a hundred blessings on their unborn child.

But now, Irymar was gone and Aldir needed to force himself to play the part of the dutiful son. He would have to don fake smiles and false courtesies. The thought of inane conversation and polite airs exhausted him. He glanced back at his bed.

If I could just go back to sleep. They do not need me there. My father will make due in my absence.

As these thoughts came to him, a light knock tapped against his door.

Gods please! Leave me alone.

"My lord," Worm, a small young boy, called from behind the door. "His Grace awaits your escort."

"Run along, Worm." Aldir grabbed the edge of a table and lowered his head. "Tell His Grace I will attend him shortly."

His chamber door opened and Worm, barely twelve years old, entered. He stood before Aldir and spoke with a lilt of self-satisfaction.

"My lord, I was commanded by His Grace, King Ulisaren, to accompany you to his palanquin myself."

I have my own pimple-faced shepherd, thought Aldir.

"Run along, Worm. Tell my father I will arrive soon." He lifted his head and glared. "There are other matters needing my attention."

Werman Gault was King Ulisaren's page and the youngest son of Lord Damen Gault of Swordfish Bay. Curly, straw-blonde hair framed his face and accentuated his youth. Why the king had accepted the boy into his own service was a mystery to Aldir, but Werman had quickly become Ulisaren's favorite lickspittle, and he was a daily irritation Aldir had to contend with.

Others of the court had privately named him Worm, but Aldir unabashedly referred to him by it. Worm did not seem to mind, though, as he never made so much as a cross face when addressed by the insult.

"What matters are these, my lord?" asked Werman. His flushed face reddened even more, as though suddenly privy to clandestine information he might relay to the king.

"You forget yourself, Worm." Aldir glared at the boy, his patience running thin. "You may be my father's puppet, but you are not my father. I owe you no explanations."

The boy straightened himself, trying to appear taller than he was. "His Grace believed you would receive me unpleasantly, but he commanded I ignore your insolence and retrieve you with haste."

Aldir laughed. *He is bereft of charm, but he has balls of iron.*

"Retrieve me?" *Yes. I am his dog after all. But I will not be his tractable dog.* "Well, let him chase after me, Worm. You can tell him I was unpleasant, and that I forced you from your duty." He placed his large hand on Werman's shoulder and squeezed tightly.

The boy's soft, un-muscled arm would be too easy to break. "Because I am forcing you," Aldir said.

He let go of Worm's shoulder and strode from his chamber and past his guards before turning down the long hallway. He turned another corner and glimpsed a stone in the base of the wall that was slightly dislodged. Someone had scattered the rushes nearest to it.

At the sight, he remembered climbing the secret ladder as a boy. Those were long years ago. *Edlen must have found my invisible staircase.*

The thought made him smile, but before he could reflect on his youth, the soft scuttle of Werman's steps filled his ears, and his vexation was renewed. Instead of yielding to his unexpected desire to descend the hidden iron ladder, he left the secret door untouched and made his way to cantilevered stairs.

He took the steps at a brisk pace, and upon reaching the landing of the second floor, he turned and made for his aunt's chamber.

Teryse Killion was King Ulisaren's only sister. Three years his junior and a woman of immense notoriety, she was known as the Iron Woman. She had been the Primacy of the Realm for over fifty years and held the respect of nearly everyone in Onyris.

At the young age of twenty-three, she had been appointed to the office of Primacy by her father, King Andaire. This announcement alone was one to be remembered for long ages, as she became the youngest person in history to hold the title. But adding to her infamy was the distinction of being the only woman ever to hold the office. And it was in her first year in this position that she gained her true fame and her new moniker.

It was during Robart Moorcroft's rebellion when Teryse Killion earned the name of *The Iron Woman*. Through her political plays and innate knowledge of military strategy, she'd been able to squash the rebellion and ensure no other upstarts might be kindled to attempt anything similar. After the decisive battle in which Moorcroft was taken prisoner, Teryse had the rebel dismembered and sent pieces of him to any lord who supported the uprising. There had been no rumor of rebellion since.

WHEN Aldir approached her chamber, Sir Oswald Graves—a bear of a man, with a face as craggy as old stone—stood still as a statue outside her door.

"The Iron Woman is indisposed." Sir Oswald barred the door.

Aldir stared up at him. "My aunt is expecting me."

As he said this, he heard Werman snigger behind him. He turned and shot the boy a look of penetrating cold.

Before Sir Oswald could respond, the door to the chamber opened inward and a young woman stood there, framed in the sunlight that filtered in from an open window. The knight dropped his arm and gawked, his eyes fixed on her bosom.

"M'lady, I apologize for the disturbance." His voice was now sweet as honeyed wine.

She smiled coyly. She was tall and copper-skinned like those of the Footsteps off the coast of Towerglenn. No more than twenty-years old, her purple, almond-shaped eyes glistened, and her long, straight black hair tumbled over her thin, uncovered shoulders. The dress she wore—a dirty, roughspun garment that common housemaids clothed themselves in—draped over her body.

Her voice held the thin timbre and musical accent of a princess of Rojiir. "Lady Teryse is expecting her nephew, good sir. Please let them pass."

Sir Oswald bowed clumsily then stepped aside.

Aldir stepped into his aunt's chamber and his eyes adjusted to the bright light that shone in from the tall windows of the room. A sweet scent of perfume filled the air.

Teryse, propped up in her bed by three large pillows, coughed. "Come close, silly boy."

In her youth, Teryse Killion would never have been considered beautiful, but in her advanced age she'd grown into something one might call distinguished. Lined with years of stress and hardship, her face resembled a weatherworn map. Her once-auburn hair had passed finally to white, and though her handmaiden had done all she could to keep it well brushed and clean, it sat atop her head in slender strands like a disheveled crown or bird's nest. Emerald-green eyes sat above a hawkish and wrinkled nose.

"Now remind me, nephew. Why have I summoned you?" Her voice, harsh and thin, was a brittle blade long past use.

She glanced beyond Aldir, her gaze landing on Worm. "I cannot remember the matter, but I am certain it will not interest our young friend here."

With that, she summoned her handmaid. "Aryanne, please escort Master Gault back to my brother. Tell him you will be attending today's festivities in my place."

"As you wish, my lady," Aryanne replied.

Werman started to complain, but Teryse cut him off. "You cannot go dressed in those rags, though," she said to Aryanne. "Please wear something more befitting of one in the king's company."

She motioned towards her wardrobe, her frail hand shaking. "I believe there are some red and green silks somewhere in there. My brother will be ecstatic to see you in it." A rueful smile appeared on her lips.

Aryanne moved toward the wardrobe and rifled through its contents. When she found the silken gown Teryse recommended, she disrobed in full view of both Aldir and Werman.

A gentleman, Aldir paid no attention to her nudity. Instead, he kept his gaze fixed entirely on his aunt.

The same could not be said for young Werman. His eyes, fixed on the beautiful young woman, followed every move Aryanne made. Dumbstruck, he had clearly forgotten any command the king may have given him.

Once Aryanne had clothed herself in green and red silks, she walked to Werman, took his hand, and said, "Show me the way, young lord." She bowed to Aldir and then to Teryse as she followed the boy from the chamber.

After the door shut behind the youngsters, Aldir turned to his aunt. "What was that?"

Teryse's laugh turned into a cough. "You boys are all the same. Your loyalties go only so far as the next pair of tits you see." She adjusted herself into a more comfortable position. "Your feigned chastity does not fool me. You are a Graymere, after all."

"You insult me." Aldir put a hand on his chest. "The only woman I wish to see is you."

Teryse slapped his hand playfully. "I have not been a woman for twenty years. I am an old lady, and I won't hear your false chivalries. When you are my age, you will learn that truth is as sweet to the ears as honey is to the tongue."

She giggled without coughing—the sound that of a young maid. "Enough about beautiful women now. Tell me why I have the pleasure of receiving my favorite nephew."

Favorite nephew? Hearing the truth may be sweet but speaking it is still bitter for you. Aldir stood and walked to the window. He stared out and asked, "Have you seen the preparations for my father's tournament?"

"I have heard them," said Teryse. "And your father-in-law has told me much and more of its magnificence."

"Father-in-law?" asked Aldir. "Laustair has been here?"

"He visits often. Which is more than I can say for my own sons...or my nephews."

"My apologies." He frowned. "But you have left a mighty big hole for me to fill. My duties to the realm seem to be all I can find time for now. And it is those duties that bring me here today."

"I may have spoken falsely earlier; your honesty is sour in my ears," she said, the racking cough continuing. "What concerns you?"

"Everything."

"I appreciate you coming to me with a simple problem." No laugh or cough accompanied her statement; instead, she gritted her teeth and stared at Aldir. "Why did you accept the role? I've told you many times I would not wish this position on my worst enemy."

Aldir pulled a seat from the table nearest the window and placed it beside her bed. He sat down. "It was not offered to me. My father *told* me I was to be the Primacy. He gave me no choice. You know him. He does not ask. He commands."

"But you are here now?" Her dark-green eyes narrowed. "Did he not *command* you to attend him? Gods! He even sent that little worm of his to see that you do not disappear."

Aldir pondered the question. "It is easier to upset him when I remember he is my father. Today is for his own self-gratification, and it disgusts me, but becoming Primacy is the decree of a king. I cannot disobey that."

"Cannot?" Teryse asked. "Or do not want to?"

Since Aldir was a boy, his aunt always knew his intentions. When he was young, he assumed it was a power all adults possessed, but as he grew into a man, he realized she was far more astute than most others. She did not guess at his feelings; instead, she asked him the questions he avoided asking himself.

"Yes." He cast his gaze to the ground and fidgeted in his seat.

"Right!" She repositioned herself again. "Now that that is out of the way, tell me, why did you come here?"

If it is honesty you desire. "The kingdom is in debt—"

"This is not news to me," said Teryse as though the matter were merely a trifle. "The way your father spends, I'd imagined we would have been bankrupted a month into my retirement." She smiled up at him. "You have done much better than I assumed."

"We are not far from bankruptcy. I have scoured the ledgers with Adept Babbit and it seems to us that my father's desire to rebuild all of Rothspire is costing us far more than it should. Why have we outsourced the work? We have men and women in Pleasant Hill who would prosper if we paid them even half of what we're paying now."

"Sometimes, Aldir, contracts for things as nominal as construction are far more political than you are aware. Give Yvonne some more time and I am certain she will discover a way to stop the bleed... She is a wizard when it comes to coin. What she lacks in personality, she more than makes up for in shrewdness."

That is a compliment to a shrew. I have enjoyed my time more in the privy after too much Straten Red than my hours with her.

He craned his head and glanced around the room to confirm they were still alone. "Our financial troubles are not the only issues that concern me." He lowered his voice to a whisper. "Raiders from the Fyrelands become bolder and now attack villages as far in as Oakblade. The Eyes of the Forest have fewer men in their ranks than they did forty years ago. We may have to bolster their forces with soldiers from Rothspire. *The Iron Horse* is not the recruitment tool he once was."

"Ha!" Teryse's eyes lit with laughter. "You mean to say our *iron* myths grow rust? How dare you, nephew? I take offense to that!"

"Not all iron is tempered the same." Her thin skin felt as though it might tear as he stroked her cheek.

She smirked, reached for his hand, and grasped it tight. "You have your mother's charm; it is so unfortunate you inherited your father's looks."

Aldir grinned. He would miss her biting humor when she was gone. He avoided the thought of this sad inevitability. "Agitators from Pleasant Hill amass in the Great Wheel to protest the King's Tournament, and the city guard request more men to silence them—men we cannot afford. Then there's the new Autark in Rojiir."

"Ah yes. Now we get to the interesting part. How are our friends across the sea?"

"Not well," said Aldir. "He takes umbrage with the levees we have raised on the ports along the Redwater. And he sends an envoy to Rothspire as we speak."

"They are not a people we want to displease, Aldir. I need not tell you the stories of how they prefer to settle disputes."

"We can count ourselves lucky they do not care about gold," he said behind a sarcastic smile. "They only set fire to those who owe it to them."

Teryse burst out in a fit of laughter. "You have a sense of humor about these things. That is good, that is good. I did not learn to laugh at such problems until I was too old and decrepit for it to help."

Perhaps that only means I am that much closer to decay.

Her light-hearted response to his worries—though it lifted his spirits—made him wonder if she took any of this seriously. "There is one rumor that vexes me, though."

She leaned forward from her pillows. "Do not keep an old woman in suspense."

"We have no definite source for this information, but the smallfolk whisper... Lord Dysternis of the Shaded Realm was murdered."

A shadow of fear flashed across her face, and though she acted as if it was nothing but the pain of her disease, Aldir could see this message disturbed her.

"Dysternis is dead?" she asked. "What evidence is there of this?"

"None that I am aware of. As I said, these are only rumors. We plan to send an emissary to Balangraide after the tournament."

Teryse sat fully up, her body stiff with concern. Or was it excitement? "It would be ill news if the whispers you hear are correct. Dysternis has proved an effective bulwark between us and the Shaded Realm since the unpleasantness his father stirred."

She closed her eyes, and when she opened them again, the stern face of the Iron Woman appeared. "Perhaps this is why the Autark grows impudent. What was Dysternis's son's name again?"

"Nekkin, I believe. Or something similar. A strange Southern name."

"Nekkin. Yes, I remember hearing about him when he

was a boy. My informants at the time told me he is Robart come again."

Robart Moorcroft, the Rebel Lord. "I have heard similar tales as well."

She squinted and waved off the thought. "Well...if he is that bastard reborn, he may have to die the same way his grandfather did."

Die?

If the legends were true, the Iron Woman had him beheaded and dismembered. Different pieces of him were then sent to the lands that took up arms against Rothspire during his rebellion. *Should I be as dismissive of this possible threat as she is?* He did not wish to question his aunt, not when he was the one who came to her for advice.

"Is there anything else?" she asked. It seemed as though her eyes were a burden to keep open.

"One other..." he started to say but thought better than to trouble her with his own personal worries. "No, it is nothing."

"Nothing?" She studied him. "I may not live much longer, my boy. Out with it."

It was a poor trick of sympathy on her part, but Aldir was too fond of the old woman to argue.

"As I said, it is a minor bother. My heart tends to worry more the older I get, but...well...it is Odain."

"Your brother? What has he done now?"

"It is not what he has done, rather what he has not done." The image of his older brother with his fair face and perfectly manicured beard flashed before his eyes. *You will make an excellent king one day, Odain... Much better than I would ever hope to be. The Gods were right in having you be born first.*

Teryse grimaced, whether from some hidden bodily ache or her own frustrations with Odain. Aldir continued.

"He sailed to Bowbreaker Bay after attending a ceremony for the Eyes of the Forest. He was to settle some issue with the Stoneworker's Guild, but we've had no word from him since then."

Teryse's brows furrowed, pale-green eyes clenched into slits. "Our prince sails to the Vines and this is the first I am hearing about it? Why was I not informed earlier?"

"Father said it was only a trivial dispute with the guilds. An issue he cared not to attend to, what with the tournament approaching. He preferred to stay in Rothspire to see that the celebration is being executed to his desires."

Teryse huffed and cursed. "You mean he wished to sit on his arse and have his successor perform his duties."

That sounds closer to the mark. "His reasons are his own. You are aware of that."

"I am aware of your father's desire to avoid unpleasant situations. But to place his own son in such danger so that he might promenade around a host of sycophants… Well, that is low, even for my brother."

"We have always maintained fair relations with the Windsongs, and this is but a quarrel between the guilds. Do you believe this to be dangerous?" Aldir eyed her.

"You are worried, are you not?" asked Teryse.

"I am worried because the sea can be treacherous, not because I believe the guilds of the Vines are." He rubbed his chin.

His aunt's face contorted into a mask of frustration. "Your brother has been sent into a wolf's den." She calmed herself and Aldir thought he heard her mumble, "Blood for blood." But then she looked up at him and said, "I do not blame you...but your father?"

Blood for blood? What does that mean, and why is she so worried about the Vines? "Do you believe Odain may come to harm while in their care? They have always been one of our closest allies." He shook his head as if unconsciously disagreeing with the idea.

"Are the Windsongs there?" asked Teryse, her eyes searching his. "I am told Lord Byron arrived in Rothspire not three days ago. Should not the prince have arrived with him?"

Now that you say it out loud, it is odd that Odain did not sail with Lord Byron.

"You must learn to trust your instincts, Aldir," said Teryse. "Perhaps it would be wise to send someone to Maresport and ensure your brother's safety. If you are concerned, you have the authority to do these things."

"But, my father..."

"But your father nothing!" She struggled under her blankets, trying to stand. "I should have never stepped down." Her body shook violently.

Aldir stood quickly and rushed to her side. "Lie back down." He helped her onto the bed, but she resisted. "Don't struggle. You do not have the strength."

"You do not have the wits!" she hissed.

Teryse ceased her attempt to stand and allowed him to assist her. "This was a horrible decision, Aldir. Your role is to think for the king, not to be his errand boy."

"It was an inconsequential matter," he said, growing angry. "I had no reason to question him."

"You must always question the king's decisions, lest all of Onyris fall into ruin."

Gods! What is she talking about?

"You understand you will never be king?" The Iron Woman's eyes bored into Aldir. "Everly's line now supersedes yours. Unless she and all of her offspring die, you and yours have no claim to the throne. If you did not question your father and stop Odain," she said, her voice growing thick with condescension, "his blood will be on your hands."

Where was this coming from? Aldir had no authority over his brother or his father. Their decisions were theirs alone.

"What are you saying, Teryse? I've no desire to rule, and no desire to see my brother come to harm. I cannot stop my father from what he desires." He stared at his aunt, confused by her accusation.

Teryse slumped against her pillows and coughed. "You are a man, Aldir, but beyond that, you are the Primacy of the Realm. No longer can you hide behind your family or fear; neither exist for you. He is no longer your father, and Odain is not your brother—and neither are they king nor prince. They are children. Your children. And like your own daughter, they must be reined in."

What has Edlen done? He knew his daughter was a handful, but he'd never shared his fatherly struggles with his aunt.

"Men who believe they wield immutable power will not cease to use it." Teryse continued. "You alone guide the realm now. I wish my predecessor told me this, but I learned quickly —much quicker than you seem to be."

His aunt's words were cold steel, and Aldir's insecurities now lay bare.

I cannot do this. My father made a terrible mistake.

"This is why I am here," said Aldir. "I need your help."

His plea tasted bitter as it spilled from his tongue.

"Help?" Teryse spat the word. She readjusted herself again, staring blankly towards an open window before grinning. "Yes, I believe we all need help in our time. Forgive me. I have played the part of the Iron Woman for far too long. It seems only now, as death is so near, I am afforded the opportunity to be the person I always wished to be. I will tell you a secret that was never told to me."

Aldir watched as the Iron Woman departed and his aunt returned. He was still her nephew; the young boy she used to sit upon her knee and tell stories to. He sat down and held her frail hands. "Yes…"

"You will no longer see a friendly face, nor listen to a kind word that does not conceal a desire. Everyone you speak to will wish something from you—from kings to shepherds—and you must be the voice of them all.

"To the king, you are the voice of the lowliest of the realm, for they have not the means to defend themselves. But to those lowly men, you must be the voice of the king, for he will not deign to condescend to them.

"And they will all hate you." Her voice grew hoarse and she wheezed, but she continued. "The king will hate you for impeding his desires, and the smallfolk will hate you for imposing more restrictions on their already-miserable lives. This is the true role of Primacy. And you will be rewarded with disdain."

"But every man and woman in the Wide-World knows who you are," he said.

"They are aware of me today," said Teryse. "Can you name the last three primacies?"

Aldir thought for a moment, but no name other than his aunt's came to his mind.

"Your silence is answer enough. How many kings do you remember?"

Ulisaren, Andaire, Alisar, Amarion, Beregon, Halstone the Fourth... and the list went on in his head.

"Why do we do it?" he asked.

"Because it needs to be done," she answered stiffly. "Onyris has and will always be held on a knife's edge. Kings are remembered for centuries beyond our lives, but they are only sharp as a tourney sword. The Primacy, though... We are the sharpened steel that slides in the gaps of armor."

Teryse Killion's eyes sharpened and then closed. Her body became limp and she slid down from her pillows.

Aldir knelt beside her, his body tense with fear. He placed a hand on her chest and felt the slight lift of her breath. She had only fallen asleep. Perhaps it was too much to ask of her to remain the powerful woman he always knew. He pulled the bedsheets over her and closed the shutters. Before he left, he stooped down and kissed her forehead.

CHAPTER

EVERLY

Before the Tournament

THE ROYAL LITTER was an enormous carriage, carved of ivory and oak—canopied by red and green silks. Drawn by eight draft horses, it swayed slightly as it lumbered down the path of Dartsuil's Keep towards the tourney field. Everly Graymere looked out one of the circular windows and noted the sun reflecting off the armor of the four knights who walked alongside them.

Inside the litter, the sweet scent of powdered sandalwood and lavender filled the air, disguising the odor of sweat and hot breath. Thankful for the masking properties of the fragrance, Everly sat atop plush velvet cushions directly across from King Ulisaren. She drummed her fingers vacantly as she minded her daughter, Princess Amara. The young girl, dressed in red and green chiffon, fidgeted in her seat and pulled at her diadem before tugging on the curtain nearest to her.

Everly nudged her and scowled. The king was in a rare temper, and she cared not to attract his ire.

"You disobeyed me!" said King Ulisaren, his finger thrust

in Aldir's chest. The lines of his face denoted that of a permanent frown, as well as the crows-feet at the corners of his gray-green eyes. "To visit her?" he roared.

Everly's brother-in-law sat grim and resolute. "I needed answers, Father." He slammed a fist onto his thigh. "You are aware how much today is costing us, are you not?"

"Costing us?" The king glanced at Everly, dragging her into a conversation she wished to evade. "He keeps me, the King of Onyris, waiting in a sweltering carriage, so he might niggle me about finances?" He started back on Aldir. "I made you Primacy, not Adept of Ledgers. Perhaps I would have done better to sit your sister-in-law in your role, eh?" He threw his hands in the air and turned to Everly.

Perhaps you would have, Everly thought but said nothing. She turned her attention back to Amara.

"She agrees but is too polite to say so," said the king. "You would do well to learn from her."

Aldir seemed to pay no heed to his rebuke. "Aunt Teryse distrusts the Windsongs. She explained our debt and has cause to believe that Odain might be in danger. A ransom is not out of the realm of possibility."

"My husband is in danger?" Everly asked, her eyes wide with fear.

She held the king in her gaze, the gold flecks in her dark-brown eyes burning. "Mind your tongues, both of you—she need not hear this." She clutched her daughter's small hands. "Your uncle only jests, my love. Same as your cousin does with you." Everly smiled down at the princess.

"Will Edlen be there today?" asked Amara.

Again, Everly stared at Aldir. In an instant, she softened her tone and stroked Amara's hair. "Yes. I am positive she awaits us now."

The king laughed. "My sweet princess, your uncle is full of jests today." He mussed his granddaughter's hair then turned to Aldir. "Your foolish actions may see you dressed in motley soon. Our buffoon, Flyspeck, will be rankled."

Aldir pressed the issue. "Teryse—"

"Let me tell you about your *benevolent* aunt," said Ulisaren. "Something she no doubt neglected to inform you of."

The litter came to an abrupt halt. A gentle knock thumped on the door. The voice of Sir Kerath Manley, the head of the King's Blades, sounded, "Your Grace, we have arrived."

The king shifted in his seat and directed the others to stay still. "One moment, Kerath."

"As you wish, My Grace," Kerath replied.

"Before I depart to enjoy my tournament, I want one thing understood." Ulisaren studied his family. "When the smallfolk name you *Iron*, they do so mockingly. It is a substitute for stubborn or pigheaded. My sister might be remembered as the Iron Woman, but do not be fooled. She is an obstinate old crone who believes daggers lurk in every shadow. Did she disclose her relationship to the Windsongs? I am certain she did not. She may relish in the adulation of her ill-gotten name, but she wishes no one discover the rust that lies underneath it. Never believe an *Iron* person is without flaws."

A small voice full of innocence asked, "What about the Iron Horse? Was Sir Matthew bad?" Amara gazed up at her grandfather.

Gods! You'd better think of something fast, thought Everly.

"Your grandfather does not mean the Iron Horse, sweetling." Everly touched her daughter's cheek tenderly. "Sir Matthew is beyond reproach; he was just as gallant and thrilling as all the legends say." She stared fixedly at the king, hoping he might remember his impressionable granddaughter was also in the carriage. "Was he not?"

King Ulisaren laughed. He stood and tickled Amara as he lifted her from her seat. "Sir Matthew Dorne was the mightiest and greatest knight to ever walk the Wide-World. Have I ever told you the story of the time he rescued Princess Helaine from the Ice Tower?"

He rapped upon the door of the carriage, and when it opened, strode down a set of stairs, his granddaughter pressed tight to his chest. He walked away from the litter, his voice booming as he regaled Amara with tales of the fabled knight.

Everly smiled while the king departed, but as soon as he and her daughter were beyond earshot, she rounded on Aldir. "How dare you say that in front of her?" Her eyes narrowed and wrinkles appeared on her pale forehead. "Your niece trusts you! You have the gall to put it in her mind that her father is in danger? What are you thinking?" She had to stop herself from slapping her brother-in-law.

Aldir dropped his gaze, his shoulders sloped. "You're right, that was unwise of me. I should have waited until Amara was no longer with us… I apologize." There was no argument in his voice.

It took great restraint on her part to not continue berating her brother-in-law, but before he turned away, Everly perceived a sadness in his eyes. She recognized this grief; it was the same she coped with every day. She placed her hand on his shoulder before she exited.

"I miss them both, too." Tears might have come to her if she stayed and dwelled on the loss of her son or Irymar, but today was not a day for tears.

Descending the stairs, she gazed upon the crush of people who swarmed the castle grounds. Everywhere she looked, crowds gathered: clusters of men and women dressed in the different colors of their families as well as smallfolk wearing their finest rough spun. Many of the commoners stopped whatever they were doing and gawked at her as she strode from the litter. She met their stares, smiled, and gave a slight wave.

The scent of roasted pork, chicken, fish, and other exotic meats mingled with garlic, onions, and turnips along with the foul odor of spilled ale, mead, and too many people. All of Onyris congregated in the field—but behind all of this excitement, Everly sensed a tension that shaded the otherwise glorious day.

She greeted her cousin, Sir Willem Thorpe, a member of the King's Blades. Tall, athletic, and cursed with a smile that could melt steel, he cut a dashing figure in the shimmering armor of his rank. His face, so near in likeness to her father's that she felt an innate obedience to him, beamed as he received her.

Together, they pushed through the crowd of smallfolk. She flashed a radiant smile and waved at the onlookers, the sun gleaming off her auburn hair, which hung in fashionable curls that tumbled over her shoulders.

"You are stunning today, my lady," Sir Willem said.

Everly Graymere knew she was stunning. Her deep-brown eyes and aquiline features were enough to make any woman jealous. She was tall, poised, and though she had birthed two children in her thirty-five years, her hips had widened only slightly, adding extra beauty to her full figure.

She was dressed in a flowing gown of green and red, which she wore to appease the king, but underneath she was ornamented in a partlet of blue and black, representing the colors of her father's family: the Thorpes of Godsbreath.

"Just today?" she quipped. Without awaiting an answer, she asked, "Do you sense their discontent?" Her eyes darted around the crowd.

Sir Willem smirked, paying no heed to her concern. "It is a tourney, dear cousin. These folk are no more than animals." He smiled vainly at a young woman who approached then continued. "And they smell blood."

"Be that as it may," said Everly, "I hear rumors of malcontents who gather in the Great Wheel."

"Malcontents?" asked Willem. He pushed past the mob, his smug smile never receding. "Who fills your head with such nonsense? Yes, the city guard was dispatched to silence a handful of scrappers, but do not worry yourself over it. Nothing more than some children armed with sticks. Our knights will flash their steel and your *malcontents* will run back to their hovels."

A hundred boys with sticks may overpower five knights. Everly kept her thoughts to herself, just as she always did when speaking to her cousin. "If you say so, Sir Willem." She locked her arm in his and smiled coquettishly.

"I will protect you, my lady, fear not." He patted her head with his free arm.

They pressed past the onlookers as they neared the grandstand—a massive box, barricaded on all sides—guarded by the King's Blades. They were the private guard of the King of Onyris and the most skilled and loyal knights in the WideWorld. The chief amongst the Blades, Sir Kerath Manley, stood six-and-a-half feet tall, with muscled arms that rippled under green and white heavy steel plate. He was named the

Sword of the King, a venerable knight in his early sixties who'd held the position for over thirty years.

"Where have you been?" Manley's salt-and-pepper beard hung just below a visored helm.

"My lady wished to receive her people." Sir Willem showed no deference to his superior. "Now she wishes to sit."

"Your duty was to escort the princess, not dawdle in her reflected glory." Kerath grimaced.

"You wound me, Kerath. Perhaps when I am your age I'll have learned not to do as our radiance requests, but until then, I believe I will defer to my lady."

Almost apoplectic, Sir Kerath lifted his hand to strike the young knight, but Everly interceded.

"My good sir, there is no cause for anger." She placed her hand on Sir Kerath's arm, her eyes wide with feigned innocence. "My cousin did his best to hasten me, but I insisted on keeping a leisurely pace. I wished to greet our fair people. If there is anyone to blame for our late arrival, it is me." Her lips pursed into that of a wounded child's.

Even Willem was taken aback. He stared at his cousin admiringly.

"My apologies, my lady. A woman's wont is a woman's wont, as my mother taught me—Her Grace more than others," said Sir Kerath, bowing.

I will have to keep an eye on this one. He's held his title for too many years. He grows stubborn. "I am not *Her Grace* quite yet, sir. Please excuse my cousin from your ire, and please excuse my tardiness. I see now His Grace is in need of rescuing." She pressed beyond the obdurate old knight and kissed her cousin's hand.

"If I need saving, I will look for you." Her curled hair

twirled behind her as she spun from the two men, leaving them to whatever discussion they might have.

The grandstand was well appointed with cushioned seats and an array of various treats. Everly made her way towards Ulisaren, past servants carrying trays of colorful foods and drinks: tarts, cakes, and pies on one; skewered boar and pheasant on another; and her favorite candied peaches and plums. She lifted one of these from a passing tray and bit into it. The peach exploded in her mouth, sending a stream of juice down her chin. She wiped the delicious effusion away as she neared her father-in-law. "My Grace, I am sorry to have kept you waiting."

Ulisaren beamed. He was still holding his granddaughter. Once he kissed the young girl on the cheek and placed her in her seat, he grabbed Everly's hand and pulled her towards a heavyset man. "Daughter, have you met Lord Brastor Archwood?"

Not daughter-in-law? He must want something from this man. Everly displayed her most brilliant smile. "I cannot say I have had the pleasure." *Gods! He must weigh over twenty stone.*

Lord Brastor Archwood was an enormous man, younger than Ulisaren by ten years, though his massive weight made him appear just as old, if not older. He kept a close-cut beard that had turned a pale white-gold except for around his mouth, which was stained almost black but tinged with a deep red. Everly knew in an instant that this man loved his wine. And she was not wrong. Before Brastor offered her his hand, he took a gigantic swig from his goblet.

"The pleasure is all mine," said Lord Brastor. He took her hand in his. A warm mitt of flesh strangled her thin fingers.

"His Grace spoke of your beauty, but I must say, it is not simple flattery." He eyed her hungrily. "I apologize for my ignorance. You are a glory."

Everly blushed—a skill she'd perfected in her years at court. "You are too kind, my lord."

I will give this lecherous old man what he desires. "I have heard many tales of your valiant deeds, my lord. My husband speaks highly of you. *The Mighty Brastor*, he names you. The man who defeated Dysternis Moorcroft in single combat. He has said that if not for your prowess in the field, we might all be celebrating a different king on this fine day." She kissed his hand. "It is an honor to hold the hand of the man who swung the war hammer that saved Rothspire."

Brastor glowed with pride. He turned to Ulisaren. "She knows her history, My Grace."

The king grinned. "Our princess consistently proves herself more than worthy of the crown."

Amara glanced up at her mother and then turned away. *I am sorry, sweetling. There will come a day where you will understand this farce.*

At that moment, horns sounded from the center of the tourney field. An explosion of cheers and shouts sprang from the crowd in a deafening roar. The tournament was about to begin.

Ulisaren tensed with excitement. At seventy-five, he was no different than a child on their birthday. He almost leapt in elation. "I believe I am needed." His body quivered with joy, and he turned to his granddaughter, Princess Amara. "Will you escort me?"

The young girl glanced up at her mother first, awaiting permission.

Everly nodded her assent.

In a quick movement, King Ulisaren swooped down and lifted his granddaughter. She pressed herself tightly against his chest and looked once more at her mother.

Ulisaren strode from the grandstand, his voice booming. "Are you ready, my lady? Onyris awaits us."

Everly loved her father-in-law for this. Though he was the king, and the most powerful man in the Wide-World, the simple fact that he cherished Amara so much made her forget any of his shortcomings—or that he'd left her with a sycophant like Brastor Archwood.

"He is Dartsuil reborn, is he not?" Brastor's voice dragged her from the precious moment.

Never forgetting her courtesies, Everly replied, "You speak the truth, my lord." She was growing bored with their conversation.

"Do you have any wagers on the melee?" he asked. "You would be foolish not to place your coin on my son, Hovaird. He is the mightiest knight to wield a sword in over fifty years."

"I was not aware Hovaird had placed his name in the ring," said Everly in mock astonishment. "Had I known, my coin would surely be on his name."

If Odain spoke truly, I would assume the Archwood stock might prove unbeatable. She smiled primly. "My husband claims your family to be beyond reproach."

"The prince is very wise," said Brastor, chuckling. "I am glad to hear you understand the strength of the Archwoods. Perhaps there is a reason beyond chance I met with you today." Brastor's voice surged with a sudden pride. "Custom states I should broach this with His Grace, first…but I never let an opportunity evade me." He took another gulp from his goblet and asked, "Is it ever too early to discuss splendid propositions?"

And so, it begins... thought Everly.

"My son Jalox," started Brastor, "is only a few years older than the princess. Have you given thought to your daughter's future?"

Everly shuddered. *Of course. It was not by mere chance Ulisaren left me with this man.*

Luckily the horns sounded again. The king was about to address his audience, but before he spoke, a small, balding Patrik Lindon approached. The Adept of Law whispered into the king's ear while handing over a piece of parchment. From where she sat, she could not hear Patrik's words, but the spasm of anger that flashed across Ulisaren's face was unmistakable. The king crumpled the parchment and shoved it back at Patrik, dismissing him with a wave of his hand.

For a brief moment, Everly met the king's eyes and thought they hinted at an apology. *What ill message is this?* As quickly as their eyes had met, the king turned from her to continue his declamation.

"Five hundred years!" Ulisaren's voice echoed above the din of the crowd. "A testament to the power of Onyris, and each of you gathered here today are a part of its history." The king held his granddaughter up, displaying her proudly. He faced the grandstands and locked eyes with Everly again. "Here, I hold the future of our lands in my arms."

A thunderous applause followed, peppered with shouts of, "Hail to the princess!"

He waited for the ovation to subside. "Our fair Amara ushers in a new era, one that will see an end to tired traditions." He whispered something into the girl's ear and a wide smile spread across her face. She giggled then whispered back into her grandfather's ear.

"She says…!" said Ulisaren.

There was a brief moment of quiet. Everly clutched Brastor's arm, though, she did not know why.

King Ulisaren placed his granddaughter down on her feet and held her hand in his. Together, they shouted, "Let the games begin!" They walked from the field, waving to the crowd.

Horns erupted with triumphant trills, drums exploded in a rapturous cadence of booms and thuds, and seventy-five knights entered the tournament field. The mass who surrounded the field cheered, and the earlier tension Everly sensed gave way to a tempest of enthusiastic hoots and hollers. The noise of the crowd grew louder than the music, and she too joined in the excitement, temporarily forgetting her noble company.

Knights armored in varying colors and flying the flags of their respective families trotted along the perimeter of the field. Landed knights, free knights, and silver swords—a slur given to warriors who refused the title of knight, instead selling their protection in return for the silver in which their name was derived—weaved about each other. The wealthiest rode colossal destriers, their caparisons emblazoned with family sigils. Others pranced upon palfreys and coursers, dressed in boiled leather and mail. Quite a few mounted no horse, instead marching behind, waving wooden swords, axes, spears, or maces. But the audience reserved their most boisterous of shouts for the last knight to enter the field.

A man of gargantuan proportions, whose red and green armor glistened brilliantly in the sun, walked onto the grounds. No horse in Rothspire could bear his weight and he wore no helm; his dark-brown skin and handsome smile could be seen by all. Long, black, curly hair sat atop his head in an untidy knot. Upon hearing the cries at his entrance, he lifted his arms over his head in a gesture of triumph.

"Gods! No," Everly said to herself. She was now the only person not yelling. Around her could be heard screams of surprise and elation, as well as violent jeers. Interspersed with these exclamations, she overheard haughty whispers and stifled curses. One of the voices she recognized was that of Lord Brastor.

"Is this some jest of the king?"

Everly hoped the old man was right. Though furious at seeing Rhen enter the melee, she knew her anger was not the same as everyone else's. "My lord, you know the king well enough. He would never jest about this." How she wished she were wrong, but her father-in-law would never intentionally disrupt the enjoyment of a tournament for his own satisfaction.

Brastor Archwood huffed, "Then this ridiculous farce must be ended before it begins." He looked around the grandstand, vainly searching for someone to fix his wrath upon.

"Men have wagered good coin on this match. We cannot allow a brocken to defile such a day as this. There are laws to prevent such a thing." The word *brocken* slid from his tongue as if he spat rancid ale.

The mere fact Brastor was so enraged tempered Everly's own frustration. She did not care about the wagers of lords, nor did she believe the boy should be refused entry due to his lineage. Her concerns were much more selfish.

Rhen was the Shield of the Princess—her daughter's sworn protector. His sole duty was to guard the heir of Onyris and to act as a silent protector. He needed no other title, no other honors. If he were to win this melee, which he most assuredly would, he could gain no more glorious a reward than that which he already possessed.

But to see a man like Brastor this upset filled Everly with a peculiar joy.

"Are you questioning your wagers, my lord?" she asked, a sly smirk curling around the edges of her lips. "Your son is the mightiest warrior in over fifty years. That *brocken* is a mere boy. Hovaird should have no trouble dispatching him."

The Lord of Straten did not answer. His face turned red, and he shuffled past her.

Amara returned, her face still flushed with excitement.

"Mother, did you see me?"

"Did I see you?" Everly embraced her daughter and kissed her cheek. "I could not take my eyes off of you."

The little princess giggled. "Grandfather told me Rhen will fight today!"

I am glad he told you, but does he know what this means? "It is very exciting. Your Shield will be able to prove his strength."

She knew her daughter was too young to understand the ramifications of his entrance. "I hope he does well," she said, squeezing Amara's hand.

"He will," said Amara, no doubt in her voice. "He will win. I know he will."

That might be even worse than him competing. She stooped and kissed the top of her daughter's head.

The knights who rode around the barricades of the field broke away from their lines and approached the lords and ladies gathered in the grandstands. Each man carried with them a single flower. Roses, marigolds, carnations, daffodils, daisies, and anemones were handed out to maidens, ladies, and a few beautiful common women. Everly herself was inundated with these gifts, as almost half the knights participating loomed near her, each one wishing to gain her favor. She smiled politely to each man who offered her their championship. Of all these great knights, she recognized less than she imagined, but her response was the same to all: "You have my affection, and I wish you luck on the field." Her voice grew hoarse after the twentieth man departed.

It was then she watched Rhen approach. *Does he believe I will accept his favor? He has grown exceptionally bold.*

Rhen stopped before he reached Everly. Instead, he bowed to Amara and bestowed upon her a ragged clump of dahlias. It was obvious he had pulled them from one of the gardens surrounding the tournament field; there was still dirt in the roots. He took the princess's hand in his and kissed it. "These are for you, my lady. Do I have your favor?"

Amara blushed. She looked to her mother and then back at Rhen. "Thank you, Rhen. Luck be with you!"

Rhen bowed and departed.

He was the only one of the many knights to ask her daughter's favor for today. Everly would not forget this. Her anger dimmed. He was the princess's Shield, and she knew he would protect her. She studied her daughter.

Amara smiled wide, and her eyes glistened with a sort of childish innocence.

If this silly boy wants to fight for his princess, I will not begrudge him. Everly grabbed her daughter's hand and said, "He will win."

CHAPTER

DARRIN

The Great Wheel

Darrin Cantlay rode in rank behind Chief Haron Ridgefront and Lord-Overseer Sir Kayvold Archwood. His backside ached as they made their way down the final stretch of the Donwar Mountains. The path took them on a twisting course, gradually descending until they passed a bend in the road and the vast expanse of The Great Wheel of Rothspire lay spread out before them.

An enormous market town encircled by smoothly paved stone covered almost the entirety of the valley floor. From where Darrin stood, he could see the ten concentric circles inside of the Great Wheel, each of these bisected by ten diagonal streets that ran from the outer perimeter towards the center. Mathematicians of old had designed the Great Wheel, and to this day, it stood as a wonder of engineering. Five roads snaked their way to the Wheel, and Darrin knew these to be the paths that led to the five townships of Rothspire. He had memorized their names as a child, wishing to one day find himself fortunate enough to visit these fabled lands.

Darrin's father had ridden to the Great Wheel in his

youth and told stories of its immensity, but to behold it with his own eyes made Lord Phillip Cantlay's words pale in comparison.

You could fit five Redruns in here. Darrin frowned at the thought. His homeland had always seemed massive, but this gargantuan city proved the insignificance of his father's holdings. He shaded his eyes and gazed in wonderment.

"She's an 'ell of sight, ay Cantlay?" said Haron, his husky voice breaking the spell of the view.

"She is." Darrin nodded.

Up ahead, Lord-Overseer Kayvold halted.

Why are we stopping? Darrin slowed his charger.

"Cantlay?" asked Lord-Overseer Kayvold Archwood, a slim man in his fifties, balding and sallow faced. He took a swig from his water skin and studied the Great Wheel. He kept an extremely tight cropped, golden-white beard, which partially masked three thin scars that ran from his right ear to his chin. The coarse hair on his face refused to grow over these scars.

"First time in the capital, is it?" asked the Lord-Overseer as he turned towards Darrin.

"Aye," answered Darrin. His voice cracked and he looked down. This was the first time Archwood had acknowledged him by name.

"We are about to enter the Great Wheel, the largest city in Onyris. Tell me, does a green boy like you have any reservations?" Archwood asked. The outline of an owl was stitched on his dark-green jerkin.

Why would I have any reservations? "No, my lord. My father has told me countless stories of the Wheel," said Darrin. "He has many dealings with the king and his council."

"Has he?" asked Archwood, his eyebrows arched in concern. He turned his attention to Haron. "And you, Chief Ridgefront? Hadley believes your last roving still weighs on you. Are you prepared to enter?"

"Aye, Hadley worries too much, my lord. It'll take more than a damned bear to keep me from my duty. Besides, I've made it this far, ain't I?"

Darrin flinched, the memory still fresh.

"Good, good," said Kayvold. "King Ulisaren is a man of little patience. He will not be overjoyed to welcome the three of us—not when we present him with your *gift*." He rounded on Darrin. "They are secure, correct?"

The severed legs Darrin had discovered in the forest were bound tightly in a hempen sack and wrapped again by a leather cloak. They'd been thudding against the side of Darrin's horse since setting out from Elmfort, and he'd grown so accustomed to their weight that he knew they were still in his possession without being asked. "Aye, my lord."

"Very well," said Kayvold. "Without them, the king will not entertain our visit." He glanced at the sack. "We bring an ill omen, boys. Do not expect a warm greeting."

With that, he tugged lightly on his reins and started back on their path. "If the Gods smile on us, today's tourney will see our king in decent humor. And Cantlay, be sure not to fall prey to the pleasures of the Wheel."

The pleasures of the Wheel?

The three men rode along the outer path of the Great Wheel, a broad stretch of rough trodden dirt. But when they entered, none of Archwood's warnings could have prepared Darrin for what he saw.

All market towns had a reputation for being lusty worlds of frivolity, but the Great Wheel must have been the architect for them all. Not only larger than that of any other realm in

Onyris, it was filled almost to bursting with shops, taverns, and inns, as well as more people than Darrin believed populated all of the Wide-World. Vendors shouted incessantly at passers-by—their voices blending lyrically into the cacophony of musicians who strolled the streets.

The smell of every food imaginable mingled with the vicious odor of unwashed beggars, as well as the perfumed nobles who meandered throughout the cobbled roads. Piles of horse shit littered the street, and store-keeps burned sage, hyssop, and rosemary in an attempt to mask the foulness.

Over the noise, Darrin heard his chief exclaim, "Get a good whiff, Cantlay. That's the scent of the Wheel. Success, sadness, and shit."

Darrin found the scent intoxicating; to him, it was the smell of freedom. He glanced around, the surging mass of people overwhelming. To his left, four scantily clad women waved at him, giggling.

"That be an Eye, ladies! Best be on your guard," one woman hollered then licked her lips.

"Aye! Maybe 'e will stain us," a round-faced redhead yelled. Her barely covered chest heaved as she giggled and winked.

Darrin smiled, his horse starting to veer off the street towards her.

Haron turned back and smirked. He checked his horse and rode back. "You ain't 'ere for pleasure, Cantlay. Archwood sees all, and he ain't the kind who'll forgive ya simple pleasures. Best look straight ahead and remember you's riding with the Lord-Overseer."

Darrin thanked him and trotted forward, away from the half-naked women. *The pleasures of the Wheel...* He smirked.

They turned a corner and followed Archwood down a

steep, narrow street. After passing a few smaller shops, Kayvold dismounted his giant gray destrier and hailed them. He tied his horse to a railing and waited.

Darrin approached, swung from his charger, and began to tie it off on the same railing.

"Let your chief finish her off, lad," Kayvold said. "You've been seeing to our mounts since we left. Ridgefront is more than capable of this task."

Out of habit, Darrin finished tying off his horse. As he finished, he apologized, "Sorry, my lord. My hands have a will of their own."

Kayvold chuckled, patted Darrin on the shoulder, then turned to Haron. "Ridgefront, keep an eye on our cargo, and see our poor beasts get some water. I'm taking Cantlay inside."

"Aye, m'lord," said Haron as he bounded off his horse and gave a curious shrug to Darrin.

What is this? Darrin looked back to his chief, his eyes wide with fear. *This is when he sends me back to Hadley. I got them here; now he has no more use for me. I should have expected this. I have no business meeting with the king. I'm barely a rover.* He kept his head down and followed the Lord-Overseer into a small, dark tavern.

Kayvold Archwood pushed open the slatted, wooden door, his slender body almost nothing but corded muscle.

The tavern was empty and strangely quiet. Darrin realized immediately why Archwood chose this forgotten spot. The room was so small that he couldn't imagine it fitting more than ten people at a time, which meant no ears might secretly listen in on their conversation.

"Quaint, is it not?" asked Archwood.

What am I supposed to say to this?

"Very," replied Darrin.

Before Kayvold Archwood could say another word, a barrel-chested man appeared from behind a counter and greeted them.

"Eyes of the Forest!" he exclaimed. His voice was rough but congenial. "What ya having? All on the house, of course." He attempted a bow, his filthy apron bunching up around his protruding midsection.

Without exchanging any courtesy, Kayvold asked, "What wine do you serve?"

"You're in fine luck, my lord," the man said. "Red from Straten; just received three barrels this morning. Best in all of Onyris. Shall I make it two?"

Kayvold eyed Darrin.

"Do you have any ale?" Darrin squeaked out.

"Aye. Ain't no Straten Red, but if it's ale you's craving, then I got more than enough." The man turned from where he stood and lumbered back to his barrels.

Ale? Why didn't I just accept the wine? Darrin kept his gaze fixed on the floor.

"A man who is aware of what he likes," said Kayvold as he led Darrin to a small table. "Sit, Cantlay. No need to be nervous."

No need to be nervous? You're not the one about to be dismissed.

As they sat on the hard, wobbly chairs, Kayvold said, "We have ridden hundreds of miles over rocky terrain and the formidable peaks of the Donwar Mountains, but this is the first time I've seen you sweat in such a way. Tell me, Darrin, am I more frightening than the wild lands?"

"I...I have witnessed what dangers exist in the wild." The memories of the enormous bear was still fresh in his mind. "I can run from them, my lord, but a beast cannot dismiss me from the Eyes."

The Lord-Overseer's laugh was explosive, the scars on his face bunched into one hideous mound of glossy, pink flesh. "So, you mean to say I am more dangerous than the wolves that stalked us during our travels? You're wasting your talent as a rover, Cantlay. I'm certain any lord missing their jester would be glad to have you in their service."

Darrin's mouth clenched, but before he could say anything he might regret, the ale-keep returned with their drinks.

"Pint of ale and a lovely red." His voice was as sweet as the wine he served.

Kayvold took a sip from his cup and smiled. "You are a man of your word." He reached into his coin purse and pulled out three noles. "For you, my good man. Bring another round when we're low."

"Bernis, my lord, but you can call me Bear," the man said as he took the three noles and bowed.

Kayvold waited for the man to leave before he said, "I've drank vinegar sweeter than this swill."

Darrin chuckled out of duty.

"I have some advice for you, Cantlay." Kayvold leaned in conspiratorially. "Be wary of any man who claims their wine is the best in all of Onyris. Those are the words of one who is trying to sell you something. Our friend, Bear, wouldn't know a fine wine from fermented horse piss—even if I held my blade to his neck.

"Do you know what makes an excellent wine?" he asked.

I would drink horse piss before I drank wine. "No, my lord."

"Character," said Kayvold, matter-of-factly. "The finest wines all have a unique character." He took another sip.

"This here, the only character it has is strength. There's

no complexity to it—there is no…mystery. Yes, it is potent, but *too* potent. It lacks a full flavor. This Straten vintage is nothing but red alcohol—it is not wine. Would you like to know the finest wine I've ever tasted?"

What are you talking about? Darrin fumbled with his mug, wondering if there was any point to the Lord-Overseer's ramblings. "Yes, my lord."

Kayvold paid no attention to Darrin's lack of interest. "Nine years ago, I found myself in the Vines… You know where that is, correct?"

Darrin nodded.

"Whitecliff, it was. I was there on a scouting mission with Gareth Penfield, my old Lord-Overseer. The Eyes were in a bad place back then—what with the red cough—and we needed as many recruits as we could find.

"The Vines were always a decent place to acquire new men, and Overseer Penfield was from Innsmaw, so he believed he might be privy to a few knights—or at least some of the free-swords who lingered there. Regardless of his misplaced beliefs, he took me to Lord Edward Halstead's.

"I was commander at Tarranfort at the time, and the Halsteads welcomed us with open arms, and better than that—open casks."

Kayvold held the cup of Straten Red in front of him. "It was there, Cantlay, where I learned what the word character meant."

In one swift gulp, he drained his cup and wiped the faintest of dribbles from his beard. "This will get you drunk, no doubt, but that's not why we drink the grape. I want every sip to tell a story; I want every last drop to own its individuality."

He pushed the cup away and stared at Darrin. "Tell me—

why did you join the Eyes of the Forest and not Rothspire's military?"

Darrin choked, ale daring to rush from his nose. "Me?" It was all he could say through his coughing.

"Well, I'm not asking Bernis, am I?" asked Kayvold. "It has been near two-hundred years since the Eyes have seen true battle. Yes, we tell ourselves that our duty is sacred, but…the vastness of the forest protects Rothspire—as well as if we've never existed."

"But the military is only active during times of war, my lord," said Darrin. "The Eyes are always vigilant. If I'm speaking honestly, I wished to be active—not held on retainer in the chance war might erupt."

Kayvold eyed him. "You mean you wished to walk the countless miles of the forest and report on fallen trees?"

"If that's what's asked of me."

"It is not out of the hope of fabled glory?" asked Kayvold.

Fabled glory? What does he mean? "No, my lord. The Eyes of the Forest have guarded the realm from raiders and brigands for centuries. With all due respect to those who serve in our army, I would rather spend my days searching out those who mean us harm than awaiting a war that may never come."

"You are certain it has nothing to do with *legends*?" Kayvold took a sip of wine. "Hadley told me your brothers call you Tin Horse… Why is that?"

Tin Horse? Darrin loathed the name even when it came from Kayvold Archwood's lips. "I…I made a foolish claim my first day in training."

Kayvold stared, unflinching. "That you wish to be the next Sir Matthew Dorne?"

Darrin was afraid to look him in the eyes. He glared at his mug of ale and said, "Yes." *How did you know?*

Kayvold looked on.

Certain the Overseer's gaze was a command, he said, "I told Chief Kittridge and the others that I was going to be the next Iron Horse, and possibly…greater." He trailed off, taking a nervous sip of his drink and wishing he could avoid the curious stare of his superior.

"Would you think me foolish for wanting the same thing when I was your age?"

You wanted to be the Iron Horse? "I would have thought—"

"That you are the only one who took the pledge in the hopes of being Sir Matthew Dorne? Darrin, my lad, the others may have laughed at you for saying it aloud, but I would wager almost every one of them joined the Eyes for the same reason."

Darrin smiled. "But none of them told Kittridge." Whether it was the ale or the fact that the Lord-Overseer seemed genuinely interested in him, Darrin continued.

"That old bastard was the first to call me Tin Horse, but soon everyone in Elmfort joined in. I should've smacked him the moment he said it. That's what my father would do."

At that, Kayvold did laugh. "You've got some fire in your belly, Cantlay. Perhaps Kittridge knew what he was doing when he saddled you with that name?"

He never thought of it that way, but Kayvold had a point. The anger that rose inside him every time he heard the nickname was exactly what pushed him to become one of the best fighters in his fellowship.

"Hadley also told me he had you pegged as a hunter—says you're a natural with your blade—yet you insisted on being placed in the rovers. Why not join Eldred's crew?"

Because the Iron Horse started as a rover. He struggled to come up with a better answer and was saved by the fortunate return of Bernis.

The ale-keep brought out another pint for Darrin and a cup of red for Kayvold. "One more round?"

Distracted by Bear's question, Kayvold recited a queer saying: "'The first is for pleasure, the second is to savor, and the third is for truth.' At least, that's what they say in the Vines."

"Coming up, sirs," said the ale-keep, nodding as though he was familiar with the adage.

I thought he said the wine was awful. "What about Harry?" He hoped he could change the subject and avoid any further scrutiny over his choice to become a rover instead of a more prestigious hunter.

"What about him, Cantlay? Is my company lacking?"

"No, sir!" said Darrin. He fumbled with his ale as some spilled on the table. *Now I've done it. I need to learn to keep my mouth shut.* "I was just…"

"Worried about your chief?" The Lord-Overseer rapped his fingers against the table rhythmically. "I am too."

Haron? Why would he be worried about Haron? They seemed old friends. "My lord, I only meant he might be thirsty."

Kayvold took a sip from his cup and swished the wine in his mouth. When he swallowed, he smacked his lips and said, "Much better on the second serve. Still, it relies too much on strength. I can't taste the oak it was barreled in." He swirled his cup and brought it to his nose. "No bouquet, Darrin. Better, but not exquisite."

Darrin was lost. He should be enjoying this rare moment with the head of the Eyes, but every time he started to relax, Archwood said something that confused him more.

"Your chief is a fine man," said Kayvold. "Has he told you that we came up in the same fellowship?"

He never said more than three words to me until we came across those accursed legs. "No, my lord. Harry never mentioned it."

"He's always been a man of few words," said Kayvold. "Makes him an excellent Eye, you know. He sees more than he says. But there are times we need to talk, Cantlay. And this is one of those."

The Lord-Overseer took another sip, his face grew flush, and his scars turned deep red. "I was struck by a bear once, Darrin. A great, big, brown one. Thought I was done for. You can see his signature on my face. I tell you, of all the things I've found in that damned forest, the bears frighten me the most. They're docile by nature, did you know that?"

He did not wait for an answer. "When they get angry, though…there isn't a creature more terrifying."

Darrin did not need to be told that. The image of the snarling, fanged muzzle, and those gargantuan claws haunted him. Certain he would see the animal's face for the rest of his life, Darrin thought to himself, *Ours was not brown, though. It was black…blacker than the nightmares of death.*

"I was useless for three months after I met her." Kayvold ran his finger against his scars. "Three months…Cantlay. Took a month before I could walk, and after that, every step was agony. Couldn't lift my arm above my head until the end of my second month. When, finally, I was ready to mount a horse again, I couldn't make it more than five or six miles before the pain came rushing back. Happened over twenty years ago, though. The funny thing is…there are days when the same aches still haunt me."

He looked at Darrin, his brown eyes aflame. "But Harry! He rode from Elmfort to Rothspire with no complaint. Loaded our horses for this journey, what…? Two days after your lot returned from the forest? Two days after he was attacked? Two days, Cantlay. Two days!"

Had Darrin not seen the man in the woods heal Harry, he would not have believed it was possible either. "He's strong, my lord. I'm certain he is simply hiding his pain."

Darrin knew his Lord-Overseer would not believe this.

"Strong?" huffed Kayvold. "He's a tough son of a bitch, I'll give you that—but your chief is not made of steel. I have watched him on our journey, yet not once have I seen him favor his arm…or give the slightest grimace when he performs a task.

"More peculiar than that…I spied him in bath while in Straten. His scars are all but vanished.

"I have carried mine for over twenty years! His are no more than faint white streaks across his chest. Tell me, how is this possible?"

We met an angry bear is all…and Haron was knocked from his horse. Nothing more, Darrin told himself.

"He was knocked from his horse, my lord. Nothing worse than that. I think the beast scratched him badly, but Bart and I chased it away."

Bernis returned with a third round of drinks and meekly placed them in front of the two men before he scurried off.

Kayvold paid no heed to the interruption. He lifted his wine. "Third is for the truth."

In one large gulp, he drained his cup. "Commander Hadley told me this same story. He also told me your companion, Bartrom, lost his wits. The boy was raving about wizards or some such nonsense?"

Darrin remembered the wild, pleading eyes of Bart as he was dragged off by his fellow Eyes. He had been shouting about sorcerers and gods. He hadn't listened to Haron. He didn't keep quiet.

"I didn't believe Hadley when he told me, and I don't believe you," said Kayvold. "The truth, Cantlay. Or you can ride back to Elmfort and be placed in a cell next to your friend."

"But…it's not like that…"

"It is exactly that." Kayvold glared at Darrin. "I brought you with us—against Hadley's recommendation—because I believed you might have character, Cantlay." His voice softened. "You have proven an adequate companion, and an adept rover, but perhaps you forget I am the Lord-Overseer. Your loyalties to your friends ended the moment *I* spoke to you. Your loyalties now lie with me—and me alone."

Gods! Forgive me, Haron. Darrin lowered his head and recounted everything: the finding of the severed legs, the enormous bear—he even told Archwood about his decision to ride off before ultimately turning back. When he got to the point where they met the strange man in the woods, he stumbled over his words.

"I can't explain it correctly, my lord, but this man… He held his hands over Haron and told us to look away.

"I closed my eyes and turned my face, but Bart looked on." Tears sprouted at the corners of his eyes. "I don't rightly know what happened, but the man began to speak in a strange tongue—and then I felt a warmth cover me—like being cradled in my mother's arms, like I was a child again.

"Then, in an instant…it passed.

"When I turned back, Haron could stand again. I know this sounds impossible, but it is the truth.

"Everything that followed is a blur. I mean…I cannot place it. The last memory I have is of the three of us riding into Elmfort." Darrin trailed off, certain the Lord-Overseer believed he had lost his mind.

Kayvold sighed. "There is no lie in your voice, Darrin." He closed his eyes and rubbed them. "Unbelievable as it sounds."

I've locked my own manacles, thought Darrin.

"So unbelievable…that it must be the truth. Either that, or you're fit to be studied by the pedagogues of Rose Isle." Kayvold smirked. "Regardless, it is more believable than the fable you and Haron concocted."

"You do not think I've lost my wits?" asked Darrin. *I question it every day.*

The sun shifted outside, and the tavern grew extremely warm. Now well past noon, the ale-keep returned again with another round. Kayvold waved him away.

"There is much to ruminate on, Cantlay. I will say this, though." Archwood tapped his fingers on the table. "The forest is changing; I have sensed it for some time now. I believe the mysterious man you met is part of this change. I am unclear on what part he plays, but I will tell you—these legs you found are the small stones that lead to an avalanche. It is not only the forest that is due change…but the whole of the Wide-World."

DARRIN Cantlay rode in silence as the Great Wheel passed by. What had he done?

Telling the Lord-Overseer all of what happened now seemed the most foolish thing possible. No decision he'd made had been correct since he'd found those damned legs. What would his father say?

"He got it out of ya, didn't he?" asked Haron.

Startled out of his silence, Darrin's horse swerved.

The two men had been riding alongside each other since he'd left the tavern, but Darrin had been too lost in his own thoughts to notice.

"He threatened to send me back to Elmfort," said Darrin as he struggled with his reins.

"Don't be such an arse, lad," said Haron. "Archwood is the Lord-Overseer. I was certain he was gonna wriggle it out of ya."

"I told him everything, Harry…" Darrin cast his eyes to the ground. "Except what Dalnor—"

"Hush yourself," interrupted Haron. "Don't go saying his name aloud." The old, haggard chief glanced up at the sky. "Makes it too real, ya know?"

"Are we going to do what he asked?" Darrin slowed his charger. "Now that Archwood knows?"

"Aye…don't think we have a choice. Archwood's a good man—Overseer or not—he's always been a decent fella. We was in the same fellowship, did I tell ya that yet?"

Archwood did.

"Aye, I think you might have mentioned it."

"Did I?" asked Haron, more to himself than to Darrin. "Regardless…he ain't like Hadley. That bastard is the blindest Eye I've ever seen. Now don't go telling 'im I said this, but ole Walker Hadley got to where he is by his family. Most useless rover I ever had the pleasure of knowing. Remind me some time, and I'll tell you some tales might make you split yer sides."

Darrin smiled. "I'll hold ya to that, Harry."

The three men rode through the Great Wheel. The buildings were no longer stacked upon each other, the crowds of people thinned. A faint odor of queer scents wafted through the air, but they no longer filled Darrin's nostrils with anything more than passing interest. The music of strolling minstrels and the rowdy shouts of the teeming masses had dimmed.

The road narrowed and the dirt disappeared, replaced by an intricate pattern of cobblestone, until, finally, they climbed up a gradual incline that Darrin knew at once to be the Trail of Kings.

In the distance, Castle Dartsuil loomed—imposing and proud.

Darrin had read countless stories that began upon this fabled road. Not a single tale regarding Sir Matthew Dorne started without him setting out on this path.

And now Darrin rode up the same stone. But he knew he was not a part of one of the Iron Horse's grand adventures. There would be no princess for him to save from a tower, no black knight for him to duel—no, he rode to present the King of Onyris with the severed legs of his son.

Something did not feel right. An eerie silence filled the air.

Something terrible happened here. Darrin's stomach rumbled.

Kayvold halted and turned to his companion. "Hands on steel."

"Welcome to Rothspire, lad." Haron kicked his horse and sped off.

Without a moment's thought, Darrin leaned down and pushed his charger into a full gallop. The severed legs of the prince bounced roughly against his horse's flank.

Three soldiers of the city guard lay upon the hard stone of the Trail of Kings. Around them a dozen smaller bodies lay, all dead, blood pooling around their limp remains.

Darrin arrived last and stared down.

A young boy's eyes stared blankly into the sky above. He wore a mask of mud, disguising any feature other than wide, white eyes.

Darrin studied the boy. *He can't be more than fifteen.*

Dressed in rags with no armor, the slash of the sword that took his life gleamed like a dark-red cavern in his flesh.

How? How could this happen? But as he maneuvered his horse past the child's corpse, he understood.

Kayvold Archwood dismounted and knelt over one of the city guard. He held his hand under the man's head and spoke rapidly.

"What happened here? Are there more? Where have they gone?"

"Scrappers…hundreds of them." The man coughed up blood and glanced at his fallen companions. "Stones…they came at us with bloody stones…"

Stones littered the trail. Hundreds of them—all of varying size. A few had hit their targets, as told by one of the guard's caved-in skull.

Archwood lifted the injured man and threw him over his horse.

Darrin stared on, astonished. The Lord-Overseer was so thin and old. He could never have imagined him able to hoist a full-grown man over his shoulder.

Kayvold shouted, "To the king. Ride!"

Haron gave a slight kick to his mount and galloped off.

Darrin, dazed by the scene, did not know what to do for a moment. He glanced around wildly; he wanted to help someone. But Archwood knew better. The soldier he took with him was the only one still alive.

Gods! Darrin pressed his boots into his stirrups and kicked. The Trail of Kings passed by at such speed, he almost believed he was in one of Sir Matthew Dorne's stories.

CHAPTER

EDLEN

Lost and Afraid

EDLEN GRASPED ONTO the barricade of the tourney field, worried she might be trampled by the sudden swell of onlookers who rushed forward. The rickety barrier swayed under their weight but did not collapse. She squeezed through a small gap in the crowd and found a section of fence that wasn't in danger of buckling.

Loathe to miss the start of the melee, she hazarded a glance behind her in the hopes of spotting Tomm. He alone was responsible for Rhen's entry, and she wished to thank him, but as she scanned the crowd, he was nowhere to be seen.

He's probably in the grandstands with the other lords and ladies, she mused. *I wager he'd have more fun down with the commoners, though.*

A sudden roar erupted from the audience, and Edlen's attention was drawn back to the field.

Two knights lay in the dirt at Rhen's feet, dazed and twitching.

Though she stood a good distance away from him, she recognized the bashful smile covering her friend's face.

"That's two!" Her shouts were lost in the torrent of jeers and curses booming from those around her.

These idiots should be cheering him on, she thought as she turned to sneer at those who levelled taunts. A mixture of body odor and horse shit wafted past her.

Nearly gagging, Edlen squinted, and as she did this, one especially loud man caught her eye.

A patchy beard barely covered the man's tan face. "Why don't ya go back and hide behind the little princess's skirt, ya filthy brocken! Tourneys are for men!" He cursed and spat.

Bold and reckless, Edlen stared at the man, ready for a fight if it came to it. But when the man noticed her glare, he lowered his head and slinked away, disappearing into the crowd.

Filled with an intrepid spirit, Edlen scowled at the others. She spun from them and hollered. "Don't listen to these buggers, Rhen! They're all craven!"

If Rhen heard her or not, it didn't matter; the crowd's disdain proved more raucous than her cheers. The smile on his face faded as he hung his head and stamped away.

Enraged, Edlen pushed away from the barricade and slammed into the throng, scolding all she strode past. Her words mattered little, though. To these people, she seemed nothing more than an insolent scrapper.

Pressing through this drunken rabble, her eyes constantly flitted back to the fight.

A knight dressed in brown and yellow rushed at Rhen, his wooden sword flailing wildly.

Edlen halted, expecting a devastating confrontation. She was not disappointed.

Rhen stood his ground as the hurried knight's blade shattered against him. He thrust his arm out, and with a mere flick of his wrist, knocked the careless man on his arse.

The knight slid a good five yards before he could stand up again and skulk from the field.

The audience erupted in laughter.

Three down, counted Edlen. She knew that if Rhen continued to knock the other combatants from the melee, the crowd might be swayed to his side.

Rhen trudged forward, his tourney sword held up as though ready for any new attack. With a few of his giant strides, he was almost beyond Edlen's sight.

She needed to get closer in order to cheer him on, but a cluster of high-born ladies blocked her path. Edlen pressed past the gaggle of simpering women, silently cursing their inattention to the melee. *Why even come to a tournament if you're not going to watch it?* But she knew the answer. This was a celebration of the king. Anyone who wished to gain favor with him must attend, and these perfumed ladies were no exception.

The loud crack of Sir Edwin Babbit's wooden sword breaking against Rhen's breastplate snapped Edlen from her thoughts. Narrowly avoiding knocking into these pathetic women, she continued forward and tried to place how many men Rhen had defeated.

Is that five or six? Gods! It's six! She grinned and ran on.

The crowd thinned as she ran further from the grandstands. This far from the royal family, only smallfolk and unworldly visitors milled about. Edlen didn't mind being counted among these people; to her it meant a better view of the fight. Out of the corner of her eye, she noticed a group of muddied children running in the opposite direction, but she paid little heed to them, her focus entirely fixed upon her friend.

From her new vantage, she marked a slender fighter—a silver sword dressed in boiled leather—sneak behind the brocken. Edlen screeched out a warning, but Rhen had already twisted around to face the stealthy man. She thought she heard her friend laugh.

Now you've done it. Edlen felt the menace behind Rhen's laughter, and for a heartbeat, she pitied the poor man. *Never try to sneak up on a giant!*

The crowd around her went silent, as though expecting the worst.

In one swift motion, Rhen grabbed the silver sword's ironwood mace. He squeezed it until it splintered into a thousand pieces then hoisted him up and flung him across the field.

Edlen held her breath. *Don't kill him, Rhen. You're not a knight yet.*

Though she didn't agree with the law, she knew the knights of the realm were exempt from punishments when competing in a tournament. As barbaric as it seemed to her, a knight could kill a man in a melee, and as long as it happened during the match, they would not have to answer for their actions. But Rhen was not a knight. He would not become Princess Amara's Shield for another year.

The silver sword crashed into the ground, rolled over and tried to stand. He wasn't dead.

Relieved, Edlen gushed. "Oi! That makes seven!"

A few voices in the crowd cheered along with her. She reckoned it would only be a matter of time until the entire audience was chanting Rhen's name.

Rhen lifted his sword and beat his chest.

Settle down...it isn't over yet. She didn't want him to gloat too early; there were still too many fighters left, and he had only defeated seven. As she thought this, three mounted knights galloped towards Rhen.

They're teaming up on him! It made sense, though; she would've done the same. Get rid of the biggest first. At least the knights who protected the realm weren't idiots.

But Rhen must have expected the same thing. He dashed towards the riders and frightened their horses.

As the knights struggled to master their steeds, Rhen came on them like a storm. He ripped one from the saddle and hurled him at the others. Horse and rider alike struck the ground in a violent heap.

A roar of excitement swept through the crowd. Hands clapped, feet stamped, and voices boomed like war horns.

Edlen laughed with relief; cheers now drowned out curses.

Utilizing the mayhem of the audience, Rhen bolted round and approached four silver swords. One of them threw himself to the ground in mercy, not daring to incur the brocken's wrath.

Rhen stepped over him but taunted the other three. He yelled something Edlen couldn't make out then smashed his sword against his chest.

Like a scythe through wheat, he sliced his wooden blade through the three fighters, knocking them to the ground in a flash.

Edlen had Rhen's count at fourteen, which meant he was definitely in the running to claim the title of champion. Though there were still men in the field, she didn't believe any of them had the numbers of her friend.

The Sins of Kings

Three mounted knights flanked Rhen on his right side, while four more closed the gap to his left. As they pressed in, two silver swords circled back and trapped his rear escape. Four more men marched forward and surrounded him.

Thirteen against one? Edlen knew her friend was strong, but this seemed an impossible task...even for him.

The crowd began to chant—and not just those around her. Edlen heard the word *brocken* from as far off as the grandstands. Whether this chant was meant as encouragement or something else, she couldn't be certain.

Rhen, it seemed, took the chant as a battle cry. For the first time since the melee started, he shouted so loudly that Edlen was able to hear him. "For the Princess!" His voice boomed and he rushed headlong into the combatants.

For the Princess? Edlen had to stop herself from laughing. She would tease him about this after the match—but it was a clever trick. If any in attendance jeered him after that, well, that would mean they cursed Princess Amara. Even the most foolish in Rothspire wouldn't be caught doing that.

Rhen moved quicker than Edlen thought possible.

Between his heavy footfalls and the scurrying feet of knights and horses, a thick cloud of dust filled the air.

Edlen ran along the border of the field to get a better view, wishing she could jump over the barricade and witness this close up. But just as she found a decent spot, the attack was over.

The dust settled, and Rhen stood victorious. Dirt clung to the sweat on his ebony face and Edlen could see splatters of blood dripping from his armor.

Gods! How did you manage that? Edlen felt tears well in her eyes. She had never felt such pride. Regardless if Rhen won the tournament or not, his victory over thirteen knights would become legend.

The melee was not over, and the sight of a knight in blue and red armor galloping at Rhen reminded Edlen of this fact.

Riding at full speed and holding his sword out like a lance, the knight slammed into Rhen, nearly knocking the brocken to the ground.

Rhen regained his footing, avoiding being disqualified. The same could not be said for the knight.

When the tip of his wooden blade met the brocken's hulking frame, it splintered apart, and the violent impact flung him from his horse. He landed with a dull thud and cursed loudly. Obviously outraged that his plan had failed, the knight got to his feet and threw the hilt of his tourney sword into the stands. Before he departed the field, he pointed at Rhen and screamed.

Edlen couldn't hear everything the knight said, but she caught the word *disgrace*. She wondered if all the men Rhen had defeated said the same thing. The thought filled her with rage. If she were ever allowed to participate in a tournament, she would show much more grace when she lost.

As the sullen knight stalked from the tourney field, Edlen noticed only one knight remaining. Having been so entranced by Rhen's exploits, she had paid almost no attention to the other fighters.

Out of the seventy-five entrants, Rhen had defeated a staggering twenty-eight. But that meant forty-five more had also been disqualified, and unless this last man had simply waited for all those others to knock themselves from the standings, he must have racked up a considerable number of victories.

Edlen stared at the final knight and thought she recognized him.

Sir Hovaird Archwood strode forward, his oak shield—emblazoned with the Tree of Straten—held aloft.

Edlen had to be honest with herself: Sir Hovaird was every inch a knight. Tall, athletic, with a tanned face and flowing blond hair, he looked like a character out of one of Laustair's storybooks.

The crowd grew silent, almost as if they had been waiting for this exact moment. Edlen could even hear Hovaird's boots crunching through the dirt on the field.

"Well met, Master Rhen," Hovaird called out. "You have won the numbers! Will you now stand against me?" His voice commanded the attention of all gathered.

"It would be my honor," answered Rhen.

Edlen wanted to shout something disparaging, but the stately manner in which Sir Hovaird carried himself stopped her.

Sir Hovaird bowed his head and walked calmly towards Rhen.

The two met in the center of the field and seemed to share words. Edlen couldn't hear what was said, but she saw a smile appear on Rhen's face. Once their conversation ended, they both lifted their tourney swords and stood at guard.

Rhen attacked first. He struck out with his wooden longsword, but Hovaird halted just out of his reach and Rhen's slash went wild, knocking him off balance. Though he caught himself before he fell, Hovaird was already on him. The knight lashed out three times in an instant, each of his strikes landing inside the gaps of Rhen's armor.

Before Rhen had a chance to counter, Hovaird lunged

at him, slashing at his calves and nearly taking him to the ground.

Forced to retreat, Rhen swung his blade defensively. His feeble blocks did nothing to slow his foe's progress. Hovaird Archwood changed his guard constantly, aiming his thrusts high then low. His feet danced forward, planted firm, and then danced again.

Edlen understood the knight's strategy—Hovaird was testing Rhen.

The brocken grew impatient. Instead of matching his opponent in technical skill, he put his shoulder down and dashed forward at full speed—a bull rushing forward, stupidly.

"No, you fool!" shouted Edlen. She buried her face in her hands. She knew Hovaird had wanted this reaction. It would be easy for him to use Rhen's massive weight against him. *Damn your temper!*

Hovaird sidestepped the stampede, avoiding the collision. As he moved aside, he placed his sword between Rhen's legs, tripping him. The giant slammed into the tourney floor, leaving deep ruts in the dirt when he fell.

Second place, Edlen thought. *Not too bad.*

Hovaird walked forward and extended his hand, but Rhen swatted it away. The gallant knight refused the insult. He leaned in, forcing a show of respect, and whispered something into the giant's ear. Rhen took his hand and got to his feet.

Cheers and insults blended together as one, the surge of noise deafening. Rhen held Hovaird's hand, and together, they lifted their arms in triumph. If Edlen believed the audience to be near frenzy before, the sudden swell of volume that exploded around her was astonishing. *You'd think the Iron Horse has returned.*

King Ulisaren reentered the field, escorted by Princess Everly, Sir Kerath Manley, and the king's page, Werman Gault. The king carried a beautiful laurel wreath, which he placed over the head of Sir Hovaird Archwood. Princess Everly handed a bouquet of blue roses to Rhen.

The king shook both men's hands then turned to address the crowd.

"Today is a glorious day for Onyris!"

The audience applauded, shouts and curses screamed from all directions.

"And a glorious day for our victor...Sir Hovaird Archwood of Straten!"

Again, the crowd responded with thunderous approval.

"But let us not forget today's champion. Twenty-seven victories—a truly remarkable feat." The king patted Rhen's lower back. "And the first man of brocken birth to compete in a King's Tournament."

Another roar from the crowd, the curses now louder than applause.

"Our very own...Shield of the Princess! Rhen, son of Rhohl." Ulisaren beamed with pride.

There was something strange about the crowd's response, and the hair on the back of Edlen's neck stood on end. She looked from side to side and noted an increasing number of youths darting in and out of the onlookers. But before she might study their movements further, she noticed something out of the corner of her eye.

A knight in blue and red galloped from the far end of the tourney field.

"Behind you!" Edlen screamed—her words lost in the swell of voices.

Ulisaren, deaf to Edlen's feeble cry, continued. "Yes, yes, history has been made, and we are all witness."

The knight Edlen had spotted, armored in blue and scarlet and mounted atop a black destrier, rode straight at the king and consort. He brandished a steel longsword.

It's too loud, thought Edlen. *They can't hear him.* She watched in horror as the knight swung his blade. *That is live steel.* Edlen only recognized the glint of sun on the edge of the sword a heartbeat before it exploded into Rhen's pauldron.

There was a bright flash and piercing snap, followed by a deep thud. None of this sounded like the brilliant noise swords made when they met on the practice yard. Instead, Edlen heard a quick but sickening murmur, the muffled yelp of exhalation before death.

The throng gasped.

In the commotion, Sir Kerath dragged the king from the field with one arm and lifted Princess Everly over his shoulder with the other. He shoved them both over the oak barricade before running back to confront the assassin. The young page, Werman, ran with incredible swiftness and leapt over the barricade just as Rhen rose to his feet.

Hovaird Archwood, who had been knocked to the ground at the horse's approach, jumped up, his wooden sword held in a front guard. He moved to assist Rhen.

A mad rage overtook Rhen as he roared, sounding otherworldly. Kicking out, his enormous boot smashed into Hovaird's chest, sending him barreling over.

For one quick moment, the crowd grew silent.

No! Rhen! No, don't! But Edlen could not shout; her throat constricted at the sight of the wound.

Blood streamed from Rhen's shoulder, covering the left side of his body in a cascade of crimson.

The knight had been thrown from his horse upon the impact of the blow and lay crumpled in the dirt only a few yards from Rhen. He struggled to his feet, but his right ankle was twisted wholly behind him, and the metal of his greaves had ripped apart, biting into his skin like a hungry dog. The moment he put his weight on his ankle, he dropped back to the ground and cried out in excruciating pain. He would surely lose his foot, if not his entire leg.

Rhen stooped down and lifted him up by the neck, spit flying from his mouth as he barked, "You! I told you I would kill you!"

The knight was Sir Hugh Castac, the son-in-law of Lord Donnel Baird of Riverfront. Edlen noted the bright blue and red armor and the emblem of a bridge immediately. The Bairds were one of the families who had raised arms against the Graymeres during Robart Moorcroft's rebellion fifty years ago.

This could only end poorly. She must stop Rhen from doing anything foolish. Before she realized what she was doing, Edlen vaulted over the barricade and bolted for her friend. Five of the King's Blades bounded over as well, their long swords drawn and their flowing green cloaks whipping behind them.

They were sure to reach Rhen and Sir Hugh Castac before Edlen could.

She gave no thought to it, though. Rhen needed her.

Less than ten steps away, Edlen felt a blinding pain explode in her head. The heavy steel gauntlet of Sir Jaymes Hallet, one of the King's Blades, had smashed into her face. She flew back, sprawled against the ground of the tourney field.

Disembodied words swirled like the echoes of a memory. "Off the field, you filthy scrapper."

I'm not a scrapper... I'm the daughter of the Primacy... I am Edlen Graymere.

But no. She wasn't. She'd purposely chosen to dress as a commoner, she'd hidden from any mention of her family's name, and now, covered in dirt, with her face swollen grotesquely and her lip split nearly in half, there was no chance of anyone recognizing her as anything but a commoner...a scrapper.

Edlen tried to speak, but blood pooled in her mouth. She spat out a wad of red phlegm and one of her teeth.

"When!" she garbled out, but as the word left her tongue, she knew it would not be understood. *Not When...Rhen!*

Sir Jaymes sneered down at Edlen and kicked her, his steel boot landing hard into soft wool and flesh. "Leave now! Or I'll give you more than a tap." He drew four feet of castle-forged steel from its scabbard.

Edlen crawled away, ashamed. Her desire to help her friend was extinguished.

Forgive me, Rhen.

Scrambling to her feet, she distanced herself from the other knight's blows. When she looked back, a more chaotic scene unfolded.

Rhen stood surrounded by the King's Blades. In his right hand, he held Sir Hugh Castac up by the throat. His left arm hung limp and bleeding. He stared murderously into Sir Hugh's eyes.

The gorget around Hugh Castac's neck crumpled like weak tin in the giant's grip. His breath came in heaving gasps as Rhen's hand tightened, steel sinking into skin. "Please," he choked.

Edlen screamed. She said no words, but hoped Rhen might catch her voice and stop.

The King's Blades held their longswords in various guards, each of them prepared to deal a lethal blow if Rhen did not relent. Their voices echoed in a chorus of commands and shouts, but before they advanced, Sir Hugh stopped struggling; his body sagged, slack and lifeless.

Rhen dropped the corpse of the blue and red armored knight and fell to his knees. He surrendered.

Thank the gods.

But the King's Blades converged on him and threw him to the ground. Three of them knelt, their knees pressing into the giant's throat and stomach. The other two attended to the motionless remains of Sir Hugh Castac.

"He can't breathe!" screamed Edlen. "He surrendered! Let him go!" As she made this vain attempt to dissuade the King's Blades, there was a sudden change in the atmosphere.

A surge of apprehension filled Rothspire.

Violence is coming... thought Edlen.

Many things happened at once.

The king shouted from the grandstands, waving his hands excitedly, his face contorted by rage. The knights who held Rhen dragged him through the dirt. Confusion roared through the crowd as a mass of bodies broke through the barricades and ran onto the field. A torrent of screams filled the air.

Edlen dodged those who rushed forward, but she lost her footing and was nearly trampled by a swarm of lords, ladies, and commoners.

Thousands of those who'd gathered earlier to celebrate now pushed and slammed into one another as they piled onto the tourney field.

Clambering to avoid the throng, Edlen got her bearings and looked around to discover the cause of this madness.

Hundreds of stones fell from the sky, raining down upon the audience. They flew from all around the field. Edlen covered her head and ran. A searing sting flamed in her arm as a stone slammed into her. She looked down at a jagged rock the size of her fist.

A thick cloud of dirt and dust rose from the stamping feet of the terrified crowd, and through this brown haze, Edlen spotted what looked like small fires blazing in the streets where the vendors had set up their stalls. Oil had mixed with flame when the shopkeepers who sold roast chicken and beef had their carts upturned.

Lost and disoriented in the throng, Edlen could do nothing but run along with the stampede. *Are we being attacked?* This was the only explanation for what was happening. *But who? Who would be attacking us?* Just as she thought this, she was forced to jump right and leap over a man who had fallen in front of her. She looked back to see the fallen man disappear under the mob. Though the noise of the crowd was at a pitch, she was certain there was an awful crunch as the poor man's bones were crushed under their weight.

Gods! What is happening?

When there was a slight break in the rush, Edlen realized this was her only chance to escape the deadly tide of humanity. She bolted through the small gap and ran for safety, faster than she had ever moved before. She raced headlong to her father. Her family would protect her. The king's litter was—at her best guess—only a hundred yards away, as she'd noted before the sudden pandemonium.

Edlen spotted her father. But Aldir was ushered into the litter before she had a chance to catch his attention. The door slammed shut and the draft horses cantered quickly on their way to the grey, stone enclosure of Dartsuil's Keep.

Sir Kerath and three of the King's Blades rode giant warhorses, their swords drawn as they guarded the litter, ready to end any threat that might arise.

The carriage moved too fast for Edlen to catch it. Her ribs began to ache, and her breath came in heaving gasps.

Would they even recognize me?

She had to stop running; she had to think of something.

Sweat poured from her brow, mixing with specks of dirt on her face. She wiped away the grime with her already-sodden sleeve.

Laustair!

Yes, he would recognize her.

But the old man's tower was on the other side of the castle, and Edlen had no idea who was causing this terror. It would be foolish for her to chance the run. No, she needed to find a place to hide and wait out the assault.

"You! Follow me!" A hand slapped Edlen on the shoulder and a girl's voice broke through the din. "This way!"

Edlen followed the girl. *I have no other option.* Dirt, smoke, and fear filled her nostrils, and her breathing became labored; every step she took pounded against her chest, but she dared not stop.

The wisp of the figure turned and gestured. Through the smoke, she could barely make out the slight frame of a young girl. Whoever she was, she waited only a moment for Edlen to catch up before sprinting off.

"Wait!" panted Edlen.

"Waiting is death. Run! Or die." Her voice echoed as it disappeared.

Running will be my death…

Edlen mustered what strength remained in her and bolted. The sudden attack subsided, and only the faintest remnant of shouts filled the tourney yard, interspersed with the muted thud of small rocks.

Smoke and dirt hung low to the ground. A few pillars of black clouds floated into the sky above. An acrid scent permeated the lower bailey, and a scene of utter destruction languished in the wake of this faceless invasion.

A regiment of the city guard marched through the residue of the day's events. One-hundred armored knights, fifty mounted and twenty archers, prowled the grounds of the castle.

A wild thought came to Edlen's mind. If she ran to one of the king's soldiers and claimed her name, they would not be able to deny her entry to Dartsuil's Keep. Aldir would be there, safe in the Hall of Glory. He would recognize her, even if no one else could.

Is it worth the risk? The memory of a steel-plated fist smashing into her face told her it wasn't. Besides, the girl who beckoned her did not attack. Perhaps she was a friend.

Edlen would not chance another meeting with any of the king's soldiers; instead, she chased after the girl.

The portcullis was closed, guarded by twenty fully-armed soldiers, yet the girl Edlen followed was running right at them.

"Left! Turn left!" Edlen shouted, hoping the girl might listen. *Friend or not, I have no desire to see any more death today.* In an instant, the girl turned left and continued without breaking her stride. *Gods! She is fast...*

A low wall ran alongside the main gate of Rothspire, and just beyond it was a large ditch—with a narrow path wide enough for one to shimmy along. Edlen used to crawl through here in order to slip unseen into the Great Wheel. It was a long, dark path which ran underneath the Trail of Kings, and Edlen hoped she was the only one who remembered its secrets.

The girl slid down the embankment and disappeared. Edlen followed, but as she neared the wall, she spied a guard at the portcullis following their movements. Without a second thought, she leapt into the ditch.

Her attempt to turn the leap into a somersault was abysmal and she crashed painfully into the hard ground. Catching the sleeve of her jerkin on a jagged rock, she slid down the incline, a searing pain running up her arm. The stone tooth dragged across her skin and left a long, deep gash that stretched from forearm to wrist. She was hurt, but well hidden.

"Now what?" the girl asked.

Edlen got to her feet, pinched the flesh around her wound, and glared at the girl.

The girl was filthy. Her face, which may have been comely, was covered in a mask of mud. "Ya got us 'ere. Where to now?" she snapped.

"I got us here?" Edlen asked indignantly. "I was following you."

"You's the one 'ooh said turn left. I turned left. Now what?" Her hair, a rat's nest of stringy brown, was tied up with a length of twine. A stink of ripe onion and rancid beef wafted from her.

Great. She's stubborn as an ass. Edlen pushed past her but did not answer. She felt for an opening in the rock. "Keep your voice down," she whispered. "Half the city guard is after us."

"Bastards couldn't find a cloud in a rainstorm," the girl

said. She wore crudely stitched trousers of the coarsest material, an ill-fitting, pale-blue tunic, and boots that appeared to Edlen to be more cowhide than leather.

Edlen's fingers found a thin gap. *There it is.* She stepped aside and grabbed the girl's hand.

"Get yer bloody hand off me." Her eyes were the color of dazzling lilac.

"Sorry," Edlen said. "Thought you might want to get out of here alive."

The girl sneered. "Ain't the first time I've 'ad to run from some steel-clad oafs." She studied Edlen. "It's yer first time, though, ain't it?"

Yes! "No!" Edlen said as she slid into the pass, her belly pressing against the cold rock. "Suit yourself."

The gap must have shrunk, she thought to herself. *That, or I've grown since I last came this way.* "Are you coming?"

The girl wormed her way in behind Edlen, her shoulder squeezing against hers. "You gonna move?"

She liked the way the girl's arm felt when it pressed against hers, but the throbbing pain in her arm pulled her mind from any pleasure she may have momentarily enjoyed; this was not the time to think on such things.

As Edlen moved forward, she remembered the times she'd taken this path. *Fifty paces and then turn right. That'll get us under the gate.*

When she was younger, the secret passage might take her an hour or so to traverse before it opened onto the Great Wheel. *But I was smaller then; I could easily walk through here. Gods! It's going to take us half the day moving like this.* "We won't see the other side until nightfall," said Edlen. "But we'll pop out near one of the taverns in the Wheel."

"Ow are ya so sure?"

"I've done this before."

"Yoo've snuck into 'Spire this way?"

Snuck into? No, I've snuck out of. "Many times." *What am I saying? Why am I trying to impress her?* Edlen turned to the right when the gap opened, the hard-stone walls no longer constricting her breathing. Her chest loosened and her wits returned.

"If right is the Wheel…what 'appens if we turn left?" asked the girl.

Left? "That leads to Dartsuil's Keep." Edlen kept to the right, almost able to walk normally. The awful odor of the girl—which she had begun to enjoy—dissipated.

"The king's keep?" the girl asked, her voice soft and distant. "Maybe we go that way, then?"

No! "No," said Edlen. "They won't welcome us there. The king is out to kill us. I know it."

The girl paused, but in the dark tunnel it was impossible to tell where she stood. "An 'ow do ya know this?"

"That's what I would do."

"Aye, and you're a Graymere, are ya?" She laughed. "I've always wanted to see the real keep, 'ow bout you?"

It's not what you think. "We turn right. There's nothing for us but pain if we turn left." Edlen squeezed her arm. The sharp sting subsided, leaving in its place a dull ache. Though it was dark and she could not be certain, it seemed to her the bleeding had stopped. She ran her finger across the wound. The deep cut had already scabbed over.

The girl's voice faded as she said, "Pain ain't never hurt no one."

She moved quicker than Edlen could have expected. All she could do was turn left and follow her new companion.

CHAPTER

ALDIR

The Hall of Glory

T HE MASSIVE DOORS of Dartsuil's Keep slammed shut. Aldir Graymere waded through the swarm of people who filled the antechamber of the Hall of Glory. Almost in a frenzy, he grabbed the nearest soldier. "Have you seen my daughter?" Sweat dripped into his eyes and his hands trembled.

"No, my lord," said Sir Dalton Yarmouth, the youngest of the King's Blades.

Aldir released the frightened knight and shoved past him. His voice was lost in the uproar, but he continued to bellow, "Edlen! Edlen!"

More than a thousand people crammed into the bottom floor of the keep, each of them shouting names of lost loved ones. The heat emanating from the crush of people was overwhelming, and the stink of fear that poured from them grew oppressive.

"Edlen!" Aldir's cries vanished in a chorus of panicked voices.

It's no use. No one can hear me through this noise.

In a moment of clarity, Aldir drove through the crowd

for his daughter's bedchamber. He no longer cared to represent the crown, and the title of Primacy meant nothing if he could not protect his only child.

He ran through the hall, past the stone in the floor that led to the secret ladder, and rounded the corner on his way to their rooms.

Sir Jayson Glenmoore and Sir Davin Loudwater stood guard outside. At Aldir's approach they both knelt. "Hail, my lord," they said in unison.

Out of habit, Aldir bowed but exchanged no further courtesies. He flung Edlen's door open, only to enter an empty room. The bedchamber was a mess of scattered clothes, books, and useless oddments. Aldir didn't care about her slovenly nature, stepping over the scraps of broken toy swords to approach an open window.

The sun glinted off an iron-hook buried into the stone ledge. He threw open the curtains and stared down. Knotted onto the hook was a length of rope that hung down the side of the wall. Aldir held the line in his hand and pulled.

Why can't you just take the stairs like everyone else?

He turned from the window and made to depart, but before leaving, he noted something curious. Mixed in with his daughter's dirty clothes—which littered the floor—was a red and green tunic and brown leather boots both emblazoned with the Graymere's sigil. He picked up the garments and folded them. *Why isn't she wearing our colors?* Placing the clothes on Edlen's bed, he realized she must be playing at costumes again. *Haven't you grown out of this game?*

Aldir closed the door behind him to address the guards. "When did you last see her?"

They regarded one another before answering.

"She came through here an hour or so before you left,

my lord. That was what…?" Sir Davin Loudwater glanced at Sir Jayson Glenmoore for confirmation. "Four, perhaps five, hours ago."

"She entered?" Aldir asked. "But did not leave?"

"No, my lord," Sir Jayson said. "You and Master Gault have been the only ones to leave the apartments today."

Aldir shook his head. "Then it might interest you to know my daughter is *not* in her room."

"Impossible, my lord."

"Impossible but true," said Aldir. "Perhaps I would do better to station one of the kennel-master's hounds at her door. I am certain she would not hide from a dog."

He left the guards in a wroth, not wishing to say another word more to them. If they could not protect his only child, he must find someone who could. *I have done no better, though.* The memory of his wife came flooding back. His last words to her were a painful regret.

I will guard her with my life. He shook his head. *Words are too easy to say—and vows too easy to break.* A thunder erupted behind his eyes. *I cannot protect her any more than I could protect you…from yourself.* He knew not whether to laugh or cry. The memory of Irymar was too agonizing to dwell on.

He neared a dislodged stone in the base of the wall and crouched to inspect it. Tracing his forefinger around a thin gap, he considered pulling the stone from its place. But a small voice disrupted his contemplation.

"My lord, His Grace calls for you," squeaked Worm.

Aldir stood, his voice full of ice. "What?" He turned slowly; his eyes burned like coal.

Werman Gault stood still as stone, caught in Aldir's gaze. No longer did the young boy present an air of conceit; he was simply a young boy, terrified by today's events, and doing his best to deliver his king's command.

He said again, through a quavering voice, "His Grace commands your attendance in the Great Hall."

He's scarcely younger than Edlen. Aldir rubbed his face. *None of this can be easy for him.* "Werman, have you seen Edlen?"

"My lord?" asked Worm.

"My daughter, Werman." Aldir's anger subsided, replaced by fear. "Please tell me you saw her today."

"I...I...I don't know."

"You don't *know* if you saw her? Is that what you're saying, Werman?" A sudden hope filled Aldir. "But perhaps you did?"

"My lord...I *think* I saw someone who looked like her, but she was dressed in rags. I didn't give her a second glance. And it could have been a boy. It was hard to tell."

"A boy?" asked Aldir.

"Maybe?" squeaked Werman. "My lord, like I said, I cannot say for certain. They looked like a commoner, and I only caught a passing glimpse."

Why would you give a second glance to a commoner? Gods! Are we so superior we don't notice those we proclaim to protect? But Edlen has always identified more with our subjects than with our family. Perhaps her costume helped her escape the riot? But it will not save her from our soldiers.

A tiredness descended upon Aldir, and his voice broke. "Where was this boy you saw?"

"On the field, my lord, crawling away from Sir Hallet. It was just before...before...the Shield..."

Killed Sir Hugh Castac? The memory was too fresh for

him to contend with. *The first man you've seen die. You will never forget the sight, you poor boy.* Tears welled in his eyes.

"Never mind that now, Werman," Aldir said, pushing down his instinct to comfort Worm. He wanted to embrace the boy, he wanted to tell him death—as terrible as it was to witness—was a rite of passage for the living. But that would be another man's responsibility. The boy would be taught the horrors of life by the knight he squired for. Aldir was not his liege; he could only pity the child.

"What does my father want?" he asked.

Werman regained what little composure remained to him. "Riders have come from the Eyes of the Forest. His Grace told me no more."

For once, Aldir believed the boy knew nothing more than he said. "Tell my father I will be with him in due time."

I must find Edlen.

Werman's eyes widened in fear. He stammered, "P-please…he insists you come with me. This is my only chance to make up for my failure this morning."

He? Not, His Grace? Peculiar choice of words, Worm. "My father will learn to live with disappointment, Werman. After all—I am his son."

"My lord," Werman said, damn near apoplectic. "He will not allow me a second blunder."

The pathetic sight of this young boy, terrified of disappointing the king, reminded Aldir of himself. How long had it been since he'd stopped caring about letting his father down? A year? Ten? Or maybe, regardless of his predilection to agitate the old man, Aldir had never stopped being afraid? Perhaps…Aldir saw himself in Worm—a child lost to an unending path of guilt and useless attempts of proving himself something more than he actually was.

If I can no longer protect Edlen, perhaps I can protect you, Werman.

I am sorry, Irymar, my love, but our daughter has chosen her path. You of all people understand this. But I will not let this boy fall into the same trap I have. Forgive me...but my father cannot be allowed to intimidate another boy who only wishes to please him.

Aldir squeezed Worm's shoulder and followed. "Lead the way, Master Gault."

THE King's Blades cleared the antechamber of most of the crowd. A few highborn lords and ladies milled about, but *lords' rights* prevented them being cast from the keep.

Aldir and Werman strode past an obese man, who upon recognizing them called out, "There's the bloody Primacy!"

Aldir stopped and studied Lord Brastor's enormous girth and distinctive pale-gold beard. A clutch of children girded around him.

"Lord Brastor. Have you been waiting for me?" Aldir asked.

"You're damn right I've been waiting," Brastor said. "Waiting for one of you bloody Graymeres to tell me what in the Gods' names happened today. Your *Shield*," he spat. "What exactly are you playing at? And just as my son receives his honors, you have him damn near killed? Then your little thugs start a bloody insurrection. Has His Grace lost his wits—or does he just hope his idiotic celebration will be remembered for all the years to come?"

"I can assure you, my lord, neither myself nor His Grace were aware of these unfortunate events. But I am more than certain we will set these matters to right."

"You were not aware?" said Brastor. "You are the Primacy

of the Realm! Are you a fool? How could you not be aware that a damned riot might occur? Perhaps you are the wrong man for the role. It is your responsibility to know anything and everything that takes place in the kingdom. Nothing like this would have ever happened if your aunt had not stepped down. Those filthy scrappers would have been strung up by their entrails before they had a chance to step foot in Rothspire."

I am the wrong man for the role, thought Aldir.

"As I said, my lord, I will ensure everything is set right." Aldir gave the slightest of bows before he pivoted on his heel to head for the Hall of Glory. But just as he made to leave, Brastor's huge hand gripped his shoulder.

"I have not given you leave, Aldir."

You do not have the authority to grant my leave, Brastor.

"Your father has already spurned me today; I will not stand here only to be brushed aside by his son. I am the bloody Lord of Straten, and you will listen to my grievances. As to your *recompense*," he spat again, "see that the Graymeres remember whose coin they spend so freely. Oh, yes! I am quite familiar with the crown's debts—and Straten is owed much more than the paltry sum your Adept of Ledgers tells you. The Windsongs are not the only family who desires to collect."

How can he possibly know? Aldir's lip quivered in a quick spasm of anger. "I will ensure that things are set right." He removed Brastor's hand from his shoulder. "My lord."

"Good, I believe you will." Brastor nodded, his many chins bunching together in comical fashion, like a row of fleshy smiles set in his thick neck. He turned and walked through the antechamber.

Upset by Brastor's last words, Aldir stood rooted to the

floor, scowling at the receding image of the fat lord and his ducklings. There was a slight tug at his jerkin, and he snapped from his ire.

"My lord, His Grace is waiting," said Werman.

From the pot to the flame. "Worm, I need you to complete a task for me."

"But the king...?"

"I will let my father know you did your duty, but what I ask is much more pressing."

Werman fidgeted but nodded.

"Do you know my father-in-law? Laustair?"

"Yes, my lord. He lives in the Tower of the Setting Sun."

"Perfect!" Aldir wondered how Worm might know this but did not let himself dwell on it. "Find him. If anyone in this place might know where Edlen is, it will be him. Please find him and bring him here."

"Yes, my lord," said Werman, readying to leave.

"Oh, and Worm? You heard nothing of my conversation with Lord Brastor."

The young boy smiled up at Aldir. "Not a word, my lord."

I am starting to understand why my father keeps you around.

THE doors to the hall swung open and a man dressed in gray finery swept past Aldir. He stepped back on his heels to avoid a collision. The man, somewhere close in age to himself yet with a head of receding reddish-brown hair, halted and made a quick apology.

"My lord," said the man, almost startled. "Forgive me."

His voice lacked any discernible accent. "My name is Tomm." He eyed Aldir, and, with a flourish, bowed low, nearly sweeping the floor. "And you must be Aldir Graymere, the Primacy of the Realm."

Aldir took a hesitant step backwards. "That is my title today." He studied the man, noticing the strange heraldry sewn into his gray tunic—a black puppeteer's rod.

Queer design, he thought to himself.

"Your apologies are unnecessary," said Aldir. "A man who *doesn't* run from a visit with my father would be a man I need to question."

Tomm nodded in jovial agreement. "Our King is a proud man…and why shouldn't he be? Sons of such renown." He smiled, his lips curling into a comforting grin. "Primacy and prince. The Gods smile on your family." He bowed. "The sun does not set on the Graymere's, as my father says."

Aldir glanced down at the puppeteer's rod and said, "And who is your father, my lord?"

"I am no lord," said Tomm. "Rather…a friend of the friendless." He grinned. "My father is much of the same. The king needs friends, and so, too, perhaps, the Primacy?" His voice dropped in deference. "I would be forever grateful to assist you in any matter you might desire."

"And what matter might that be?" asked Aldir, suddenly suspicious.

"Blood was spilled on a day of celebration. For that, we must all be sorry. Blood, regardless of who it belongs to, is a sacred thing, my lord." Tomm glanced behind him and caught the eye of someone in the antechamber. "Many apologies, my lord, but it seems you and I both have previous engagements we must attend to. Pleasurable as our meeting has been, neither of us should forsake our commitments."

Tomm took Aldir's hand in his and said, "I will be in Rothspire for some time…please search me out. There is much we might discuss." With that, he turned and darted through the waning cluster of people in the antechamber.

Aldir watched Tomm's lithe figure disappear and pondered his words. For a moment, he contemplated following the strange man, but the king was waiting for him. He allowed himself one last fleeting glance before entering the colossal doors of the Great Hall. Aldir walked underneath the massive statues of King Bradain and King Berad the Vicious. Their stone swords met at their tips and created an archway that framed the entrance to the hall.

He gave only the most cursory of glances up at the incredible structures, the solemnity of the imposing edifice having worn off when he was a young man. The stone reeked of centuries of unwashed inhabitants. Aldir loathed the scent. He shivered. Not only was there the unpleasant odor to contend with, but the Hall of Glory was always too damn cold for his liking. No wonder he avoided coming here unless the king commanded him to.

Deep inside of the hall, Aldir studied his father who sat on his throne atop a raised dais. Next to him, in a much more modest chair, was Princess Everly, her daughter Amara placed firmly on her lap. Sir Kerath Manley loomed behind the throne, solemn as ever. Two of the King's Blades stood sentry on either side of the dais.

As he neared, Aldir recognized the two knights. Sir Willem Thorpe and Sir Barret Fendyke. This set him at ease. He'd known Fendyke since childhood and had recently struck up a friendship with Sir Willem after sharing a flagon of wild-fyre whisky in celebration of their new appointments.

In front of the dais, with their backs turned to Aldir, were two men dressed in the tan livery of the Eyes of the Forest and one other garbed in the luxuriant finery of a lord.

Gods! Another Archwood.

Lord-Overseer Sir Kayvold Archwood whirled around

and strode forward, his hand outstretched. "My lord." He bowed deferentially.

"Enough," said King Ulisaren. "No need for courtesies, Archwood." He gripped the arms of his throne. "My son enjoys the benefits of his new title too much as it is. He has an annoying habit of tardiness." A sneer appeared on his face as he gazed fixedly at Aldir. "Off to get more *answers*, I assume?"

"No, Your Grace," said Aldir as he took his place in the seat next to the king. "I was looking for Edlen…your grandchild, if you haven't forgotten?" He met his father's eyes. "She has not been seen since the Shield of the Princess murdered Sir Hugh Castac."

"How dare you!" Ulisaren rose from the throne in a rage. "As though I condone the boy killing that knight?"

"You let him fight!"

"The law let him fight!"

"You are the king! You make the law."

"And the law will see that he stands trial."

The blow from Castac's sword would have cleaved any other man's arm clean off, but Rhen barely flinched. "How do you propose to punish a brocken, Your Grace? How do you punish a Shield?"

"He will sit in a cell until I am ready to determine this. Perhaps the Primacy of the Realm may enlighten me as to the best way to deal with this matter," the king said, his voice oozing with disdain.

At that, Everly moved her daughter from her lap, stood, and whispered something into the king's ear.

"Once again, your sister-in-law protects you, Aldir." Ulisaren sat back down and apologized to the men from the Eyes of the Forest. "This is not a time for our family's squabbles.

These men have ridden a tremendous distance to present us with something."

Though he acknowledged the men, Aldir said, "Perhaps gifts can wait, My Grace." He glowered at the king. "People have died today. Our own people. And those responsible are also *our* people. Am I the only one who believes this to be of far greater importance than a gift?"

"Beggin' ya pardon, m'lord." A gruff voice belonging to an even gruffer man interrupted. "It ain't no gift we bring."

"Mind yourself, Haron," said Kayvold. The slim man put his hand on his companion's arm then addressed Aldir. "My lord, first let me apologize for Chief Ridgefront's disruption, but what he lacks in courtliness, he makes up for in truth. We do not come bearing gifts, and though the timing may be inopportune, I believe it is of profound concern."

"Of greater concern than an uprising in our own castle?" asked Aldir.

Kayvold bowed his head. "Yes, my lord."

Aldir took a deep breath and turned his attention to the king. "My Grace, I think it folly to ignore what happened today."

"We have ignored nothing," said Ulisaren. "While you were searching for my granddaughter—" he let the word hang in the air—"your sister-in-law and I dispatched a company of the city guard to close the gates of the castle and hunt down the rabble responsible for this ridiculous outburst. Sir Kayvold and his men rode through the Great Wheel earlier today and were able to describe the offenders. It was those damn scrappers, Aldir. The ones you said would be nothing more than a small mob of agitators. Well, it seems they did more than agitate. Two of our soldiers lie dead on the Trail of King's and one more is now in the care of High Divinator Erabil."

Another mistake, thought Aldir. "What are the guards' orders?"

"To kill any man, woman, or child who lifted a finger against the realm."

"That is barbaric!" said Aldir. "Scrappers are but children! We cannot sanction the butchery of our own people!"

"Scrappers stopped being children the moment they took the life of a city guard. They are dangerous vermin who carry a plague of revolt. The faster we snuff them out, the sooner Onyris may heal from the wounds they inflicted upon us," the king said, resolute on the matter.

"Everly, please. You cannot agree with this?" Aldir stared at her.

She looked back at him through impassive eyes. "Discontent is a snake in the grass, dear brother. It hides in the overgrowth of complacency, slithering silently, ever closer to its prey. And then it strikes. Its fangs pierce the goodness that lives inside the smallfolk and poisons them with thoughts of rebellion. Yes, I agree with His Grace. We must remove the head of this snake and leave its corpse in the field to rot in the sun."

Gods! I am surrounded by tyrants. "Lovely metaphor, but you seem to forget that if our family is responsible for the death of our own city's children, it will not be snakes we must be wary of but the outcry of all the smallfolk—and after that the reaction of all the Wide-World."

"No more of this!" Ulisaren slammed his hand down. "They are dirty orphans from Pleasant Hill who grow too bold. I will listen to no more. You are the Primacy! You will make certain the realm is protected." He turned aside, returning his attention to Kayvold. "Lord-Overseer, again I have to apologize for my son's distractions."

That's all I am to you, Father. A distraction, an annoyance. This entire proceeding is a farce. You don't need a Primacy; you need a mirror. But I'll wager after your decisions today you won't be able to stomach the sight of yourself.

"No apologies necessary, My Grace. The king must rule his court how he sees fit. I envy you not. I am but your humble servant," said Kayvold.

Ulisaren smiled and then glared sidelong at Aldir. "I am pleased to have someone understand this. We may continue with no more interruptions."

Aldir smiled back with stilted irony. His smile faded when one of the Eyes lifted a sack and set it at the foot of the dais. He leaned forward in his chair and studied the offering, and then studied the man who had placed it.

He couldn't have been more than eighteen or nineteen years old, but already his rover's uniform was covered in patches of black, brown, green, and the unmistakable stain of dried blood.

What has this boy been through at such a young age? Aldir noted the blotches of acne that covered the boy's light-brown skin, most severely clustered where his tightly curled black hair met his forehead. "What is your name?"

The young man looked to his Lord-Overseer before answering. When he received a reassuring nod, he said, "Darrin, my lord. Darrin Cantlay of Redrun."

"Cantlay?" the king said. "Phillip Cantlay's boy?"

"Yes, My Grace." Darrin seemed to squirm.

"The prince and I were down in Elmfort not two weeks ago to observe your fellowship receive your honors." He laughed. "Two weeks a rover and you're already stained in such a way?" He pointed at Kayvold. "What are you doing to these poor boys, Archwood?"

A sad grin appeared on Kayvold's face, the scars on his cheeks twisting slightly. "Perhaps our young princess should be excused, My Grace." He looked at Everly. "And begging your pardon, my lady, but might I suggest you take your leave as well? This is not an appropriate discussion for a woman as fair as you."

Aldir had to choke back a laugh. *Poor wording, Archwood.*

Everly only smiled, but Aldir knew the contempt that smile concealed. Her voice was thin and hard as an assassin's dirk. "My good lord. I do not believe it is under the jurisdiction of one, even as exalted and revered as you, to determine what is appropriate for a princess to discuss. I understand your sentiment, and it will be regarded as nothing more than the misplaced tenderness of a courteous man. But in the future, please be mindful of your false assumptions as to my constitution." She folded her arms and rested them in her lap, then called for her daughter.

The young princess, who had been strolling through the cavernous hall, heard her mother and came running. As she was about to take her place on her mother's knee, Everly spoke softly to her and then motioned for Sir Willem Thorpe to take her away. The young girl did not protest.

Edlen would have argued with me if I'd asked her to leave, thought Aldir. *Even when she was her age. Gods! She has always been so willful.* He closed his eyes for a moment and said a silent prayer for his daughter's safety.

"I will heed your warning, for my daughter's sake," said Everly. "Let her absence be a sign of respect for your concern."

"Your Majesty," said Kayvold.

"'My lady' will suffice."

Aldir hid a smile.

"Well, young Master Cantlay," said Ulisaren. "Your Lord-Overseer thinks you are the most suited to present this strange gift to us. Let us get on with it, then."

"Your Grace…" started Darrin. The boy's voice cracked slightly. "We found something in the forest that bears the seal of the Graymeres."

"Please do not tell me you have ridden hundreds of leagues to return something carelessly jettisoned from one of my carriages." The king grew impatient.

"Aye, Yer Grace," said Haron, stepping past Darrin and lifting the sack. "The boy 'ere is too polite to tell ya straight." He untied the rope that bound the outer layer of leather.

A sickly-sweet odor wafted from the hempen sack before Haron removed its contents. Aldir winced; it was the smell of rot and decay. *What in the Gods?* "What is in there?"

Ulisaren covered his nose, almost choking. "Is this some jest, Archwood?"

"I wish it were."

The laconic old rover, Haron, took a knife from his belt and slashed open the top of the sack. He reached in and pulled out the festering remains of a severed leg, and adorning the putrid flesh was a polished leather boot.

Aldir nearly retched. His initial reaction was to recoil, but the ghastly sight was too intriguing to turn from. Everly groaned, and the king gasped.

He could not take his gaze from the hideous image. The corrupted skin that sprouted from the opening of the boot reminded him of the nightmare he'd awoken from this morning. *But that was just a dream.*

"Is that the Wheel?" Aldir saw it plainly now. Fine threads

were sewn into the leather—the sigil of his family. "Is that my brother?" His bowels roiled, and thin, fiery saliva filled his mouth.

"Aye, my lord," said Haron, pulling another leg from the bag.

"Gods…" murmured Ulisaren. "No more. Please tell me there's no more."

The young rover, Darrin, knelt to one knee and said, "My Grace, we are uncertain if these remains belong to the prince, but we have good reason to believe they do."

Everly took a deep breath and said, "You are wrong."

"The third man in our company agrees with you, my lady. He rode with Chief Ridgefront and me when we found them. He suspects the boots might be a forgery," said Darrin.

"A forgery?" asked the king. "Yes, of course they are." A wave of relief crossed his face. "Now tell me, Cantlay. Why then would your Lord-Overseer bring this hideous mockery to my attention?" Ulisaren glowered at Kayvold. "Answer me, Archwood."

What if they do belong to Odain?

"Your Grace," said Kayvold. "The doubt Cantlay speaks of comes by a young man who has gone mad. Darrin, I'm certain, only wishes to provide the court with all the information we possess. Forgive his false hope, but I am of the mind these truly are the remains of the prince."

Aldir could no longer sit idle. He stood and approached the legs, lifting one to inspect it. The cut was remarkably precise, he noted, performed by one with exceptional skill: no blood stains, no ragged skin around the edges, not a hint of coarseness. "Why did your companion suspect the boots might be a forgery?"

"He was his father's apprentice, my lord," said Darrin. "A

tanner in Hiltsport. He didn't believe the leather was castle quality. But he could not be sure."

"You say he's gone mad, though?" asked Aldir.

"Aye," said Haron Ridgefront, lowering his head.

Aldir noted a solemn glance pass between the two rovers but paid it little mind. "Lord-Overseer, what are your thoughts?"

"I did not wish to spend unnecessary time investigating this, my lord. Regardless if the boots are a forgery, there is a message behind it. One the royal family must be aware of."

"What bloody message?" said the king as he rose. "We have killed the prince. What kind of damned message is that, and which damned fool would send it?

The Iron Woman, thought Aldir. "Aunt Teryse did something similar with Robart Moorcroft, if I am not mistaken." He looked at his father.

"Your aunt's exploits are greatly exaggerated," replied Ulisaren. "Besides, that was fifty years ago. Moorcroft's son is a lamb, not the wolf his father was."

"Dysternis Moorcroft is dead, or so it is reported. Perhaps the new Lord of the Shaded Realm wishes to rekindle the embers of his grandfather's rebellion?" Aldir stole another glance at the boots. "It may be a sign."

"Odain is in Maresport with the Windsongs," said the king. "And unless you expect me to believe they are in league with this upstart in Balangraide, you should refrain from wild conjecture."

"It could be the Voress Ní..." said Darrin, almost whispering.

Haron elbowed the young rover. "Cantlay's got an imagination on 'im, Your Grace, and he forgets who he speaks to." He glared at Darrin. "Bad nerves is all."

The king eyed Darrin. "The Voress Ní?" He scowled and grew quiet.

"The Shadow Kings?" asked Aldir. "Why do you say that?"

Kayvold interjected, "He's too young to know myth from truth, my lord. He's an excellent rover, but he is still green."

"Young, yes, but perhaps he's keen to something." Aldir gestured for Darrin to stand. "I want to hear why you think this."

"The cut, for one, my lord," said Darrin, not waiting for his chief's approval. "Even Haron says he's never seen such a clean cut. The Voress Ní were known for having blades of surpassing keenness. And, strange as it sounds, we found no footprints near the…legs.

"A large storm passed over the forest a few days before, and the ground was still muddy, but when we came upon the boots, my lord, there were no footprints. An odd detail, I know, but if I may—all the old stories involving the Voress Ní claim they did things of this nature.

"Severed limbs, pardon me for saying it, left in strange locations, with no sign of how they got there. They would leave them as a kind of token, wouldn't they? A message before a…" The young rover trailed off.

"War?" asked Aldir. "Is that what you were going to say?"

"Yes, my lord." Darrin shuffled slightly. "But as I say it out loud, it sounds rather daft."

"You're damned right it sounds daft!" Ulisaren bellowed. "Who would want to go to war with Rothspire?"

Rojiir, Balangraide, the Fyrelands…the list goes on.

"I think we are forgetting something," said Everly, still sitting in her seat. "My husband is currently in the Vines, under the protection of the Windsongs. If any harm has come to him, they would be responsible for it, and as avaricious as they might be, they have the wisdom to never openly defy our friendship.

"A scratch on the prince would be a sign of aggression, but this—this is an act of war. None of the families in the Vines have the strength to assail Rothspire, and they know they would achieve nothing but utter annihilation if Odain does not return. No, I do not believe this."

She pointed at the boots. "This is a mockery—a malicious jest. Take this away and incinerate it. I no longer wish to see them."

"My lady, I do not think it wise to dismiss the meaning behind these," Kayvold said.

"And I do not think it wise to spend another moment debating the significance of an insult," said Everly. "Not when our city has experienced a riot on the king's birthday. If you will excuse me, I must see to the actual safety of our realm." She stood and walked past the fetid legs, not giving them even a casual glance. She curtseyed slightly to Ulisaren and strode from the hall.

After the princess's departure, a pall hung over those who remained. Her outright dismissal of the importance of the boots left the others to ponder her words.

Aldir broke the silence. "Though my fair sister-in-law deems this discussion beneath her, as Primacy of the Realm, I find it folly not to consider the veracity of your suspicions."

"Thank you, my lord," said Kayvold. "I promise I would not have ridden here to present nothing more than idle conjecture."

"Idle conjecture?" snorted the king. "What else have you brought, Archwood? The only answers you supply are the fanciful notions of a child. I will grant no more time on the matter unless you can tell me the meaning of this."

Kayvold bowed his head and said, "With your leave, Your Grace, I believe we must consider the role Lord Byron Windsong and his family may have played in this. My lady disallows the possibility of their participation, but I must respectfully disagree. The Windsongs came to Rothspire by way of the forest; it is possible someone associated with them may have placed them there... Not all of the Seven Families of the Vines are known for their absolute devotion to the Graymeres. I believe one may be connected to this."

"If you expect me to openly question Lord Byron Windsong, you are a bigger fool than I give you credit for," Ulisaren said.

"Not openly, Your Grace. Perhaps there is another way. If the Primacy is amenable?"

If I am amenable? Aldir stared at the Lord-Overseer.

"Go on," said the king.

"Lord Byron arrived to attend today's tournament, but after the unfortunate events that waylaid these festivities, he will be most desirous to return home as quickly as he may. It is not without precedent that the Primacy might accompany him on his journey back to Maresport—given the nature of what transpired. Lord Aldir's presence would be seen as nothing but the good faith of the crown."

"And when is Aldir to make this request of Lord Byron?" the king asked.

Kayvold grinned. "Windsong keeps a manse in Towerglenn where his enormous galley is docked. If the Primacy were to arrive in the port before Lord Byron departs, he could then ask to accompany him, leaving him no choice but to accommodate."

"What will my presence achieve?" Aldir asked.

"The prince is supposedly still in the Vines and under the care of the Windsongs. If you are aboard his ship, there will be no time for messages to arrive in Maresport of your coming. No chance to alert anyone."

"But if Odain is not there?" Aldir asked.

"If the prince is not in Maresport, then..." Kayvold glanced at the severed legs. "Then we must assume..."

He is dead? "What would stop them from killing me once I discover this truth?"

Kayvold smiled. "The Shield of the Prince."

"Sir Rhohl?" asked the king. "Would it not appear a queer choice to send the Shield of the *Prince*...with the Primacy?"

"Queer?" asked Kayvold. "It would be queerer if a Shield did *not* accompany one of the Graymeres."

Ulisaren stayed quiet.

"As long as the Primacy stays in Maresport, he will have access to the royal fleet, which will sail as guards alongside the Windsong's ship. There should be no reason Lord Aldir and Sir Rhohl would not be able to board at any time and sail back to Rothspire if they discover the worst." Archwood frowned. "You will be protected day and night by the strongest man in the Wide-World, and you will have immediate access to a portion of Rothspire's naval strength. If our suspicions hold and this tragedy is truth, the officers aboard our ships can take Windsong into custody in order to stand trial."

"Remarkable!" said Aldir. "There is not a chance you had devised this plot prior to our meeting, is there?"

"I am an Eye, my lord. It is my sworn duty to see things before they happen."

Aldir smiled appreciatively. "Remind me to speak to the Adept of Ledgers and revise your salary."

Rising from his throne, the king asked, "Can you ensure my son's safety, Lord Archwood?"

"I cannot ensure anything, Your Grace, but I vow to you that I ask nothing of your family I would not do myself."

"Very well," said Ulisaren. "Sir Kerath," he addressed the knight for the first time. "Find Sir Rhohl and Lord Byron. If the Lord-Overseer's plan is to be enacted, we must be certain all our pieces are in place before this game begins."

Without a word, Sir Kerath Manley bowed and departed.

"Before we adjourn, is there any other business to be discussed that cannot wait for a proper council, Lord Archwood?"

Aldir thought about everything that had happened since he'd woken up this morning and prayed the day might finally be at a close.

"Aye, Your Grace." Haron nudged his young rover. "A simple request Cantlay 'ere forgot to ask."

Exasperated, the king asked, "Master Cantlay? Make it quick."

Darrin's eyes darted between them. "Your Grace, it's only a simple inquiry."

"Let's have it, boy. You have earned at least one."

"I was wondering if I may speak with a man named Somath who supposedly resides in the castle?"

"Somath?" the king asked aloud. "My dear boy, over ten-thousand people call Rothspire their home. You cannot assume I am familiar with each of their names."

Somath? Aldir closed his eyes and for a brief moment saw the rotting corpse of his dead wife, her mouth opened as a viscous black sludge trickled down her chin. Her voice hissed in his ears, its deathly rattle choking out the word, "*Somath...*"

"I apologize, Your Grace. I was asked by a friend to find him." Darrin Cantlay bowed his head and turned.

"Darrin," said Aldir as he stood. "Who asked you to find this man?" He approached the boy.

The rover was hesitant to answer.

Aldir turned to address his father. "Your Grace, I ask your leave to speak with Master Cantlay. I believe I may be able to assist him in his request." *Or he may be able to answer a few of my questions.* "I see no need to waste your time or the time of the courts with such a mundane task." He twisted and faced Kayvold next. "With your permission as well, Lord-Overseer?"

The king rose from his throne and said, "I have no interest in spending another minute on our young rover's fancies, but if you deem this of any value, I see no reason to deny it." He stepped down from the dais and awaited the customary reverence to be shown. Once all the men in the hall had knelt and bowed their heads, he strode down the aisle and exited, not saying another word.

"My lord," said Kayvold, "I have no reason to oppose your desire, on the stipulation that myself and Chief Ridgefront accompany our young charge."

Aldir cared little who accompanied him. If this man could provide any insight into the name his dead wife hissed, the entire realm might as well be present.

"I am certain Master Cantlay will appreciate your company."

"My lord," said Darrin, his voice a whisper in the enormity of the Hall of Glory. "Perhaps we might speak in private?" He gazed around the hall as though the walls themselves might overhear. "I made an oath."

An oath? To whom? "I respect your candor, Master Cantlay. We will hold our council in my chamber. I am hoping we may both find an answer to our queries."

Chapter

EVERLY

The Timid Wolf

*F*OOLS, THOUGHT *E*VERLY *as she strode from the Hall of Glory. Both of the Archwoods. The Lord-Overseer—the man placed in charge of maintaining the realm's greatest defense—is nothing more than an overly-suspicious dullard, and his gluttonous ass of a brother, Brastor, believes I might for a moment entertain the notion of mixing my daughter's blood with his ludicrous family? Gods! Is this the kingdom I must inherit? Sycophants and idiots.*

She swept through the antechamber, forgetting her courtesies as she ignored the displaced lords and ladies who littered the hall. Her frustrations were a mask of rage, a deterrent from unwanted conversation—as Lady Calvert of Pinefall learned when she attempted to approach the princess.

Everly only had to glance at the elderly woman before Lady Calvert twisted away and interjected herself into a group of high-born women who clustered themselves into one of the antechambers' many alcoves.

Let the old wretch and her gaggle of crones gossip on that rebuke. Perhaps she will choke on her curses. Everly laughed aloud and continued down the corridor that led to the doors of the keep.

As she stepped across the threshold of Dartsuil's Keep and strode through the upper bailey, she studied the aftermath of the riot.

But what if the Eyes are not wrong? The young one was almost terrified enough to make me believe their story. What if Odain...? No, it is not possible. He is heir to the throne; he is a father. No one in Onyris is senseless enough to commit such an act of treachery. The king will regain his wits. I am certain of it. He will not succumb to this fallacy.

It was quiet, which was unusual. Instead of the laughter and drunken clamor so common to an evening in Rothspire, the only sounds she heard were the heavy steel footfalls of the city guard. The fires that had erupted from overturned carts in the yard earlier were now extinguished, and only a faint acrid scent lingered about the cool summer eve.

A voice cut through the rhythmic stomping of soldiers' boots.

"My lady."

Everly stopped and searched for the man who called her.

One of the King's Blades broke from his ranks and marched towards her. His polished steel armor reflected the setting sun. He raised his visor and said, "My lady, it is not safe to be out alone."

"Is it not safe for the princess to walk the grounds of her own castle?" She frowned. "The only people I see are the city guard and a King's Blade. Do you mean to tell me I should be worried about you, Sir Hornbrook?"

The knight stammered, "M-my lady, we have not finished rounding up the criminals. I would not be upholding my oath if anything happened to you."

Did your oath protect my son? Did your sword end the red cough? No. The Gods are cruel, and as much as you men believe your steel cocks may ward off danger, you are merely frightened children playing at hero. Everly fixed her gaze on the man's face. "Roger," she said his name affectionately. "If you feel the need to protect someone, look to your family. I am certain they are worried about you."

The knight cast his eyes down and said, "My lady, I mean no offense, but I am sworn to the safety of the royal family, and I cannot allow you to place yourself in danger." He lifted his arm in an attempt to grab her shoulder.

Everly slapped his hand away. The crack of her flesh on his steel plate rang in the evening air. Her fingers throbbed, but she allowed no sign of pain to be seen on her face. "Do not *ever* presume to touch me!" Her eyes became slits, and her mouth tightened with indignation. "Resume your post now, or I will strip you of your title immediately. And the only *family* you may deem to *protect* will be the toothless whores so blind with age they cannot see the shame that will so plainly cover your face."

Sir Roger Hornbrook stared at her agape. He dared not say another word. His red and green cloak whipped behind him as he spun and marched back to his men.

Protect...guard...shield...the words these men use are not meant to defend. They are a justification to withhold and dominate. To them a woman is no different from a child, a babe too fragile to even walk. But where is their honor or gallantry when true pain, true devastation is on their doorstep? Off fighting imagined threats, off drinking in alehouses, off finding weaker women to control.

The memory of her first son, Prince Bradain the Third, came rushing back to her. He was only seven, a year younger than Amara was now. She remembered his thin frame pressed against her chest, the violent convulsions of every cough thundering against her breast.

She remembered his eyes the most; they were gold, like sunshine glinting across the sea. So beautiful, so full of innocence at one time. But they had become almost hollow; black pits set into dim, gray flesh.

After he lost his ability to speak, she had forgotten what his voice sounded like. She could only hear the rasping, guttural rattle, and the choking. And then…the blood.

How many died during that plague? Does it even matter anymore? It took Bradain, my son, my heart.

She pushed the memory back; it did her no good to remember. She still had Amara, and she would destroy any man who might cause her daughter pain, be it a lord, a king, or a God.

Her feet had been moving while she was lost in these thoughts, and though she was not conscious of it, she soon found herself standing at the entrance of the sacellum. And though custom dictated her presence at this holy temple on the tenth day after every new moon, she had not willingly passed through these doors in over nine years. Not since Bradain had been laid in its crypts.

What drove her to this place, she did not know, but she entered nonetheless.

The air inside the sacellum was thick with incense and burning sage; she wrinkled her nose at the overwhelming scent. The soft patter of her feet echoed throughout the room, magnified by the impressively high, domed ceiling. When she looked above at the mosaic of cloudy skies and twenty radiant stars, she bowed her head in instinctive reverence.

"Gods," she said aloud. "It has been too long since I

prayed to you, but please accept my supplication. Protect my husband, and I will forgive your abandonment of my son."

"The Gods do not bargain, my child," a thin, nasal voice answered.

Everly lifted her head. "Your Glory," she said in surprise. "I thought I was alone."

"We are never alone, my child," the High Divinator, Erabil Varna, said as he shambled towards her, an enormous black dog following closely behind him. "The Gods fix Their gaze on us wherever we go." He stood only a breath away from her now and placed a fragile hand on her cheek. "And though They may know all, Their servants are left to question. Why does the princess find herself under the shelter of the Ten?"

She shuddered at his touch but made no attempt to remove his hand. The prelacy stood higher than royalty, and though she despised their authority, she was powerless to their sovereignty. She responded, her voice that of a guilty child, "I seek the assurance of my husband's safety."

"I did not know you kept the faith of the Gods, my child. I have seen you during sermons, and though your body kneels, I do not feel your soul bending to Their grace."

He disgusted her. The yellowed, emaciated skin, which barely clung to his face, reminded her of a snake in the process of molting. His ill-fitting gray robes hung from his skeletal frame, and his breath, perfumed as it was, scarcely masked the rot that dwelt in his mouth. But it was his eyes—an anemic shade of brown, waxen and almost devoid of color—that sickened her the most.

She stiffened her resolve and smiled, piously.

"Yet," said Erabil, "we are children of All, and even the most wayward of us find a path to Her, eventually. I am glad to be the torch you hold as you stumble away from the darkness of Naught."

I did not come here for a lecture on scripture. "Thank you, Your Glory."

"I need no praise, my child. The Ten will recognize your devotion."

"I can only hope my atonement will please Them." She bent to stroke the dog. "She is quite beautiful."

The dog drooped at her touch and presented its ear.

As much as Everly detested the priest, she could not help herself from petting the animal. Its soft black fur filled her hand, and she soon forgot her previous anger.

"They were wolves, once."

"What?" Everly asked, more out of shock than interest.

"Dogs, my child," said Erabil. "They were wolves. True, it was long ago, at the intersection of history and legend, but at one point in their journey, this gentle creature was just as dangerous as a wolf in the wild."

Her hand rubbed the dog's mane absentmindedly.

How she had wanted one when she was a girl. But her childish pleading fell on the deaf ears of her father. *Only priests keep a dog, Everly,* her father had said. They are *hunters, shepherds, and guards. Not pets.*

A sharp twinge of pain shot through her hand.

She couldn't have been more than eight years old, if she remembered correctly. After her father's refusal, she had run to the kennel-master of Godsbreath and demanded he let her play with the hounds. *I didn't heed his warnings.*

It had been a big black and tan shepherding dog. The one with the glossiest of coats. She'd thrown her arms around the thing and hugged it with all the love she might have shown her mother. But the animal was fierce, the lord's most prized hunter. After she'd let go of it, she had assumed the dog would be her best friend.

I was a fool. A child, but a fool.

In one quick moment, after tugging on the beast's tail, its sharp fangs had sunk into her hand. The only thing she remembered was running back to her father in tears. And after that ... the beautiful creature had been slain. She'd cried more at the fate of the dog than her own pain.

To this day, she would not forgive herself.

"Do you know why we keep them?" Erabil asked.

Everyone does. "They are your protectors."

"That is but a small part of their duty." The High Divinator reached down and stroked his dog. "In the time before memory, the most timid of wolves came to man, as we come before the Gods today. They bowed to their masters and accepted such scraps as they deemed within their means, and the meekest of their kind received the acceptance of man. But as submissive as they might have appeared to us, they were still savage creatures. No other beast in the Wide-World dared approach these groups of men if a wolf stood by their side."

"They were the original shield of man?"

Erabil laughed. "Ah yes, one in your position would understand it that way." He released the dog and glanced up towards the dome of the sacellum. "But we keep these glorious animals as a constant reminder that man is but a beast, and the most timid and humble of us might be accepted by the Gods, and those who feast on the scraps left by Their divinity will ultimately find themselves let into the towers of the holy." He took her hand in his. "My dear child, do you see the imprudence in believing man is anything but the shield of the Gods?"

His hands were slick with perspiration; she fought back the instinct to immediately release herself from his grasp. "There are those who believe the Gods have rejected us, Your Glory." His grip tightened ever so slightly. "Our princess is not one of those, I pray."

Can a fable reject someone? "No." She smiled and gracefully removed her hands from his. "But there are moments when I question Their desires."

"As we all do in times of great uncertainty, but perhaps it is best I leave you to converse with Them alone. It is said that on rare occasions, one of the Ten may listen to the weakest of prayers uttered by the gentlest of mice."

They will not hear a gentle prayer from me. "Thank you, Your Glory. I would appreciate that."

Erabil grinned, his smile never reaching his milky-brown eyes.

At that moment, the doors to the sacellum opened and a man dressed in dark gray appeared. He strode confidently through the room. As he neared, Everly noticed the sable stitching of a puppeteer's rod on the front of his exquisitely tailored doublet. He wore a deep-gray cloak that shimmered in the faint torchlight of the room and the rapping of his gray leather boots echoed under the massive dome. "My lady, I have been searching for you." His voice was laced with concern.

Everly stared at the man suspiciously. "And who are you?"

"My name is Tomm Harken, my lady. I held council earlier today with His Grace and you." He knelt to one knee. "I have come to inform you that your daughter's Shield has escaped."

Rhen? That's impossible. She laid her hand on his shoulder and tried to remember his face. A moment passed in silence, and then she gestured for him to stand. "You must be mistaken, Master Harken. Rhen was taken to the Dark Cells. It is impossible for one to escape."

Everly, though knowing Rhen could be rash, never believed her daughter's Shield would do something as foolish as attempt to escape. "Your Glory—" She turned to Erabil. "Please tell Master Harken that no one can escape the Dark Cells."

Erabil rubbed his dog's neck, looked at Tomm Harken, and said, "My child. You have been given false information. Prior Melwin, a student of the faith, was dispatched upon our young Shield's arrival to tend his wounds."

"Your prior is dead," said Tomm. "Along with Sir Ethan Canby." He turned his gaze from the High Divinator and peered at Everly. "My lady, I need you to come with me."

The air in the room grew thick, and Everly struggled to understand what had just been said. "Excuse me, Master Harken," she said, attempting to regain control of the situation. "You are not in the charge of my family, and you have no authority to ask anything of me."

"Be that as it may, my lady, more of your people now lie dead and it would seem rather careless if the princess of Rothspire believed it more important to discuss courtesies than to see to the capture of *her* servant."

Who does this man think he is? "I might find your accusations more believable if you arrived in the company of one of the King's Blades or a soldier of the city guard."

"I must agree with our princess, my child. Your manner does not befit one with the interest of our realm in his soul." Erabil frowned.

Tomm bowed his head. "It is for the interest of the realm that I came to my lady first. I do not believe it wise to alert the city guard or His Grace of your Shield's betrayal before you assess his crimes. The moment the smallfolk learn of a brocken's deceit, the leadership of the Graymeres may be called into question. I only wished to save Our Magnificence from further humiliation."

"But *you* are somehow privy to this information?" Everly glared at the man dressed in such peculiar finery. "Why would I place my trust in a stranger who so flippantly disregards their station?"

In an almost reluctant fashion, Tomm Harken removed the glove from his left hand.

Everly stared at the man's tattooed hand. "*You* are a pedagogue?"

"It is against my sacred oath to deceive, my lady. But you must forgive a man who seeks trust in his words alone." He eyed Erabil. "And one would suppose a man of faith might be willing to extend their belief to their fellow man."

"My dear child, the Gods do not instill in me Their clarity in such matters. My apologies."

Everly looked at Erabil in disbelief. *And I bow to you? Does a pedagogue exceed your glory?* "Master Harken, I am not so easily swayed as Our Glory. Though I respect the esteem a pedagogue is deserved, I do not know you, and I desire more than a few tattoos and rings to account for the validity of your claim."

"My lady, I have not come here to argue over status." He slipped a shimmering, silver glove back over his hand. "I had hoped you might regard my integrity, but it seems your pride outweighs your duties. I am obliged with seeing to the preservation of our realm, and if your mistrust of a pedagogue is any indication, it would appear my assessment of your propriety was misplaced." He knelt once more. "My lady, if you would excuse me."

"Stand up," said Everly. "Lead the way, Master Harken. I will not have it said of me that I am one to ignore my commitments."

Tomm Harken stood and spun away from her. He did not wait for Everly to follow him.

Gods! Are you testing us? What has Rothspire done?

She left the sacellum, her prayers unanswered. If Rhen had committed the crimes this man alleged, there would be more than a riot and a dead knight in a melee to answer for.

This is the kingdom I must inherit. Broken. Our Shields have become swords and our people have grown so restless that they no longer quaver at our might. And Odain? Perhaps those boots were his. My husband… His last steps were the footfalls of our doom.

She heard a dog's howl pierce the still night air. The shield of the Gods bayed in the coming dark.

CHAPTER

RHEN

The Dark Journey

"How'd we get so lucky to be the ones to lug this bloody monster all the way down to Towerglenn?"

"Right place, right time, I figure."

Towerglenn?

Rhen had barely regained consciousness, but he was certain one of these men had said Towerglenn. Their voices seemed strange to him. Their accent was not that of Rothspire.

When he opened his eyes, blackness filled his sight. It was as though he had not opened them at all. He gave a sudden jerk, but that was useless as well. Cold iron rings bit into his skin.

Why am I in chains? He writhed frantically. *Where am I? Where am I being taken?*

His breathing came in short, shallow bursts, obstructed by a dirty, fibrous braiding of hempen rope stuffed in his mouth.

They've gagged me? The thought caused him to convulse with fright. He gnawed at the rope—teeth gnashing into bulky cord—but it was too thick for him. He must think of something.

With immense exertion, he flexed his massive arms, hoping to snap at least one of the links in the hefty iron chain. His muscles rippled and bulged. A blinding blaze of pain shot from his left arm and coursed through his body. He shook violently, the cold iron of the chains sliding against the open wound made by Sir Hugh Castac's sword. Rhen screamed in agony, his cry muffled by the rope.

A loud *thwack* thundered in his ears, the sound of a fist slamming against a wooden box. He rolled from one side to the other but found his movements restrained to less than an inch in either direction. In one last surge of terror, he attempted to sit up, but again, his strain was met with immediate denial as his head crashed into a heavy board. A lid.

I'm in a coffin...

"You'd best keep quiet if ya know what's good for you," the harsh voice of a man said.

Rhen stopped struggling. If he couldn't break through his bonds, he must regain his wits.

"Sounds like our friend is coming to. So much for Hallet's powders."

"Shut yer mouth, ya damned fool. We was told not to use any names."

Hallet? Sir Jaymes Hallet? The King's Blade?

Memories flooded back: the melee, Sir Hugh Castac, the King's Blades, his surrender, and then...nothing. Where was he? And who were these men?

"Besides, we ain't wanting *him* hearing us."

"Bugger this bloody monster. A brocken don't got the

brains to figure who we're talking about. May as well be a bear we got caged up here."

"Not the damned brocken, ya nit." He lowered his voice and said, "*Him.*"

Him? Rhen didn't care about the men's insults—their scorn was as natural to his life as the buzzing of flies—but these two sounded genuinely terrified when it came to whomever this *Him* was.

A long stretch of silence passed. Rhen could discern the distinctive breathing pattern of the two men, but not a third; at least not someone near enough for him to catch. Beyond the strained breath of these men, the steady clopping of hooves on hard dirt and the consistent whirl of iron-studded wheels continued unabated. As he settled his own breathing, the gentle sway of the floor he lay upon grew familiar.

We're traveling, but we're moving slowly. If I'm being taken to Towerglenn, these men are in no hurry to arrive. Rhen listened attentively, but the soft rustle of wind that usually accompanied travel in a wagon bed was suspiciously absent. *The wagon is covered. Whoever is doing this is doing so in secret.*

He wiggled his fingers; his right hand—though bound to his side—tensed and loosened with ease, but those of his left hand bore little strength.

The memory of Hugh Castac's sword swinging through the air clouded his mind. The laceration in his arm flamed anew. He stifled a groan.

"Been a few hours. We must be close."

"Aye, I s'pose yer right. Can't be too long now."

The wagon bed creaked as one of the men got to his feet. Rhen heard the sound of a heavy canvas flap opening.

"What the bloody hell ya doing? *He* said to keep down 'til we got there."

A loud thud shook the wagon as the man who'd opened the flap was dragged to the floor by his companion.

The cadence of hoof beats slackened then halted. Both men muttered a curse. Rhen marked their rapid breath.

"Now ya've done it," one said aloud, like a child caught by an angry father.

Slow, deliberate steps struck the ground outside. A soft rustle of steel clinked with each sinister footfall.

Him, thought Rhen. *Perhaps I'll recognize his voice.*

The quick rustle of heavy canvas being thrown open peeled through the silence. Not a word was squeaked from either man, but Rhen sensed their fear. The flap closed with a clap, and the uniform steps of the third man sounded once more.

The wagon lurched forward, and the rhythm of hooves resumed their steady drum against the road.

Another hour or so passed in silence before Rhen perceived an incline in their journey.

This is the descent into Towerglenn. We are near.

Towerglenn was the stronghold of Rothspire's army and home to their naval fleet. It was a vast and sprawling coastal city built along the shore of the Brockhead Sea. Not only the central hub of Onyris's maritime strength but also the epicenter of commerce and trade. Many wealthy lords kept manses upon its towering cliffs, overlooking the sparkling sea. Unlike Rothspire, Towerglenn had become a unified divergence of military, market, and magnificence. But why was Rhen being taken here?

The road from the Great Wheel passed between two enormous towers on either side of a narrow lane. These towers, from which Towerglenn derived its name, held a history that everyone in Rothspire learned in childhood.

Rhen remembered his father's own explanation of their importance.

It is said that when one stands atop these towers, they possess the view of the Wide-World. Day or night, you can identify an enemy's approach from over a thousand leagues away.

If only I stood atop one of them this morning. Rhen laughed to himself.

The thought of his father made him clench his teeth tight on his gag. *What a failure I am.*

Rhohl, the Shield of the Prince, had done more to engender the people of Onyris's goodwill towards the brocken than even that of Rhoan, the very first Shield of the King.

And in one act, I have squandered everything my father worked so hard to build. Perhaps I deserve whatever fate awaits me?

His father's assumed disappointment enraged him. *Why should I care? You have spent your life striving for an unachievable vision. For all the good you've done, I'm still here. Wherever this is. Would Edlen be attacked by her family's guards? For trying to protect them? No! Would a Graymere be thrown in a cell for killing a man who meant them harm? I have sworn my life to them, and this is how I'm repaid? You are the idiot, Father, and I'm the one who suffers for your loyalty.*

Tears ran down his cheeks, mixing with the bitter rope in his mouth. He shook again. The memory of his best friend crawling away from him on the tourney field sparked a wrath previously unknown inside of him.

I would die for you, Edlen… His eyes burned.

But you…you frightened little…you ran from me. You disappeared when I needed you most. Why did you not declare yourself? You are a Graymere! Hallet would not have struck you! You could have…you should have…done something.

The wagon stopped and his guards made a clamorous noise as they got to their feet. It seemed to Rhen that they were uncomfortable moving in heavy armor.

"Get yerself ready—*He's* gonna want to move this bastard quick."

"Yeah, yeah," the other man grumbled in response. "Steady on...I'm still sore from loading 'im."

"Sore or not, *He* ain't gonna hear your belly aching. I'll wager he sticks yer guts if he catches wind of yer complainin'."

The coffin scraped against the hard wood of the wagon bed as the two men slid it forward. Their grunts reverberated in the small space.

Rhen stiffened in anticipation, certain they would let it crash to the ground below. But the sharp, violent pain he expected never came. Instead, he overheard the uniform steps of Him advancing; his slow, calculated movements harsher than the racket caused by his escorts. His casket was lifted up and then placed carefully onto the ground.

How many men are here to unload me? There's no way these two would be able to lift me, even if Him helped them.

Rhen listened intently to his surroundings once again.

The recognizable panting of the two men was easy to distinguish, but *His* breathing was altogether foreign. As though the man lifted nothing heavier than a crate of goods, his breath remained slack, almost non-existent. Other than his approach, Rhen might not have detected his presence. Beyond the puffing of the men, Rhen noted the lapping of waves and the subtle grinding of a large ship at port. When he focused, the muted croak of dock lines chattering became clear.

They brought me to a boat. Why?

The fear he stamped down earlier roared back.

No! Why am I here?

He rocked back and forth again to no avail. *Let me out! Let me out!* He tried to scream, the rope in his mouth choking him.

"Powder's worn off, sir," said one of the men.

"He's too big for it," added the other. "We ain't gonna be able to pick him up now, not thrashing about like that."

Pick me up? Do they mean to load me onto a ship? An idea came to him. *The fool is right; they won't be able to lift me if I don't stop moving.* He mustered all his strength and slammed himself into the side of the coffin. The rope lodged deeper into his mouth, though he was no longer concerned with discomfort.

The lid of the coffin flew off. Rhen's hood was ripped from his head.

Thank the Gods! I can see again.

His attempt at destroying the casket had failed, but his plan had worked. The darkness he grew accustomed to vanished—replaced by blurry starlight. He drank in the vision of the night sky. This paltry gift of sight was worth whatever future woe might come.

A figure stood over him, hooded and cloaked, its features disguised by a mask of shadow. Still chained and unable to move with the gag set firmly in his mouth, he stared up in disbelief.

Him towered over Rhen's prone frame. He glanced down impassively, unimpressed with the brocken.

The two men, who Rhen still could not identify, laughed nervously. One of them said, "He's all yours, sir. Just let us know how we can help ya."

The unmistakable shriek of steel drawn from its scabbard

rang out, followed by a quick thwack and a faint gurgle and then the thud of a heavily armored body hitting the ground.

Just after that, Rhen heard the fumbling clatter of a man too horrified to draw his own blade. He saw the faintest image of someone dressed in the garb of the city guard stumble past. The dim outline of a longsword flashed under the starlight and the severed head of a man wearing a silver and red helmet landed against his face.

Rhen screamed. Long twine strands slipped down his throat. He twisted and writhed about, no longer noticing the iron chain that bit into his wound. The man's face, which now snarled silently, gaped at him, the warm blood seeping from its bodiless neck pooling in the wooden box.

Oh Gods! Oh Gods! No! No! No!

Two cold hands grabbed onto him, and he was lifted from his coffin.

No! This is not happening!

Him hoisted him over his shoulder. Rhen tried to wriggle free, but the man placed a firm hand on his neck and steadied his movements. He carried Rhen up a short ramp then entered the hull of an enormous ship. The world turned black once more.

He dropped Rhen unceremoniously onto a hard surface, iron chains gnawing at his flesh. Before he could react, the strange man thrust him against a wall and the sound of clinching locks echoed in his ears. Rhen inhaled a scent of stale wine, sweat, and perfume.

He was standing, but his muscles no longer seemed to work. His legs gave out, but he did not fall; instead, thick iron tethers held him upright. No longer in control of his body, Rhen hung there, terrified and confused.

The distinct clang of cage doors slammed shut. And like a beast's jaws biting into its prey's neck, the thin clink of a lock snapped closed.

A slow, gravelly voice said, "He…comes."

Chapter

DARRIN

The Primacy's Chamber

Darrin walked slowly, keeping his head down; the magnificence of Dartsuil's Keep was beyond anything he'd imagined.

As a child, the stories he'd most loved to read concerning the castle painted a picture of drab, cold stones stacked upon each other to impossible heights. But moving through its ornately decorated corridors now, he understood how misleading those tales were.

Every direction he glanced was filled with more delicate finery or subtle pieces of woodwork that far surpassed the skill of any craftsman of his homeland. The sight of such impeccable technique embarrassed him, reinforcing the notion that he was in a world removed from his upbringing. In his youth, he believed Redrun to be but a quainter version of Rothspire, but the reality of his surroundings mocked him.

My father's land is a hovel. It is no wonder Haron holds him in such disregard. Phillip Cantlay…Lord of Haystacks, the Master of Dung.

He shuffled closer to his chief. "Is all of Rothspire like this?"

"This be but a part, Cantlay. Ain't never been further than 'ere myself. Leaves an impression, it does. I'll say that much."

The corridors of Dartsuil's Keep were warmer than the Hall of Glory, and small beads of sweat ran down Darrin's forehead. A sweet, familiar scent wafted towards him. *Fresh-baked bread?*

It reminded him of home. Though the majesty of the king's capital shamed him, the pleasant aroma would always remind him of his mother. A pang of sadness crept across his heart. *I'm sorry I left without telling you.* He wished he'd had the courage to say goodbye to her—but if he meant to defy his father and become a rover, her words would have stopped him. *I hope you're well, Mother...and that you don't hate me.*

He pushed his thoughts aside as a bent old man cloaked in heavy gray robes, followed by a young boy, approached the Primacy of the Realm.

"Who are they?" Darrin whispered to Haron.

"No clue, lad," said Haron. "But the Primacy's interested in what they 'ave to say."

Darrin noted the odd pairing of the elderly man and the young boy, assuming they must be some noble grandfather and grandchild seeking audience with Aldir. For a moment, he pitied the Primacy. *A man in his position must have to pander to everyone in the kingdom.*

But just as this thought flitted through his head, the Primacy pointed in his direction. "Master Cantlay." Aldir's voice was a command.

Darrin grabbed Haron's arm. "Do they want me to come?"

"Aye." Haron shoved him forward, chuckling. "Ain't no use keepin' 'em waiting, my lad."

I never should have asked that ridiculous question. What have I done?

Darrin stepped from behind his chief and walked forward. "My lord." He knelt.

"Master Cantlay," said Aldir, "I would like to introduce you to my father-in-law, the wisest man in Onyris—Laustair Mostah."

"My pleasure, Lord Laustair."

"Stand, boy." The old man tittered. "I am no lord, and I desire none of your courtesies." He smiled, the wrinkled skin around his lips creasing into a million folds.

A wave of relief washed over Darrin; his nervousness disappeared. "I am sorry for your loss. I have been told Lady Irymar was an amazing woman."

"That she was."

Laustair reached out a wizened hand, the bracelets on his wrist clattering as he clutched Darrin's shoulder. "But let us not speak of such sadness. Our Primacy tells me you seek someone."

"Yes, sir." Darrin marked the young boy who Aldir had not yet introduced. "But I was sworn to keep this request secret. I apologize for my rudeness, but I have already told too many people." *I should not be telling you this.*

Laustair laughed again, his age appearing to fade. "Young Master Gault was just departing." He knelt laboriously and whispered into the boy's ear.

The young boy nodded enthusiastically and bowed. Without a peep, he darted away.

"A man's secret must be held sacred. If one is not trusted with their word, the entire structure of secrets may come crashing down upon them." Laustair winked. "Darrin, is it? My boy, *no one* in the Wide-World is more respectful of one's secrets than myself. After all, I have been the confidant of not only our Primacy but his daughter as well." He turned to Aldir. "Is this not so?"

"A better vault I have not met," agreed Aldir.

"Very well!" said Laustair. "It is decided. You may share your secrets with me, Master Darrin."

An immediate fondness for the old man settled in Darrin's heart. "Thank you, sir."

They walked together through a corridor. The Primacy, though, kept quiet conversation with the old man.

"We may retire in my chamber," said Aldir. "It is well stocked with food and drink. My father-in-law wishes to join us, and I have agreed to his request."

Darrin took the many steps to the Primacy's apartments and soon felt the ache in his muscles. He watched Laustair and wondered how he must be faring. *This must be murder on the old man. Why was he so intent on joining us?*

THE soothing scent of the old man›s pipe filled the Primacy's chamber. Darrin breathed it in and smiled. After recounting the details of his and Haron's trials in the forest again, the comforting fragrance was a welcome distraction.

"That is when he asked me to search for this…Somath." Darrin eyed Lord Archwood. He had kept this part of the story from him. "I must apologize to you, Lord-Overseer, but I was to tell no one but Somath."

Kayvold took a sip of wine. "Do you recall what I said concerning character, Master Cantlay?"

"Yes, my lord. And I am sorry."

"On the contrary," said Kayvold. "I was quite certain you possessed the qualities required to make for an exceptional rover. And your adherence to the sanctity of this man's secret proves me right." He chuckled and turned to Haron. "You have taught him well, Ridgefront. Just like you, he sees more than he says."

"Aye, my lord. He's earned his stains."

Laustair set his pipe on a table beside his cushioned seat. "Did this man give his name?"

"Yes, sir."

"Well. Let's have it."

Darrin's eyes narrowed. "Dalnor, sir, but he insisted I not say his name to anyone but Somath."

"If you have kept this name secret, why are you telling me?" Laustair stared at Darrin.

"I…do not know," stammered Darrin. He had no explanation for why he'd just divulged this to a stranger. *Perhaps my character is not to the standard my Lord-Overseer assumes.* He stared at the floor. "I sense…well…you are supposed to help me find Somath."

Laustair searched the faces of the men and inhaled sharply, a billowy white cloud of smoke hanging in the air as he exhaled. His gaze settled on Haron. "Chief Ridgefront, you too met this Dalnor character, correct? What did he look like?"

"Aye, sir." His bushy eyebrows furrowed. "But if ya mean to ask me to describe 'im, I ain't gonna be much help."

"Did you not see him clearly?"

"Clear as I'm looking at you now. But it ain't no use me try an tell ya." He cast his eyes down. "Memory ain't what it used to be, if ya understand."

"Rubbish to that, Ridgefront!" Kayvold bellowed. "Not three nights past, you and I discussed our first roving." He turned to Laustair. "And this man here remembered the smallest details of an unremarkable event that happened over thirty-five years ago." He faced Haron. "I won't have any more on your memory. You are speaking to the Primacy of the Realm, and you represent the Eyes of the Forest. Give these men the courtesy they deserve and answer Master Laustair's question."

"Aye, my lord," said Haron. "Mind you, it'll sound a lie."

Darrin tapped his foot rapidly and stared at his friend.

"He looked…" Haron paused, catching Darrin's glance. "Well, old. My lords. But not old. Mind you, I was in a wee bit o' pain at the time, but as I first saw 'im, I took 'im for some ole hermit, ya understand? One of these coots who've grown tired of cities and moved into the woods. We find 'em more oft than naught just as they're 'bout to die. The forest ain't the safest place for these folks. But that weren't the case with 'im. When I got a better look at the bloke, he couldn't 'ave been older than our Primacy 'ere." He frowned. "Strong, healthy-looking…and huge."

"Huge? How so?" Laustair peered at the grizzled man.

"Now, I ain't never seen one of these brocken, but tale of their size is legend. Can't say he was tall as one o' them, but near enough made no damn difference. But…" Haron shook his head as though afraid to say something.

Say it, Harry. If you say it, perhaps Archwood might realize that Bart hasn't gone mad.

"Then in a blink, he seemed a child; no bigger than a lad of five or six." Haron slammed his fist on his leg and tears rolled down his cheeks. "Every time I looked at 'im he was different—only his voice never changed. Always the same, ya see? Deep and full. It was my father's voice."

Are you crying, Harry? It wasn't possible, not Haron. Darrin had seen him mauled by a bear. He'd stood over him while Haron had lain in a pool of his own blood—a damned bone sticking out of his leg—and the old bastard had still managed to eke out a laugh. Why was he crying now?

Laustair eyed Darrin. "Was this the same voice you heard?"

What was his voice?

"Begging your pardon, sir, but I can't rightly say," said Darrin. "His words were more...in my head, if that means anything to you? I'm certain he spoke aloud, but it was more like...I heard him in my mind. Now, though, if you're asking—I heard my mother's voice."

The air in the room grew thick. Darrin noticed how when they'd first entered Lord Aldir's chamber, the brazier in the corner had provided plenty of light, but even though the fire still raged, it had grown dim.

Aldir stood and lit two lanterns. A soft, amber glow filled the chamber.

"Interesting," Laustair muttered as he tapped ash from his pipe. "Are you men of faith?"

Darrin studied his company. This was not something discussed in the Eyes of the Forest. He'd wondered if Harry followed scripture, but had never dreamed of broaching the subject. He assumed Lord Archwood to be a man of the faith (most lords were) or at least that was what his father had told him.

To receive the honor of lordship, one must proclaim their servitude to the Ten. But perhaps the title of Lord-Overseer was nothing more than a rank?

"Aye," said Haron before bowing his head.

"Yes, sir," Kayvold responded with the same reverence.

Aldir nodded.

Darrin grew nervous. "My father is." He lowered his eyes. "But my mother keeps to the Elder Gods." He drummed his fingers on his thigh. "I have not decided for myself, though."

Laustair grinned. "Brave of you to admit, Darrin." He rose from his chair and shambled to a cabinet near the windows. Pulling a tall, thin bottle from inside, he filled five goblets with a reddish-brown liquid and served each of them.

"A young man in the attendance of three highly ranked individuals—all attesting to being men of faith—yet he shows courage enough to admit indecision." He raised his glass. "I salute you, Master Cantlay."

In one swift gulp, Laustair finished his drink. "Let the shared indulgence of this spirit fortify us all with the bravery of our youngest."

Each lifted their goblet and drank, toasting Darrin.

Nearly gagging as the liquid burned down his throat, a calm soon washed over him. He smiled timidly. *Gods! I did not ask to be saluted.* Darrin bowed his head. *What is the old man after?* "I have done nothing remarkable."

"Have you not?" Laustair poured the last of the bottle between the men's goblets. "Gentlemen, how deep is your understanding of the Ten?"

Each bowed their heads in reverence.

"I see," said Laustair.

"Yes," said Kayvold. "The Ten shelter us all."

"They do?" asked Laustair, with a hint of suspicion.

"Aye, sir," Haron answered matter-of-factly.

Laustair grinned. "And you, Aldir? Do you also understand the faith as our guests do?"

Darrin recognized the pained expression on Lord Aldir's face.

"I understand the faith in my own way, Father. In the way you have taught me."

"Enlighten us all, my lord," said Laustair. "What have I taught you?"

"The Ten are the vassals of All. Creators of Her vision, protectors of Her children, and stewards of Her realm."

"Perfectly stated." Laustair took a deep draw from his pipe.

"Is Dalnor one of the Ten?" asked Darrin.

"Ah!" said Laustair, his voice booming in exclamation. "I believe he is."

"It is not possible," whispered Kayvold. "The Ten are Gods seated on the High Throne of the world. They do not walk amongst us."

Darrin noted uncertainty in the Lord-Overseer's voice. The struggle between what he believed and the longing to be seen as an equal of Laustair.

"My lord, can you tell me what separates myth from truth?" asked Laustair.

The Lord-Overseer took a deep breath but did not answer the question.

"Can anyone here tell me?"

Darrin studied the others. None were willing to speak, none willing to appear foolish, but a word came to him in a flash. "Time?" He did not know why he said that aloud.

Laustair clapped his hands and said, "Master Darrin, my boy, you are wise beyond your years!"

His face reddened, Laustair's praise filling him with such warmth he thought he might burst.

"Time is right." Laustair laughed again. The sound echoed off the walls. "Who here is familiar with the Valdryz?"

No one answered.

"None of you?" Laustair giggled. "A room filled with men of the faith, and none of you recall the name of the Valdryz?"

Aldir interjected. "If the name is of any importance, why have you not mentioned it before?"

"There has never been a need," said Laustair. "One would hope those of the faith might be interested in learning where their devotion originated."

"Sir," said Haron, "I 'ave been a student of the faith since I was a boy, but I ain't never seen that name mentioned in any o' the books I've read."

"And I doubt you might find a book that does speak of them. The scriptures were written by men…and it is men who changed the fate of the Valdryz."

Aldir gripped the arms of his chair. "Why would you ask us about something that has never been taught?"

"Never been taught?" puzzled Laustair. "I did not say it has never been taught. I said no books speak of them."

"What is the difference?" Aldir shifted in his seat. "Father, if this is another one of your riddles, I fear we do not have the time to waste on unraveling it. Who is Somath?"

Why does the name mean so much to the Primacy? thought Darrin. *He seemed overly intrigued when I mentioned it to the king. Does he seek him as well?*

"History is one grand riddle," said Laustair. "If you have not the time to unravel my question, I doubt you will ever find the man you search for."

"Fine!" said Aldir in exasperation. "What are these bloody Valdryz you deem so important?"

"The Valdryz are the Ten…or rather…who the Ten have become." Laustair eyed the men. "They *are* the faith, my lords: emissaries of All, creators of the Wide-World. But time has shrouded their being in myth. The Valdryz descended from their thrones and condescended to walk amongst men." He glanced at Kayvold. "Lord-Overseer Archwood recites a falsehood—so widely claimed to be a truth it makes no difference. Time distorts facts and creates in its place... history. It is true; the Valdryz have not interfered in the lives of men for thousands of years. Long before King Dartsuil, long before the breaking of the lands, and long before memories faded into myth. But just because none remember a thing does not make it false."

"What proof of this is there?" asked Kayvold.

He wishes to question him. Is this how the Lord-Overseer desires to be seen as his equal?

"The story of these rovers is proof, my lord." Laustair nodded at Darrin. "Proof enough for me."

"Perhaps it is nothing more than a shared hallucination. Stories have been told of such things," Kayvold said.

"Yes, yes," said Laustair. "Tales of this phenomenon are well documented. In those tales, though, both parties afflicted tell the same story. It is not so with our good men here. Master Ridgefront and Master Cantlay experienced similar visions, but each note subtle differences. I am of the mind that they have neither corroborated their tale nor been afflicted by mutual delusion."

The simple act of agreeing with Laustair made Darrin feel wise. He studied the others and observed Aldir and Haron consenting as well.

Kayvold also nodded in agreement, as though he understood the old man's statement was beyond reproach.

He still has not answered my question. Darrin struggled to find the right words, but all he could contrive to ask was, "Who is Somath?"

"Have I not told you?" asked Laustair.

Darrin's chin sank into his chest. The shame covering his face turned his light-brown skin scarlet. "No, sir. You have not."

Laustair's laughter was louder than ever before. "Ha…" He stared at Darrin, his brown eyes burning with the cozy warmth of an evening fire. "Must I knock the answer into your head, my boy? Somath is one of the Ten—one of the Valdryz."

I am no great lord, nor am I chief rover; perhaps my ignorance will be seen as nothing more than green folly. Darrin hazarded to question Laustair. "Then…is Dalnor also a Valdryz? Are you saying I stood in the presence of a God?"

Haron eyed him ruefully but said nothing.

"Yes, Master Cantlay," said Laustair, drawing from his pipe.

Blood rushed to Darrin's face and he lifted his hand in an attempt to conceal his amazement. The others in the room didn't seem to accept Laustair's answer as readily as he did, but it did not matter. He knew the old man told the truth.

Lord Aldir interjected, drawing the men's attention from Darrin. "If this Dalnor is a God, why wouldn't he simply seek out Somath himself? Why trust a young man—no disrespect, Master Cantlay—but a young man who might never arrive in Rothspire? If Dalnor is truly one of the Ten…one of the *Valdryz*…there is no doubt he himself could make it here."

"You heard our fair rover's descriptions, did you not?" said Laustair. "A Valdryz in their true form would find it exceedingly difficult to blend in with those around them. Man is no longer as understanding when it comes to the Gods as they once were. Not when the very concept of the Ten has changed so drastically in the minds of the people."

"If I comprehend Chief Ridgefront and Master Cantlay

correctly," said Aldir, "Dalnor had no single form. If this is the case, would not the people simply disregard him? An old man, a child, a young man; the people of Rothspire would not look twice at any of these."

"Aye, my lord, but beggin' yer pardon," Haron interrupted. "It ain't as simple as all that. Cantlay and I was trying to describe what we saw, yes, but it's more like trying to say what was in a dream, if ya get me? Dalnor was a memory, though he stood before me. He existed, plain as I spoke, but Master Laustair's got the right of it. There ain't no way Dalnor could just prance on in through the Wheel and up the Trail of Kings. As good as he makes ya feel when you're with 'im, I think the idea of 'im might be too terrifying. 'Haps he knows this too, and that's why he asked Cantlay to relay his message."

Laustair smiled thankfully at Haron. "Chief Ridgefront, you do see more than you say." He drew on his pipe and puffed out ten small white ringlets of smoke.

A tide of clarity washed over Darrin. Wherein being in the presence of Dalnor was as comforting and peaceful as being held in the arms of his mother, being in the presence of Laustair was like experiencing complete lucidity. Perhaps this was a power of the Valdryz? They would not just come out and tell you they were Gods, no, they would urge you to discover something like this for yourself. They shaped the Wide-World, they did not build it...this was what the others in the room could not comprehend. Darrin took a deep breath. "Are you Somath?"

Laustair frowned. The fire in the brazier erupted in a rage, the dying lanterns flamed anew.

Chapter

EDLEN

The Voice Underground

Edlen lost track of time as they crept through the dark tunnels of Rothspire. Lost in a web of crisscrossing paths and false trails, her eyes finally adapted to the utter black in which they wandered. She had always relied on her ability to see clearly in the dark, and now, able to perceive her companion's silvery outline as they neared some vast pit, she leapt forward and grabbed the girl by the shoulders.

If not for her quick action, the girl may have stumbled in, only to discover its true depth with her mangled bones. The girl only shrugged a meager thanks as she continued down another path.

Too much time had passed since Edlen had traveled by means of these forgotten roads, but she distrusted the steepness of the path they were on.

This goes down too quickly; we're no longer heading in the right direction.

"I think we should turn back," said Edlen.

"Are yoo fraid?" the girl said, unfazed by her near-fatal fall.

"I'm not afraid. I'm..."

What? Terrified? There might be more pits, or worse, lurking down here. And what if we're caught? I'll be beaten by the city guard until someone realizes I'm the daughter of the Primacy, and you...well, I don't want to think about what they'll do to you. And that's if we even find our way to the damned keep. "It's illogical to go traipsing back into their fortress, isn't it?"

"Illogical?" the girl asked.

Edlen paused. "I mean rather, well...it's foolish, don't you think?"

"Foolish..." The girl laughed. "After what those bastards have put us all through? I don't think this *illogical* at all." Her voice shifted, a different accent slipping across her tongue. "If yoo ain't got the steel in ya, turn back. But I'm going on. I ain't wasting a chance to see the Graymeres. Hap's I'll grab me some of their gold 'fore I turn back to the 'Stock."

"You won't find any gold in the keep. They don't leave their riches lying around in piles."

"Lying round or not, I ain't leaving without taking something from them. They've taken enough from us, don't ya think?"

What is she talking about? We haven't taken anything from her? The more she spoke, the more confused Edlen became. Who was this girl, and why did she hate her family so much? A thought arose in her mind: *Did she have something to do with what happened at the tournament?*

"What happened back there, anyway?" Edlen asked.

"Exactly what was supposed to happen. You was in the Wheel, weren't ya?"

She stepped back and mumbled, "Course I was."

"You saw what they did!" Again, the girl's voice slipped from its low-born accent. "Those Spire-ights got more than they bargained for. Thought they could just slit Ollie's throat and the rest of us would run off. Well, it was 'bout time some of us did something, don't ya think?"

Gods! "Who was Ollie?" asked Edlen.

"Ollie was my best friend," the girl said quietly, but then her voice became a rage. "And them Graymere thugs killed him! With no question. They attacked us first! They came for anyone ain't lucky enough to be born with coin flowing in their veins." She started to laugh. "But they never expected us *scrappers*," she said the word with a hint of pride. "They didn't expect us to come for them, did they?"

The girl sniffled. "Blood for blood. And we bloodied their noses pretty good today, if ya ask me."

"Is this why you want to sneak into the keep?" Edlen asked. "To get back at the city guard?"

The girl's voice grew thick, as though attempting to mask tears. "Those bloody guards didn't act alone. Yer a fool if ya think so. They take their orders from the Graymeres." She spat. "I ain't turning down a gift from the Ten. They brought me to you, and you brought me here. Must be for a reason."

The Ten? What do they have to do with this? "Perhaps it *was* chance that brought us together. I was only looking for a way to escape." Edlen put a hand out, searching through the dark. "But I thank the Ten you came along."

The girl shirked from her grasping hand. "You call it chance; I call it divine. The Graymeres are due a reckoning, and regardless if you want to help or not, I'm gonna make it happen." She moved in close to Edlen. "What's your name, anyway?"

Edlen shuddered.

Her nearness turned from calm to sinister. Too afraid to speak the truth, Edlen answered, "Harris." The false name hadn't fooled Tomm Harken, but she prayed this girl wasn't secretly a pedagogue. "What's yours?"

"Harris, eh?" She reached for something at her side. "Where you from, Harris? I don't think I've seen you in Fairenstock before." Any trace of the smallfolk accent had vanished.

The girl's sudden closeness filled Edlen with a mix of dread and joy, but not a modicum of trust. *Seen me before? You're no better than blind down here.* Not wanting to appear as a terrified child, Edlen mustered what courage remained to her. "I asked you first. You tell me your name and I'll tell you where I'm from."

The unmistakable sound of steel drawn from leather split the silence. "Fair enough, Harris." The girl's voice had a lyrical quality. "My name is Vairet." She twirled a small dagger in her hand. "Where are you from?"

"Pleasant Hill," said Edlen. The ghostly glint of steel sliced through the darkness but stopped a breath away from her face. "Put that down!" she demanded. "I saved your life. What are you playing at?"

"You saved my life?" asked Vairet. She spun the blade mere inches from Edlen and then thrust it forward, hilt first, into her hand. "If I remember correctly, you were standing still as stone in the center of a field when I found you. I'm not certain how that equates to *you* saving *my* life?"

Equates? Who is this girl? No scrapper would ever use a word like that. "I showed you the entrance to this tunnel, didn't I? I stopped you from falling into that hole." But as she said this, she began to question if she had actually done more than Vairet had done for her.

"Well, regardless of who saved who, we're both here now, aren't we?" She pressed Edlen's hand around the handle of the knife. "Keep this with you, if you're afraid. I swiped it off one of those city guard bastards after we took them out on the Wheel. He's not gonna need it anymore." She sneered. "Besides, I got one of my own. I'm thinking you might be a wee bit bolder if you have a blade on you."

Vairet turned away and continued up the path. Once she was a few paces on, she called out, "By the way, no one but a Spire-ight calls it Pleasant Hill. Might do you well to remember."

Edlen stood, mouth agape, the heft of the dagger weighing down her arm. She clenched her fist around the leather grip. Even in this darkness, she could tell it was castle-forged.

What did she mean by 'swiped'?

Edlen redoubled her pace and fell in beside Vairet. Too many questions raced through her mind to ask anything useful, so instead she recited a poem she remembered from childhood.

Five lands are in but these ten mile
Rothspire, Straten, Towerglenn, Pleasant Hill, and the Barrowile
The King keeps an eye from his great throne
Forest guards, Towers on the Sea, Smallfolk, and Home of King's Bone
Rothspire stands tall to protect All
From Ill Threat, or Her Distant Foes, Sadness, which may see Her Fall

"Beautiful," said Vairet. "Perhaps your crow-eyed wet nurse will teach that to me one day."

"You said no one calls it Pleasant Hill, but every child in Rothspire sings this song."

"First time I've heard it," said Vairet. She stopped walking and turned toward Edlen. "Have you ever been to Pleasant Hill?"

"I'm from Pleasant Hill!" Edlen demanded.

"No, you're not!" Vairet grabbed her. "I've told you the truth when you asked, but you…" Her voice teetered on rage. "You've done nothing but lie when I ask you a question. Why you think you need to lie…I honestly do not care. But do not insist you have any idea about where I come from. Do not, for one moment, think I believe a word you say." Her last words held a quavering tone, but she clearly stamped down any other emotion besides anger. "No one from my home calls it *pleasant*."

Edlen slinked away. She took a breath. "Why do you hate the Graymeres so much?"

"You know your poems, Harris, but not your history," Vairet hissed. "The Graymeres have done *everything* in their power to deny the blight of Pleasant Hill. Who do you think stripped us of our contracts? The people of *Pleasant Hill*," she spat. "We are ten times the builders of those who now construct the towers of Rothspire. But the royal family pays men from the Vines to despoil the works of Dartsuil."

"Why not petition the king?" asked Edlen.

"Petition?" Vairet laughed. "It is the king who signed the contracts! He stole our people's livelihood and put it in the pockets of the rich. No, there is no *petitioning*, the king. He has decided to turn a blind eye at the mere mention of my people. But no longer. No! After today the Graymeres will no longer pretend we don't exist." Vairet's voice swelled with anger. "With only a few children, we destroyed the King's Tournament. Imagine what will happen when all of Fairenstock rises up!"

"There will be more attacks?" asked Edlen.

"More?" Vairet grew indignant. "This was just the start, Harris. You cannot deprive people of their basic needs forever. If the king thinks he can simply ignore an entire realm—" She laughed. "Well...he has misjudged us. You lot up here, you do not know poor. You do not know what it is to have *nothing*! If I ever have a chance to take something precious from that disgusting family, I will. Maybe that pretty princess of theirs, Everly." She spat again.

Everly? "What do you mean by that?" asked Edlen.

She patted Edlen on the shoulder then walked away and said, "Nothing, Harris. Nothing."

Edlen followed Vairet in silence as they made their way through the tunnels. The path they walked narrowed and shrank. Where, for the past two hours or so, they'd been able to walk upright, they now found themselves crouching, until ultimately, they had to crawl up a winding passage.

Up ahead, Edlen noticed a small staircase set into a shallow wall.

We must be under the keep now. But I have no memory of this entrance.

Remorseful over their last conversation, Edlen grabbed Vairet's shoulder and squeezed it lightly. She signaled that she would go forward to inspect the stairs.

"I can see better down here than you. I'll go first," Edlen whispered.

Vairet only nodded.

No fight? Maybe she is afraid after all.

Edlen stared at Vairet through the darkness and noted thin tear stains streaming down her cheeks. She longed to embrace her companion and apologize for all the wrong her family had done, but she understood Vairet was not one to accept condolences.

Perhaps I can still help, whether she trusts me or not.

Edlen squeezed Vairet's shoulder again and scrambled ahead towards the stairs.

Vairet smirked at this act of contrition but did not flinch away from the touch. Her voice was a whisper, "Your turn, Harris. Whoever you are."

Are we by the Dark Cells? Edlen had never snuck from Dartsuil's Keep through here. She never imagined that there would be an entrance this far down. *How deep are we?*

As she reached the bottom step of the stairs, she was able to stand again, but she stayed crouched, knowing that even the slightest of movement might give her away. Staring up at the small flight of stairs, Edlen realized that they came to an abrupt end underneath a dark ceiling. She moved slowly and cautiously up the stones until she could no longer move forward. Touching the ceiling above her, she tested the thickness of the roof. *A trapdoor? Who would put a trapdoor in the Dark Cells?*

As her finger slid across a splintery wooden door, Edlen heard muffled voices. Keeping as silent as possible, she listened intently.

"And Castac?" a voice asked.

"What about him?"

Edlen did not recognize either of the men's voices. One was deep and low, where the other was high pitched and nasally, as though he were ill.

The nasally man continued. "He did what he was supposed to. Him dying was nothing but a blessing of the Gods."

"A blessing?" asked the man with the deeper voice. "Baird

is gonna want a full investigation. We'll have half of Riverfront in the capital once word gets down to them."

"As I said." The other sniffed. "All part of the plan. Castac was an arse—his corpse will be much more useful to us than his hateful simpering."

Edlen glanced back at Vairet but refused to take her ear from the door.

The man with the deep voice grunted. "Hateful or not, he wasn't supposed to die. He's a damned knight for All's sake. How do *they* expect anyone else to support *them* if a knight's death is held with such disregard?"

"Disregard? Is that what you believe?" the man with the thin voice asked. "Castac is a martyr, you fool. He died for *the cause*. This is how the other families will understand it. Need I spell that out for you?"

"And they think this whole farce will be believed?"

Edlen wished she could see these men's faces. They spoke like those of high rank, but she could not place them.

"Why would it not?" The nasally man sniffed then sneezed. "You've done your part, haven't you? The brocken is gone—that was all you needed to achieve. Well, that, and the Sword of the King."

"The Sword will not leave his sheath," the man with the deep voice said, almost annoyed. "You can tell our friends that the old steel is rusted."

A thin laugh exploded. "Good, good. That will make *them* very happy."

"Were the scrappers part of the Voress... I mean *their* plan as well?"

The nasally man paused then said, "A fortuitous accident."

"Accident?" the man with the deep voice asked. "Word

has it a couple of your men perished down on the Wheel—surrounded by some dirty scrappers."

"My men acted of their own accord, but if their actions helped stoke the flames of a riot…all the better, wouldn't you say?"

The Wheel? Edlen remembered what Vairet had told her. Ollie? The city guard did kill her friend. Gods! What is happening?

The man with the deep voice asked, "What do we do now? I was given no other instructions."

"You need not worry about what's to be done next. With the brocken gone and Castac dead, our friends will be certain to guarantee your compensation."

"And that will be the end of it? I've heard rumors about our friends."

"What rumors are those?"

"*They* do not tolerate loose ends."

"Do you believe *we* are loose ends?"

"Gods! Randall. We're talking about the Voress Ní." The man with the deep voice whispered his last words.

A loud smack cracked above Edlen. One of the men must have slapped the other.

"Do not say that name aloud again! Forget it entirely. *They* do not exist. Do you understand?" the nasally man hissed. "Or *we* will be seen as loose ends."

The Voress Ní? What is that? Edlen pressed her ear against the door. When she felt Vairet's soft touch on her arm, she almost shouted.

Edlen jerked away from the trapdoor and stared at Vairet. Quiet as she could, she asked, "What are you doing?"

Vairet grinned, her voice but a slip of wind. "You don't get all the fun."

Fun? This is a plot against my family. You cannot share in this. "Go away. There's not enough room for both of us."

"Of course there is." Vairet squeezed into the cramped space and put her ear against the door. In a mocking gesture, she put her forefinger to her lips.

I am beginning to hate her, thought Edlen.

The two men paused their conversation. For a brief moment, all Edlen heard was Vairet's soft breath.

They know we're down here! She tried to back away from the door, but Vairet grabbed her shoulder and smiled.

The voices resumed their conversation.

The nasally man whispered, "I have it on good authority you'll be repaid handsomely for your assistance."

"You mean?"

"Yes, my friend. If you stay quiet, the Sword is yours."

"How do we know *their* plan will succeed?"

The nasally man sneezed. "The Eyes have brought *their* gift to the old man. And everything *they* said would happen is happening."

"Then…he is leaving Rothspire?" the man with the deep voice asked.

"Sooner than we imagined."

Who is leaving? Edlen couldn't imagine anyone leaving Rothspire after today's events. *Not the king…my father?* No. The Primacy would have too much to do… They must be speaking about someone else.

"How can you know this?"

Vairet clutched Edlen's elbow and asked, "What are they talking about?"

"Sshh…" said Edlen. "If we can hear them, they can hear us."

But the two men made no sign that they noticed their voices.

"The walls of Dartsuil's Keep have ears," said the man with the nasally voice. "It is my job to listen."

"Fine," said the other. "Keep your secrets. But just because he is leaving doesn't mean everything else will go according to their plans."

"Do you doubt them? It matters not. The wheel is in motion, and we need do nothing more than play our parts."

Just then, she heard the sound of rapidly approaching footsteps padding down stone stairs in the distance, and a voice came thundering from the other side of the trapdoor.

Who is this? Edlen wondered. Her body clenched.

It was a woman's voice. Her aunt's voice.

"What is happening here?" Everly Graymere's voice rang through the stone walls of the Dark Cells.

A long moment of silence followed. The receding sound of the men's boots echoed underneath the trapdoor.

Edlen's heart throbbed in her chest. *No! Aunt Everly, get out of there!* She grabbed Vairet, though she did not realize it.

"Who is in charge?" commanded Everly.

The nasally man answered, "My lady, you should not be here. Your glorious eyes need not be sullied by this horror."

A voice, which Edlen recognized, responded, "Our lady is not so fair that she cannot be present to witness the treason that exists in her own realm."

Tomm? Thank the Gods! Edlen felt relief wash over her.

CHAPTER

EVERLY

The Missing Giant

Everly surveyed the horrific scene; the gnarled remains of a barred iron door slumped on broken hinges and resting against a black stone wall. Fresh gouges in the rock shimmered, indicating where the door had been violently flung open.

Outside of the cell, Sir Ethan Canby's corpse lay face down in a pool of blood. Whoever had killed the young King's Blade had done so in a ferocious fashion; the sword—having skewered him as it passed through his torso—had ripped into the chainmail covering his stomach and plunged out of his back, leaving pieces of kidney or pancreas to slip from the rent flesh, metal, and leather.

She choked back her repulsion and peered into the cell.

Slumped in the corner was the thin, fractured body of Prior Melwin. His head lolled to one side, revealing pronounced bruising on his neck. His bloodshot eyes had rolled back slightly, creating a ghastly image that looked like two black half-moons floating in a red sky. Small blotches of brownish-red dots speckled his scarlet face. Blood trickled from his open mouth and congealed around the cleft of his chin. It reminded her of jellied strawberries left in the sun.

This was a world wholly unknown to her. Far from her birthplace in the fields of Godsbreath, and even further removed from the gilded halls of Rothspire.

The Dark Cells were just that. Dark. Other than the faint orange flicker of torchlight, the shadows around her gathered hungrily. The tragedy she'd stepped into solidified the otherness that lived deep behind the black stones of the dungeon.

Two men appeared from the shadows, and it took Everly only a moment to place them. "Sir Jaymes, Sir Randall," she said without bowing. "Which of you leads this investigation?"

"That would be me," said Sir Randall Ostrom, captain of the city guard. He was thin and hard as the blade he carried. Though he sat on the other side of forty, his face was sharp, chiseled, and clean-shaven, like a man half his age. He stood only slightly taller than Everly. His voice was constricted, as he was though ill. He sneezed then asked, "But I must ask, how have you come to be aware of this?"

Tomm spoke first. "I alerted Our Lady."

"And who are you?" asked Sir Randall.

"My name is Tomm Harken." He bowed.

Sir Jaymes Hallet leered at Tomm through the torchlight. Where Randall Ostrom was thin, Sir Jaymes was broad. Built like a warrior from children's tales, he filled the space he stood. His heavily bearded face scrunched in suspicion. "I do not give a bloody damn as to who you are, Master Harken. How is it you were alerted of this crime before the city guard?"

A fair question, Sir Jaymes. She'd assumed Tomm had learned of Rhen's escape after the authorities. But if they had only recently discovered the scene, how could he possibly have come by this information?

Tomm lifted his head. "I desired to have a word with your captive. And assuming he had not been graciously escorted to some soft, comfortable chamber where he might receive proper attention for his wound, I naturally reasoned that a brocken—who so carelessly slayed a man who meant to kill him—would find himself a guest in the fabled Dark Cells of Rothspire."

Everly glared at him.

"So, you admit to conspiring with him?" asked Sir Jaymes.

"I admitted no such thing, Sir Jaymes Hallet." He smiled. "Though you care not to know who I am, I am quite familiar with you."

"Are you threatening me?" Sir Jaymes moved forward, his hand perched atop the pommel of his sword. He towered over Tomm Harken. Torchlight danced in reds and oranges as it glittered off his armor.

"I make no threats, my good sir. I am simply stating that it is my duty to know things that you do not." Tomm gazed up at the knight, unflinching. "Perhaps if you gave the same attention to your duties, you would not be threatened by a man who merely wishes to assist you after your magnificent blunder."

"My blunder!"

"Yes," said Tomm. "What else would you call this?"

"Treason," said Randall Ostrom. "It is quite clear what happened here."

Tomm walked to the body of Sir Ethan Canby and knelt. "If it is so clear, you wouldn't mind explaining what you believe transpired."

Sir Randall exchanged a look of exasperation with Everly. "If my lady wishes to hear it?"

"Explain." Everly glared at him.

The captain of the city guard strode to the mangled iron door of the Dark Cell and began. "The brocken was brought here by the King's Blades and placed in this cell. Shortly after arriving, the High Divinator was called upon to care for his wound. In his place, he sent Prior Melwin—who we were assured was as masterful a healer as the Divinator himself. The brocken was calm at the time...most likely in shock. Once the prior began his healing, I withdrew my men to search for the rioters.

"Sir Ethan stayed behind to keep watch over the prisoner. But that bastard brocken was only biding his time. Once he was alone with the others, he acted. And, as you can see, he strangled the prior first. Then, using his strength, he ripped the cell door apart and attacked Sir Ethan Canby."

"So, a trained knight in the King's Blades had his back turned to a boy who single-handedly defeated over a score of men earlier today?" Tomm asked, smirking.

"I did not say he had his back turned."

"Then, is Sir Ethan blind?"

Sir Jaymes Hallet exploded, "Do not sully the name of my brother!"

"Sullied or not," said Tomm, "the captain believes your brother took no action while a *nine-foot-tall beast of a man* strangled a prior of the realm? Do you know how long it takes to strangle a man to death? Over three minutes. By Sir Randall's estimation, that means a King's Blade stood idle for three minutes while a helpless man struggled for his life? Now I ask again, was Sir Ethan Canby blind as well as deaf?"

"Master Harken!" Everly said. She grabbed Tomm's arm.

"You do yourself no favors with these insults. Tell us what you believe happened."

Tomm chuckled. "Fair." He stepped into the cell and peered down at the stack of hay that acted as a bed. "Perhaps, he was never actually brought down here."

"Do you mean us liars?" Sir Jaymes could barely restrain himself. "I might have your tongue for that."

"This is a serious allegation," said Everly. "What evidence do you possess to make this claim?"

The soft clink of Sir Randall's boots tapped on the stone floor. "He has no evidence, my lady. This man is an interloper. He wishes to muddy the waters of the king's justice." He approached Tomm. "To accuse the captain of the city guard—as well as a King's Blade—with no proof is an act of *pure* treachery. The name of the Leonardis family may strike fear in the people of the Vines, but let me tell you, Tomm Harken, it holds no sway in the capital.

"Oh yes! I am familiar with you…and I suggest you recant your accusations before another body is discovered down here." Randall sneered as he glared at Tomm.

Unconcerned with this threat, Tomm smiled. "A question is not an accusation. It is possible I misread the entire affair."

"As I am certain you have," said Sir Randall. "Now! If you will kindly answer my question. What business did you have with the prisoner? And remember, answer plainly. It seems rather odd to me that a visitor from the Vines might have dealings with the Shield of the Princess."

"It does seem rather odd, now, doesn't it?" Tomm answered. "Nevertheless." He stepped away from Sir Randall and continued.

"I had the privilege of becoming acquainted with young Master Rhen earlier today. You may say his plight was one that rang near to my heart. I was made aware of a niggling matter that prevented him from participating in the celebration of his kingdom, and I took pity on the boy. I know something about being *ostracized* by a family. I wished only to check on his welfare. He was in need of a friend." Tomm grinned.

"You are the one Patrik Lindon spoke of?" asked Everly in astonishment. "You are the one who discovered the law?"

"My infamy precedes me," said Tomm. "I might say only that I am the one who *aided* your adept in correcting a flaw in your records. Nothing more."

Everly curled her hands into tight fists. "A flaw? The only flaw is your meddling. You might say only that you are *responsible* for this terrible act."

"And you would be wrong, my lady," said Tomm. "My *responsibilities* lie directly in the service of justice—which is something I fear these men are not well-versed in.

"After his exploits in the melee, I grew concerned for Rhen's wellbeing." He glanced back at the carnage. "I assumed the King's Blades would not be overly kind to him, and being familiar with the laws of the land, I presumed he would be held in a dungeon—or some other barbaric form of prison."

"Barbaric?" Sir Jaymes said derisively. "He killed a knight. The Dark Cells are a luxury for one convicted of such a crime."

"Convicted," said Tomm and turned to Everly. "It appears the king's capital conflates conjecture with conviction."

But Rhen did kill Sir Hugh Castac. "Master Harken,

as much as I appreciate your concern for the safety of my daughter's Shield, the entire realm witnessed him murder Sir Hugh Castac."

"Did we?" His voice contained a hint of conspiracy. "The realm *witnessed* a deranged knight attack a boy with live steel *after* the melee concluded. Regardless of Rhen's actions, my lady, he is due a fair trial."

Is he? she thought. The events of the day whirled through her mind.

A brocken had murdered a knight. Not simply a knight. Sir Hugh Castac was an ordained knight in the service of Lord Donnel Baird. A man whose loyalty to the crown was well-known to be tenuous at best.

Despite the fact that Sir Hugh attacked Rhen first, the killing of a knight in such high standing would cause ripples throughout the kingdom. And to add to the displeasure of the other noble families, the bloody scrapper riot would be seen as nothing less than the Graymeres loss of control on the lands they proclaimed to protect.

Worse than any of this, though, was the revelation that her husband might be in danger while still under the shelter of the Windsongs.

If anyone were to overhear that the prince may be dead, how long before the power of the crown might come under dispute? She steeled herself against the thought. Her eyes hardened to a pinprick.

Everly stared at Sir Randall Ostrom, her dismissal of Tomm's statement apparent to all. "I do not care if a trial will be considered fair; I want you to find him."

Sir Jaymes practically leapt to her command. "Yes, my lady. Consider it done."

"I will not consider anything done until I look into his eyes," she growled.

Both Sir Jaymes and Sir Randall bowed.

Before they departed, Sir Randall stepped close to her and whispered, "My lady, it is not for me to question the company you keep... I only warn you to be cautious." He glowered at Tomm. "His family's name holds a black reputation in my homeland, and as you witnessed, one willing to defame the men who risk their lives to protect the realm is one willing to do things even more unsavory. I advise you to hold him at an arm's length. For your safety, my lady." He bowed again before marching up the stairs of the Dark Cells.

Thank you, Sir Randall. I will remember your words.

Tomm sighed heavily. "They will not find him."

Everly snapped, "Who are you to know?" She'd had enough of his snark. Her lips tightened as she scowled, her voice stern and commanding, she spun around and stared into Tomm's eyes. "You have told me nothing! You make veiled accusations about the king's men, turning me into a fool in their eyes! Do you not understand the severity of this situation?"

"My lady...you hurt me," said Tomm. "I am more familiar with the implications than you comprehend." He frowned. "How well do *you* trust these men?"

What does he mean? "I trust the men in my service more than the vague suspicions of a stranger."

"Be a tad more perceptive, my lady. You know Rhen better than anyone else. Do you believe he is capable of this..." He stared down at the dead body of Sir Ethan Canby.

Tomm was right. Everly had known Rhen from birth. Though he'd grown into an enormous, muscled giant, he remained the sweet boy she'd always known. He was no monster.

Their last interaction—his favor to Amara—flashed through her mind.

"He is kind…"

She forced back tears. Rhen was as close to a son as she'd had since losing Bradain. "Why would he do this?" Her voice quavered.

Tomm neared her; his voice soft and comforting. "Perhaps…he did not?"

"What are you suggesting?" She wished he stopped speaking in riddles.

"As I said, my lady." He peered down at the hay. "Our friends were quite defensive when I suggested he had never been brought here—and I had no desire to end up one of the slain. But please, look closely." He pointed. "What do you see?"

In the corner of the cell, opposite the lifeless body of Prior Melwin, a thick pile of scattered hay lay undisturbed. She studied the area. *Dirt and hay? What does he want from me?* "I see nothing strange." Her voice was tired and sad.

"Exactly," said Tomm.

Everly grew impatient, "What are you getting at?"

"Blood. My lady," said Tomm. "Do you see any on the straw?"

She squinted and stared through the dim torchlight. *There is nothing.* "No. There is none."

"The boy's wound would have been severe. Brocken or not…he would bleed. But there is no blood. Tell me, if we are to believe the captain's account, then Rhen laid in this very spot for some time before the prior arrived. If this is where they brought him, would we not find at least a *drop of blood?*"

Gods! He is right. "What are you suggesting?"

Tomm paced from the cell to the stairs. "For that, I have no answer, my lady. Not at this moment at least."

"Why would both of them lie? They said they brought him here. They must've certainly been aware someone would be alerted to this."

"Ah, of that I agree," said Tomm. "But I doubt they expected anyone to be alerted before they were finished setting the scene."

As Tomm said this, a faint creaking came from the shadows. He put his finger to his lips to signal silence. A heavy thud rang throughout the Dark Cells. Tomm slid to the nearest wall and grabbed a torch. The shadows receded. Everly noted what looked to be a door in the floor of the dungeon. From the black square in the ground, two hands appeared.

Everly slipped close to Tomm and stared in quiet fear. *What now?*

Neither of them had a weapon. If this was the person responsible for these murders, they stood no chance of defending themselves. Without knowing she did so, Everly clutched Tomm's arm.

Slowly, a figure appeared, dragging itself up from the black pit. As it lurched out of the dark recess, Everly noted how small it appeared. *There is no way this thing killed a knight.*

It paid little attention to them—more interested in reaching back down into the hole it slithered from.

Everly dare not speak, but she tugged on Tomm's arm and pointed.

He nodded and took a cautious step forward.

The thing breathed hard as it pulled itself up, and as it did this, another form emerged from the black door. Alike to the first, this new shadow was thin and small, but it did not struggle as it pulled itself into the room.

Tomm, not waiting for a third enemy, thrust his torch forward and shouted, "Speak!"

The two figures cowered and covered their faces. A small voice croaked from one of them.

It was a girl's voice.

"Aunt Everly?" It sounded hopeful.

Edlen?

Everly ran forward. "Edlen? Is that you?"

Tomm grabbed at her, trying in vain to stop her, but she broke from his grasp.

"Edlen?" she asked again.

The thing crept forward, shielding its eyes from the torchlight. But as it came into the light, any fear Everly had disappeared. It was her niece, Edlen.

Edlen rushed forward and threw her arms around Everly. "Gods! Aunt Everly! I was so worried."

Everly squeezed her niece tightly and studied her.

Edlen's face was filthy, streaked with sweat, blood, and a thick layer of grime. Her tunic stained so severely she could not discern its color—but it was definitely neither green nor red.

"Where have you been?" asked Everly, her voice equal parts relief and suspicion.

Edlen slunk away. "The two men? Are they gone?"

"Sir Jaymes and Sir Randall?" she asked.

"I do not know their names," said Edlen. "But they were here only moments ago."

"They are gone," said Tomm. He walked towards Edlen. "But I must say, your aunt has more right to ask questions than you."

"They took Rhen!" blurted Edlen. "They took him to someone called Voress Ní."

"The Voress Ní?" asked Everly. "Edlen, what are you saying? Where have you been? What happened to you?" For the first time, she took notice of the other person who appeared from the trapdoor. It was a young girl, even more disheveled and dirty than Edlen.

The girl took a step closer and sneered.

"This is—" started Edlen, but the girl interrupted her.

"Do not say my name…Edlen." Her voice teemed with venom. "You are one of *them*."

"One of who?" asked Everly. "Edlen, what is she talking about? What is happening?" She stared from her niece to the girl. All this was too confusing, and she began to feel overwhelmed. "Someone tell me what is going on." No longer did she present the stoic queen she so wished to seem; instead, her last statement was more a plea than a demand.

"Aunt Everly, we have to do something. They took Rhen. They said he's leaving sooner than they expected."

"Edlen," Tomm said. "You must calm down. We cannot help you if we do not understand what you're saying. Are you suggesting Sir Randall Ostrom and Sir Jaymes Hallet are conspiring with the Voress Ní to ransom Rhen?"

A ransom? Yes. Thank you for making sense of this, Tomm. "Is that what you heard, Edlen?"

The strange girl moved quietly. Edlen stepped aside and now nothing was in between them. Everly caught a glint of orange flame dancing upon a small object in the girl's hand. *What is that?*

The girl struck with the speed of a viper.

"Vairet! No!" Edlen shouted and leapt between Everly and the girl.

The thrust of the dagger was quick and violent. It sank into Edlen's belly. She dropped to her knees and fell to the ground. Blood seeped from underneath her dirty green and yellow tunic, and she grabbed at the wound.

The girl hissed. Was it a hiss or tears? She vanished back down the black pit of the trapdoor.

Everly screamed and threw herself on top of Edlen.

Her hands slid around Edlen's stomach—which was now slick with blood. She knew not what to do but hold her and scream. "Edlen! No! Edlen!" Tears streamed from her eyes. She pulled her niece close and rocked back and forth.

"Tomm! Do something! Help me! Help me!"

Tomm sprang forward and knelt beside them. He grabbed at Edlen's face and pulled her eyelids open. In one fluid motion, he removed his dark-gray cloak and rolled it into a tight ball then placed it firmly against Edlen's stomach.

"Apply as much pressure as you can. Keep the wound from bleeding out, and keep her calm. I will get help. Do not move her." With that, he ran from the Dark Cells.

Oh Gods! Gods no! Please. Please. Please. "Edlen, my sweet girl, please, please." She held Tomm's cloak against Edlen's belly and stroked her brow.

"My sweet little girl, you're going to be fine. I promise you." But she knew she had no right to promise such things.

She sat in the shadows of the Dark Cells of Rothspire, far below the comfort of her future throne, and sobbed. Her voice cracked as she cried.

"Bradain…not again. Please Gods…not again!"

CHAPTER

ALDIR

Gods and Demons

"How do you expect us to believe this, Laustair?" Aldir asked. A sudden flash of light from the brazier caused him a moment of uncertainty, but he regained his wits sooner than the others. He pressed his thumb and forefinger into his eyes to sharpen his focus. Did his father-in-law just admit to being a god?

He shifted in his seat, understanding he must reassert his authority over this ludicrous conversation. *I am the bloody Primacy of the Realm! I cannot have these men thinking I condone my own family's impudence.*

"These men rode many leagues to discover an answer to an issue of utmost importance, yet you offer them no more than absurd cheek." He apologized to the men of the Eyes of the Forest and stood.

Laustair glanced up. "Excuse me, my lord, but only a fool responds to a matter they do not comprehend with anger."

Does he wish to goad me into an argument? "I have made a rather comfortable life for myself by accepting matters I do not comprehend. It is not my lack of perspicacity that irks me, *Father*. It is your graceless disregard for our guests' purposes."

Though the others maintained a quiet respect, Aldir was acutely aware of their discomfort. This was an inappropriate conversation, but he would not have it said of him that he allowed such disrespect, not even from one as revered as Laustair.

"You give them no more than fables or conjectures, yet anticipate acceptance. I demand proof." Aldir slammed his hand on a nearby table.

"What proof would suffice, my lord?" Laustair eyed him. "For it seems my words no longer command the trust they once did."

Exasperated, Aldir shook his head. "According to Chief Ridgefront and Master Cantlay, this Dalnor refuses to come here himself." He approached Laustair. "I have known you near thirty years. Am I to understand you somehow neither changed your appearance nor revealed the slightest of variances in your façade during this time?"

He faced the others; his voice laced with derision. "Has my father-in-law altered his appearance in any way tonight?"

Their silence and unease spoke louder than words. Perhaps they were wise not to answer. Caught between himself and a self-proclaimed God, Aldir did not envy their position. He scrubbed his hand across his face and turned to confront Laustair, but a soft voice interrupted him.

"Perhaps, my lord," started Darrin, "we cannot distinguish the divine unless it is willed?"

Edlen would get on well with this boy. Neither of them knows when to keep quiet. The thought of his daughter gave him pause. *Come home, Edlen. Let me see your face once more before I leave. Let me be certain you are safe.*

"The Valdryz are not travelling magicians," answered Laustair. "They do not perform *tricks* for a lord's amusement or *illusions* for coin. Young Master Cantlay hits near the truth. Though I have known you for many years, I excuse your lack of perception...but your distrust *irks* me."

Laustair stood, taking shambling steps towards the brazier. Once in front of the raging fire, he bent down and reached for an ashen log buried deep within the flames.

Aldir instinctively lunged forward in an attempt to protect his father-in-law. But as he thrust his hand out, his body stiffened and he was unable to move. Frozen where he stood, his heart raced, sweat bathing his body. *What wickedness is this?* he tried to say, but his words were stilled.

A reddish-orange light emanated from the burning brand Laustair now held that cast his arm in an otherworldly glow. A thick bracelet, or manacle, adorned his wrist. He gave the fetter no more than a passing glimpse as he said, "There is one who might salivate at your desire of proof, Aldir. But I shall never reveal myself to him."

Let me go! Aldir shouted in his head, but no sound left his mouth.

Kayvold Archwood leapt from his seat and rushed to aid the Primacy but was stopped by an unseen force. He stood still, halfway standing from his chair.

"You may resume your seat, Lord-Overseer." A grim smile spread across Laustair's lips.

With a loud thud, Kayvold fell back into his chair. A dreary silence filled the room.

"The Primacy is in no danger, I assure you," Laustair said. "He asks for proof of my claim, and I mean nothing more than to provide it."

A surge of energy spread through Aldir's body. He lurched

forward, tripping over his feet, unbound from whatever invisible chains previously held him.

Gods, he thought to himself. *It can't be true.*

"It is," Laustair answered, as though he read Aldir's thoughts.

Shaken and confused, Aldir backed away and sat in his chair. "This is not possible…" he muttered.

"Did you not ask for proof, my lord?"

"I…I…never," said Aldir, embarrassed. "How?" He ran his hand over his face, hoping to mask his shame. If his father-in-law spoke the truth, then why hadn't he been able to save Irymar? Why had so much tragedy fallen on his family? No. Laustair was playing some trick. He was not a God.

Light drained from the brazier. The lanterns on the walls extinguished themselves. The room was thrust into darkness and a scent of fresh lilacs and rosehips wafted through the air.

Irymar? It was a scent Aldir knew only too well. It was the scent of home. The smell of happiness. The smell of her. He squinted through the darkness and glared at Laustair. *I do not know how you are doing this, but Gods hear me, I will not forgive you.*

Laustair caught Aldir's gaze and frowned. "I am afraid my brother Dalnor's desire to find me can mean only one thing." He tamped ash from his pipe. "There would be no other reason to jeopardize his safety…or mine." He looked at Darrin. "What was his message? Did he mention another name? I must know."

Darrin squirmed in his seat, his scant figure illuminated by a faint gray effulgence.

He is but a child. Aldir brimmed with rage. "Laustair!" he shouted. "Leave the boy be!"

"I must know," said Laustair, imploringly. "Did Dalnor speak of another?"

"Yes," said Darrin in a whisper.

'Who?" asked Laustair. "What name did he say?"

Aldir gripped the arm of his chair. "Enough, Laustair! Leave it for the morning. Let these men rest."

"No!" Laustair dismissed Aldir's command. "I must know. We all must know."

Darrin made to say something but stopped himself.

"Please, boy!" urged Laustair.

Frightened, Darrin answered. "Malighaunt..."

"Malighaunt," Laustair repeated, his lips tightening. "What were his exact words?"

Aldir reached over to grab Darrin's shoulder, acutely aware of how uncomfortable the boy was. "You do not have to answer, Master Cantlay." As much as his interest was piqued, he could not sanction the boy being coerced into a conversation he wasn't comfortable with. "We will revisit this in the morning." He glowered at Laustair. "When we are not as prone to fancy."

"My lord," said Darrin. "I was told to speak to Somath. I will not shirk from my responsibilities."

"That's my lad," said Haron, his bushy eyebrows alight with respect. "Tell 'em."

Tell them what? Aldir knew this conversation was slipping from his control, but he was more concerned with learning how any of this connected to his dream. Why did Irymar say *Somath*? Was she warning him? He gazed eagerly at the young rover. *How is Darrin a part of this?*

Darrin tapped his foot incessantly and stared at the floor. "I was told to repeat these words to Somath." He closed his eyes as if trying to recall something. "*Je'tulin mali'por yl Nei-lad gu'stair. Turi hal yl kalen dor Akull'dine.* He is coming… Malighaunt comes."

The language, though wholly foreign to Aldir, terrified him. A heaviness crept across his heart, and he gazed at the boy with pity. *Whatever your role is, Master Cantlay, you are playing it extremely well.*

Laustair dropped his gaze, stared into his lap, then took a deep breath. "You have done well, Darrin…extraordinarily well. I have much to think on." He lifted his pipe and drew in a lungful of smoke. "I believe the Primacy spoke the truth. It is best to continue our conversation in the daylight."

It was Aldir's turn to disagree with this hasty conclusion. The words Darrin recited seemed to give Laustair pause, and he had to know what they meant. "Who is Malighaunt?" he asked. "What did Darrin say?"

The other men appeared just as curious as Aldir. They leaned forward in their chairs, their eyes fixed on Laustair. All but Darrin, who had shrunk in his seat.

Aldir noticed just how young the rover was and wondered if he was asking too much of him to continue. *My father would not care if the boy was uncomfortable… Gods! Am I turning into him?* The thought made him shudder. *No. The king would rake a man over burning coals for an answer. I am simply asking for clarification.*

Laustair caught Aldir's eye and shook his head. "I will not force Master Cantlay to suffer through anymore tonight. I have pushed him too far already. Suffice it to say, he has just spoken a language that has never been uttered by man." He reached out and patted Darrin on the knee.

"I am alright, Laustair," said Darrin as he wiped at his

eyes. "It is a relief to speak those words aloud. They have repeated themselves in my head for over a fortnight."

You are stronger than you appear, my boy. Aldir gazed at Darrin with a new appreciation. "If the boy gives his leave—"

"*It is not up to the boy,*" hissed Laustair. He stared fixedly at each man as though measuring them. When his eyes landed on Aldir, he softened. "There are many subjects that should not be openly discussed in the dark. The information Master Cantlay provided tonight is the *reason* why those topics should only be spoken of in the light."

The wind blew gently through Irymar's hair, and she pressed herself against him.

Aldir smelled lilac and sage. He loved the way she felt when he held her. Her embrace was not a thing he deserved; it was a gift he relished.

This was the woman he loved. And she loved him.

They stood there: entangled, laughing, and playful.

They gazed out from the high tower and basked in the glory of Rothspire underneath them. Irymar jabbed a finger into his stomach.

Aldir pulled back immediately and peered down at his new bride.

She cackled silently, childishly mocking his grimace. The moment he made to say something, Irymar flung her arms around him, enveloping his mouth in a passionate kiss. As their lips met, Aldir slipped from their tender embrace and tickled her. She squirmed away from him and stared back, her lips drawn into a comical pout.

Her dark, windswept hair framed her face and her scowl instantly turned into a mischievous smile. They met again, and now, almost as though they were of one mind, clasped hands around each other and danced to the music in their heads. They swayed in unison, smiling. Words no longer needed.

Eleven years had passed since Irymar first arrived in Rothspire, and since that day, she and Aldir had spent most every day together.

At first, the two could not stand one another, but in time, a childish attraction had formed. In adulthood, their youthful flirting had blossomed into a deeper more experienced love. No longer were they children forced to study together, instead, they'd craved each other's presence. Their attraction had been impossible to dismiss, and, if not apparent to them, the families of both had started to discuss their forthcoming union.

So it was that Aldir Graymere and Irymar Mostah had wed. A more beautiful ceremony could not have been imagined.

But as they stood atop the tower, no pretenses existed between them. Aldir understood his wife more than anyone else in the realm and was secure in the knowledge that she understood him as well. They danced silently across the roof of the turret; he clutched his bride's waist and lifted her from the ground. The sky was bluer than sapphire. And as he held her against the unending expanse, she laughed silently, throwing her head back.

Clouds gathered overhead, seemingly out of nowhere. A summer storm threatened to end this glorious day. Aldir placed Irymar back down and pointed towards the growing black and gray sky. She frowned at the idea of their revelry ending.

Whether a trick of the clouds or not, her face took on an ashen pallor. The white gown she wore now held the faintest cast of yellow.

Thunder erupted and the skies burst forth in a torrent of rain and hail.

Aldir reached out to grab her arm, and as his fingers met her flesh, her skin sloughed off under his touch. He pulled his hand back immediately, but where he had grazed her, dark-purple bruises formed and a trail of black, pustulous rings sprang up. He gazed at his hands in horror, only to see bits of her flesh underneath his fingernails.

She backed away; her mouth opened in an expression of torment. Her teeth, which were once ivory white, became the awful greenish brown of rot. One by one, they fell from black gums, leaving bloody pits in their absence. Her black hair turned to stiff straw and dropped from her scalp, now a jagged dome of scabs and open sores.

Too much for Aldir to watch, he covered his eyes and turned to flee, but a bony hand thrust forward and caressed his fingers. Frozen where he stood, he let the hand uncover his gaze.

Irymar stood before him, but she was no longer the woman he fell in love with. In place of the beautiful young maid, a horror of mottled flesh and blood-stained bone walked disjointedly near him.

The sky turned darker than night, an impossible blackness that shimmered in ghostly grays with every flash of lighting. The only light in the storm was that of two dim stars, like the hungry eyes of a starving beast.

Aldir dropped to his knees and screamed, but the fleshless fingers of Irymar's hand groped through the darkness and covered his cries. Like some sort of rigid worm, her fingers slid into his mouth and choked his shouts.

He stared blankly at this ghoul, unable to look away.

Once certain he could not run, Irymar hobbled backwards, the creaking of her putrefied joints louder than the thunderclaps overhead. She arched her back until she walked bent on the ground—more spider-like than human—and cackled. It was the sound of death mocking the living. It was the sound of decay.

From her festering, moldy womb sprang an infant: pink and lively. The baby's cries split through the thunder. And as the cord of life that tied the child to the decomposing mother turned black and crumbled, Irymar hovered over the infant and attempted to feed on it.

Aldir knew instantly that this was Edlen. He would not let this dreadful thing touch his daughter. His wail, which emanated from somewhere deep inside of his soul, rent the tower itself.

Cracks formed across the floor. The stone tower began to collapse, but before he could reach Edlen, the ghastly figure of his bride enclosed itself around the baby. Her voice hissed and one of her arms became a dagger that pressed against Edlen's throat. Blood spurted from the point where the bony blade pierced the child's neck. Irymar screeched, "She is for Malighaunt!"

A LOUD rapping echoed throughout Aldir's chamber. His eyes shot open. Sunlight poured in from his open window.

What time is it? He rolled to his side, away from the window. His head throbbed in pain.

The rapping continued. Followed by a man's voice.

The voice sounded distant and muffled, as though he imagined it.

Imagined or not, it did not go away.

"My lord, your daughter…"

My daughter? Edlen?

Aldir struggled out from beneath his sheets. He was dressed in the same clothes that he'd worn yesterday, his body ached, and the musty, day-old sweat of his tunic and trousers clung to his sleep-dampened skin. "Edlen?" he asked aloud, his voice still groggy with slumber.

"Permission to enter?" the man on the other side of the door asked.

As he placed his feet on the floor, he noticed he still wore his boots. "Enter, enter." He stood and shook his head—a vain attempt to dislodge his weariness.

A man in his mid-thirties entered, clad in the colors of the King's Blade's and the green and red cloak of the Graymeres. "Sir Willem, what is it?" asked Aldir.

"My lord, you must come with me. Now!"

Now? "Give me a moment. I am just waking."

"No, my lord. You must come now. Edlen is in grave peril."

"Edlen? What are you talking about?"

"Follow me; I will explain along the way."

Though Aldir's body ached, Sir Willem's tone gave him no option. "Lead the way." He mustered his strength and followed the knight from his bedchamber.

Edlen, what have you done?

With every footstep, his senses came back. The two men dashed down the stairs towards the antechamber of the Hall of Glory, the previous night replaying in his head. *Laustair? Who is Malighaunt?*

"What happened to her?"

Sir Willem ran ahead, his pace unflagging. He turned his head. "Stabbed, my lord. By a scrapper."

Aldir's heart thumped in his chest. A fog filled his mind and he nearly stumbled. Sir Willem grabbed him, saving him from falling to the hard, tiled floor. He had a thousand questions streaming through his mind, but he could not bring himself to ask even one. The world around him blurred, and it was all he could do to stay on his feet. He would not lose her. He would not let his fear cripple him like it did with Irymar.

They tore past the crowd of people who filled the antechamber. He thought he heard muttered shouts, but the voices of those who cluttered the hall were but a low hum in the cacophony of sounds that raged in his head.

Sir Willem threw open the doors of Dartsuil's Keep, and they raced through the courtyard.

Aldir cared not if he was seen in such a panic. He cared for nothing other than Edlen's safety. The Gods would not take her too.

He chased after Sir Willem, his wits slowly returning. He recognized the street they ran down. They were nearing the sacellum. The same place he had dreamed of two nights ago.

Once they stood at the threshold of the holy building, Sir Willem grabbed Aldir's arm and spoke in a hushed whisper. "They do not need me down there as well, my lord. My charge was to bring you here. If you go past the dais, there is a small door just beyond it. They are expecting you."

"Willem. What happened?"

"I have told you all I know, Aldir." Sir Willem grabbed Aldir's hands in his and apologized. "The High Divinator and my cousin are with her. They will answer your questions."

"But…"

"Go now, my lord. Be with her."

"Is she…?" asked Aldir, unwilling to say the last word. The thought of seeing his daughter lying on the cold stone of the burial altar nearly made him freeze. *I can't…not again.*

"She was not dead when I left. But I make no promises. Go now! Speaking with me will do nothing."

Aldir embraced Sir Willem, thanking him for all he'd done. When the knight departed, Aldir entered the sacellum, his footfalls reverberating in the empty stone hall.

He paused, noticing how dark it had become, as if his dream was somehow manifest. The sacellum…Somath…

Malighaunt. Was Sir Willem a part of this? He had just been presented with his brother's severed legs, and now, he had been awoken with another catastrophe. *Why wouldn't Willem come with me? He was more than ready to bring me here.*

Aldir turned to the door. It was not possible his daughter was here. Edlen was willful, but she would never find herself in a position to be 'stabbed' by a scrapper. *And I am now expected to walk into the deepest chamber of this place?* Someone was hoping to end the line of Graymeres. He would not be taken so easily. *But...what if Edlen truly is hurt?*

As he paused, unwilling to go any further, a large black figure appeared from beyond the dais and stalked forward. It moved slowly, walking on all fours.

Is this Malighaunt?

In his panic, he stepped backwards and reached for a sword at his belt. There was nothing there. He'd left his chamber in such a madness that he had not armed himself. *Gods! You are clever, Willem.*

This was a trap.

Willem had lured him here under false pretenses. Someone wanted him gone, and they sent a monster to dispose of him. Irymar had tried to tell him, but he'd been too daft to understand her warning. *I am sorry Edlen...*

If he were to die, he wished only that his last thoughts were of his daughter.

The black creature slinked forward like some dark beast out of his nightmares. Like Irymar did before she'd tried to kill Edlen. *She knew what hunted me.*

Aldir shouted, "You will not have her!" He would not die quietly. "She is my daughter! She is not for Malighaunt!" His rage was enough to cause the creature hesitation.

Filled with sudden bravery, Aldir moved forward.

The black creature hesitated, but after realizing this man was no danger, it bounded towards him. With every step it took, it grew larger. And just as it came near enough for Aldir to understand what threat it posed, the beast leapt forward and put its paws on his shoulders.

An enormous black dog stared at him and then opened its mouth. It had no intentions more menacing than to drag a long pink tongue against Aldir's face.

Gods! Be good, thought Aldir. He struggled to stand. The hound must have weighed nearly as much as him, and as it stood on its hind legs, it surpassed his height.

His fear vanished, and he began to laugh at the story he had concocted. Playfully stroking the dog's muzzle, he mused, *I can no longer see the difference between a hound and a devil.* "Good girl!" he said, dancing with the giant animal for a moment.

The dog jumped back down and stared up at him, her tongue lolling out of one side of her mouth.

If you are not a monster... Aldir immediately realized what this must mean. *Edlen!*

He rushed forward, the dog bounding playfully behind him.

CHAPTER 15

RHEN

The Cage Opens

Even with his blindfold removed, Rhen could not see through the darkness of his cage. Chains rubbed against his wrists, slowly flaying his skin. The soft, steady creak of the ship lulled him into a trance—a musty scent of cabbage and salted meats filled his nostrils.

Though he'd strained against his iron shackles when he'd first arrived, the wound in his arm had become too agonizing to dismiss. The less he'd struggled, the less it hurt. He had given himself over to a pattern of deep breathing and feigned sleep.

Two hours or more had passed since *Him* announced the coming of another, but as the time wiled away, no one appeared.

I have been missing a long time. Surely the Graymeres are searching for me?

Rhen had taken to saying this thought so often the words became a comfort. True or not.

After the first hour of his captivity, Rhen had called out

in frustration, only to be prodded by *Him*—with what he believed to be the blunt end of a fire iron. A gag had been fastened across his mouth, turning his shouts into the unintelligible neighing of a horse.

After his last bout of screaming, his jailor had thrown a bucket of icy water over him.

Whether an act of punishment (or *Him's* attempt to provide Rhen with something to drink), he'd sucked at the fibrous rope in his mouth, grateful for what little sustenance it delivered.

That had been more than an hour ago, and Rhen thirsted for more to drink. The thought of shouting raced through his mind, but he held no trust that *Him* would be so kind as to offer a second draught.

I have been missing a long time. Surely the Graymeres are searching for me?

The moment came when he no longer cared about imagined punishment. His thirst outweighed his dread. In a quick, forceful motion, Rhen lifted his arms above his head and swung down violently.

The wall of his cage groaned but did not give way. His bonds ripped against the tender skin on his wrists, tearing open the flayed skin. He howled in pain but received no penalty for this action.

Him laughed, a terrifying laugh. One of derision, enjoyment, and silent knowledge.

"He is coming," *Him* said.

Who is coming? Rhen wanted to scream. The cuts on his wrists flared, but the terror of waiting for the unknown pained him more than a thousand steely strikes.

"Who?" asked Rhen, finally, through the grit of his gag.

"Who is coming?" His words were nothing more than a jumble of inarticulate sounds.

The slow tap of leather-soled boots descended from a stairway somewhere deep within the blackness.

Him strode past Rhen's cage. "He is come," he said.

Rhen cocked his head to the left and stared. Though his eyes could not penetrate the dark, his hearing became more attuned. With each step he heard, an image of this stranger grew clearer in his mind.

The footsteps were slow but not plodding. This was not a man of substantial girth. The clacking of his boots was whip-like. New leather. Perhaps this man had wealth? As he neared, Rhen heard quick, shallow breaths. Thin, as if they belonged to one who had been athletic in their youth but now carried the weight of age. The man must be over fifty, nearing sixty.

Who are you?

"Thank you, my friend. You may light the torches now?" The man's voice—cordial but stern—held a hint of an accent. The word *friend* came out as *freend*.

The bastard had light with him this whole time? Why keep himself in the dark? Rhen thought. *Is he afraid of this man?*

"Belo, you may unbind our friend," said the stranger.

Belo? At least he has a name.

Belo removed his hood, and in a quick, fluid motion, unlocked the door of the cage and strode close to Rhen.

No longer blind, Rhen was finally able to see the face of the man who had carried him into this prison.

A hideously grim and scarred face neared his own. The right side of his face was a slick, vestige of burned flesh—coupled with a colorless, white eye—making Rhen shudder.

Belo removed a small, golden dirk from within his black

cloak. He slid its blade between Rhen's cheek and the rope-gag in his mouth. The edge of the knife was honed so finely that the thick hempen braids gave way at the subtlest of strokes.

Rhen could breathe freely again. He gasped for breath. His lungs burned, but he didn't care. *Let them burn*, he thought. *I can breathe.*

This also meant he could scream. But what would be the use? If any allies aboard the ship existed, they surely would have heard his noisy, albeit muffled, shouts from earlier. Besides, Rhen had learned rather hastily this evening, that any of his struggles would only be met by, at best, passive indifference. Whoever this man was, he had seen to a degree of secrecy that Rhen was quite unfamiliar with.

Instead of fighting, Rhen decided to continue with his previous plan. He would watch and learn. The hours in which he had been blindfolded and gagged had taught him patience and a certain level of intuition he never knew he possessed. Rhen squinted.

The hull was the size of a great hall. The ship he was in must be enormous. In the center of the room stood a table, set with food and drink, flanked by two chairs. One was large enough for a brocken, and the other, though much smaller, was ornately upholstered—a sort of throne.

Belo then unlocked the manacles on Rhen's wrists.

He was freed.

Rhen instinctively rubbed at his wrists. Though no longer bound or gagged, he knew he was not truly free.

The man who sat at the table beckoned him over, not fearing Rhen's unchaining.

Rhen stared at Belo. *I will make you pay for this.*

As though he could read his thoughts, Belo smiled and said, "Must not keep our lord waiting."

If Belo was capable of lifting him from the ground and throwing him over his shoulder, Rhen understood his thoughts of revenge may be nothing more than a fanciful dream. Neither of these two seemed to fear him in any way. And that worried Rhen.

He stepped past Belo shakily. Though unencumbered, Rhen's body was still sore and tired. Had he wanted to fight, he didn't believe he could achieve anything other than getting himself killed. He lumbered from his cage and warily approached the offered seat.

Upon nearing the table, Rhen studied the man.

He was short. And though all men were short compared to him, this man was shorter than even Edlen. He had a dark olive complexion as well. Not as dark as one from Rojiir, but possibly one descended from that bloodline.

Rhen might have shared a laugh over the man's appearance if he were back home with Edlen.

Even more pronounced than the man's nose was the odor that arose from him: acrid and cloying but masked by flowery perfume. The scent of aged wine left in the sun.

The man gestured towards the empty chair and said, "Sit, my friend."

His speech was thick and slow—a voice graveled by years.

He removed a pipe from a pocket within his cloak and lit it with a candle. He inhaled languidly then breathed out a robust plume of smoke. "I apologize for any discomfort you experienced tonight, Rhen."

How do you know my name? Rhen slumped into his chair; a dull, throbbing pain shot throughout his body. The simple comfort of sitting was enough to relax his muscles to the point where he felt every wound he'd received throughout the day. He grimaced but forced the agony away before he said, "What discomfort?" He would not allow the man to see his pain.

The man smiled slightly at Rhen's jest but gave it short shrift. "You are at a disadvantage, so I forgive your frustrations. But I do not suffer disrespect. I made my apology. It is custom for you to either accept it or deny it." His eyes hardened. "What is your decision?"

Rhen scowled. The memory of Sir Hugh Castac's face as life drained from it flashed in his mind. Such terror in his eyes. *I have killed a man. Perhaps I can do it again.* He clenched his fists and said, "I accept your apology, on the condition you tell me what's happening."

The man took a draw from his pipe. "I believe that can be done." He reached for a bottle of wine on the table and poured a drink for both of them. "Where I am from, it is customary to drink three times before discussing a matter of importance. Will you respect this tradition?"

"Only three?" asked Rhen. He drank the offered wine in one gulp. "Where I am from, we do not kidnap people." An incredulous smile spread across his lips.

Paying no mind to Rhen's quip, the man refilled their goblets. "The first is for pleasure. The second, to savor." He sipped at his drink. "The third is for truth."

Rhen attempted to chug the wine again, but the man stopped him.

"The second is to savor, my friend," the man said. "The tradition must be upheld."

Rhen glared over the top of his goblet then set it down. "As you wish."

He glanced around the hull, noting Belo standing silently a few steps behind. *Best keep my humor to myself.* As he tasted the wine on this second round, he understood the meaning behind this strange custom.

When he first sat down, he'd been famished. The thought of any drink was enough to make him salivate, but once he drank the contents of his first goblet in one swig, his had thirst dissipated. This second serving was glorious, and the slower he partook, the more it sated him. *Perhaps this man knows of what he speaks?*

A few moments passed in silence as they finished their wine. When they were done, the man poured the third round.

"My name is Byron Windsong."

The third is for the truth.

Byron Windsong continued. "A great injustice took place today. Do you know of what I speak?"

Rhen knew the name Lord Byron Windsong, but until now had never seen him. The Windsongs were a powerful family from somewhere down in the Vines. But other than that, Rhen cared little to learn anything more about them.

Rhen took another sip and said, "Would abducting the Shield of the Princess be considered an injustice to you?" No matter how much he attempted to hide his anger, it seemed it was impossible to not call this man out for what he had done.

"Your frustrations have been noted, Rhen. But it will avail you little to insist my actions are anything but charitable."

"I was put in a coffin, blindfolded, and gagged. Do the people of the Vines consider that charitable?" Rhen wished to slam his fists against the table, but the pain in his arm was too intense to do anything but shout.

"The means by which you were saved may have been uncomfortable, but drastic measures were needed to preserve the secrecy of your escape."

"What are you talking about?" asked Rhen. "I did not ask to be saved."

"I make no more apologies," said Byron Windsong. "Are you aware of the danger you were in?"

"Obviously not."

Byron sipped his wine. "You are very young, but youth is no longer an excuse for ignorance. It pains me to realize how little you know of the Wide-World. But a boy raised in Rothspire need not be aware of struggles beyond the capital, I assume."

Rhen had no response to this accusation. He knew how sheltered he was, but he believed himself to be rather well-versed in the history of Onyris. "And what struggles are these?"

"My dear boy," Byron said, laughing for the first time. "The Graymeres' time is at an end. Even a fool is aware of this. The sins of a king are not forgiven by the gods. Do you think it an accident Sir Hugh Castac attacked you? Donnel Baird of Riverfront keeps mighty friends in Balangraide—or what your folk call the *Shaded Realm*. Sir Castac's actions were but the first strike against the royal family. You were meant to die; are you aware of this?"

No. Hugh Castac was nothing more than a drunken ass who wanted revenge for my threats before the melee. The memory of Rhen's words outside of the ale-tent rang in his head. *"I will kill you." That is what I said to him. And that is what I did.*

"When you survived his attack, there were those who desired your head in repayment for killing a knight. Luckily, I have my own men in the capital. And they acted faster than those who wished you ill."

This is all a lie. "I am the Shield of the Princess. I would not be killed for protecting myself and the Graymeres."

"That is a child's reading of the issues, Rhen." Byron Windsong smoked his pipe and sipped at his wine. "The Graymeres would be forced to execute you. Regardless of your title, the Southern realms would petition your punishment. And a king is reliant upon his lords.

"There are more lords in Onyris who wish to see the brocken stricken from their place as Shield than those who might support you. In a matter of time, King Ulisaren would be placed in a position where he could either take your head…or lose the support of an entire region of the realm. Our king desires maintaining his *legacy of peace* much more than standing behind his *Shields*."

He poured more wine for them. "Do you not see? Despite your survival, the crown was sure to kill you. Those who planned this strike cared not to see you live—what they cared for was to see the king lose strength. And they accomplished their goal.

"I achieve nothing by ensuring your safety. The crown will crumble. Yet I *did* save you."

Rhen was taken aback by Byron Windsong's words. "Why should I believe you? Why would a man whom I have never met care for my survival?"

"Simple," said Byron. "Though I stand to gain much by the dissolution of the crown, I stand to gain more by introducing you to a king who vows to guarantee your safety. A king who commissioned me to see that you come to no harm. A king who places your welfare far above that of a decrepit family who strives to retain as impossible an ideal as that of peace. A king who will put an end to the hatred of the southern lords. Blood spilled for what is right is blood spilled for prosperity. Peace has a price, and our new king is willing to pay for it."

"There is only one king," said Rhen. "King Ulisaren Graymere. Or have you forgotten?"

"Why do you believe that, my boy?"

Believe? It is not a question of belief. It is a certainty. Same as day follows night. "It is truth. A fact. The Graymeres have been king for five-hundred years. Or do you speak of rebellion?"

"Ha!" Byron Windsong reached for a strip of beef. He bit into one end and tore at it. Spit flew from his mouth as he said, "Rebellion!" Wine washed down the greasy food. "It is not rebellion I speak of. It is war."

Chapter

DARRIN

The Morning Run

Cold wind whipped across Darrin's face as he sprinted up the stone steps of the curtain wall. The brisk, gray, morning air was refreshing, a welcome change from the staleness of the Hall of Glory and the smoke-filled chamber of the Primacy. Last night's conversation replayed in his mind as he ran along the level stone and came upon two of the city guard on patrol.

One of them held up a hand to halt him as he approached. "Where you off to in such a hurry?" He eyed Darrin suspiciously. "And what is an Eye doing up here anyway?"

Darrin slowed his pace and bowed. *Do they not train?* He stood upright and said, "Exercising, sir."

"Exercising!" The man turned to his partner and laughed. "Perhaps you would do well to get some exercise too, Henry."

Henry, a rather bulky soldier, chuckled. "Got enough of that yesterday, I say." He considered Darrin for a moment and said, "Could've used a fit rover like you, though, boy. Those bloody scrappers were too damned fast for me and Karl here."

"Too damned fast for most of us, eh?" said Karl. "What's your name, rover?"

"Darrin, sir."

"Your captain a prat like ours, Darrin?" Karl glanced over his shoulder as though he believed his captain might appear at that moment. "That bastard Ostrom put Henry and I up here as punishment. Can you believe it?"

"For what?" asked Darrin. It had been weeks since he'd been able to share in the gossip and gripes of fellow soldiers. He wondered what these men might say if they knew that he'd kept no company other than his chief and the Lord-Overseer for over a fortnight. Though the city guard was not the same as the Eyes of the Forest, Darrin believed all men who served in the military of Rothspire must share similar experiences.

Henry lowered his voice. "One of them filthy scrappers stabbed the Primacy's daughter in the gut. Word is the girl is near dead, but ya didn't hear anything from us, ya get me?"

The Primacy's daughter? Does this mean we'll have no chance to continue our conversation? Darrin nodded in agreement but asked, "Why would he only punish the two of you?"

"Only the two of us?" Karl shook his head. "No, boy. Ostrom has changed all our patrols. Says he can't trust none of us now. Thinks someone in the guard is responsible for helping the scrappers. He don't want us getting too comfortable with the folks we're meant to watch over, ya see?"

"And the Primacy's girl is just the beginning," added Henry. "I 'spose there ain't no harm in telling a rover, but the Shield of the Princess gone and run off too. A brocken on the loose!" He lowered his head. "All save us! What's the world coming to, eh?"

Astonished that these men would divulge so much to a

stranger, Darrin began to question the truth of their claims. But his father's words came back to him. *"Unhappy men are prone to share their misfortunes freely. For it is the only currency they possess that accrues interest."*

The gray morning vanished as Darrin raced atop the curtain wall. Drenched in sweat and lungs burning, he completed the vast circle that ringed Rothspire. An hour or more had passed since his conversation with the city guard, but their comments lingered.

If Aldir's daughter is in danger, I cannot trust I'll have another audience with him. Perhaps I should seek out Laustair myself? But what would Archwood say to that? I don't even know if he believed the old man. Do I? It actually sounds quite foolish now. Gods! But what if it is true? I have to find out.

He strode down the steps from the curtain wall, remembering his promise to meet with Haron over breakfast. If he was lucky, old Harry might just be waking up. Though his muscles throbbed from the morning run, he darted through the bailey towards Dartsuil's Keep.

For a brief moment, he could not help but think of Sir Matthew Dorne. Did the Iron Horse ever have to contest with the possibility of a God demanding anything of him? Darrin could not remember any story like that.

Haron bit into a rasher of bacon, grease dribbling out the side of his mouth. "The Primacy's girl?"

"Yes. They say she's close to death," Darrin answered.

"And these men who told you were city guard?"

"Aye." *Why do I always say that when I'm with Harry?*

"Well...I don't think we'll be 'aving any more chats with 'im then," said Haron. "I'll talk to Archwood about it. Perhaps it's time we head back to Elmfort. We've done what we set out to."

Darrin peered around the feasting hall. Most of the king's guests had departed, but there were still a few scattered groups of late comers who seemed rather content to pick at the scraps of their morning meal. "I'm thinking about talking to Laustair by myself," said Darrin. "Am I being foolish?"

"Aye," said Haron. "But it ain't never stopped you before." He laughed. "As your chief I'm supposed to tell ya that you ain't to do nothing unless ordered to by myself or the Lord-Overseer. But—" he pushed his plate away and stood—"if this ain't all some big jest, I'd say a God outranks Archwood."

Darrin smiled. "Thank you, Harry."

"Don't go thanking me yet, lad. Neither of us know what this all means. You might be cursing me in the future."

After he excused himself from the table, Darrin rushed from the hall in the hopes of finding Laustair.

Chapter  17

ALDIR

The Sins of Kings

The high divinator's chamber was immense and appointed in a manner of grand magnificence. A fire in the brazier kept the room warm to the point of hot, and the overpowering scent of various incenses battled in the air.

Erabil had done all he could to stop the girl's bleeding. Now, swathed in strips of cloth that were steeped in boiled wine and other medicines, Edlen lay atop a divan, her bloodstained tunic crumpled on the floor.

She's asleep. Thank the Gods. Though Edlen's breath was labored, she did breathe.

Aldir expected to be greeted by a far worse scene, his thoughts having drifted to a grim place. The sight of his daughter, so frail and thin, filled him with rage.

If Edlen does not survive this... Aldir gritted his teeth at the thought and made a silent vow that whoever did this would find themselves gored upon a lance in the center of the castle.

"Who is responsible for this?" shouted Aldir. He knelt over Edlen then searched the eyes of the others in the room.

Everly clutched Aldir's arm and said, "A scrapper girl."

His sister-in-law's eyes were crimson with tears. It was apparent to him she had not slept in some time. He gazed up and asked, "Where?"

"The Dark Cells. Edlen came out of—"

"The Dark Cells!" Aldir was furious. "What in the name of All was she doing down there?"

"I do not know," said Everly. She drooped her head in embarrassment.

"Perhaps I can attempt to answer, my lord." A man dressed in gray and silver with a puppeteer's rod sewn into his tunic stepped forward.

"And who are you?" asked Aldir. He stroked Edlen's brow and glared at the man.

"My name is Tomm Harken, my lord. We met…"

Aldir remembered meeting this man outside the Hall of Glory. "Yes, yes… I recall. Why are you *here*?"

"He is a pedagogue," said Everly. "He is a friend."

A pedagogue? A friend? It was all too much for Aldir. He rubbed at his temples and sighed. "Someone just tell me what is happening."

"I was with your daughter yesterday, my lord, prior to the tournament. She aided me in seeing to the righting of an injustice. With her help, we were able to set a matter to rest, but we lost company at the start of the melee. When the scrappers started to throw rocks, though, I lost track of her completely. Far too many people rushing about. I fear the city guard might have mistaken her for a scrapper. She must have attempted to escape them. Your daughter delights in avoiding scrutiny, but I am certain you already know this."

Pedagogue or not, Aldir bristled at another man's explanation of his child. He would question Tomm in depth at another time, but now he desired nothing more than to be alone with Edlen. He rested his hand on her chest. "This does not explain what she was doing in the Dark Cells."

"Until she awakens and regains strength enough to tell this part of the story, my lord, I am operating under the assumption that she and this scrapper tried to escape the riot by using the tunnels under the castle. As we speak, men swarm the tunnels. They will rout out the scrapper."

"By what authority do you command the men of Rothspire?" Aldir asked.

Everly frowned. "I gave Tomm temporary jurisdiction over this investigation. There is much you and I need to discuss, Aldir. Edlen is not the only victim of yesterday's events."

"What does that mean?"

"Perhaps that conversation might be held another time, my lady," said Tomm. "The Primacy has just arrived. He needs to attend to his daughter."

Poor Tomm, thought Aldir. *No one suggests a thing to Everly Graymere.* For the first time in what felt like forever, he laughed silently to himself.

"Agreed," said Everly. "It is time I find *my* daughter. Edlen is in the safest hands possible now."

Agreed? She has never agreed to anything she did not suggest. "Tell me, who else is hurt?"

"When we are alone, brother. Your thoughts should stay focused on Edlen." Everly embraced Aldir and whispered in his ear, "Be careful, please."

She swept up her gown and departed, leaving Aldir with Tomm and Erabil.

He stared at them but decided to say nothing. Instead, he found a chair and dragged it to Edlen's side. He grabbed his daughter's hands and wept, unconcerned with anyone's reaction.

An hour passed in painful stillness, punctuated only by his brief sobs. Edlen occasionally moved in her sleep. Each time this happened, Aldir grew hopeful she might wake, but the nepenthes elixir given to her by Erabil was exceptionally potent; she would remain asleep for hours to come.

Aldir mumbled a soft prayer, but after what he'd witnessed last night, he no longer knew which, if any, Gods to pray to. His only solace came in his half-uttered apologies.

"I have failed you," he said, his voice soft and pained. "I have failed you. I have failed your mother. I have failed the realm. Forgive me…forgive me."

"You have failed no one," said Erabil, his robes brushing against Aldir's face. "She will survive."

Aldir whipped his head around, his eyes burning with hate. "I was not speaking to you." His body tensed into one rigid muscle. "I do not ask for your absolution."

Erabil backed away, his head bowed.

Aldir leaned over Edlen and kissed her forehead. He wiped tears from his eyes and stood. In two strides he was in front of Tomm, close enough to smell the day-old perfume the man wore. "I want her brought back to her room before sundown. *No one* is to hear of this. Do you understand me? Not one word of this is to be breathed throughout the castle."

"Yes, my lord," said Tomm.

Aldir did not move. His eyes simmered as he stared at Tomm. "You and I will speak soon. Do not leave the city. If you do…I will have you dragged back by your bowels."

Tomm smiled. "It is not my intention to depart, my lord. Besides, I am rather fond of my bowels."

"It is not wise to move the girl in this condition, my lord," squeaked Erabil. "Not, at least, until the wound starts healing."

Again, Aldir's wrath was extraordinary—Laustair's antics from the previous evening still fresh in his memory. "I am no longer interested in the *wise counsel* of old men, Your Glory," he growled. He opened the door of Erabil's apartment, studied the High Divinator, and said, "My daughter will be in her chamber come nightfall."

He slammed the door and marched through the sacellum.

As he made to exit, the massive black dog traipsed after him. Before he left, he spun around and patted the animal's head. "Will you protect my precious girl?"

The dog gazed up at him, its doleful brown eyes filled with loyalty. A long, wet tongue lolled out and lapped at Aldir's hand.

"Perhaps you will."

Is all of this an ill omen? How can the events of one day spell such disaster? Aldir's thoughts swirled in a storm of confused questions as he entered Dartsuil's Keep. Everything had gone awry since he'd stepped into his father's litter yesterday.

He pressed through the growing throng that filled the antechamber, paying no mind to voices calling his name.

Lord Brastor Archwood sauntered towards him, his obscene stomach bouncing with every step. "Primacy!" The man stepped directly in front of Aldir, purposely blocking his path. "A word, Primacy. My son's justice has yet to be addressed."

Annoyed, frustrated, and enraged, Aldir thrust his finger into Lord Brastor's ample chest. "I have not the time to waste on your trivial requests, Brastor. If your rancor is severe enough, perhaps you should petition an audience with the king. For now, though, your tedious complaints do nothing for your cause. Kindly let me pass, or I shall see that your son is stripped of any glory he does or does not deserve."

Aldir leaned forward and whispered, "I am the Primacy of the Realm. *You* are but a troublesome man who derives a grotesque sense of personal accomplishment through the actions of his child. If your son is truly deserving of such acclaim, mayhap he himself will seek me out."

"I will not forget this, Primacy." Brastor huffed and strode forward, slamming his meaty shoulder into Aldir as he passed.

Add that to the list, mused Aldir. *Who else might I anger today?*

Free from any other distractions, Aldir quickened his pace and bound up the stairs of the keep. He decided to see his aunt. Why he needed to see her, he could not answer, but the compulsion to receive her guidance was too crucial to ignore.

Sir Oswald Graves blocked the door of Lady Teryse Killion's chamber. At Aldir's approach, though, he stepped aside and bowed. "My lord, she will be pleased to receive you again so soon."

No attempt to stop me this time? Interesting. He smiled at the hulking knight and bowed.

The overwhelming scent of saffron and sage permeated her chamber. Someone had recently lit the herbs. Aldir glanced around the room but saw only his aunt, her emaciated frame outlined in light silk sheets. She twisted in bed and stared at him—then with great effort, she lifted a bony arm and beckoned him closer.

She looks far worse today, he thought. *I should leave and let her rest.*

"Are you going to stand there gawking at me, or will you come help your dear aunt?"

The disease that ate away at her body seemed not to affect her tongue. "Coming," he said. He was a little boy again—dutiful and accommodating.

She groaned when he lifted her head but insisted he prop her up with a few pillows.

"I expected you earlier. I grew tired of waiting."

What? He eyed her curiously. "Why would you be expecting me?"

Teryse sighed. "The Lord-Overseer of the Eyes of the Forest brings you your brother's severed legs, The Shield of the Princess murders a knight in your father's tournament, those scrappers you were worried about have caused a riot, and your daughter has been stabbed in the stomach—am I forgetting anything?"

"How?" Aldir stared at her.

"My boy. I was the Primacy for nearly fifty years. Do you think I no longer retain my own eyes and ears throughout the realm?" She lifted herself slightly. "You will learn soon enough—it is your responsibility to be aware of *everything* that happens here. There was a time your father could not break wind without me being notified." She snickered. "But I fear your current worries are a tad more distressing than an old man's flatulence."

"Well, I see I cannot keep any secrets from you." He attempted a smile.

"No, you cannot. And it would be folly if you tried."

"Then you know why I am here." He found a chair, set it beside her, and sat. A long moment passed. He rubbed his forehead in contemplation. "What do I do?"

"It is rather obvious, is it not? You do what you told your father you would. You sail to the Vines with Lord Byron Windsong and find your brother…the Prince of Onyris. Everything else is but a niggling annoyance to the crown. This is why adepts exist." She winced in pain, or was it annoyance? "They will see to the other issues. But if the Windsongs are in any way connected to the prince's murder. Well…" She stared at Aldir. "I need not tell you what would come of that."

"But …my daughter."

"Is *not* the Prince of Onyris."

Anger arose from somewhere deep inside his gut; he did his best to suppress it, but his voice raised in volume and pitch as he said, "Someone tried to kill her!"

Teryse was unyielding. "She is not dead. Your brother, though, *is* the Prince of Onyris and will one day be the king. It is your duty as the Primacy of the Realm to ensure the might of the crown. Edlen—as lovely a girl as she is—is not the future of Onyris."

What was she saying? *Am I to leave my only daughter as she struggles for life?* "How can you…I mean…you have children—would you not?"

"No!" she said. "I would not put my own craven needs before that of the realm."

"Craven?" asked Aldir aloud. "My place is here! My place is with my daughter."

"Is your place to sit idly by and pout? Is your place to leave the prince's fate in question? Your place, Aldir, is to do whatever is necessary for the Graymere family. For the crown.

"Edlen does not need your simpering and moroseness." She squirmed beneath her blankets as she pulled herself to a position where she no longer appeared weak or sickly. "I know the black thought that lingers in your mind. I know what sadness avails you. But I tell you now, Aldir—your child will not be aided by your cumbersome grief. She will not be mended by your anguish. If you mean to help her in any way, you will leave on the next ship to set sail for Maresport. You will find your brother—alive or not—and you will return to Rothspire with an answer. If war is coming, you must be prepared. A kingdom does not survive by reacting to aggression; it survives by destroying those who mean it ill."

If war is coming, you must be prepared... His aunt's words terrified him.

War with whom?

True, Onyris had enemies, but their force and history must be enough to dissuade any realm from declaring open hostility.

Aldir made his way to his father's royal chamber.

Two of the King's Blades stood sentry at the base of Ulisaren's floor; Aldir saluted both as he neared. One was Sir Dalton Yarmouth, a robust man in his earlier thirties, clean shaven, and clear eyed, and flanking him towered Sir Maron Darlow.

Darlow held the distinction of being the only member of the King's Blades to slay a man while in the service of King Ulisaren. Ten years ago, when Sir Maron was nearing forty years old and had been a Blade for twenty of those years, he'd discovered a plot to assassinate the king.

Sir Maron Darlow, now fifty years-old, smiled at Aldir and placed his hand on the hilt of his sword and bowed.

"My lord," he said. "Been an age since I saw you up here. Are things well?"

Aldir bowed his head in return and said, "Well as a spring day, Sir Darlow. Is my father still around?"

"Yes, my lord. Just seen Master Werman running from his room to fetch him his breakfast. Shall I let the king know you're here?"

Worm, thought Aldir. *He moves around this castle faster than anyone else.* "I'm glad the old man is awake." He smiled. "But I am in no need for an announcement; I think I can make my way to his chamber."

"As you wish, my lord," Sir Maron said and gestured for Sir Dalton Yarmouth to stand aside.

Aldir pushed lightly on the intricately carved door of his father's chamber and entered.

The room hadn't changed at all since his mother had passed, and Aldir realized that was the last time he'd spent any time here. Along the outer-facing wall, an enormous tapestry depicting the lineage of the Graymere family still hung—musty and worn. Above the brazier, mounted yet covered in years of dust, was the Graymere crest.

It depicted the Great Wheel, golden in the center, hemmed by a green chevron that was speckled by red stars. On either side of the Wheel sat a two-headed eagle, wings splayed, and a downward attacking bear. The oppressive heraldry of his family's crest made Aldir uncomfortable. He averted his eyes and searched the cavernous room for his father.

A small door far within the chamber opened, and Ulisaren shambled from out of the privy.

He stared, mouth agape, as Aldir approached.

"I see you are dressed for visitors," Aldir said.

The old king was dressed in thin nightclothes, his age

starkly apparent now that it was no longer hidden under the guise of his royal attire. Aldir was shocked by how fragile his father was.

The king straightened his back and stood upright until he almost resembled the powerful man Aldir knew him to be. He strode forward, found his green and red robe, and then threw it over his delicate frame. "Aldir?" He peered through aged eyes. "It is you."

Why does he sound glad to receive me? This must be some game of his. Aldir took a timid step and said, "Yes, Father. It is me." *He is so frail. What happened to the hale man I sat with yesterday?*

"So many years have passed since you visited me in my chamber." The king fell into a large chair and smiled placidly. He ran his hand across his face. "You are now witness to the man behind the king..."

He is so old.

The king's face sagged in a thousand wrinkles; heavy bags pulled at the skin under his eyes. His lips drooped, and his neck was like that of a turkey's waddle, not that of a king. His voice, husky and sapped of life, continued. "Do not fret, my son. I am old. It is well that you finally see me for who I truly am."

"I apologize, Father. Perhaps I should return another time."

"No, no, no..." said Ulisaren. "You will, Gods willing, be my age someday. My body refuses to listen to my mind, but I will defeat these aches and pains. I always do." He looked at Aldir. "Yesterday was an extremely trying day, was it not?"

"It was."

"We will overcome our setbacks, though. We are Graymeres."

We are.

Ulisaren craned his neck to either side, the snap of his joints loud enough to be heard by all of Dartsuil's Keep. "I am glad you are here, but why have you come?"

Uncertain that this discussion might now be appropriate, Aldir lowered his head and said nothing.

"Aldi..." said the king. "I am no fool. You have not stepped foot near here since we lost your mother. Whatever it is you wish to speak of, I am positive it is important." He frowned, his face wilting to a sad memory of his former glory. "Tell me, do you come as my son or my Primacy?"

Aldi? He has not called me that in over thirty years.

Aldir walked to a chair and pulled it close to his father. He sat and stared at his hands before taking a deep breath. "Is it possible I come to you as both?"

The king grabbed Aldir's hand. "You are both."

And my daughter...what is she to you, Father?

"Edlen," he started, "was attacked last night."

"Attacked?" The king squinted. "By whom?"

"A scrapper. Or that is what I am told. Everly believes the girl meant to kill her, but Edlen got between the two and..." It was too difficult to say the words aloud again.

Ulisaren sighed and shook his head. "I see. Perhaps your sister-in-law is not too severe in her desire to punish the lot."

Though Aldir had sworn revenge against the one who'd nearly killed his daughter, he still could not reconcile the thought of butchering an entire group of children—dangerous or not. He mustered his grief. "Vengeance is a contagion, Father. As angry as I am, the idea of waging a war with our own people is a measure I cannot condone."

There is the word again—war.

"'Vengeance,'" said the king as he lowered his eyes. "It

is an interesting phrase you use. I have been pondering this exact notion since last night." He sniffed the air and looked at Aldir. "Saffron and sage?"

"What?"

"Saffron and sage. I thought I recognized the scent as you entered." Ulisaren grimaced. "You've come from your aunt's chambers."

Aldir, puzzled by his father's deduction, answered, "Yes. But how did you know?"

"Who do you think lit the herbs for her?"

"You? But why were you with Aunt Teryse?"

"She is my sister, Aldir. And she was my Primacy for nearly fifty years. I need no reason to visit her, do I?" asked Ulisaren. "We may not always see eye-to-eye, but her counsel is still valuable. I assume you are of the same mind, seeing as you sought her out as well."

"Well," said Aldir, smiling at his father's frankness. "Yes, I lean on her quite heavily these days."

"As you should."

That is not what you said in your litter yesterday. "You were of a different opinion before the tournament, if I remember correctly."

"Ah," said Ulisaren. "Aldi, I am the King of Onyris. There are times I must flex my authority lest I lose it. You disobeyed my command, and though we rode with family, I mustn't ever be seen dismissive of something. Even something as slight as your tardiness. Kings are men—nothing more. When you strip us of our finery, our crowns, and our scepters—we are merely men. Men who carry a great burden." He frowned, his fleshy lips twitching as they strained to turn themselves into a smile. "I am certain Teryse would revel in this admission."

"What did she and you talk about?" *Now it is my turn to play the role of Primacy.*

"The young rover."

Darrin?

"He mentioned a name I wished not to hear," said Ulisaren. He drew a deep breath. "The Voress Ní."

"But their existence is nothing more than legend. Why would you—"

"A foolish claim indeed, yet…" Ulisaren stretched his back and rolled his head in a slow circle. He reached for a pipe that sat atop the table nearest him and lit the brown leaf in the bowl. As he exhaled, he said, "But it is not without merit."

"You don't believe they are responsible for Odain, do you?"

"If you cannot prove one's existence, does that mean they do not exist?" He puffed on the stem of the pipe. "The sins of kings." The words mixed with smoke in his mouth. "Does the name Ichaem Leonardis mean anything to you?" he asked.

Aldir thought on the name, but he could not place it. "No. I cannot say it does."

"Of course not. His name has never been written into our histories—and for good reason," said Ulisaren. "I desired never to think of him again, but…those legs from yesterday. I am now certain.

"Perhaps the Voress Ní are not the myth we wish them to be…perhaps the Voress Ní is a single man. Perhaps the Voress Ní is Ichaem Leonardis." The king spoke as if solving a puzzle long fretted over.

"Who is he?" asked Aldir as he leaned closer to his father. He was a child again, eagerly awaiting a story.

The king sat up straighter. "Who is he? I asked myself

that same question many times in my youth." His eyes narrowed to slits; his words came out in a whisper. "He was an extremely dangerous man."

Was? "Is he dead?"

"Mayhap. Yet his actions, I am certain, may extend beyond death." The king sighed. "The truth of Robart's rebellion finds itself greatly distorted over time."

The tale of Robart Moorcroft's rebellion was taught to all in Onyris and perhaps to the lands beyond the sea as well. Its importance had grown through the years, evolving from history into legend. Every child knew the story.

"Ichaem Leonardis," said the king, "proved more responsible for our victory than myself or your aunt."

"How so?" asked Aldir.

Ulisaren's face wilted. "The Puppet Lord, we named him in secret. But had we been aware of his ruthlessness, perhaps *demon* would have been more appropriate." The king wiped at his brow and continued. "We believed him nothing but a traveling puppeteer: a low-born performer from Waterbridge in the Vines. Had we only known…"

The air in the king's chamber became still. Aldir clenched his fist in nervous anticipation. "What did he do?"

As though in a trance, the king's body stiffened. "Ichaem Leonardis killed Robart Moorcroft. Not I, not Teryse—Ichaem Leonardis." Sweat dripped into the king's eyes, though he did not wipe at it. "He delivered Moorcroft's head to us during a private performance for my father. A puppet show he titled *The Sins of Kings*."

And you've been hiding this for fifty years? Aldir looked at his father with pity and disdain.

The king avoided Aldir's gaze. "It was he who brought that bastard's butchered body to all who opposed Rothspire.

It was he who ended the rebellion; yet *we* declared victory. Ichaem Leonardis did not ask for glory. The Puppet Lord only asked for payment, but…the payments never ended."

Ulisaren's voice shifted. No longer a soft monotone, it became frantic. "They never ended! Fifty years of payments, Aldir! Fifty years! The crown could no longer afford his silence. I had to do something. I had to stop it! I had to!"

"What did you have to do?" Aldir leaned forward and grabbed his father's arms. "What did you do?" He was not certain he wanted his father to answer.

"Odain!" the king shrieked. "Your brother went to the Vines to settle our debt with the Leonardis family." His head dropped to his chest. "They meant for someone to find those legs, certain they would be brought before me. The sins of kings, Aldi, have come home to roost. Ichaem Leonardis does not forget his debts, and neither will his children…whoever they are."

"You sent Odain to his death!" Aldir backed away from his father. "Teryse was right."

The king stared at the floor. "War is coming, Aldi. Yesterday's tragedies were but shots over the bow. They will not stop. Not unless we destroy him. You must go to the Vines, now! You have to find your brother. You have to find out if Ichaem Leonardis is still alive, and if he is not…you have to find the new head of the Voress Ní. Take Werman with you, and find Sir Rhohl. If we act quickly—there is a chance we may disrupt their plans."

CHAPTER

DARRIN

The Mermaid's Kiss

THE COURTYARD OF Rothspire teemed with activity. Vendors barked from behind their stalls, courtiers mingled with commoners, and lords—both high and low—jostled at the entrance to Dartsuil's Keep, eager to receive an audience with King Ulisaren. The events of yesterday had vanished into a memory as the prospect of a new day in the king's capitol dawned.

Where did all these people come from? Darrin thought as he slipped through a crowd of young women dressed in fine silks. He had only been in the feasting hall for an hour at the most. The castle grounds were all but empty when he'd run the wall this morning.

Lost in the pulsing mass of Spire-ights, he stared in every direction, hoping to spot a familiar landmark. This being his first time in the bustling city, he had only the vaguest of ideas of where he was.

When he'd arrived yesterday, the upper bailey had held but a handful of scattered attendants and drunken tournament guests. He tried his best to map the path they'd taken in his head, but it was now no more than a blur.

Hopeless. I should go back to Haron and tell him I'm lost. The thought made him shiver. If he wished to call himself a true Eye, he must always be able to get his bearings. *Sir Matthew Dorne was said to have a compass behind his eyes.* With that, Darrin shook his head and studied his surroundings.

Behind him loomed Dartsuil's Keep, which must mean the sacellum was to the east. He peered through the throng. In the distance, the domed roof of the holy building peeked out. *East.* Yes, that would make the tower in that direction the Tower of the Setting Sun. With that bit of assurance, he slid between the throng of people cluttering the courtyard.

Why he assumed Laustair would be that way, he did not know. But his instincts were rarely wrong.

A host of people halted before him, forcing Darrin to stop and watch the spectacle unfolding in the streets.

Horns blasted and drums thumped as an enormous carriage—pulled by no less than twenty horses—rolled through the crowd, followed by a detachment of mounted soldiers and trailed by at least a hundred smallfolk: minstrels, cooks, servants, handmaids, butlers, kitchen staff, and an assortment of nurses and priors.

Atop the carriage flew an elaborate flag of yellow and green, a massive tree growing from within a great house that was emblazoned upon it.

Darrin stared in awe at the enormity of this traveling realm. He turned to one of the other onlookers and asked, "Who is that?"

"Lord Archwood of Straten, ya git. Ain't the flag enough to tell ya?"

Embarrassed by his lack of heraldic knowledge, he snuck

away from the woman who so brashly answered his idiotic question.

Lord Archwood? The Lord-Overseer? Does he have a brother? Darrin, you fool. Of course, he does.

Why the fact that his Lord-Overseer having a family was such a foreign concept to him at first, Darrin could not answer. Instead, he waited for the train of people to pass then continued on his way to find Laustair.

Though the tall tower he headed for grew closer, the intersecting streets he wandered confused him.

It should be an easy task to reach his destination, but somehow, Darrin had to backtrack a few times before he found the correct path.

And I call myself a rover...

After a frustrating start, he soon stood at the arched entrance of the Tower of the Setting Sun.

He gazed up at the foreboding tower. Its immense height worried him. A tower of this size would not be simple to navigate, especially when he had no clue where Laustair's chamber was.

Trusting the same instinct that brought him there, Darrin entered the tower, only to become immediately overwhelmed.

Three separate staircases greeted him, each stretching into unknown heights. *If I choose the wrong one, how much time will I waste before I find the old man? And that's hoping he's even here.*

The sudden desire to retreat filled his mind. What was he doing here, anyway? *If my father were here, he would certainly have some choice words for me.*

Sticking your nose where it don't belong, eh, Darrin? I told you that joining the rovers was a mistake.

Much less populated than Dartsuil's Keep, the Tower of the Setting Sun seemed home to lower nobility. People milled about the ground floor, but Darrin never sensed the cajolery that seemed second nature to those who mingled about the antechamber of the Hall of Glory.

A surge of clarity washed over him. He dashed up the staircase to his left. This was not an action brought on by any rational conclusion; it was merely a gut instinct that he chose not to ignore.

After sprinting up nearly a hundred of the tower's spiraling stairs, Darrin reached the topmost floor. His heart beat rapidly against his ribs and his breath came out in shallow panting gasps. If he'd guessed correctly and he now stood before Laustair's chamber, he marveled that one as old as him might be able to make this climb with any regularity.

The sweet, pervasive scent of dried nicotiana drifted from underneath a closed, iron-banded oak door. *That's the same leaf he smoked last night.*

Darrin, his energy redoubled by the fact that he must surely have chosen the correct flight of stairs, strode forward and rapped his fist against the door. The moment his knuckles sprang back from the heavy oak, sweat poured down his sides from his underarms and his mouth grew dry.

What am I going to say to him?

With no time to think, the door creaked open and a familiar voice spoke from within the room. "Cantlay...we wondered what took you so long."

Lord-Overseer?

Darrin took a timid step forward and pushed at the door.

Inside the room, both Lord-Overseer Archwood and Laustair sat in high-backed chairs, their eyes fixed on him.

But if they're both sitting...who opened the door?

"Come, come, Master Cantlay," said Laustair. "I was certain you would seek me out."

The chamber seemed limitless as Darrin stumbled across its threshold. The Primacy's chamber was but a child's nursery compared to this tremendous hall.

A mountainous bookshelf ran along an entire wall of the room, containing more volumes than all of Redrun's library, and then some. Scattered across the sea of carpeted floor were an innumerable number of peculiar instruments—which, had he simply been visiting as a guest, he might have speculated courteously at their uses. Darrin meandered towards the two men, gazing casually at the dizzying assortment of oddities.

"My lords." Darrin bowed. "How is it you knew I would come?"

Laustair was the first to answer. He drew from his pipe and said, "Your dissatisfaction with the hasty conclusion of our conversation was quite apparent." He smiled.

Darrin eyed both men. A brash courage erupting in him, he said, "Malighaunt." The fear of forgetting his purpose coursed through his blood. "Dalnor commanded me to tell Somath that Malighaunt has discovered the last of the Valdryz."

The jovial atmosphere of the room vanished. Though near midday, a sudden darkness descended upon the chamber. Laustair's eyes narrowed; a cold fire blazing behind them. "He said those exact words?" The abrupt change frightened Darrin. "Why did you not say this last night?"

I was afraid? Was I? Did I believe your claims? Was I nervous? Yes, of course I was—I am out of my depth.

"I...I do not know," said Darrin. "But I am telling you now. I apologize if this comes too late, but this is why I am here. I am not bold. I am terrified. I do not know why I was burdened with this task. If I have failed you... Perhaps Dalnor entrusted this information with the wrong man, and for that I am sorry."

Laustair waved his hand. The darkness receded and the bright sun reentered the room. "You have not failed, my boy. Your endeavor is truly formidable. You hold no responsibility in these matters.

"I believe the time has come to tell you that which I wished never to say aloud," said Laustair as he grabbed a bottle filled with a turquoise liquid and then poured its contents into three ornately carved goblets.

"My friend," said Kayvold, "I have not slept since the night before last. Please...I have not the constitution for more spirits."

Thank you, Archwood. It is not even midday; I cannot stomach another sip of that foul-tasting stuff.

Laustair frowned. "This is no spirit, Lord Archwood." He took the slightest sip from the drink and grinned. Pleased with his concoction, he lifted the other two goblets and handed them over.

"The Mermaid's Kiss," he said. "A more delightful tonic I have never ingested. The privateers who sail between the God's Sea and the Redwater tell tales of its invigorating properties." Again, he sipped at the beverage and gestured for them to do the same. "I prefer to drink it slowly. It has the tendency to excite the tongue."

"I appreciate the offer, Laustair," said Kayvold, "but I simply cannot drink anymore."

"I do not force this upon you, Lord Archwood, but if you indulge me, you will see I do not deceive you. And for what I am to discuss, this may be a salve for your doubtless troubles."

"And what troubles are those?" asked Kayvold. He held the drink to the light and inspected its contents. With slight unease, he tasted the Mermaid's Kiss.

His eyes flashed like a freshly kindled fire; he hooted and stomped his feet. "Gods! This is delicious!"

Darrin followed suit and sampled the light-blue elixir. A rush of energy surged through him, as though a bolt of lightning had struck him in that exact moment. The hair on his neck stood on end, and his body tingled. His face grew flush and had he been asked to, he might have sprinted down the tower stairs and run the circle of the wall three times over, never needing a rest.

"What is in this?" asked Kayvold. "I feel ten years younger."

Laustair chuckled and resumed his seat. He tilted his goblet back. "That, I cannot answer. Precious little stores of this elixir remain to me. Mayhap I will find myself in the company of the person who gifted me such a miraculous thing, but until that day, I refuse to tinker with perfection."

"I completely understand," said Kayvold, taking another sip.

A sudden fear gripped Darrin, and he clutched his goblet with both hands, not daring to spill even a drop. *This is surely the secret to the old man's unnatural vitality. And he serves it freely.*

"Who is Malighaunt?" Whether it was the bottled vigor of the Mermaid's Kiss, or simply his own youthful impertinence, Darrin asked the question which had plagued his mind since he'd left the forest.

"I believe this an appropriate time to explain, Master Cantlay. I can only hope you reserve some of your drink for my telling," said Laustair.

Kayvold snuck one last swig and then placed his goblet on the table nearest him. "Yes, Laustair. I believe it is time you clarify this mess Darrin unwittingly created."

That I created? Darrin gaped at his Lord-Overseer. *I have done nothing of the sort.* "I...I had no intention..."

"Of that I am certain," said Laustair. "You created nothing, Master Cantlay. This is a quagmire that stretches far beyond anything you or even your grandsires can claim responsibility for. I will not waste either of your time with a history lesson, when it is obvious you are both aware of it."

Laustair took a deep draw from his pipe and continued.

"The Valdryz, having forfeit their previous form, swore an oath that they might only guide the fortunes and futures of man. But there was one of their order who secretly desired to control man. He kept this desire hidden from his brothers for thousands upon thousands of years—long after man turned from their teachings and humanity proclaimed themselves the *true* rulers of the Wide-World.

"Malighaunt is his name. And he deemed the time rife for what he believed to be the reclamation of his power. The Sundering War, as it is known today. The rupturing of the land itself." Laustair's eyes narrowed.

"During this cataclysmic event, Malighaunt shed any pretense of servitude. He declared his intentions and waged a singular war against man.

"But his arrogance led to his downfall. The other Valdryz learned of his black mind. Together, they stood against Malighaunt and defeated him. They imprisoned him for an age in the Towers of Allevghaunt.

"But pity for their brother gnawed at the spirit of the others, and before the agreed time of punishment passed, Malighaunt was released. It was not until much later, though, that they discovered he had corrupted the minds of his jailors: Inganar, Scryta, and Dalnor.

"Together, Malighaunt and his thralls developed a weapon that might extinguish the worldly forms of their brothers. They called it the Black Flame."

Darrin tapped his feet and scratched at his nose but would not break eye contact with Laustair. The old man seemed to notice Darrin's unease but continued with his story.

"The wisest and foremost of the Valdryz, Begrafaine, fell under the sway of Malighaunt. He took for himself a mortal woman, and from their union they bore a child.

"Of all the laws and oaths that the Valdryz held sacred, this was the most egregious. To mate with a mortal was seen as an affront to All. The Gods—the guides of man—were never to surrender their power to those they were bound to foster.

"Once the other Valdryz perceived Begrafaine's dishonor, they held a trial in which it was determined his offense beyond that of even Malighaunt's wrongdoing.

"Imprisonment in the Towers of Allevghaunt—such as was sentenced before—would not be a satisfactory punishment. The Council of the Valdryz agreed that the debasement of their kind could only be answered with banishment. And Malighaunt devised the perfect means in which to expel a Valdryz…the Black Flame.

"In front of all assembled, Malighaunt performed an execution… an execution that each of the Valdryz agreed upon." Laustair grimaced but continued.

"A hideous display followed. The Black Flame did not

cast Begrafaine from the Wide-World; it ate away at his essence—a terrible fire engulfed his body and gnawed at his flesh. His skin blistered and popped like a beast on a spit. The intense heat from the blaze was far beyond anything imaginable, it was as though All herself dragged the sun from the heavens.

"Begrafaine screamed, but his words caught fire as they seared from his mouth. His frame crumpled under the heat.

"This was not the punishment promised. This was sadistic torture. The Black Flame was not a means to banish a brother from their corporeal form. It was a threat to the entire order of the Valdryz. It was a declaration of intent—and Malighaunt was the only one who might wield it."

Kayvold took a large gulp of his drink and asked, "What became of the woman and the child?"

A shadow crept along Laustair's face. He lowered his eyes. "Malighaunt's most trusted thrall, Dalnor, searched out the woman and her babe—for Malighaunt dared not sully himself in the pursuit of a mortal. In a small fishing village on the outskirts of Hearthsblow, Dalnor discovered their whereabouts.

"The woman was quite striking—raven-haired, with eyes the color of ice. The babe was no more than a swaddled bundle of pink flesh. Even as young as it was, it had a smile that might never be tarnished. Dalnor was overcome with remorse. Had he not performed the next simple act of kindness, we might not be having this conversation now."

"What did he do?" asked Darrin. "Did he free them?"

"No," said Laustair, a grim frown pulling his lips down. "If he came back to Malighaunt without his quarry, Malighaunt's shadows, Inganar and Scryta, would be dispatched. Not only would the life of the woman and child be forfeit, but so would that of any village suspected of holding them as well. No...Dalnor knew he must bring them to Malighaunt. Their crimes must be punished."

"Crimes?" asked Kayvold. "What crime might a babe be guilty of?"

"In the eyes of Malighaunt, the babe was an abomination. Men turned their backs on the Valdryz, remember. For him, the mere fact that the blood of a Valdryz mingled with those he believed unworthy was a crime that must be eradicated from the history of our order.

"But in one last act of compassion, Dalnor did a thing unexpected, one that I am certain still haunts him.

"Upon his arrival in the village, he learned of the birth of another child, crippled and deformed—a babe who would not live to see its first birthday. Dalnor reasoned that the sacrifice of this twisted, monstrous child would satisfy Malighaunt's retribution... and perhaps stay any further harm to the world of man.

"He returned to Allevghaunt with the woman and both babes. But he kept the healthy offspring of Begrafaine secret. He sought me out before presenting his plunder to Malighaunt. Terrified of what may come of his treachery, he begged me to leave with the child. He believed I might be able to disappear before our brothers learned of his deceit."

Laustair lifted his arm and displayed an iron band wrapped around his wrist. "I was presented with the child... and this bracelet—if I agreed to wear it, my thoughts would be clouded to my brothers and my appearance would be disguised to all.

"I weighed the choice for some time, but the plight of my brothers and the fate of this innocent child swayed my decision. Thirty-seven years, I have worn my false shroud, and in that time, I have spoken no words to *any* of my brothers. Perhaps the time has come for me to break this silence. Perhaps the time has come for me to search out the one who swore me to my purpose. Perhaps it is time I answer for my role as *executioner*. For that is what I am, an executioner—not only of my brother, but of those innocent souls I did nothing to save."

"Dalnor?" asked Darrin, astounded. "He is the one who took the child?"

The thought of the poor, crippled babe suffering whatever torment Malighaunt had inflicted upon it made him ill. "Were they killed?"

Laustair grimaced. "I have no doubt, Master Cantlay. Malighaunt would not be one to show mercy."

"You are no better!" said Darrin. He stood and pointed a finger at Laustair. "They did nothing wrong! How could they be punished for a God's mistake? How could you allow it?"

"Sit down, boy!" said Kayvold, his anger swift and forceful.

"But—"

"No! Sit down, now! That is an order!"

"He is right in his condemnation, Lord Archwood." Laustair rubbed his chin. "Our decisions were abysmal, and I will carry the weight of my role in those executions for eternity."

Kayvold frowned. "Though I appreciate your sorrow, Laustair, Cantlay is a rover in the Eyes of the Forest and must at all times abide by our rules of conduct." He turned to Darrin. "You will behave with respect, regardless if I am in the room or not. Do you understand?"

Respect? The old man just admitted to being complicit in murder. "Aye, sir." Darrin sat and stared at Laustair.

"We are leaving Rothspire come daybreak on the morrow," said Kayvold. "If you wish to join us, Laustair, I will see that you are accompanied for a time. Perhaps the Eyes can assist in setting some of this to right." He glared at Darrin. "You were sent by this Dalnor to relay your message, and unless there is anything else you're keeping from us, I believe the message has been received."

Darrin nodded.

"Then we are in agreement. We will escort Laustair—if he wishes—to meet with Dalnor. I will not have it said that the Eyes of the Forest do not see their obligations through to the end."

What? Escort him back into the forest? That was never asked of me. "Lord-Overseer—"

"An order is an order, Cantlay."

Laustair shook his head. "I will appreciate the company, Master Cantlay. I only hope you will begrudge me less by the time we part."

What choice do I have? Darrin stood, his hand sweeping against the goblet at his side. The last drops of the Mermaid's Kiss spilled onto the carpet. "May I be excused until such time as we depart?"

Kayvold glanced at the fallen drink and then back to Laustair. The old man nodded. "Find that you are saddled and ready by daybreak, Cantlay. We leave straight from the stables."

"Aye, sir." Darrin marched through the chamber, paying no mind to the extravagant instruments that had so enthralled him when he'd first entered.

Chapter

EVERLY

The Glory of Youth

Everly opened the door to her chamber slowly. It was early morning, and she did not want to wake Amara. It felt like ages since she'd last seen her daughter—and after all the misery of last night, the gentle peace of crawling into bed beside Amara would be a much-needed comfort.

The curtains were drawn and any candles lit during the evening had all but burnt to their wicks. Slivers of morning sun colored the room in diffused grays, Amara's tiny frame barely noticeable under thick blankets.

The glory of youth, thought Everly. *One day you will be burdened with the troubles of the Wide-World, but today, sweet girl, I envy your ignorance.*

She sat on the bedside, too tired to undress but not too tired to cry.

Her tears poured in an unstoppable torrent. It was all too much. Why must she have to contend with all this tragedy? She did not ask for any of this. She did not choose to be wed to the prince. If anyone should be tyrannized by these struggles, it was her father. He was the one who had orchestrated this union.

But where was he?

Dead. The coward. Like some sly-handed merchant who'd sold his wares and accepted his payment only to vanish before the purchase proved faulty.

I hope your titles and gold kept you warm when death clasped its icy grip on your heart.

She pressed her face into her hands and wept in silence. Amara need not be disturbed by her mother's failures. No— those shortcomings belonged to her.

When her stomach grew tight and her throat raw, she pushed those thoughts aside and crawled in beside her daughter.

Before sleep could greet her and wash away her sadness, she pulled the blankets back and wrapped an arm around Amara.

Wet? Why is she wet?

Everly ran her hand down her daughter's back, assuming the young girl had wet herself during the night. As she placed her hand upon Amara's lower back, she noted the thickness of the liquid. *This isn't urine...*

She threw the blankets off, but the girl did not stir.

Fear replaced her gloom. Frantic, she pushed at the little girl. Nothing.

No! No! No!

She grabbed her daughter by the shoulders and shook. Nothing.

No! Please... No!

The gray light made it impossible to see anything but a dark stain covering the girl. A mad thought flashed into Everly's mind.

She is too young to have flowered. But it is possible, isn't it?

"Wake up, sweetling," said Everly. "Please wake up. Please." She rocked the girl violently. "Please…wake up! This game is not funny. Amara!" she shouted. "Amara! Wake up now! I command you! Wake up! Wake up! Wake up!"

The girl did not move.

Gods! Gods! Gods! No…no…please Gods, no…

She sprang from the bed and ripped the curtains from their rods. Sunlight filled the room.

Blinded momentarily, Everly rubbed her eyes, but before she dared open them, she spoke a prayer. She had not said a prayer since she was a child. Would the Gods listen to her now?

Slowly, hesitantly, she removed her hands from her eyes.

Red.

There was too much red.

For a moment, Everly thought she might faint.

But she didn't.

Instead, she dashed to the bed, falling upon her daughter and screaming. Her hands slid against Amara's nightclothes, growing sticky with congealed blood. The young girl's face was pale—all life had drained from her once rosy complexion, her hair lying dull against the bedsheets.

Everly howled again, the sound more bestial than human. She pulled the girl up and enveloped her. Whether she believed she might be able to hold her tightly enough to undo this horror or that by grasping the child firmly enough her life might be traded for her daughter's, Everly did not know. The only thing she was certain of was that she no longer wanted to feel this agony.

Sir Willem Thorpe flung open the door and rushed into

the room, but as he approached, his steady footfalls faltered. He took a quick step backwards, bowed his head, and whispered, "Gods."

The sunlight streaming in from the window lit the scene in dazzling horror. Mother and daughter entwined, both covered in blood.

"Everly," said Sir Willem as he neared. His cousin did not respond. Her cries devolved into unintelligible sobs. He reached out to touch her arm.

"Do not touch me!" she snapped. "Do not touch me!" Her voice was a mixture of terror and sorrow. "Do something, please!"

She released her daughter slowly and raised her head. When she finally turned and stared blankly at Sir Willem, her face was smeared with blood and flush with tears. "Do something," she said again, almost pleading. "Do something… save her…save her. Please, Willem…please."

Sir Willem pulled at the young girl's nightclothes and pressed his hand against her belly. He lowered his head and held his ear to her mouth in the hopes of hearing even the faintest of breaths. But there was nothing.

Everly watched his eyes harden as he stared down at his niece's throat.

A fine slit ran across the soft pale skin of her neck. Blood had clotted around the wound and ropy strands of death slipped in red tendrils down her chest.

He inspected her stomach and found three puncture marks dotting her abdomen.

"She is gone," he said.

The room spun around Everly. She wanted to scream but nothing came out. Her heart beat rapidly and her limbs grew numb. Had she not been in bed, she surely would have fallen to the floor. She curled into a tight ball and started to gasp, quickly and violently.

Her eyes closed and the only thing she remembered hearing before the world went black was the distant sound of her cousin's voice calling her name. But that was impossible; the world had ended.

CHAPTER

ALDIR

The Rising Tide

THE ROAD FROM Rothspire to Towerglenn ran through the Great Wheel and then stretched south-west for fifteen miles over smooth, well-trodden roads. It passed over a wide green dale then rose upwards into the lush highlands that overlooked the Brockhead Sea. The final descent, though, after turning east at the gap in the Agrion Hills, twisted down a treacherously steep, narrow, and rocky trail.

Aldir pulled back on the reins of his courser and steadied it for the sharp descent.

He turned to look at Werman Gault who had been struggling with his pony earlier in their ride. "Worm, you must gain control or the beast will grow defiant."

"Yes, my lord," said Werman as he kicked feebly into his pony's side.

"Don't kick!" said Aldir. "Squeeze with your legs." *Has your family taught you nothing of riding?* "If I catch you doing that again, I'll pull you down and kick you in the belly. See how you enjoy it."

"Yes, my lord." The young man squeezed, but his legs had almost no strength.

Why did my father force me to take this twit? He may have a knack for running messages, but he is wasted in any other pursuit. He has been useless since we left the castle.

"Better, Worm, better," said Aldir, in the hopes the young boy might do well with some encouragement. "It takes years to master yourself in the saddle, and this is no jaunt through the Great Wheel." *Is this why Lord Damen Gault sent you to foster with us? It would not be the first time a father prizes his eldest yet leaves his runts to beg for scraps.*

After leading them safely down the path, Aldir rode alongside Werman and said, "I pushed us hard today, Worm, but I am impressed with your resilience. I know this was not one of the leisurely rides you are familiar with, but ours is a task that requires great haste." He patted the boy on the shoulder. "The king would be proud."

Worm looked up at him and smiled. But Aldir noted a shadow of unease behind the boy's eyes.

A curious one he is. Perhaps my father wishes for him to harden on this trip.

They trotted over the cobblestone walkways of Towerglenn as they approached the serpentine coastline. Fleets of ships swayed in the port, rocking against one another as they played a discordant symphony of soft creaks and knocks. Aldir gazed out at the vast sea and bowed his head. The sun was setting, cutting a sharp streak across the horizon. The last light of day faded, leaving shimmering ripples of pink and yellow to sink below the inky surface.

His brother was out there somewhere, hidden beyond lapping waves and bottomless waters.

He forgot how much he despised the sea.

It was in the nethermost darkness of this immeasurable tomb that Irymar, his beloved, had leapt to her death. His family clung to the story that she'd died during childbirth, but he had been there with her atop the Tower of Seafall. He alone had witnessed the madness and grief that assailed her, and he'd been powerless to stop her.

Now, staring into the fathomless depths of her watery crypt, he wondered where her once beautiful form had washed ashore. Or, if her body sank still, never reaching a final resting place.

Lost in dreamlike memory, he only just noticed Werman slowly trotting away. *Where is he off to?*

"Worm!" He spun his horse and followed after the boy. "Where are you going? I told you to stay by my side."

"Apologies, my lord, but were we not supposed to find Sir Rhohl?"

I am well aware of duties. "I am to find Sir Rhohl. You are to squire for me."

"Yes, my lord, but..." said Werman as he squirmed in his saddle and pointed in the direction of a weather-worn tavern across from them. "I believe Sir Rhohl might be in there."

"Why do you say that?"

Worm closed his eyes and said, "Sir Kerath told the king that Sir Rhohl was holed up in a tavern in Towerglenn. If I were attempting to hide from someone, I would think such a sad place would be the best spot."

Quite astute, Worm. "When did you overhear this?"

"Last night, my lord, before we left," said Werman. "The king held a private meeting with his Blades."

Private, eh? "A private meeting where you were allowed?"

Werman stared at the ground, unwilling to meet Aldir's eyes.

You keep many secrets, Worm. I will wring them from you one of these days. "Very well, Master Gault. You are excused for now, but a time will come when I may press you for all the secrets you hold."

The young boy's eyes welled with tears.

Gods, boy, collect yourself. Aldir calmed his voice. "I will suss this out. But I am thankful for your help." He hoped his young squire might become less vulnerable before they reached the Vines.

The tavern must have been there for a hundred years or more. The wooden boards on its outer walls were so beaten by salty air and mist they had become almost black—except for the thick white coat of seabird droppings that spattered the surface like melting stars. Orange light danced through broken windows and landed on the planks of raised decking.

Aldir tied off his horse outside the shabby inn and helped Werman do the same. He looked up and studied the rotting sign that hung limply from one of two rusted chains. Painted upon the sign in faded red letters—which he had to squint to see—were the words, 'The Rising Tide.'

Lovely place, Rhohl. I'm certain the men in here will be overjoyed to host the Primacy. He shook his head and glared down at Werman. "Stay with the horses, Worm. This is no place for a boy." *This is no place for me either.* "I will not be long…"

Werman nodded and gave no fight. It was obvious to Aldir that the boy held no desire to enter the tavern. Neither did he.

From outside, Aldir heard shouts and curses. He pulled his cloak around him, hoping to disguise the heraldry emblazoned upon his chest. *My tunic is worth more than these folks might earn in a year.* With that thought swirling in his head, he entered the Rising Tide. He lowered his head and attempted to squeeze past three men who stood with their backs to the entrance. As he tried to wriggle past them, he accidentally hit one with his shoulder.

The man snapped around and bellowed, "Aye! Mind yer bloody self!"

Gods—there goes my quiet arrival.

The other two turned around and glowered at him. Both had faces like carved mastheads and deep-set eyes, that, if not completely black, were close enough. Their hair was a bright orange, a reflection of the fire that burned in an open pit in the center of the tavern. One of the brawny men wore a shaggy red beard, but other than that distinction, they were near identical. They stood shoulder to shoulder and blocked Aldir, studying him as though a man not covered in sweat and filth was a curiosity.

The bearded man pinched Aldir's cloak. "What's a Spire-ight doing 'ere after dark?"

"You're a long way from the 'all 'o Glory!" added the other, sneering.

"I am…" *The Primacy of the Realm*, he wanted to say, but at that moment another man stepped from behind these burly guards.

"Lost," the new man said. "Poor fella must've wandered off ole Windsong's ship. Don't you lads be giving him no grief, ya hear me?" He pulled at their shoulders and separated them. "Don't go scaring off our friends from the Vines now."

"He's wearing green and red like the Graymeres, Stav! He ain't no bloke from the Vines," the man Aldir had collided with a moment ago snapped.

"He's a bloke from the Vines if I say he is. You understand me, Sam." The man rounded on the three and said, "Get yer arses back to the game and stop blocking my doorway. I'm running a 'stablishment 'ere. It ain't no help to me if you three bastards terrorize everyone who walks in 'ere."

The red-bearded man snorted and spat on the floor. "He shoved right into Sam. This the kind o' people ya want in the Tide?"

"Mayhap I shove ya three troublemaker's outta 'ere? This gent might actually spend some coin."

All three men laughed and plodded away, but before they passed beyond hearing, the clean-shaven twin shouted over his shoulder, "Best mind where ya walk, fella. Not everyone 'ere is as decent as my brothers and I."

The man who interceded waved off the threat and bowed slightly. "My lord," he whispered. "Many apologies for my patrons, but they're not as bad as they seem. They ain't any more dangerous than a bloody seagull; twice as annoying, mind ya, but no more dangerous." He smiled and introduced himself.

"Stavron Glade, at yer service, my lord. And I welcome ya to the Rising Tide."

Aldir took a step back and bowed his head. "Thank you, Master Glade. I'm not certain I could have taken all three of them."

"Ah! They would've started crying for their mum if ya popped one o' them in the nose, my lord." Stavron laughed, and it was a hearty sound. "Specially if our friend came out ta help ya."

Our friend?

He studied Stavron's face.

The man was older—in his sixties, thought Aldir. Wrinkled from ear to ear. The wrinkles were healthy, though, possibly etched from years of laughter. His eyes were a bright green and brown, which reminded Aldir of the highlands he'd just come from. Stavron was not tall, but he carried himself in a way that might command whatever room he found himself in.

"Who is our friend?" asked Aldir. "And why did you tell those men I am from the Vines?"

"Ha," laughed Stavron. The sound was warm and made Aldir smile. "My lord, I've been 'ere damn near forty years now. Had my share o' lords and ladies pass through. Ain't take much to realize when one is 'ere for their own purposes, if ya get me?" He winked and the folds around his eyes creased into a map of a thousand intricate roads.

"Now take no disrespect, but when a lord ain't 'ere for some *personal* reason, they wear their colors and symbols like a flag, ya see. It's the ones like you—if ya don't mind—who cover themselves up as best they can… Well, they're the ones needing my help. Ain't no disrespect now, ya see?"

He would do well in the capital. Aldir smiled and said, "No disrespect, Master Glade. You seem to have the right of it." He lowered his shoulders and breathed in deeply. The stench of dead fish and human odor was no longer stinging his nostrils. "But you said, *our friend*—who do you speak of?"

"Why the Shield o' the Prince, my lord," whispered Stavron. "Been 'ere since yesterday. I don't think I'm wrong in thinking you and he know each other—what with both being part o' the royal family and all."

Fair assumption. "But…he's—"

"Ah yes! He's a rather big bloke, ain't he." Stavron laughed again and gestured behind the bar. "He asked to stay out o' sight, if ya get my meaning?"

"Would you take me to him?"

"O' course, my lord. Stavron Glade ain't nothing if he ain't loyal to the Graymeres."

He ushered Aldir past dirty mugs and drained barrels of

ale. The attentions of the other patrons were fixed on a rather exciting game of *Bloodied Queen* being played by two swarthy men in the far corner of the tavern. Even the red-headed twins dared not take their eyes from the cards now dealt in front of the competitors.

At least my new friends seem to have forgotten about me. He glanced over at the game. *I wonder which one will walk out with all of their fingers.*

The door behind the bar opened, revealing a conspicuously large room. *If a brocken were to desire a place to hide, this would be it,* thought Aldir. *But how could Worm know he'd be in here?*

"Glade!" a rough voice bellowed from behind a shaded archway. "I told you not to disturb me."

"Pardons, sir," said Stavron, "but I only thought, well, this being the Primacy and all—"

"Primacy?" A colossal man stepped out from the shadows.

Sir Rhohl, the Shield of the Prince, stood over twelve-feet tall and wore steel plate the way some men wore linen nightclothes. His ebony face, framed by white whiskers, turned from a frightening grimace into a glowing smile in a breath. He plodded forward and knelt before Aldir. Though he lowered himself to one knee, he still towered over Stavron and the Primacy.

"My lord, what are you doing here?" When Sir Rhohl spoke, the ancient wood walls vibrated. "Shouldn't you be celebrating your father's tourney?"

Stavron Glade bowed to both men. "I still got business to attend to, and no game o' *Bloodied Queen* ever ends without a little spilled blood, eh?" He made a quick apology and left the two men to their conversation.

"Rhohl!" said Aldir as he reached out to shake the kneeling giant's hand. "Gods! It's good to see you."

"Better to see you, Al," said Rhohl. He got to his feet and lifted Aldir in a massive embrace. "How do you find yourself in the Tide of all places?"

Always slightly embarrassed when Rhohl lifted him from the ground like a child's toy, Aldir nearly wept. *Why are you here? Why are you not with Odain?* His eyes reddened as he fought back tears. "Rhohl…it's all falling apart."

"Al," said Rhohl, placing his massive hand on Aldir's shoulder in an attempt to comfort him. "What is falling apart?"

He doesn't know anything. Gods, I'm going to have to relive it all. "Is there wine?"

"Plenty," said Rhohl. "Just a moment." He stamped back behind the archway and returned a few seconds later with two handfuls of various bottles.

"Reds, whites, or ales?" he asked. "If I remember, you're partial to red."

Good man, thought Aldir. "Yes, let's open one of them."

"Only one?" Rhohl smirked.

"Ha!" said Aldir, forcing the laugh. "I will start with one but might as well open a few more. Best to let them breathe." There was no way he'd be able to keep up with the brocken's appetite for wine. He remembered an evening he, Rhohl, and Odain had shared when they'd nearly emptied the stores of Dartsuil's Keep. The Shield of the Prince had drunk four bottles for everyone Aldir and his brother had shared. It was a miracle that any of them had survived that night. Aldir grinned at the memory.

An hour passed, and more than five bottles had been emptied. Aldir told Rhohl all that had transpired—making certain to avoid any mention of Rhen being the one to kill the knight. There was no need to anger Rhohl, not when he needed him to sail with him. If he were to tell him that his son had been taken prisoner by his own people, the Shield of the Prince would fly into a rage and rush back to Rothspire. Instead, Aldir finished his story with the scrappers' riot and Edlen's injury.

Rhohl stared on in quiet disbelief at this litany of problems. His response to each tragedy was to open another bottle of wine. A quake of a burp erupted from him, and he gazed off blankly, a scowl of utter bewilderment etched into his face. "You are certain the legs belonged to Odain?"

"I believe it true," answered Aldir. "One of Archwood's rovers, a tanner, questioned their authenticity—but I assure you, they are no forgery."

"A forgery? Why would the tanner assume this?"

"For that, I have no answer. It is possible the poor rover wished he never found them. Would you be willing to suggest regicide? Perhaps he desired not to be a part of the affair?"

"Interesting," said Rhohl. "You inspected the boots?"

The putrid scent of festering flesh arose from somewhere in Aldir's memory. He would rather never think of them again.

"As well as I might. I've worn the same leathers for more years than I can count. Trust me when I tell you…they were a Graymere's."

"But you did not touch them? You did not bring them to the cordwainer? How can you be certain they are not a forgery?"

Gods, Rhohl! Why are you fixated on this detail? "No, we

did not. But what does that matter? My father and I both agree they belong to Odain."

"I do not mean to imply you did not do your duty, my lord, but," said Rhohl, taking another swig of his wine, "as soon as you mentioned the boots, well, I...I remembered something rather unusual."

"And what might this be?"

Rhohl lowered his head as though ashamed. "When your brother and I arrived in Bowbreaker Bay, Lucien Penfield escorted us to his manse. In his carriage, well... There was a man in Penfield's service who shined Odain's boots. Some servant of Lucien's—a ruddy little fellow—who spent the entire ride fixed on his task."

"It is not strange for a lord receiving the prince to offer such pleasantries," said Aldir.

"We did not think it queer either. But since you say the boots might be a forgery—the more I think on it, the more I question the intention of this courtesy." Rhohl wiped at his lips. "A two-hour ride from the port to Penfield's manor, and this shiner never lifted his head, never said a word. That alone is strange, is it not? I have traveled the whole of Onyris with your brother and not once have I met a bootblack who did not fancy himself a master of gossip, or at the least, a failed poet."

"What did he look like?" asked Aldir.

Rhohl laughed. "Gods, Al. They all look the same, don't they?" He smiled and poured another flagon.

"Wiry, dressed in gray, balding...red hair." Another burst of his laughter echoed in the room. "But if we're being honest, *all of you* look the same to me!"

"Do we now?" asked Aldir with a grin.

He reached over and lifted the last bottle of red. The description of the shiner lingered in Aldir's mind. "Did the man wear an odd sigil?"

"A bootblack, Al. Why would he wear a sigil?"

A thin man with red hair dressed in gray? Is it possible? Aldir lifted the wine and savored the vintage. *No, it could not be.*

"No reason," he said. "Are you supposing this shiner studied Odain's boots?"

Rhohl sighed, a queer glint in his eyes. "It is most likely nothing. Not a tanner nor cobbler in the Wide-World—not even your cordwain—might possess the skill to recreate the pattern on a Graymere's boot from memory. Pretend I didn't mention it." He leaned back on his stool and sighed. "This is why you've come to Towerglenn, is it not? You suppose I played a part in your brother's misfortune."

Astonished by the accusation, Aldir nearly fell from his seat. Was it surprise at Rhohl's frank question…or the wine? He could not be certain.

"Not at all," he said as he regained his balance. "I am to sail to the Vines, Rhohl, and you are to come with me."

Clearly relieved by Aldir's unflagging trust, Rhohl chuckled, a throaty sound that threatened to raze the Rising Tide. "To find your brother? Or his killer?"

"To find the Prince of Onyris," answered Aldir. "Or to bring woe upon our enemies."

"Your balls are bigger than mine." Rhohl smiled, the creases of his face blending into an onyx canvas of relief. Or was it worry? His voice dropped to a hush.

"That bloody place is a den of vipers, make no mistake. Your brother changed once we landed. I won't be a part of that again. Not with you."

"What happened over there, Rhohl?" Aldir grew grim. "Why are you here and he is—"

"Not?" Rhohl tapped his gargantuan foot on the wooden floor.

"He turned on me, Al. Thirty-odd years of loyalty, and he turned on me." Rhohl clenched his massive fists. "Dismissed…was the word he used. Dismissed." He stared wildly. Drink or anger, Aldir could not tell.

"Can you believe it? The little prat *dismissed* me from his service." Rhohl's bulky hand landed on his thigh. "The Shield of the Prince…and I was *dismissed!*"

A scream echoed from the main hall of the Rising Tide, followed by a chorus of shouts and curses.

The Bloodied Queen takes her due.

Chapter

DARRIN

The Greathouse of Straten

Daybreak came and found Darrin packing a fresh palomino charger. He shoved dried meats and nuts into a leather satchel attached to its simple saddle. The horse appeared healthy and stout—a small grace. He would not have to contend with a lame or sickly beast on their return journey.

Haron fed and watered his blood bay destrier. "Ya look outta sorts, lad. Things didn't go well yesterday, I gather?"

Darrin was in no mood to jest. "They went."

"Ha!" bellowed Haron. "They went?"

He strode forward and patted Darrin on the back. "I'll leave it alone. Best raise yer spirits before Archwood arrives. Ain't no fun riding long miles with a sullen lil' twit."

Haron's humor did nothing to lighten his spirit.

The two-day journey to Straten was uneventful; Darrin rode most of it with his head down and answered questions only when directly addressed. The ride held none of the excitement that had filled him when they first entered Rothspire. Even the Great Wheel—the grand hub of commerce and frivolity—offered him nothing but aggravation and a pervasive sense of wasting daylight.

Kayvold forced a halt as they rode through the circling roads and crush of people. But Darrin insisted he would tend to the horses while the three men—Lord-Overseer Archwood, Haron, and Laustair—entered a tavern and spent what he believed to be far too long drinking and carousing.

Haron was in unusually high spirits as they rode on from the tavern. His voice—gravelly and gruff—sang a song Darrin had never heard:

Though I ain't heard her voice
In twenty nights to pass
I close my eyes and wonder
If my hand ain't me new lass

Darrin smiled for the first time since leaving the stable of Rothspire, but the moment his chief caught his eye, he dropped his head and stared dismally at the uneven cobblestones sprawled out before him.

Can't we just get this over with?

They set up camp on a flat ridge of the Donwar Mountains and made a small fire once night drew close. Darrin sat some distance from the flames and gnawed on a hunk of dried meat. His frustration with Kayvold's orders remained unabated.

Though the others acted as though nothing was amiss, Laustair glanced over at Darrin occasionally, a shadow of grief hidden somewhere deep within his eyes.

The Lord-Overseer issued first watch, and Darrin leapt at the opportunity to take it. He longed for the lonely task; his desire to sit in complete quiet—away from the others—might be the only solace he could get on this miserable trek.

As Kayvold and Haron rested their heads against their bundles and drifted to sleep, Darrin turned his back to the fire and stared out at the black sky.

"You have been awfully quiet, my boy," a voice muttered nearby.

Darrin spun and grabbed the hilt of his sword.

"No need for that," said Laustair, finding a large rock to sit against. "Do you mind if I join you?"

Yes, I mind. Go away, old man. "If you choose to," he said.

"A gracious host." Laustair pulled a pipe from his pocket and lit the bowl. The scent was sweet and comforting, somehow removing the chill from the night air.

Darrin shifted his gaze and turned his body from his unwanted guest.

"Your vexation is not unfounded, my boy," said Laustair.

Stop calling me 'your boy.' I am a rover.

"You are a rover, Master Cantlay. Of that I am certain."

What? Did you?

"Yes. I apologize if it seems uncouth, but in this darkness—well, I find it rather difficult to tell if you spoke aloud or…"

"Have you been able to do that this whole time?" asked Darrin.

"Yes and no," answered Laustair. "You see, voices are often a jumble that I find no interest in discerning, but given you and I are the only ones awake, your voice becomes much clearer."

"Can you stop it?" Darrin's question was double-sided. Laustair's skill amazed him, but he also felt naked and vulnerable.

"I ignore them at times, much as you might ignore crickets or wind. But to stop it? I am afraid that is beyond my abilities."

Darrin twisted around to face the old man, the light from the fire just enough to make him visible. A sadness washed over him. His thoughts became unintelligible as he listened to the nightly music of the mountains. "Perhaps I have been unjust in my accusations."

"Ha." Laustair inhaled a heavy plume of smoke and breathed it out in a myriad of shapes. "Perhaps—perhaps not." He stretched his legs out and crossed one over the other. "You are unlike most men I have met, Master Cantlay. There is a fire within your soul. You struggle between what is moral and what is expected. Most men choose one or the other. It is possible they also struggle, but none I have met bounce so effortlessly between the two. Tell me: What is it you want most from the life granted to you?"

"To do what is right," Darrin said without thinking.

This had never been a question for him. His father had taught him that morality was the gift of the Gods—the very thing that separated man from animal.

"Ah...I see," said Laustair. "But what is right, when all that is left is wrong?"

"I don't understand the question."

Again, the old man puffed at his pipe. "How do you decide you have made a correct choice when both options given will surely end in disaster?"

Darrin tapped his fingers against the dirt and gazed back into the night sky. "I would hope I choose the least of disasters."

Sparks erupted from the fire as a thick log guttered out and fell amongst the remaining kindling.

"I need to tend to the wood," said Darrin.

"Do you?"

A blaze roared from the campfire. Bright red and yellow fangs snapped at the black sky. It was as though he had stoked it with fresh logs and kindling.

"How do you do that?" Darrin asked.

Laustair smiled, his face glowing in the newly lit flames. "You know how." He handed his pipe over and nodded. "It will set you at ease."

Darrin inspected the pipe and timidly placed the tip against his lips. He drew in his breath and allowed the smoke to fill his lungs. He coughed harshly; his eyes watered, but he took another draw. This time, though, his mind cleared and his body relaxed. He handed the pipe back to Laustair and thanked him.

"As we were discussing, Master Cantlay—"

"You can call me, Darrin." He smiled. The anger and frustration that had coursed through his veins earlier—like a bowstring pulled taut enough to snap—had vanished. He felt as though he sat across from a friend. "Please, my father is Master Cantlay." He grinned.

"Well...Darrin," said Laustair, returning the smile, "is not the least of disasters still a disaster?"

It is... "It..." Darrin struggled to keep his eyes open. "Is."

STRATEN appeared different to Darrin as they rode towards the Greathouse. When they'd travelled through this realm five days ago, it had been empty, with only a handful of people there to greet them. How much it had changed in so little time.

At that time, they'd stayed only a few hours before sleep and even less than that as they'd readied their horses in the morning. Lord-Overseer Archwood had insisted that they stay at an inn instead of the Greathouse. But now that Darrin beheld the luxury they'd avoided their first time around, he wondered why Kayvold withheld this majesty from him.

The Greathouse of Straten did not come by its name lightly. More than great, this house was a castle. Enormous, almost absurd. A sprawling structure of intricate workmanship nearly five stories tall. Built of every wood that might be found in the forest, the Greathouse was a marvel to the eye.

A gargantuan oak tree grew in the center of the house and exploded from the roof, its immense branches reaching far beyond the roofline. If Dartsuil's Keep was the largest building Darrin had ever set his gaze upon, the Greathouse of Straten was the most beautiful.

Dozens of servants rushed in and out of the magnificent structure through enormous rosewood doors, each carrying trays of varied size. A feast was most assuredly underway. And by the commotion, this was a feast of unparalleled extravagance.

"Mind your tongue," said Haron as they rode towards the impressive doors of the Greathouse. "Lord Brastor Archwood is a prickly twat. And he ain't gonna be overjoyed ole Kayvold is bringing his rascals with 'im."

This is the Lord Archwood I watched leave Rothspire? He had more people in his retinue than the entirety of Redrun!

"Aye..." said Darrin, absentmindedly.

"Aye is right," said Haron as he dismounted. "And don't ya speak up unless asked, d'ya get me?"

"Aye."

A vast room opened before him, its walls made up of shimmering silver birch and brilliant golden oak. Hearths and braziers littered the space, and from the looks of it, they'd never been extinguished. Thick black clouds of smoke billowed overhead and escaped through slanted slats in the roof. Centuries of smoke had left a coat of black tar that oozed from the ceiling.

Underneath the pitch, a crowd of hundreds frolicked to the raucous music: harp, drum, flute, and fiddle played a rendition of, *O'er the Mists of Midnight.*

All those not swaying or dancing to the tune busied themselves with the splendid food and drink served by countless servants. Unlike the somber feasting hall of Dartsuil's Keep, this banquet was the liveliest affair Darrin had ever beheld. He spied roast mutton, flame-broiled chicken, whole-cooked pheasant, an entire hog turning on a spit, and vegetables of every color imaginable. Ale spilled from barrels into mugs and landed on the rushes. Wine splashed about as guests clinked goblets to each other's health. The laughter in the Greathouse rivaled the music.

Lord Brastor Archwood presided over the entire event from the center of a stupendously long table. Flanked on either side by two men who must surely be his sons, the Lord of Straten bobbed drunkenly in his seat and waved his tremendous arms about. He only stopped this obscene dance to drink from an impressive goblet and shout orders to those near enough to obey.

Dazzled by the opulence of Straten's celebration, Darrin barely noticed his chief's elbow when it jammed into his side.

Though he could not hear Haron's voice, he slowly realized what the gruff old man was attempting to make him notice.

Brastor had noted their entrance and now hailed them to his prodigious table.

The four travelers must have been rather conspicuous.

Lord-Overseer Archwood's finery, the two rovers in their stained uniforms, and the bent old man, Laustair, shambling behind them in ancient gray robes—what a comical sight they presented.

The Lord-Overseer led them forward and bowed to the Lord of Straten.

Music faded, and the only sound left was that of the ribald talk and jests of the assembled. Brastor Archwood stood and greeted his uninvited guests.

"Welcome, brother!"

Darrin kept his head bowed but caught Laustair's eyes; they shared a smile.

"To what do we owe the pleasure?" asked Brastor. "The Lord-Overseer of the Eyes of the Forest comes forth with his louts and..." He stared at Laustair. "Is that our fair Primacy's father-in-law? Why yes! The same who taught our Primacy his *grace* and *wisdom*." He laughed, his voice a terrible snarl of contempt and arrogance. "Straten is fortunate to host such noble company." Brastor slapped the backs of both his sons and then gestured for them to stand as well.

"It has been long years, brother, but I hope you might still recognize your nephews." He dropped a fat hand on the shoulder of the man to his left and said, "Do you remember Hovaird? He's grown into quite an impressive man, wouldn't you say? Took the King's Tournament from a brocken—did you know that?" He glared in the direction of Laustair. "Only our splendid Primacy can't find the time to acknowledge this. But Lord Aldir's gratitude is difficult to come by. Never mind that now. Sit, boys, sit."

The two men sat. Brastor's neglect in introducing the youngest of his sons was not lost on Darrin.

"Never could I forget my nephews, brother," Kayvold

said. "Hovaird's achievements are legendary, and Jacken..." He studied the other man for a moment. "Well, you've come into your own, haven't you? The Eyes are always searching for new talent. Perhaps your father might finally allow you to join our ranks."

A drum beat out an excited rhythm, and the other musicians followed with matched enthusiasm. The guests in the hall reprised their earlier frivolity and soon the din of music drowned out all other voices.

Lord Brastor glared at his brother but reluctantly invited him and his companions to sit.

Darrin glanced around the room and took in the sights and sounds of the celebration. Amazed by what he saw but worried about their current situation, he pulled at his chief's cloak. "What are we doing here?"

"It's Archwood's game, lad. I ain't got a clue." Haron was clearly annoyed.

Archwood's game? Which Archwood? Darrin grabbed at a tray of greasy pork and potatoes and did his best to busy himself with food and drink. If this was between his Lord-Overseer and his brother, he cared not to be a part of it.

"Boy!" Brastor leaned over the table and called to Darrin. "What's your name, boy?"

I guess I am a part of it now. "Darrin Cantlay of Redrun, my lord." He had to shout over the pounding drums and screeching fiddle.

"Cantlay, eh?" asked Brastor as pieces of pork flew from his mouth. "Philip Cantlay's boy, am I right?"

"Yes, my lord."

"Good man, Lord Cantlay," said Brastor. He turned to Hovaird and grinned. "Have I ever told you of the time Lord

Cantlay stayed with us?" He burst out laughing and then eyed Darrin. "Your father is a decent man. A bit of a scamp in his youth but decent, nonetheless. Has your old man told you any stories of me?"

The only story his father had ever told him of Lord Brastor Archwood was the same told by the whole of Onyris. In the year of Robart Moorcroft's rebellion, the army of the Shaded Realm had marched towards Rothspire and Prince Ulisaren rode to meet them with a host of knights. At the time, Sir Brastor was regarded as perhaps the finest knight in all Onyris, yet he'd broken rank from the prince and charged headlong into the advancing army.

The battle that ensued—now known as the Battle of Daggerpoint—had lasted less than ten minutes. The mighty Sir Brastor, heedless of his prince's commands, had rushed forth and slain ten men in ten seconds and severed the arm of Robart Moorcroft's son, Dysternis. At that, the army of the Shaded Realm had given way around him, and he'd carried the limb of his victim back to Prince Ulisaren.

This, at least, was the story the people of the realm told. True or not, Darrin had never inquired to find out.

"Yes, my lord," Darrin shouted over the music. "He's told me much of your prowess in war and your bravery at the Battle of Daggerpoint."

Haron kicked him beneath the table and stifled a laugh.

"Very well he should have!" said Brastor. "Glad to have his boy at my table. You are welcome in Straten any time. A boy of fine stock, I'm certain you are."

Yes...if blatant flattery is what passes for nobility, then I most assuredly come from the finest stock.

The feast continued in this manner for some time, with

Brastor barking questions at all who sat in earshot. The music blasted or receded throughout the night, and the food never seemed to stop coming. Most of the men at the table had drunk themselves into a stupor, except the four travelers and Brastor's sons.

Though neither man said much during the festivities, Darrin studied their behavior.

Hovaird Archwood was a true knight. His hair—coiffed and luxurious—was trimmed short so as to never fall in front of his eyes. His face was knightly, stern and resolute. He smiled when the occasion called for it but, other than that, he kept a measured look of respectability. His posture was excellent, and he sat upright, only tasting the wine in front of him and never drinking more than one or two servings. He ate his food with the impeccable grace of a high lord.

The other son, Jacken, though less muscular than his brother, was no less knightly. He had the same sharp features and striking eyes as Hovaird, but without the pretense. Jacken had a natural presence—congenial and outgoing. He was nowhere near as stiff as Brastor's eldest, and it seemed to Darrin that he enjoyed the conversations he was in; they were not simply a duty to be carried out.

Several hours passed, and by that time, most of the guests had wandered drunkenly from the Greathouse, leaving only a few stragglers to plunder what little food remained. The musicians had departed some time ago, and the enormity of the room only grew in the absence of their chords and melodies.

Darrin glanced around and realized that they and the Archwoods were the only ones who remained. Surely it must be time to retire? If they were to head back to Elmfort in the morning, the Lord-Overseer would want them to get as much rest as possible. As he thought this, Kayvold's raised voice pulled him from this belief.

"That is not the case!" said Kayvold. "You have done nothing for the Eyes!"

"Nothing?" Brastor rose from his seat. "Who provided your precious Eyes with weapons and armor?"

"Rusted iron and rotten leathers—what a grand gesture! And even then it was only by the king's orders!"

"Ingratitude, like always." Brastor glared at Kayvold and then smiled at his sons. "I supply your blighters from my own armory, and you have the gall to complain? And to question my integrity as well. The king's orders contained the right of refusal…were you aware of that? I would say not."

"Oh! I am to be thankful you did not refuse to arm the men who protect your realm?"

"Protect our realm?" barked Brastor. "You play soldier and sleep in trees. The Eyes of the Forest cart deadwood to-and-fro and call that protection. It is the army of Straten that protects Rothspire. It is the forest itself that protects the realm. It is me who protects the realm."

"You?" Now it was time for Kayvold to laugh. "And what, dear brother, do you protect the realm from, eh? Perhaps you protect the people of Pleasant Hill from having any food by eating it all yourself!"

Darrin lowered his eyes and tugged at a loose thread on his doublet. He should not be present as these two exchanged barbs. He glanced up surreptitiously and noticed that Brastor's sons acted as though this was commonplace. Their vacant stares did nothing to set him at ease.

Brastor seethed and slammed his goblet to the floor. It

shattered, spilling wine across the rushes. Flustered, he glared at Kayvold and, without saying another word, stormed from the hall.

A palpable tension filled the room. After a long moment of silence, Hovaird stood.

"Uncle, we are pleased to host you and your men, but the night grows long, and it is best we all turn in. I will see that you are put up in our finest rooms."

"Now, now Hovaird," said Jacken, not rising from his seat. "Let our father fight his own battles. He is the mighty Brastor, is he not? I am certain he will return. Perhaps he and Uncle will close the evening with a duel." A sly smile appeared on his lips.

"Your jests are in poor taste, Jacken," said Hovaird.

"I suppose you wish to fight Uncle then? Father will be so proud."

Gods! Do any of these men care for each other? This must be why Archwood never speaks of his family.

Kayvold rose and addressed Hovaird. "Your courtesy is appreciated Hovaird, but the Lord of Straten has made his desires abundantly clear. I will take my men and ride for Elmfort. We are no strangers to *sleeping in trees*."

A CHILL crept into Darrin's bones as they rode swiftly across the open plains before the entrance of Nauringale Forest. He pulled his cloak tight and thought of warm fires and a cozy bed. Four hours had passed since they'd left the Greathouse of Straten, and the longer they rode, the more likely it was that the Lord-Overseer was not jesting about sleeping in trees.

At this pace, they would reach Elmfort before dawn, but he worried their horses might collapse if they did not rest soon.

The dense tree line of the forest appeared over a ridge: a black wall looming sinisterly in the distance set against the silver night sky.

"We stop at the archway of the forest," Kayvold said, his voice echoing in the vast expanse of open field. "Get what rest you might, but until then…"

Darrin galloped towards the black wall. Far in the distance, stretching out high above the trees, a dark cloud filled the sky.

CHAPTER 22

RHEN

The King You Are Meant to Be

"Parry, boy!"

A short sword flashed in front of Rhen's face. He stepped back, narrowly avoiding the strike. *That one almost took my nose off.*

"Parry! Don't step away. Your back leg is weaker than a tittering lass," said Belo. The disfigured man did not relent in his attack. He slashed once again. This time, though, his blade met Rhen's violent counter.

"Better, but you used your edge. You must always use the flat or your steel will be useless." Belo lowered the tip of his sword and huffed. "Enough for now. You have much to learn."

Rhen had only rested for a few hours during the night. After his dinner with Byron Windsong, he'd been told that his training would begin in the morning. His captors had tended his wound, and though the poultice they'd used had stung terribly, when he'd awoken, the gash in his arm had closed and scabbed over. Belo had muttered something about special herbs from Rojiir. Rhen cared not where the herbs originated, though he was relieved to no longer wince in pain every time he moved his arm.

"Lord Byron is impressed with your strength, lad—which I must admit is damn difficult to withstand—but you wield a sword like a touched toddler." Belo sat on a bench against the wall in the hull of the ship. "No wonder the Archwood boy bested you."

"He is a knight!" said Rhen. "He's been trained by the greatest swordsmen in Rothspire."

"Bah to your knights," huffed Belo. "And bah to your Rothspire. Those men fight as though their opponents are bloody trees. They hack and slash with no thought to the art of the discipline." He wiped his blade down with an oily rag. "If you are to compete in Lord Nekkin's tournament, you must learn the proper way to fight. And there is very little time to teach you."

They'd started their training after an early breakfast, and after four hours of constant battle, this was the first time Belo had said more than *parry*, *thrust*, *block*, or *dodge*.

Rhen grabbed one of the rags and oiled his sword, just as Belo did. He looked up and said, "Lord Byron did not tell me of any tournament."

Belo finished applying the oil and stared at Rhen. He lowered his voice and said, "Lord Byron will tell you only what you need to know. He has left you in my charge and given me *my* orders. If he chooses not to speak of the tournament, his reasons are his own; regardless, your skills must be improved."

Those were the last words shared between Rhen and his trainer before they resumed his instruction.

Hours passed, filled with one-word shouts and grunts. Live steel sparked and the ship swayed beneath their feet.

Over and anon the two met—metal on metal singing in the vast hull. Rhen's arm throbbed and his legs grew weak, but Belo never tired. The more vulnerable Rhen became, the harder his aggressor pressed him, forcing him to find a wellspring of energy.

"Enough!" cried Rhen. "I'm going to collapse."

"Collapse with your sword held up, boy!"

Gods! He means to kill me.

Rhen gripped the hilt of his sword and roared. He strode forward, blade held in a window guard, and thrust the point with all of his might. Belo blocked the attack and sent Rhen's sword flying from his hands. He twirled the edge of his steel around and stopped his thrust only a hair's breadth from Rhen's face.

"Tomorrow, we condition," said Belo, a hint of disappointment in his voice. "Your breath is dismal. I expected more from a brocken."

Belo reached out and helped Rhen stand. He sheathed his sword and placed it against the wall. Without saying another word, he departed. A gentle wail of rusted hinges creaked out from the stairs, and the dim thud of Belo's boots patted away. Though muffled, Rhen heard the recognizable clink of a heavy iron lock.

Once his one-eyed friend was gone, Rhen shouted, "I didn't ask for this!"

He bent his head and brought his breath under control. His lungs burned, his heart beat rapidly, and his fingers were numb. "I didn't ask for any of this," he said again in a whisper.

He was a prisoner. It mattered not what name Byron Windsong gave it. He was being held captive in the hull of this ship against his will and forced to duel with a man who might kill him at any time. Once again, his thoughts turned to Edlen. *Where are you? Are the King's Blades on their way to save me? Does anyone even know I am gone?*

If the daughter of the Primacy had been abducted, there would certainly be a force of men searching for her. But a brocken—why would the king care?

Yes, the Graymeres might pretend to love him and his father, but when put to test, they were men. The same who wished to eradicate his kind from the Wide-World.

Perhaps Lord Byron was correct? Perhaps Sir Hugh Castac was just the symptom? The disease was the Graymeres.

Did Edlen actually care about him?

She says the words...but... She was not there when he needed her. Edlen was not there when Patrik Lindon—the Adept of *Law*—told him that the Graymeres made mandates to restrict his kind from being a true member of his own family.

My family? Who is my family? My mother was one of you, and you knew she would die giving birth to me, but you called it an honor. Oh yes, you said it was the highest honor, but death is death—what honor is that?

It is you, Oh! Lords of Onyris, who would sacrifice one of your own race in order to breed my line...in order to diminish the brocken...in order to turn us into...you.

Rhen stumbled to an enormous chair and fell into its soft cushions. Three bottles of wine sat unopened before him. He pulled out the golden dirk Lord Byron had gifted him and uncorked one of the reds.

The first is for pleasure.

He tilted back the drink and gulped. Red liquid drizzled down his chin, and he exhaled loudly.

The faint snap of a lock being unclasped echoed above, followed by a groaning screech of rusted hinges.

Rhen snapped his head to his left and squinted through the dark opening to the hull.

The familiar clack of leather-soled boots clicked against wooden stairs.

Lord Byron Windsong entered. He sniffed at the air. "You have started without me?"

He carried two bottles, and upon his approach, set them on the table next to Rhen. Wasting no time in uncorking one, he said, "For pleasure." He took a sip, and with the bottle still held to his lips, chuckled. "No matter. You are more than allowed to enjoy our grape."

Unsure of how to respond, Rhen merely held his bottle aloft and smiled.

Wasting no time with pleasantries, Lord Byron Windsong said, "Belo tells me you are improving. That is good—very good."

Rhen, having not eaten since this morning, suddenly noticed the effects of the wine. Still angered by his thoughts of the Graymeres, he spoke abruptly. "You have entered me in a tournament?" He glared at Lord Byron.

"Ah, ah…" Byron filled a jeweled goblet with wine and continued. "Third is for truth, my dear boy. We have not even savored our drink." He motioned for Rhen to open his next bottle. Once they both held their next round, he downed the red in one swig and said, "Tell me what you taste."

"It tastes like wine," said Rehn, growing tired of this tradition.

"Master Rhen…" said Lord Byron. "If I cannot trust in your description of our shared drink, how am I to trust anything else you may say?" He placed his goblet on the table and studied Rhen. "I will ask once more. What do you taste?"

Bloody fermented grape. What do you want from me? Bring

me ale and I will talk for hours. He took another sip and swirled it in his mouth.

The memory of his father and Prince Odain sharing a few bottles of Straten Red earlier that year came to him. The terms they bandied about as they got progressively drunker echoed in his head.

Rhen mumbled, "Currant and blackberry with a hint of tobacco."

Byron leaned back in his chair and laughed. "You have just described a red from Straten, my dear boy. Wine from Maresport has no hint of tobacco... Try again."

This is ridiculous. He sipped the wine again, this time sincerely attempting to discern its flavor. A moment passed as the drink sat on his tongue. He focused his thoughts on the taste. Then suddenly he realized why savoring the flavor was so important.

He no longer agonized over his predicament. His mind, now focused purely on the intense tartness in his mouth, thought of nothing but discovering the complexity of flavors dancing across his palate.

Tricky bastards. This is why the second is to savor.

"Cherry and red plum, a subtle taste of cranberry, and aged oak." He marked Lord Byron's smile and asked, "Perhaps the smallest hint of strawberry as well?"

"Astounding!" said Lord Byron. "As I told Belo—you are capable of learning."

What does he mean by that?

"Now, for truth," said Byron as he poured another round. "I did not wish to fill your mind with misplaced worries. Today was meant to be a true test of your abilities, and according to Belo, you have proven quite the apt pupil."

"But there is a tournament?"

Lord Byron sipped at his wine and grabbed a slice of salted pork that still sat on the plate from last night. "I wish Belo had not mentioned it to you, but yes, Lord Nekkin aims to hold a tournament next month, and I have promised him a champion of monstrous proportions."

"Who is Lord Nekkin?" *And why would I care to impress him?*

With a deft hand, Lord Byron filled his goblet and another for Rhen. He inhaled deeply. "Why, Lord Nekkin is the true king of Onyris. The same I mentioned last night. He will replace the Graymeres and their rabble of unworthy successors." A proud smile crossed his face, turning his eyes to slits.

"Lord Nekkin is the student of a Valdryz. He is blessed by the Gods, my dear boy. His will be the rule of All and Naught—he is the *Chosen King*, not a pale memory of greedy conquerors. And it is he you will find yourself in the service of. The brocken will rise under his rule, my boy. You will be made a lord—a lieutenant in the army of the Gods. No longer will your people be subject to the whims and loathing of man. Once you prove yourself in the Arena of Destiny, Lord Nekkin and Malighaunt will give you any realm you desire. You will be counted among the high."

Rhen smiled at the thought. His wine-stained teeth appeared red in the candlelight.

Chapter

EVERLY

After Death

Everly stirred.

Where am I? She rolled to her side and opened one eye. *This is not my bed.* She stroked the sheets against which her face lay and cautiously opened her other eye. Something was wrong. Why was she not in her bed?

Her nightmare had been terrible, but waking to this strange sensation was worse. Once she regained her bearings, she lifted her head and gazed groggily around the room.

It took only a moment for her sight to come into focus, and she recognized the face of her cousin, Sir Willem Thorpe, sitting in a chair pulled beside her.

"Will?" she asked, her voice rough with sleep. "Where am I? What are you doing here?"

"Everly…"

Why does he sound so odd? It was only a nightmare. Am I not allowed even those?

"Everly," he said again, his voice filled with relief. "I thought for a moment we'd lost you." His hand stroked her brow, and there were tears in his eyes.

"Where am I?"

He took her hand and said, "We are in the High Divinator's chamber. You have slept for two days now."

Two days? No, he is wrong.

Before she could respond, her cousin jerked his head and shouted, "Your Glory! She is awake!"

Your Glory? "Willem," she said quietly. "Where is Amara?"

The High Divinator glided forward then knelt painfully over her. The close smell of sage and clover that wafted off of him was somehow both comforting and repellent.

"My dear, we were quite worried. Two days with no food or drink. I was beginning to believe we would lose you as well."

Lose me as well? What do you mean by that? "Where is my daughter?" Everly crept back in the bed to distance herself from the High Divinator's rankness. "Where is Amara?" Her voice became stern. *It was only a dream. It could only be a dream, couldn't it?*

"She is with the Gods, my dear. You need not worry for her anymore."

With the Gods? What is he saying? "No," she said. "You are mistaken. She is in my chamber. And that is where I should be as well."

"Ev…" said Sir Willem. "She… Amara…she is…"

No! Don't you say it. Don't say it. Don't…

"Dead."

Everly backed herself further into the mattress as though she might be able to escape through its feathers. It was not a dream. It was not a nightmare. It was…real?

"No, it can't be. You are all mistaken. You are wrong. You are playing an awful joke. Who would do this? And why would you play along? Willem, why are you playing out this jest?"

"It is no jest, cousin."

The world about Everly grew hazy again, and she struggled to keep her eyes open. *No!* she thought to herself. *I will not close my eyes again. True nightmares exist only when you are awake. I will not be lulled by the dangers of sleep.* Resolute and stiff, she sat up and gazed into her cousin's eyes. "Who must I kill?"

Chapter 24

EDLEN

The Girl in the Walls

Edlen sprang up, her face bathed in sweat. Each breath bit deep into her wounded abdomen. She grunted.

"No!" she screamed, her body trembling. "No! Vairet! Don't!"

A large black dog leapt from her bedside and howled, frightening Edlen. She jerked her head to stare at it. The moment she met the animal's eyes, it ceased its roar and approached her. A long, slobbery tongue drooped from the hound's mouth and lapped her arm.

What?

She reached her hand out and patted the dog's massive head.

Who...who are you?

The shock of waking, along with the sudden appearance of this strange beast, forced Edlen from her frenzied dreams. She pet the dog, scrunching its soft fur between her fingers.

"Good boy," she said.

"She is a female," a familiar voice said.

"What?" Edlen asked, unable to discover the source of the statement.

"She is female—and she would not be parted from you."

Tomm Harken stood over Edlen. He bent over to stroke the dog's muzzle, but it responded with a warning growl. He backed away. "She is quite protective."

"Tomm?" Edlen asked, attempting to understand where she was. Her head was fuzzy with sleep and her eyes had not regained focus. "Tomm, is that you?"

Tomm's body was no more than a soft blur, but as he stooped over the foot of Edlen's bed, his face grew in clarity.

He smiled. "Yes, my lady. I cannot say I have ever been more pleased to see someone wake."

Gods! Edlen winced in pain, her slightest movement agony. She lay her head back down against her pillows and asked, "What happened? Why are you here?"

"Your father asked me to escort you safely to your chamber, my lady," said Tomm. He strode towards the window and tugged at the curtain. "You've suffered a grievous wound. Mayhap playing scrapper proved more dangerous than you believed?"

Playing scrapper?

Edlen looked down and noticed she no longer wore the drab clothing she'd dressed in earlier. Her stomach was naked but for a dark-red gash below her ribs.

Her memory came in flashes: the melee, Rhen, the riot, the tunnels, Vairet, the hidden door, Everly, Vairet again...a blade...and then nothing.

I do not think I was playing anything.

"Where is my aunt?"

Tomm sat in a chair by the window and dragged his hand

across his face. "Much has happened since you last saw your aunt, my lady. None of which should be spoken of until you regain your strength." He fiddled with the edge of his cloak. "It is more than three days since you last ate; I will ask one of the guards to fetch a meal."

More than three days? What are you talking about, Tomm? That is not possible. Perhaps a day, at the most… There is no way I have slept for three days.

But at the mere mention of food, her stomach roiled with emptiness.

"Tomm?" she asked weakly. "What happened? Please tell me she did not hurt Everly." Her eyes swelled with fear.

"Food, my lady. I will tell you everything, but not until you eat."

It was not long before a suitable meal arrived, and Edlen devoured the hot stew. She dipped stale bread into a steaming mixture of beef broth and mushrooms.

This was not to the quality she was accustomed, but as she pulled the last bit of meat between her teeth, Edlen decided she'd never tasted anything quite as exquisite. She looked at the huge dog lying beside her and felt a pang of guilt.

Grabbing remnants of food from her bowl, she lowered them to the appreciative animal.

The dog took them gently in her mouth and carried them to a corner of the room. Her tongue licked at the offering as if it were the grandest treasure she'd ever received.

The meal sat uncomfortably in Edlen's empty stomach. She moved awkwardly in her sheets and attempted to sit up. "Thank you Tomm." She frowned. "Now tell me what is happening."

"There is too much to tell while you are recovering," answered Tomm. "Let it suffice that your accomplice did not harm your aunt. It is a miracle you survived, Edlen—your attacker carried Rojiirin steel. How do you suppose a scrapper from Pleasant Hill got her hands on a blade as precious as that?"

"Where is she?" asked Edlen with a start.

"Lady Everly?" Tomm eyed her. "Or your slippery friend?"

Both. "Everly...of course."

"Your aunt is currently under the care of the High Divinator."

"You said she wasn't hurt," said Edlen, grunting. "Why is she with him?"

Tomm gazed thoughtfully at Edlen. "Perhaps that part of the tale is reserved until you are stronger. I assure you...it is not enjoyable to hear."

He reached over to a kettle on the table and poured himself some tea. "I answered one of your questions, Edlen. Will you not answer mine?"

Is this a game? "Tomm, I know nothing about the girl."

"You know her name." Tomm sipped at his drink. "Please do not lie to me. Our game was fun when we met, but the world is changing" He glared at Edlen, his eyes a searchlight.

"You and I must trust one another. If not... I fear our friendship will come to an end."

What are you saying? "I am not lying to you," Edlen answered in panic. "She gave me her name, but that must have been a lie? She is scrapper; that is all I know."

And she despises the Graymeres. But all of Pleasant Hill does, it seems.

Tomm eyed her suspiciously. "She is wanted by the crown, Edlen. The King's Blades and the city guard are searching for her. If you can recall *anything* about her, it would greatly assist their efforts."

Edlen lowered herself back against her pillows; Tomm was right, she did not possess the strength for conversation.

"I am tired, Tomm. I'm sorry…but I can't remember anything else."

Her stomach hurt terribly, and her body ached. Sleep overtook her as she asked, "Who does the dog belong to?" Edlen's voice trailed off.

"You," answered Tomm. He rose from his seat and placed his hand on Edlen's brow. "She would not leave your side while you were in sacellum. The High Divinator agreed with me that maybe it would be best if she stayed with you for a while." He smiled again. "Many things might have changed if she were with you during the tournament. Alas! The Gods write their stories—and we must but play out our parts." He stroked Edlen's face. "Get rest, my lady. I will bring news to the king that you are awake."

The king? Edlen could no longer fight off her tiredness. *Why not my father?* She closed her eyes and fell into a deep sleep.

Hours passed before Edlen stirred.

A dim silver moon shone into the chamber. She opened her eyes slowly and searched the room. Tomm was gone. Edlen was alone—save for a large black hound. A strange realization dawned upon her.

Though it was night and candles no longer lit the chamber, Edlen could see her room clearly.

She rubbed her eyes until they stung, but the light did not diminish.

Her body no longer ached either. The weariness that had

filled her earlier had vanished. She felt refreshed and ready to leap from her bed.

What is happening?

She stood, and as she did, the dog craned its neck and pricked up its ears, bounding towards Edlen, panting. The moment she reached Edlen, she sat obediently and gazed up, expectantly.

Edlen scratched her head and looked into her lovely-brown eyes. She knelt down and wrapped her arms around the dog's neck. The dog nuzzled her and licked her forehead.

"What am I going to call you?" she asked while petting her.

The dog's massive size made her appear more horse than hound. Edlen stared at her a moment longer before saying, "Larla!"

The dog scratched a hind leg and rolled onto her back, presenting her belly.

"You're a sweet girl, aren't you, Larla?" Edlen continued to pet her.

In the old stories her father had read to her about Sir Matthew Dorne, the Iron Horse had kept two gigantic destriers he might ride into his adventures. Larla and Rew. They were nearly as important as the knight in those tales. Larla, the largest of the two, was all black except for a patch of pure white on her chest. The resemblance to her new friend was uncanny.

A sudden warmth filled Edlen. She sat on the floor and played with Larla, her joy almost enough to forget about the strangeness of her newfound sight.

Edlen stood and gazed about her chamber, noticing something resting at the foot of her bed. She walked towards it.

A book? Her eyes needed no adjustment.

Where did this come from?

Afraid to touch the thing, she peered down and read the title aloud, "*Laws and Decrees of Onyris: Year Fifteen of Graymere Ascendency.*"

Year fifteen? This book is almost five-hundred years old. What is it doing here?

She studied it; the cover was a deep-red leather, the script made of delicately sewn green letters. *Was this the same book of laws that Tomm found?* A scrap of dirty cloth hung between the pages in the center of the book—a marker. If Tomm left this book for her, he meant for her to open to this specific page.

Edlen looked around the room anxiously—she was still alone.

Nervously, she opened to the page marked by the cloth. Though it was surely midnight and she had lit neither torch nor candle, she found no difficulty in reading the text.

The page she opened to was a slog of a read. She skimmed the text twice.

The aged ink, though artfully drawn, spoke only of laws pertaining to royal succession. A paragraph near the end stated:

In the event a lawful succession of power hath attend neither foremost scion nor seed; thou consort shall secure regency in steed. Thus, ministering thy kingdom under rule of proper custody. Such as succession is reserved, said consort may appoint those to cabinet deemed climacteric for preservation of welfare.

The words were gibberish to Edlen, but somehow the detail of the cloth strip proved more important than the whole of the book. She knew this cloth. And as she stared at the rough stitching upon it, she noticed a thin script appear.

Try as she might, she could not discern the scribbled letters. She needed more light. Perhaps if she held the strip over a candle, the fire might reveal some hidden text.

Quietly—unsure of who might be watching or listening—she snuck towards a table and grabbed a half-melted candlestick. As she searched frantically for something to light the wick, she heard footsteps padding from behind the door.

No, no. Go away. Give me a minute, she thought as she attempted to read the book.

Muffled voices broke her concentration. The guards were speaking to someone.

Dammit all.

She bounded across the floor of the chamber. Panicked, she thought, *Where can I hide you?*

The answer came promptly.

The chest.

The voices outside her room stopped—and in one fluid motion, Edlen lifted the top of her chest and stuffed the book inside. But as she looked down, the sparkling mother-of-pearl axe on the cover of her grandfather's tome seemed to wink at her.

Without thinking, she swapped the two volumes and leapt back into her bed. She opened *The Executioner's Lament* just as the door clicked open.

Tomm Harken strode in, stopping as he noted the large book Edlen held. He peered down and laughed, "A little light reading, my lady?"

Edlen glanced up from the page she was pretending to read and greeted Tomm. A sudden fear rose inside of her as she realized she'd left the scrap of fabric sitting on the table beside the unlit candle.

Unlit!

There was no firelight in the room, so how could Tomm believe she might be reading?

It took no time for Tomm to address this simple fact. When the door snapped closed and the chamber plunged back into darkness, Tomm said, "I've always found it difficult to enjoy text—no matter how riveting—when read in the dark." He smirked and sauntered over to the table lighting the candle. "There you go, my lady. Now we may both learn from these pages."

"Thank you," Edlen whispered. *Maybe he won't see it?*

Edlen's luck did not hold.

"What is this?" asked Tomm. He lifted the fabric from the table and held it between his fingers, eyeing the strange designs etched upon it. *"Peculiar…"*

The way he said it made Edlen's skin crawl.

"What?" asked Edlen.

If she acted dumb, perhaps Tomm might not think anything of it.

But Tomm held the strip of cloth over the candle and frowned. "Quite strange," he said more to himself than to Edlen. "Quite strange indeed."

Unsure of what Tomm meant, Edlen closed her book and leaned forward. "What do you have there, Tomm?"

I will continue to play ignorant.

"I was hoping you might tell me," Tomm asked suspiciously.

"Can I see it?"

"Certainly, my lady," answered Tomm. He handed it to Edlen then sat on the edge of the mattress.

Larla lifted up her head and slowly got to her feet. She growled lightly, but even a light growl from her was deep and threatening.

Tomm stood at once, backing away from Edlen's bed. "Your friend doesn't seem to care for me." His tone attempted to hide his unease.

Why is that, Tomm? Perhaps Larla sensed something in Tomm that she had missed.

"Heel," said Edlen. That was a command she'd heard the kennel-masters use.

The imposing black hound stopped her deep-throated warning but continued her approach. She stalked past Tomm and stood between them, her lips pulled back in a snarl that exposed a mouth of ivory daggers.

"Heel, girl," Edlen commanded again.

Larla sat upon her haunches. She turned her attention to Edlen and lapped a thick tongue against her hand. Like an immovable statue, she set herself between Tomm and her master.

Edlen ran her fingers through Larla's coat absentmindedly. As she studied the strip of fabric, a laugh fell from her lips. "I have not seen one of these in years!" Edlen dangled it in front of Larla. "When I started my lessons, Rhen grew so jealous he actually pleaded to Sir Rhohl that he should be allowed to study with Laustair too!" Edlen giggled like a girl half her age.

"But once he was in the class, well…" She placed the cloth into a random page of her grandfather's book. "He immediately regretted his decision. We wrote each other secret notes. In order to avoid Laustair's scrutiny, we passed them to one another as *bookmarks*. This must have been one he hid inside this old thing." She slapped her hand on the cover of the text.

Tomm's lips curved into a smile, but his eyes stared on implacably.

"Rhen used to call me *Laustair's Puppet*; that would explain the puppeteer's rod. And the face—" Again, Edlen broke out in a fit of laughter. "It was his idea of a joke, wasn't it? He was trying to say I was his unhappy puppet, wasn't he? Can you imagine if Laustair found this?"

Edlen grabbed her stomach and coughed. Gasps of remembered joy mixed with pain. "Gods! Rhen would have been carried to the Dark Cells!"

Tomm smiled appreciatively, like one who listened to a friend's dull story that did not involve them. "He was dear to you, was he not?" His smile faded and his eyes grew stern.

Pretending not to notice the change in Tomm's expression, Edlen answered, "He is like my brother."

"Then it would pain you to know that he is now an escaped criminal?" Tomm no longer feigned any half-hearted appreciation.

"What do you mean, Tomm?"

Tomm crept back to the chair beside the candle, his face distorted by some inner torment. "Your *brother* is wanted for the murder of Sir Hugh Castac." There was no humor in his voice. "And your new *friend*, Vairet—" he glanced at the torn cloth in the book—"is wanted for the murder of your cousin."

"What?" shouted Edlen. She could not stop the question from exploding from her mouth.

The chamber blurred and she grew dizzy.

Edlen leapt from her bed—though she did not know she'd done so—and glared at Tomm. In the corner of her eye, she noticed another scrap of fabric slipped between the wall and floor of her chamber.

"What...it's not...possible..." Was she speaking to

Tomm or questioning the legitimacy of the scrap she'd just noticed?

"You keep an interesting assortment of friends, my lady," said Tomm. "Let us all hope your new bitch—" he eyed Larla—"is loyal to the crown." He stood and walked in a wide circle away from the humongous black dog. "I trust you, Edlen, but trust is fickle," he said. "For your sake…do not let my trust turn to suspicion." Tomm glided from the room.

Once certain Tomm no longer lingered outside, Edlen approached the scrap of cloth on the floor and bent to inspect it, but when she tugged at it, it would not budge.

"What in the gods name?" She pulled at it again, but the cloth slid under the wall and vanished.

Edlen stepped back and stared in wonder.

Slowly, one of the stones in the wall seemed to dislodge itself. A small gap appeared, and from within, a pair of hands reached out, followed by a body slithering against the floor.

"Vairet?" Edlen whispered.

Larla moved and lowered her head in a playful manner.

You are not afraid of her? Edlen wondered how it was that the hound reacted so harshly to Tomm but treated the girl who stabbed her as a friend.

Vairet crawled forward and then knelt before Edlen. Dirt and tears smeared her face. She bowed her head and said, "I'm not here to harm you."

"Had enough of that, have you?" Edlen asked, her voice a mixture of surprise and betrayal. She turned away, but as she was about to call for her guards, a faint voice drifted into her mind.

"Forgive me, Edlen…please…"

Edlen spun and stared at Vairet. "What did you say?"

Vairet lifted her head and said, "I didn't say anything."

The voice in Edlen's mind spoke again, but the words were unintelligible. She eyed Vairet and asked, "What are you saying?"

Vairet said nothing but looked at Edlen quizzically.

"You...you just said..." Edlen trailed off, not finishing her question. Perhaps her mind was playing a trick on her?

"I am sorry," she said. "I, I thought I heard you say something."

In that moment, Vairet's voice rang loud inside Edlen's head. *"I never meant to hurt you, but when I saw Everly Graymere, something inside of me snapped!"*

"You never meant to hurt me? You stabbed me," Edlen shouted. "You tried to kill my aunt. What did you expect to happen?"

Vairet's eyes opened wide and she said, "How did you hear that?" She backed away from Edlen.

Edlen stood still, but her body trembled. She closed her eyes, and a chorus of words erupted inside her head—a thousand thoughts swirled around like a swarm of insects. Her and Vairet's thoughts hued and cried in a flood of echoed thought. This was no trick, no illusion. Not if they sat and talked for hours would she have heard all Vairet expressed at this moment.

Edlen thought she was going to faint. She staggered forward and grabbed Vairet's arm. When she looked up and saw the fear in the girl's eyes, she let go.

In the brief moment she'd touched Vairet, Edlen was able to feel every emotion the girl had. Her fears, anxiety, pride, and desires coursed through Edlen as if they were her own.

But the most powerful feeling the girl possessed was remorse. Remorse for stabbing Edlen, remorse for wishing to kill Everly, and remorse for everything she had ever done to hurt anyone.

Edlen wept. She knew that Vairet did not deceive her. There was no more callousness in her mind or her heart. A blackness descended on her when she lunged at Everly, but this blackness was gone.

Stepping away from Vairet, Edlen sat on her bed and cried.

Larla leapt up beside her and licked her face, trying in her own way to comfort her.

Vairet knelt beside the bed. "I have come to repay my debt to you."

She did not need to tell Edlen why she was there. Edlen already knew. "It is I who owes you. You saved me during the melee, and now you've come to warn me about Tomm."

"Is that his name?" Vairet asked. "The puppeteer?"

"Yes, but I thought he was a friend." Edlen gazed at Vairet and whispered, "He is searching for you."

"He will not find me," said Vairet, smiling for the first time. "But I need to return that book, or he will know it is missing."

"Where did you find it?" Edlen asked.

"In the library." Vairet cast her gaze to the floor. "He was writing in it."

"How did he not see you?"

"Same as you did not see me bring it here." She glanced back at the opening in the wall. "The entire castle is connected."

Edlen was well aware of the secret passageways inside

Dartsuil's Keep but had never come across any paths that led inside of the rooms—let alone one that could take you as far as the library. "But...how?"

"You may have taken them when you desired, but I have been living inside of them for days now." She lowered her voice. "And I am not the only one."

What does that mean? "Who else?"

"I saw a boy in one of the corridors the night I..." Vairet trailed off.

Stabbed me? Edlen grimaced.

Vairet looked at her pleadingly but continued. "Couldn't have been more than ten or twelve."

"A boy? Are you sure" *There are very few children in the keep.*

"Yes," she said. "Very certain. It was he who showed me the loose stones inside the chambers, though he did not know he did so. I caught him speaking with the man who wrote inside of the book. The man, Tomm, gave him something, and though they hid it...I know a knife when I see one. I thought maybe he was coming to find you, so I followed him."

She placed her hand on Edlen's. "The boy snuck into a room, so I hid myself and watched what he might be doing."

"What did he do?"

Vairet's voice became shaky. "He killed a little girl, Edlen. I do not think he wanted to—he cried the entire time, but I watched him do it. And then I left as fast as I could, but I heard him weeping when he slipped back into the walls."

A little girl? Amara? Edlen's face sank and her body sagged. *Tomm did not lie about that.* "What did the boy look like?"

"Curly blonde hair, but other than that, it was difficult to see his face. Young, though, I know that."

Edlen thought about all the boys in court, but very few had blonde hair and even less had curls.

Werman? Could it be?

She sat on her bed and wrapped her arms around her knees then began to rock gently back and forth. Larla curled in front of her and lay her head on Edlen's lap.

"Why?" asked Edlen, mumbling. "Why would Werman want to kill her? Why would anyone want to hurt her? She was so young, Vairet. She never hurt anyone. She would cry if I stepped on a bug in front of her. Why…why?"

Vairet sat next to her and put her arm around her shoulder. "I do not know. But if I do not return that book now…I don't know what else might happen."

Chapter

DARRIN

The Empty Fortress

Something was wrong.

Where is everyone?

The sun set behind the western range of the Donwar Mountains as Darrin passed through an unmanned gatehouse and entered Elmfort. The enormous fortress of the Eyes of the Forest had been all but abandoned. Sword-pells and practice dummies stood stranded in the clearing—an area that rarely hosted less than twenty men honing their skills. He had never thought to see Elmfort empty, and its ghostly quiet made the hair on his neck stand on end.

"Where is everyone?" he asked Haron. The crusty old man only shrugged. Their horses' hooves patted noisily in the empty grounds.

Are we at war? He stared into vacant, shadowy windows of deserted towers. Their lidless black eyes stared back, answerless.

Has everyone left? That would be impossible! Elmfort must always be guarded—or so the Rovers' Vow stated.

They trotted through the clearing, making their way towards the watchtower. If anyone remained in Elmfort, they would be there, safe behind fortified walls.

"Be on guard, lad," said Haron. "None of this sits well with me."

As if it sits well with me?

"Ho!" a voice cried out from behind an arrow slit in the Watchtower.

Darrin spun in his saddle.

"Ho," answered Haron. "Is that you, Will?"

A moment passed before a man in a dark-green and brown uniform scuttered out from the Watchtower's archway. He held a torch aloft. A heavy, rough-spun hood distorted his features.

Darrin squinted as he tried to make out the man's face.

Will wore a long, black beard flecked with white; the skin around his eyes and mouth—drawn and sagging—was pulled back in a wrinkled grimace. He looked as though he had not slept in days. "Haron? It is you! Thank the Gods! I hadn't hoped to see one of you bloody rovers again."

Haron leapt from his destrier and ran to the man, grabbing his hand. "Ya look like 'ell, Will. What 'appened 'ere? Where is everyone?"

At that moment, Kayvold rode through the gatehouse followed by Laustair. They galloped straight to Haron.

"Where is Captain Hadley?" asked the Lord-Overseer without as much as a hello. "Where are the others?"

"My lord." Will bowed.

"Stand up, William," said Kayvold. "Answer me."

"My lord," started William. "Hadley—"

"*Captain* Hadley," Kayvold said, or was it a demand?

"Yes, yes... Captain Hadley," said Will, correcting himself. "Well, it's all gone to pot now, hasn't it? Day after you three took off for Rothspire, one of his hunters came back from some errand they was on—only thing, he was all burned up, wasn't he? How he made it all the way back I got no idea, but he was screaming about some fire. I think he meant ole Leddenwell was burning. Then he started ranting about blood drinkers. Well, you know Hadley...I mean Captain Hadley. Well, once he heard that, he tells the stewards to bring the poor sap down to the Roots."

"Is the man there now?" asked Kayvold.

"He's dead, my lord," said Will. "And that ain't the worst of it, if ya get me. Some hours later, two of those hunters' horses come galloping back—one of them singed down to the bone. Well, a few of us run up to the top of the watchtower, and bloody 'ell if smoke ain't rising from down the way of Leddenwell."

"Raiders again?" asked Archwood.

"Ah! Well, that's what we thought too. Then the captain tells the rest of us not to worry. He's gonna send his best men out to handle it. Soon, we got Chief Penmar and Major Knell riding off with all their men..."

"Hadley sent rovers?" asked Haron, his anger barely concealed.

"Aye," said Will. "Thought they might know some paths the hunters ain't ever found."

Well, that could be true, thought Darrin.

"My rovers are too green!" shouted Haron. "They ain't no use against raiders. Penmar knows that better than anyone!"

"Well, if that ain't the truth." Will continued. "But Hadley, er, Captain Hadley, commanded it, ya see. Fifty men he sent out, ya understand, but only three come riding back."

"Only three?" asked Kayvold.

"Aye, my lord." Will bowed his head and lowered his

voice. "Two hunters and a rover. Only thing, that poor rover's the only one still alive—and him just hardly."

"Who?" demanded Haron. "Which one of my lads?"

Will closed his eyes as he searched for the man's name. "Bartrom, I think his name was."

"Bart!" Darrin bellowed, forgetting his rank. "Bart Norwhich?"

Will hesitated to answer, but when the Lord-Overseer did not rebuke Darrin, he agreed. "Aye... that's the one."

Darrin stared at Haron imploringly. *Did Hadley pull him out of the Roots only to send him to his death?*

He turned back to Will, too afraid to ask, but he needn't worry.

"Where is he now?" Haron asked.

"Well..." said Will.

"Where is he, Will?" Haron asked again, his voice a silent rage.

"He's up with one of the stewards," Will said. "The poor lad... He ain't well..."

"What happened?" Darrin asked as he studied the windows of the watchtower, hoping he might guess the room Bart now lay in.

"Lost an arm and most of a leg..." Will stared at the ground before continuing. "Like some beast made a meal of it."

Darrin became dizzy; he choked back the hot sick that rose in his throat. *Eaten? Was it the bear again?*

Kayvold reached out and grabbed Darrin by the shoulder. "This was the same man who accompanied you two on your first roving?"

Fighting his urge to vomit, Darrin steadied himself. "Aye, my lord."

Haron spit a wad of phlegm on the grass and stomped a foot. "What bloody right did Hadley have in sending 'im back out?" He stared at the Lord-Overseer; his eyes bulged with disgust. "Bart is an excellent rover, but he ain't no warrior!"

"Hadley didn't discriminate," said Will. "But it ain't the worst of it." He mimicked Haron and spat on the ground. "Your lad—and I'll give him this—is one strong bastard. No leg, no arm, but still managed to warn us all. Gave a name to what got him; kept shouting out the word... I won't forget it. *Akkuladine*, he says. *The Akkuladine are coming.*" The name dripped black from his tongue. "*The Akkuladine are coming...*"

Silent until now, Laustair dismounted and approached Will. "The boy said, *Akkuladine*? He named them this?"

Taken aback by the directness of Laustair's question, Will tilted back on his heels and studied him before answering, "Aye, Grandad. I'd forget my own father's name before I forget that bloody word... *Akkuladine.*" He spat.

Laustair stepped away and held his hand to his brow. "This is ill news, Master Erwin. This is ill news indeed."

Erwin? Will never gave his surname. Darrin caught Laustair's eye and grinned.

The other men—if they made notice of the use of Will's full name or not—clustered in an almost secret council.

Kayvold spoke, his voice a confused hiss. "What are the *Akkuladine*?"

Laustair sighed. "The word is from an ancient language— one that has not been uttered by men in a thousand years." He eyed Darrin. "*Blood Drinkers,* you name them. A name given to the acolytes of Malighaunt—those contorted and disfigured by *Dark Wisdom*, and more beast than man.

"They were a tribe of man enslaved by terror. Through them, Malighaunt ravaged the Wide-World in the Elder Days before this land was known as Onyris. The Akkuladine were a black terror—a marring of the works of the Valdryz. It is because of this that Malighaunt was imprisoned in Allevghaunt.

"If they now walk freely in the world again…there is little you can do to stop them."

Blood Drinkers? Darrin had known the myth of them since childhood but had only ever believed them to be a fable told by nans and drunken uncles. A story used to scare children into following rules.

Best eat yer' veggies or the Blood Drinkers will get ya, he heard his grandmother's voice say. *Best listen to yer mum, or the Blood Drinkers will get ya.*

"This is ill news," said Laustair. "Ill indeed."

He stared at the ground—and then, as though he'd decided something after weighty debate, he looked up at Darrin. His eyes then snapped to Kayvold. "Lord-Overseer, your company is much appreciated, but I must be off now. Though I arrived too late, even the last rays of sunlight might illuminate a dreary road."

"Aye, Grandad," said Will. "It ain't safe to travel alone; did ya not listen to what I said?"

Laustair smiled grimly. "I assure you, Master Erwin, I will come to no harm."

"It is not wise, Laustair," said Kayvold. "I will not say no to your leaving, but your counsel is still needed. Perhaps you will reconsider?" He tugged on the hilt of his sword almost nervously. "At least until daybreak. Will you not grant me this request?"

"I have tarried far too long," said Laustair. "If the Akkuladine truly walk amongst us, daybreak will only see more death."

He leapt atop his horse, circled close to Darrin, and said, "Keep to hope, Master Cantlay…keep to hope."

A thin vial of icy blue liquid slipped from his robe, which he handed over surreptitiously. "The last drops of the Mermaid's Kiss," he whispered. "Use it wisely."

With that, Laustair rode off at a terrible speed.

T HE Lord-Overseer ordered the men who remained in Elmfort to light as many torches and braziers as they might—but with nothing more than a handful of stewards and woodcutters, there were too few to satisfy his command. What fires were lit cast the sprawling fortress in a dim glow, their shadows creeping across the floor like a small host of black insects.

The Akkuladine? The name took on an almost magical property. Darrin sat at a long table in the drearily-lit feasting hall. He pondered the old man's riddle. *Keep to hope?* What did he mean by that?

Rothspire? thought Darrin, hopefully.

Did Laustair ride back to the capital? Would the king send his army?

He stabbed his knife into day-old beef. "Do you think Laustair is telling the truth?" Darrin hesitated before biting into the gray meat.

Haron answered, his mouth full of boiled onion and beef, "Aye. I ain't got no reason not to believe 'im." Discolored gravy slopped into his beard. "We've seen some things in the past few days, ain't we? And Hadley riding out 'imself… He ain't risking his own skin chasing ghosts, eh?"

"Chasing ghosts?" Kayvold said as he sipped his ale. "Mayhap that is exactly what he has done?"

"Beg yer pardon?" Haron said. "I was only just sayin'."

Kayvold downed his drink. "The woodcutter said Captain Hadley sent his men looking for these Blood Drinkers, right?" He stood and poured more ale into each man's cup. "Never once did he mention that Walker Hadley actually *believed* these reports." He paced the hall and entered into a dialogue with himself.

"If an enemy attacks your scouts, would you send your troops into the brunt of their force?" Kayvold did not wait for a response. "No general would. You would send an emissary. Yes, you might send an attachment to defend this parlay, but you would not show your hand." He grew more animated as he spoke. "Hadley…Captain Hadley…say what you will, but he had more sense than this. What madness forced him to make such a rash decision?" His question trailed off, as though he hoped silence might provide an answer.

Haron spoke up, breaking the silence. "You don't think he believed any o' this?"

Kayvold smirked. "Tarranfort is half a day's ride, Ridgefront. Yet the Woodcutter made no mention of Hadley's attempt to alert them."

"Aye, my lord," said Haron. "But Captain Hadley pulled the entire force of Elmfort. If he didn't believe the threat worth it, I can't reckon he would empty the place."

"Unless he wished to gain favor," said Kayvold. He slammed his mug onto the nearest table.

"Favor for what?" Darrin asked, hiding behind his ale.

"Never underestimate a man's desires, Cantlay," said Kayvold. "If I know Hadley half as well as I think I do, he would never believe these ghost stories. No! He—and this I am quite certain of—suspected to find nothing more dangerous than an extremely bold band of raiders. Your captain did not receive his title based on his skill or foresight. He is an enterprising man. If he thought it possible to handle this menace alone, he knew the Tribunal of the Eyes would look *most* favorably upon him. He would not share this victory with Captain Weyburn willingly." Archwood took a set and grabbed at his chin.

"I fear his desire to replace me has proven ill for all of Elmfort."

He would risk all of our lives for his own gain?

Darrin fingered the vial in his pocket and then took a long drink from his mug. He stared from Kayvold to Haron, attempting to further understand their thoughts.

"Ya think 'im that selfish?"

Kayvold frowned. "You're too old not to think that, Harry." He poured more ale into his mug. "We are all selfish, aren't we? In our own ways." With a look of conspiracy in his eyes, he slurred, "It's unfortunate Elmfort is under his command. Selfish, foolish, rash…"

"Aye," said Haron, a drunken smile appearing on his lips. "So, what do we do?"

"We clean up his mess," said Kayvold. "We are still Eyes of the Forest, are we not?" He poured another round of drinks.

Chapter

EDLEN

The Blank Page

The hours after Vairet snuck from her chamber dragged on. The sun rose, Rothspire awoke, and still she had not returned.

What is taking her so long? Edlen's thoughts turned to dark imaginings. *If she is caught? What then?* But she had evaded those who'd searched for her this long.

Edlen looked at the book on her bed and, desiring to take her mind from her worries, sat in a chair beside the window and opened to the first page:

Before thought! Before the beginning,
There was Naught—
Of Naught existed nothingness
All—but a glowing white fire; a bitter point in ever-expanding blackness
Small though this flame burned, ever it grew hungry for the nothingness
Suddenly, fire erupted! Tearing through Naught—
filling the void with cleansing White Flame

Naught; subdued—receded to the edges of All
And it was: All birthed Time
In Time's infancy—All blazed radiantly
Giving substance to the nothingness

Edlen closed the pages and studied the title once more, certain she'd read from the wrong book.

The Executioner's Lament.

Why had Laustair given her a scripture of faith? She opened the book and continued, hoping there might be some secret hidden in the text:

And it was All's reign
From All came the Neilad—Ten bright rays: colored, terrible
And the Neilad shone throughout All and Naught—in their wake: creation

The words grew tedious; and in her frustration, she flipped the pages, reading little but a sentence at a time. All of it was written in the same manner.

He wanted me to read this in three days? thought Edlen, almost cursing her grandfather. But just the thought of Laustair made her smile. She could never be angry with him, though she did wonder why she hadn't seen him…why none of her family had been to see her. She pushed the thought aside and focused on the book.

Edlen turned to the last page; perhaps if she learned how the story ended, she might be intrigued enough to start from the beginning?

Blank.

She thumbed back a few more of the pages.

Blank.

Faster and faster, she scrolled through empty pages. More than half the book was unwritten. It was then she found the last written line. But…

She slammed the book closed and fear crept into her body.

That isn't possible.

Edlen opened it again, cautiously turning the pages until she found the ghostly writing.

She watched in dread as new lines of text—written in the author's fine script—appeared on a blank page. *The Executioner's Lament* was writing itself.

She stared at the page in horror, but her curiosity soon outweighed her fear.

"Yes, Somath. He found her. And now his thralls turn their attention to us."

"How is this so?" asked Somath. "She is dead."

"She is Valdryz, brother. She cannot die; not unless he desires it."

"But she is also mortal. It is not possible her body survived the fall."

"We do not know what is possible. She is the only one."

Somath bowed his head. "She is not the only one. A child was born."

"How?" asked Dalnor. "Somath, you were to protect her, study her, not breed her. It was for that reason we banished Begrafaine. Why allow that to happen again?"

"Malighaunt did not banish Begrafaine," said Somath. "He slaughtered him. And we did nothing."

Dalnor grabbed Somath's arm and said, "And now he desires to slaughter all of us. Allevghaunt is no longer safe. We had to flee Valendir, brother. It was luck I found you, but I know not where the other four have gone. But if Malighaunt finds her, how long until he discovers the rest of us? Where is the child?"

"She is safe," said Somath. "Hidden behind the walls of Rothspire."

"Safe?" asked Dalnor. "There is no safety behind walls, Somath. Malighaunt sends Inganar and a throng of Akkuladine. Even now they press through the forest."

"So, it is true? The Akkuladine crawl forth again?"

"Yes," said Dalnor. "I have seen our brother and his army. Rothspire does not possess the might to stand against them."

"Is this why you sent the boy to find me? Do you wish to fight them?"

"We defeated them before, Somath. But I do not have the power to do it alone."

"We were nine then, Dalnor. Scryta and Inganar had not wholly turned to Dark Wisdom…and Begrafaine had not been executed."

"It is but a small battalion of these foul beasts, not the entire host. I count less than a thousand," said Dalnor.

Somath stared through the forest, the distant blaze beyond the horizon an orange portent of despair. "Mayhap we can keep them at bay. But I would have to reveal myself… You are certain it is only Inganar?"

"Quite certain," said Dalnor. "Our brother Scryta still lays hidden somewhere, and Malighaunt will not appear until he is sure his shadow spreads. He still fears you."

"Ha," laughed Somath. "Malighaunt has not feared me for some time. Not since Begrafaine."

"Begrafaine was the weakest of our brothers, Somath, and though you wished never to acknowledge this fact, it does not make it untrue." He bowed. "Clear Wisdom is yet to be tested against Malighaunt's Black Flame, but…" Dalnor's form began to shift, but before his body entirely changed, he said, "We must do what we can for these men." And as these words left his mouth, a bear of colossal size now stood where Dalnor once had.

Edlen's door creaked open and Tomm Harken stepped into her chamber, but she did not lift her eyes from the book.

"Must be an engrossing read," said Tomm, peering down as he approached.

"Tomm?" Edlen asked, startled. "What are you doing here?"

"I told you I would come back," he said as he studied the pages. "Do not stare too long at a blank page, my lady; wiser men have lost their minds doing so."

Blank page? Edlen looked at Tomm and then back to *The Executioner's Lament*. Delicate script, clearly visible, etched itself into the pages.

"Do you mind?" asked Tomm as he lifted the heavy book from Edlen's lap and thumbed through the pages. He chuckled to himself and said, "I fancied myself the next Therod Halwell when I was your age." He closed the book and handed it back. "Might I give my humble advice, though? You may want to start writing on the first page."

"But," started Edlen. *Can he not see the writing?*

"My dear Edlen, are you feeling well?" He removed his glove and placed his hand on her forehead. "Your fever does not subside. I will ask the High Divinator to visit after today's services." He poured the last of the tea. "Until then, you should drink this and rest."

What fever? Edlen held her hand to her brow. The skin was hot to the touch. *But I feel better than well.*

She fixed her gaze on Tomm, and as she did, the discordant echo of a thousand voices all speaking at once flitted through her head. But she could not understand what these voices said. This was nothing like the experience last night with Vairet; she could make nothing of this mess. A chorus of mutters, mumbles, shouts, and whispers all spoken in different tongues. The voices swirled, and she grew dizzy.

Edlen closed her eyes, attempting to shut out the noise. She shook her head and asked, "What services, Tomm?"

"Your cousin's, my lady," said Tomm, staring intently at Edlen. "I've come to escort you to the sacellum, but I fear you might not be up to the strain." His voice softened. "I will give your regards."

The story Vairet had told. Tomm gave Werman the knife used to kill Amara. *And now he comes to bring me to her funeral?*

"It is a tragedy," started Tomm, his voice full of compassion. "But I swore my service to your aunt. Her killer will be found and brought to justice." He leaned over and patted Edlen on the shoulder.

"I apologize for my tone last night, my lady. I have given much thought to my actions and pray you might forgive me. I was rash, and even I am not immune to fear. But I hold no ill towards you, and I hope you hold none for me."

"Tomm?" asked Edlen. "Why did you come to Rothspire?"

Tomm smiled, or was it a frown? "Another day, my lady. I promise to tell you all you wish to know, but today is a day of grieving; my story would seem inappropriate."

He patted Edlen's shoulder again and said, "I will apologize to your aunt and your grandfather for you." With that, he glanced back down at *The Executioner's Lament*, and his mouth twisted into a smirk. "Interesting title, but as I cautioned, do not stare at the blank page too long…"

Once Tomm departed, Edlen grabbed the book and furiously opened to the page she had been reading. The script no longer wrote itself, but nonetheless, writing filled the page.

Did Tomm truly not see anything? It is not possible.

She flipped back to the beginning, and there, etched in thin ink, was the same passage she'd found so dull to read only a short time ago. *He must have seen this.*

Edlen closed the book and gazed around her room. The stone in the wall had not moved. She no longer wished to wait for Vairet.

Shall I search for her?

She stared at the hidden door and then swung her head around until she caught sight of Larla, curled into a ball on her bed.

You will not be able to follow, girl.

As though the dog read her thoughts, she lifted her head and perked up her ears then leapt down and leaned against her.

Edlen scratched behind Larla's ears and made up her mind.

I'm sorry, Amara. I must find Laustair. She studied the book one more time. Her grandfather had given it to her for a reason.

He told me not to go to the tournament. He wanted me to read this. But why? If I had listened to him, none of this might have happened. I would not have met Tomm, and Rhen would still be here. Were you aware of this, Laustair?

She could not change what happened to her cousin, but she might be able to do something. Though what that might be remained unclear.

Stripping off the last remnants of her blood-stained bandages, she dressed herself in the green and red colors of her family.

If any of what Tomm had said was true, half the castle

would be attending Amara's funeral, including Tomm himself. She might be able to reach Laustair's tower without being noticed. But no, those were the thoughts of a child.

I am a Graymere; I care not who sees me. This is my home. I will not let you force me to slink about like a criminal.

After she finished pulling up her leather boots—stitched with the detailed etching of a giant wagon wheel with many spokes, all bleeding into trails that ended in stars, suns, and moons—she scribbled something onto a piece of loose parchment and slid it under the loose stone in case Vairet returned.

"Come, Larla," Edlen said. The dog bounded towards her in response. "It is time we stop hiding."

With that, she and the enormous black dog stepped through the door of her chamber, into the open corridor of Dartsuil's Keep.

She only hoped she knew what she was doing.

CHAPTER

EVERLY

The Queen

HUNDREDS OF PEOPLE crammed themselves into the sacellum. It was hot and sticky. The foul scent of rancid perfumes mixed with perspiration and the spoiled smell of what passed for holy incense. Everly's nose crinkled.

Bad enough she must sit silently on a crude stone bench while the High Divinator recited passages from sacred texts. But to pretend this noxious odor was an acceptable part of her daughter's funeral was too much to bear.

King Ulisaren sat beside her. His face drawn, sallow, and unhealthy. She glanced at him once or twice during the ceremony, but each time she caught his eye, he pressed her hand in his. After this happened three times, Everly pulled away from his sweaty clasp.

The king's soft grip repulsed her, too clammy and frail.

She was the grieving mother. It was a disgrace for him to require her condolence.

After an hour of Erabil's plaintive speech, Everly grew restless. She rose from her seat and strode to the dais where Amara lay. Her abrupt movement caused a stir from those assembled, but she no longer cared what this feckless rabble deemed crass. This was her daughter. This was her pain.

She stood over the princess and stared down, heedless of the gasps in the audience and deaf to the High Divinator's words.

So small, she thought. *Smaller than Bradain.*

The young girl lay in a tiny coffin, her prostrate body covered by three silk sheets. The first and second layer were green and red. The top sheet was a thin, opaque dressing of white. As the three shrouds blended into one, the colors mingled into a sober union devoid of hue or splendor.

Everly noted the miserable costume. She hated that she was here. She hated Erabil. She hated her family. She hated her husband. She hated her brother. She hated everything…

You are too beautiful for this.

"Wait for me, daughter," said Everly, her voice a whisper. Or was it a plea? She turned and glared at the High Divinator.

His burnished silver coronet sat across his forehead like a noose not yet slipped to his neck. He halted his prayer and addressed her. "My lady—I understand the difficulty of this, but to ensure our princess's safe passage to the Ten, we must all remain seated while I grant her final rites."

She stalked towards him, pressed her finger into his chest and hissed, "You understand nothing." Her voice seethed with disgust.

"If we could not see to her safety in this realm, do not fool yourself into thinking that she is entitled to *anything* in the other." She spun away from Erabil and swept past the shocked faces of the gathered. Her strident footfalls echoed in her wake.

Outside of the sacellum, a throng of onlookers—unable to pack themselves into the holy chamber—amassed. Only satisfied by another's woe, they eyed Everly hungrily.

Whether these were merely curious spectators or the low-class lickspittles who dreamed of one day owning lands and wealth, she cared not to know. To her, anyone who desired to witness her child's funeral was a loathsome creature incapable of dignity.

But these were her people—*her* loathsome creatures.

A few grabbed at her as she stormed past, some attempting to clutch her gown, others mumbling halfhearted apologies. She did not need apologies. She needed vengeance. This was the third funeral in as many days, and the people of Rothspire had turned their grief into sport.

The first—a somber, underattended affair—was held for Prior Melwin, the unlucky young man strangled to death by the Shield of the Princess (or so the story was now told). King Ulisaren had been one of only a few devout followers to sit at the poor boy's rite of ascension.

Everly counted herself blessed to have avoided that ceremony.

Yesterday, though, as she'd reappeared in court, her first duty was to sit vigil for the deceased member of the King's Blades, Sir Ethan Canby.

By that time, the people of Rothspire—ever enterprising—had turned these morbid exploits into something of a venture.

Along the road to the sacellum, cunning vendors had sold small, hand-carved toy swords—emblazoned with Sir Canby's name—to passers-by. Strictly to memorialize the loss of one of King Ulisaren's most valued men. But as Everly had ridden back to Dartsuil's Keep with the king, she couldn't help but notice the lines of people gathering about.

A vast mob had formed, willing to spend their hard-earned coin on a variety of fried foods and freshly brewed ale. The tents, which had miraculously popped up nearest the solemn temple, were never less than half full. It was the tournament all over again.

Today, though…the people of Rothspire's ability to turn calamity into commerce made her ill.

Three days of death. Three days of mourning. Three days. Three people.

And now she must depart from her daughter, but these people cared not for her pain—not if they might earn an extra nole or two.

EVERLY walked down a deserted stretch of road. It was a dusty, unused path that circled behind abandoned shops before opening back up to the main throughway of the keep. Had she ever taken this street? She could not recall.

But there were no false-condolers to pester her, and that simple fact, at least, was something to be glad of.

Let them gossip, she told herself for the umpteenth time. *If a mother's grief is the height of my people's chatter, let them chatter.*

A man's voice hollered behind her, "My lady."

She paused and collected herself. Before turning to chastise the unwanted pursuer, she took a deep breath and readied herself for confrontation.

"Your words are appreciated," she said in a practiced response. "But I would appreciate them more if I might be left alone." This was the voice of a queen. A woman who would never be daunted by anyone's desires.

The man halted; his footsteps ceased. He spoke again, his words unaffected by Everly's passion. "We found your daughter's killer."

Everly turned around, her heart near bursting. "Tomm?"

Tomm Harken bowed. He kept his distance, but when he lifted his head, Everly noticed a familiar smile.

"Her name is Vairet, my lady…and she remains somewhere in the keep." He sauntered towards her.

"So…she is *not* found?" Everly stepped forward.

Gods! Please let him tell the truth. Her shoulders loosened, and her stomach lightened. "Where in the keep, Tomm? Where is she?"

"In the walls, my lady." He moved closer and dropped to one knee, his face lined with concern. "I am sorry I do not have happier news to report." He averted his eyes. "My previous suspicions prove unfounded."

"How so?"

"Sir Randall Ostrom, my lady…and Sir Jaymes Hallet. I cleared them both of any indiscretion. There is no evidence of their involvement in the disappearance of your daughter's Shield."

Rhen? Gods, how could I forget about him? "Then you believe he escaped?"

"Not without assistance…but…."

"But what?" Everly shook her head and said, "You may stand."

Tomm rose and breathed deeply, pausing before he said, "Edlen, my lady.

Edlen? But how? No…this is ridiculous. "That is impossible."

"Is it?" he asked, his gray eyes clouded in anguish. "I have watched over her since the Primacy departed; the girl speaks in her sleep."

"Dreams. One does not speak truth in dreams."

"One with innocence in their heart, perhaps. But your niece has all but confessed to her treachery."

Everly closed her eyes and choked back tears, her breath pounding against her chest. *No...please no. Not sweet Edlen.* "She saved my life."

"Ah," said Tomm. "I asked myself that same question. I do not think she believed her accomplice capable of murder, but even if her last act was one of attrition, she remains culpable for her crimes."

Crimes? She clenched her fists by her side, unable to accept this indictment. "She took a blade for me, Tomm."

"Perhaps..." said Tomm.

He glanced from side to side, making certain their words were still secret. "Ostrom's men spent an entire day traversing the paths under the castle. They found a trail that leads from the Dark Cells to...." His lips curled around clenched teeth. "An opening in the Great Wheel."

"And what would that matter?" But she knew the moment she said the words. *An unguarded pass into the castle.* "No." Her voice came out in a gasp.

"Yes, my lady. Edlen must have shown this scrapper a secret way into the castle." He took her hand. "Why do you think they were under there?"

His tone changed; he said his next words like a man approaching the gallows. "The day I met your niece, she introduced herself as Harris Rayfield—a false name—but one I recognized immediately. It was apparent she desired to avoid any association with the Graymeres. Why else would the daughter of the Primacy keep her identity hidden?" He let his question sit unanswered. "It pains me to say, but I believe Edlen is actively working against the best interest of the royal family."

Tomm shook his head in disbelief. "But I now hold proof she worked alongside this scrapper and aided in Rhen's escape...and the murder of your daughter."

No, no, you are lying. "No!" said Everly. "Not Edlen. She is a child; she is not capable of...she is not...No!"

A crash came from behind the boarded-up window of an abandoned shop. She jerked her head towards the sound and whispered, "It is not safe to speak here." Her eyes danced between Tomm and the abrupt noise. "Meet me in my chamber."

Tomm laughed. "Beg your pardon, my lady, but there is no place less safe in all Onyris than your chamber." He peered in the direction of the sound and lowered his voice. "You must continue to uphold your role as queen regent, my lady, but you must not return to your chamber." A slip of parchment appeared in his hand. "I have seen to your safety, but if you do not follow my instructions, I promise nothing."

Queen regent? What are you talking about? "Tomm," she said, a quiver in her voice. "I am not the queen regent. We still have a king."

"For how long, my lady? He grows no younger, and the events of the past few days weigh heavy on him." Tomm touched her chin. "Your children are gone." His hand pulled back from her face and pressed against his heart in a sign of grief. "Your husband's safety lies in question. If the worst proves true, you alone are the heir-apparent. You are the prince's wife, which makes you the queen regent. As long as you are safe, neither Aldir nor Edlen have any claim to the throne." He bowed.

"I swear to you my fealty." With head lowered in supplication, he said, "My life for yours…my queen."

Queen, she thought again. Tomm may not speak with tact, but his honesty came as a refreshing change from what she had grown accustomed to in court. How would any of those people broach these subjects? Simpering at best, but coddling or reticent would be nearer the mark.

"My lady?" a new voice boomed from around the bend in the road.

Everly turned and Tomm got to his feet. A tall knight in white and green plate trotted forward, mounted atop a beautiful brindle charger. He wore no helm as he approached.

"Sir Kerath," she said, "well met."

"Well met indeed, my lady," said the Sword of the King, bowing to her while eyeing Tomm mistrustfully. "Master Harken." He nodded his head slightly but only out of duty.

"A pleasure, Sir Kerath," said Tomm, a wry smile cracking his lips.

The mounted knight ignored Tomm's sarcasm and addressed Everly with something of annoyance in his voice. "King Ulisaren worries over you—I am come to escort Your Grace to the Hall of Glory." He studied the empty buildings that surrounded them. "The streets are no place for you, my lady. Especially back alleys with no city guards to protect you."

Yes…the protection of our mighty city guard has never proven futile. "I appreciate my father-in-law's concern, but it is my choice to wander our realm, and unless I am mistaken, I am well within my right to walk along any road I desire."

"I do not question your rights, my lady," said Sir Kerath,

the irritation in his voice veering dangerously close to impertinence. "But I answer to the king, and his desires come before any other in Onyris...even you, my lady."

Perhaps the Sword of the King finds himself too long in his position; he is stubborn as an old mule. She smiled—forced and unconvincing. But still, when Everly Graymere smiled, men tended to forget their duties.

"His Grace awaits," said the old knight, oblivious to her feigned charm.

He's grown too old for courtesy as well. "As you say, Sir Kerath. Who am I to disobey our king?"

***

"Everly, my dear," said King Ulisaren, "I was worried you may have..."

Died? No, Father, not me—only my daughter. "I am well, Your Grace."

The king's face, even more grave than it had been only a short time ago, hung loosely in folds of ashen wrinkles. *When did he get so old?* she thought.

Is it possible Amara's death has stripped him of his strength? I was her mother. Why must I be strong? You are the King of Onyris, yet you steal my grief like some common thug.

"Sit, Everly, please." He motioned towards the seat next to his.

Everly strode up the steps of the dais and took her rightful place beside the king. She glanced over and studied him.

Ulisaren sat slumped in his throne, his red and green mantle draped over his rapidly diminishing frame. He held his head up with a fist underneath his chin and peered through tear-stained eyes at those assembled. His voice, though, still retained something of its former power. "Now that my daughter joins us, we may commence."

Commence with what? She noted the men who sat before them in a semicircle. This gathering was the King's Cabinet, or what Aldir referred to as his father's wardrobe. A group of five advisors who convened only upon rare occasions to administer council that the king himself deemed too difficult to decide himself.

Of the five men, three were adepts: Richhard Marsen, the Adept of Combat, Jefforsyn Isabel, the Adept of Sovereignty, and Patrik Lindon, the Adept of Law. Along with these adepts, the other two were lower-ranked lords who represented the affairs of varying realms. Lord Edmund Eldred of Sharkspeak and Lord Brandin Lasaine of the Spine.

"Your Grace," started Patrik Lindon. "An ancient text within *The Laws and Decrees of Onyris* states that if the bloodline of succession ends—" He gazed up at Everly and then back down to a gigantic book on his lap. "Well, it states quite clearly that the crown goes to the spouse."

What are they talking about? Everly stared at the king. *Why are they discussing this today?* "Father?" she asked in a whisper. "What is he talking about?"

"Ssh," hissed the king. "Continue, Patrik." He twisted his head slightly and frowned at her.

Disoriented by the interruption, Patrik Lindon ran his finger along the page and said, "In nearly five-hundred years, this has never occurred, Your Grace, but it appears Dalantis the Wise prepared for just such an occasion."

"Ancient bloody texts," said Richhard Marsen. "The Wide-World hadn't even split apart yet when that was written, Pat." The Adept of Combat was a bulky man in his mid-forties; previously a general in the army of Rothspire, he carried himself much like any younger soldier might. His thick black hair, which he kept cut incredibly short, covered a thicker head that sat atop a neck of pure muscle. Though he had lived in Towerglenn for nearly twenty years, his accent was pure Fyrebreak. "How are we gonna hand over the crown to a bloody Thorpe?"

Hand over the crown? "Excuse me?" asked Everly. She disregarded the insult thrown against her father's name. "Who is handing over the crown?"

"Apologies, my lady," said Richhard Marsen. "I meant no disrespect."

"No, Richhard," said the king. "I am the one who must apologize." He turned in his seat and gazed at Everly. "My dear girl." He frowned, almost like a child who had been caught taking the last sweet cake from his mother's cupboard. "I had no intention of ever thrusting this upon you, but you must understand. Onyris must always have a Graymere in power. The Wide-World knows nothing else. But with the passing of Amara, our kingdom is without a line of succession. Every king or queen for the past five-hundred years was born into their future. Groomed from birth, as you know all too well. But...we no longer possess the time in which this may be upheld."

Queen... Tomm did not lie. "You are still king, Father," said Everly, a sudden love for the man rising inside of her. "And Odain..."

"Begging your pardon, my lady," said Lord Brandin Lasaine, an aged man who looked as though death had merely forgotten of his existence. "The prince is now an uncertainty, and Onyris cannot deal in uncertainties."

"Gods, Lasaine!" shouted Jefforsyn Isabel, the Adept of Sovereignty. "The poor woman just buried her daughter. You need not throw her husband's disappearance in her face." A younger man, nearest in age to Everly than any other in the hall, Jefforsyn bowed his head in deference and said, "My lady, forgive our good Brandin, his tact has been eaten by his prostate."

Brandin Lasaine laughed heartily. He pulled a coin from his pocket and threw it at Jefforsyn Isabel. "And Isabel's balls have been eaten by his mistress."

All of the King's Cabinet exploded in laughter at this. And in that moment, Everly understood that these men were nothing more than a ribald group of drinking partners. The king had surrounded himself with people who cared more for frivolity than frankness. Tomm's words from earlier resounded in her mind. *I need more men like you, Tomm. Not these pathetic drunkards.* She smiled at the men's jests and then cleared her throat.

"Gentlemen, though I appreciate the vast knowledge you have of one another's genitalia, my father summoned you here for a purpose." Her smile faded, her lips leveled in stern authority. She reached over and placed her hand in the king's. "Your Grace, please ask your men to return to their task."

Ulisaren's mirth vanished, and he squeezed his daughter-in-law's hand with what strength remained to him. "Everly is right. This is a serious situation and demands our utmost attention. Please...we must resolve this."

Every man in the hall bowed their heads, their gaiety replaced with a mixture of embarrassment and solemnity.

Patrik Lindon scratched nervously at his book and said, "There is one last article in Dalantis's *Laws*."

Edmund Eldred, a man of 50 years whose lifetime of drinking had wreaked a terrible toll on his face, coughed. His bulbous red nose drooped over a face marked with patches of rosacea. His voice, hefty and sonorous, punctuated by throaty growls, bellowed, "On with it then! You heard the king!"

"He claims…" Patrik sighed and looked anxiously between his friends and then back up towards the king and Everly. "It states—rather unambiguously—that if a spouse of the heir should claim the crown…" Again, he paused, his face flushed, his voice uncomfortably shaky. "They have the right to replace their cabinet with those they see fit."

Replace the cabinet? Everly smiled. It was the most serene smile she'd mustered in years.

The men in the room exploded in fits of indignation.

Quarrels broke out.

The king collapsed in his throne, exhaustion finally laying its tiresome claws into the old man. None of his cabinet noticed their king's slouched body; the anger and confusion this archaic law created played out in an uproar of wealthy men who refused to accept this unforeseen certainty.

Everly surveyed the scene with a hint of satisfaction. Men—even of such high standing—fell prey to grief.

True, their grief was in no way commensurate with the loss of a child—but still. She no longer hated herself for the way she'd reacted when her daughter had died. If these men would tear themselves apart under the fear of losing privilege—while still maintaining wealth and land —then her desperation was no more than the purest pain of loss. She possessed nothing these men could take from her now. She cared not for the crown, but if these men must be forced to grant it to her, then there could be no sweeter reward for the anguish she'd survived.

The Gods took her children but gave her a kingdom.

Just then, she noticed the king sunken into his throne.

Numbness bathed her body.

She moved steadily to him, pressing her hands against his face. Cold. She slid a hand down to his neck and held it there for long moments. Nothing. His skin had turned a pale blue, and his tongue lolled out from his mouth.

"Father!" she screamed, but the action was reflexive. She felt neither fear nor pain.

"Father!" she shouted again. Still, no worry. Was it possible that when one had experienced so much pain, they might lose the ability to fear? Was it possible that she had grown indifferent to death?

She clutched him and screamed. "The king!"

Her knees hit the floor of the dais with a thud; there would be a bruise tomorrow.

"The king!" She fell backwards and landed hard on her rear end. It was a dull pain.

"The king…" she screamed again, and again, and again.

The others rushed forward, their shouts echoing throughout the Hall of Glory, but Everly's mind drifted far away. Tears fell from her eyes, but she was unsure of why they came.

The clouded memory of a hundred people thrashing about mingled with an audible hum of cries and curses—a blur of commotion. Sir Kerath Manley lifted the king and carried him from the hall.

Half-awake, Everly dragged herself from the floor. She gripped the edge of the nearest seat and pulled herself up. The soft cushion of the throne helped ease the pain in her backside.

Everly gazed out at the remaining men in the Hall of Glory.

Queen?

The word appeared in her mind.

Queen?

The men quieted themselves.

Queen... She straightened her back and her eyes grew stern.

Slowly the men in the hall knelt before her and cast their gazes to the floor.

How did Tomm know?

CHAPTER 28

DARRIN

The Two Rovers

Haron departed for Tarranfort before sunrise. If fortunate, he might reach the northern garrison of the Eyes of the Forest before nightfall. The old rover still had friends up there, and the Lord-Overseer held hope he might parlay this goodwill into a mustering of action.

Prior to his leaving, the three men climbed to the top of the Watchtower and gazed out into the depths of the forest. From this height, they watched a bright orange light rim the edge of darkness—a false dawn. An ever-growing fire ate away at the horizon and the pillars of black smoke that rose from the far-off canopy looked as though the land itself had vomited midnight into the heart of the sky.

"Our forest burns," said Kayvold. "The Gods walk amongst us, and we three stand here, a fool's hope shared between us. I would never willingly send a man to his death, but the days of decency and honor have passed into blissful memory. What this new day brings, I cannot say. Yet I promise you both—it will be unlike anything we have ever dared imagine."

"Aye, m'lord," said Haron. "But we made a vow, didn't we?"

"Vows," said Kayvold, almost as a curse. "Vows are meant to bind, old friend. They may bolster the will of some, but in others—I have seen it shatter their resolve. No, it is not a vow we make this day, for whatever comes, none of us are bound to defeat. What I ask, I do not expect to be accomplished—I only pray that it might."

He put a hand on both men's shoulders and eyed them with fatherly concern. "If Laustair is correct, and I do not doubt that he is, we may be riding to our deaths. I will not have a vow be the last thought that goes through our heads." A smile crept across his face. "We embark on a journey that has no end. I can only hope we meet again before our parts are over. It is hope that I want you to trust in, not a vow. Hope may prove stronger than any oath we might swear."

Keep to hope... Darrin thought. *Those were Laustair's words.*

"It's a bloody decent plan, m'lord," said Haron. "The best us three could come up with, at least."

Darrin laughed. The Lord-Overseer's words, though true, did not fill him with hope. But Haron's jest made him understand Archwood's intentions. No vow might secure their safety, but hope—hope in their plan, hope in the strength of the Eyes, and hope in each other—that was all they now possessed.

They had spent most of the night devising a plan to confront the Akkuladine, even though they were uncertain if these monsters actually existed.

Haron would ride to Tarranfort and rouse Captain Weyburn's force of over five-hundred hunters and rovers. This group would secure the northern pass that led from Leddenwell, hopefully stopping the Akkuladine from breaching the realm of Evermoore.

Kayvold and Darrin would spend the morning gathering what men remained in Elmfort and setting them to the task of fortifying the fortress. Fifty men, manned with long-range weapons, might hold the walls for a short time. If it came to this, they held hope that a siege might provide time for the army of Rothspire to arrive.

After this, the Lord-Overseer would send a small group of stewards to ride to Straten and plead for assistance. Lord Brastor, though prickly and proud, must agree to dispatch some of his men, if only to gloat over Kayvold's need. The stewards were instructed specifically to speak with Sir Hovaird. The Lord-Overseer was certain he would have the wherewithal to send for help from the king. A threat to the forest was a threat to all of Rothspire.

Once these measures were seen to, Darrin and Kayvold would ride with great haste to meet with Captain Hadley before his company reached Leddenwell. At that point, the Lord-Overseer would take command from Hadley and stop them from riding heedlessly into slaughter.

If they could change their course and come to Leddenwell from the south, they might be able to funnel the Blood Drinkers into the narrowest part of the forest, at which point Elmfort's strength would smash them against the might of Tarranfort.

It's the best plan we can come up with. And the only thing they could do was hope it worked.

Hope. What an interesting word.

Shortly after Haron rode off but before the sun rose, Darrin received permission to go in search of Bart. The story told by Will the woodcutter yesterday gnawed at him.

A lifetime ago, when he'd left Elmfort for Rothspire, Bart had been down in the Roots. Why would Hadley release him only to ship the poor man back into the forest? It made no sense. Did his captain expect him to die?

An hour or so passed before Darrin found anyone to speak to. By this time, the sun had broken through the dawn and filled the sky with gray light. He wandered up a staircase in one of the smaller barracks and bumped into a steward who was coming down.

"Ho," said Darrin. "I'm sorry, I thought I was the only one awake." He eyed the man, recognizing him as one of the recruits in his fellowship. "Stephan? Gods! I'm glad to see you."

The steward held a strange instrument, clutching it close to his chest. "Cantlay?" He shook his head as though seeing someone he never expected to see again. "It is you!"

The tool he clasped nearly fell to the floor as he reached his hand out in greeting. "I thought you were dead."

"Not yet," said Darrin, studying the serrated blade of the strange object. "What is that, Stephan?"

"Amputation saw," he said as though Darrin should know.

"For what?"

"Amputating," said Stephan. "Got a rover up there needed some bad flesh removed."

"Who is up there?"

Stephan stared quizzically at Darrin and held the horrific tool at his side. He appeared to be puzzling out this interest in his patient. "Gods!" he said, suddenly figuring it out. "Bartrom Norwich... You knew him, didn't ya?"

Knew him? Do you mean he's dead? "Is he still—"

"Alive?" asked Stephan. He gazed around the stairwell uncomfortably. "For now. But whatever got him, well..." His eyes closed as though the thought frightened him. "Seems like his body has gone bad, rotten and all."

"Rotten?" asked Darrin. "What does that mean?"

Stephan would not elaborate; he only gestured to the room where he'd come from, made some feeble excuse for his haste, and continued on his way.

Desperate to speak with Bart, Darrin ignored the steward's abrupt disquiet and darted up the stairwell to find his former companion. The chamber door remained open; a gentle breeze blew into the hall from unfastened windows. The morning air was chilly, and a faint sour scent drifted alongside it.

Darrin halted before entering, his nose wrinkling at the unpleasant odor. It reminded him of spoiled meat. He stepped inside and gasped.

In the center of the room, laid atop a stone table and covered in bloody bandages, was Bart. Or what was left of him. Will had not exaggerated. His right arm was missing and his left leg ended just below his knee. He stirred.

Gods! He's still alive.

Darrin moved closer. As he neared, he noted blackened flesh—like the charred skin of over-cooked chicken—around the edges of Bart's missing limbs. Sweat ran down his face and beaded on his upper lip. "Bart?" he asked, his voice a thin whisper. "What happened to you?"

Bart's head rolled to one side; his eyes opened in slits. His face was dirty, stained with mud and blood, and his lips, cracked and dry, were drained of all color. He spoke in a soft wheeze. "Tinny?" He struggled to open his eyes more. "Tinny...is that you?"

"Yes, Bart, it's me." The old insult no longer offended Darrin; if anything, it made him smile. He leaned down and stroked Bart's forehead. "What...what happened?"

Bart coughed, his chest heaving violently. "Did ya find Somath?"

"Yes," said Darrin, tears welling in his eyes. "We found him."

"Good, good," said Bart. "Me mum is gonna be upset, ain't she? I can hear her now." He coughed again, and this time small flecks of blood dribbled from his nose. "'Why can't you be more like that boy, Tinny. Now ya gone and got yerself killed.'"

Darrin grimaced; his tears mixed with the sweat on his face. He grabbed Bart's only hand and squeezed. "You can tell her that Tinny was only trying to be a good rover, just like her son. And, besides, you're not dead yet."

"Yet," said Bart, laughing and coughing in one hideous spasm. "Don't make me laugh, ya bastard. It hurts."

"What happened out there?" asked Darrin, unsure of how much longer he might have with him.

Bart groaned and convulsed slightly. "Blood Drinkers, Tinny." He closed his eyes and lay silent. But when he re-opened them, he stared wildly at Darrin.

"Akkuladine... They are real, Darrin." He coughed once more and shut his eyes.

Darrin placed his hand on Bart's brow. His skin was aflame. The hissing of the poor man's breath relaxed.

Sleep, Bart. Perhaps this will all be over when you wake again.

Branches lashed against Darrin's face. He and Kayvold galloped at incredible speed through the forest. Never before had he ridden this fast, but never before had he ridden with such urgency. The heavy smoke of fire filled the air, causing Darrin to choke. They would not be able to keep up this pace for long, but they had no other choice.

It might take six or seven days to reach Leddenwell on a normal roving, but that was broken by nightly camps and slow-placed trots along a maze of paths.

Certain Hadley would not take the road at a leisurely trot, and Kayvold pushed them in the hope they might reach him before nightfall two days from now.

A day into their journey, they approached the spot where Darrin had found the prince's legs, and as they sped along that road, he couldn't help but think of the bear. He glanced through the dense trees and thick bushes. How much had changed in those two weeks? The memory of Dalnor crept into his thoughts.

After a short rest on their second night, in which they shared little food and less conversation, they awoke early and resumed their trek. A few hours into the third day of this exhausting ride, the ground sloped downwards at a dangerous angle. They came upon a deep ravine and steadied their horses, surveying the land before them.

Ramblon River, the fast-flowing waters that streamed down from the Talon Mountains in Evermoore to the north, stretched out beneath them. This river split the forest between its mountainous western edge and its more condensed yet flatter eastern territories. On the other side of the river, the land rose steeply into craggy hills passable only through slender trails that were flanked by deadly cliffs.

In their haste, they must have veered too far south and now needed to backtrack ten or so leagues. By doing so, they could cross the land bridge at Tuckhollow, a small village raised against the calmest section of the Ramblon River. The people there were friendly to rovers and could provide them with fresh horses.

Darrin assumed Hadley would have passed through the town, and perhaps, if they were lucky, they might also catch word of their departure. Though this detour would add hours to their ride, it would ensure they would come across his captain and fellow rovers safely—and refreshed.

"We cross here," said Kayvold, peering down at the rushing water.

What? That is ridiculous; the horses will never be able to cross. "But Tuckhollow is only a few hours away."

"A few hours we cannot spare," said Kayvold. "We cross here and take the lowest pass through the mountains. When we come out from beyond that trail, we'll be ahead of Hadley. He will have stayed the night at Tuckhollow and spent most of the morning seeing to his gear and mounts. This is the fastest way, Darrin."

And the most dangerous. "Aye, my lord."

They found the least steep part of the ravine to lead their horses down, but still, the going proved incredibly slow. Each step they took, they needed to dig their boots into soft soil and use all of their strength to keep their beasts from tumbling down into the river. Half an hour passed as they made this difficult descent, but once they reached the rocky ground, the roar of the water frightened Kayvold's horse, and if not for their combined effort, it may have darted off into the river and drowned.

Gods, thought Darrin. *We will all drown in this.*

He stared at the swift-moving water and noticed jagged stones sticking out like gnarled fangs. *How are we going to do this?*

Kayvold glanced at Darrin and patted him on the back. "Do you trust me?"

No.

Not waiting for a response, Kayvold climbed atop his horse and bellowed a command. He squeezed his legs tight around the beast's sides and leaned forward. Like an arrow let loose from an archer's bow, man and animal blurred into a hazy dart lost in the white mist of the hungry river.

Darrin stared on in a mixture of horror and hope. The loud crack of hooves smashing against wet rock faded and after a few seconds—which seemed an eternity to him—Kayvold turned his horse in a long circle on the other side of the riverbank.

Though dimmed by the noise of rushing water, Darrin heard his Lord-Overseer hooting in triumph. Then the hoots turned into faint words.

"Don't think about it, Cantlay!" Kayvold's voice boomed over the din. "What would the Iron Horse do? Stay to the stones! Your horse will do the rest!"

Would Sir Matthew Dorne do this? I never a read a story about him doing anything this dumb.

Darrin mounted his horse and took a deep breath. He stroked her mane and spoke soft words of encouragement. Whether those words were for the animal or for himself, he did not know. He screamed something inaudible, and in pure mimicry of the Lord-Overseer, pressed his legs tight against the horse's body and leaned forward, his face smashing against his charger's silver coat.

The moment he left the pebbled shore, his horse slipped

on slithery algae that coated the smooth river rock. His heart pounded, but his mind went blank. Without thinking, he grabbed the reins tighter, and with deft motions he'd never been taught, pulled the horse out of its fall and straightened their course. Before he understood what he'd accomplished, they were on the other side of the river. He halted his gallop.

He sat there, shaking with adrenaline. Kayvold rode up to him and slapped his shoulder. "Bloody amazing, lad!"

Darrin smiled and then burst into a fit of uncontrollable laughter. He could not say why he laughed, but he could not help it either.

"I thought for sure you were going to drop," said Kayvold. "That was the most extraordinary thing I've ever seen, Cantlay! How in the Gods' names did you recover from that?"

The Gods' names. Darrin grabbed at the pocket where he kept the vial Laustair had given him. The Mermaid's Kiss was still there.

"I haven't a clue," he said. "I just...well...I just did what the Iron Horse would do, didn't I?"

"Matthew Dorne never did a thing like that, boy. Maybe the time is come we start calling you *Iron Horse*," said Kayvold, a grin of pride spreading across his face. "If we make it through this, people will be telling stories about you."

He slapped his shoulder again and said, "After that, the rest of this ride is gonna seem a prince's promenade."

TRUE to Kayvold's words, the journey through the mountain pass proved no more difficult than a pleasure-ride along the road from Redrun to Oakblade.

They crossed over the steep trails in only a few hours, finding no more trouble than a damp midday meal. The dried meat and bread they carried with them had become soggy after their river run, but even wet food could do nothing to dampen their joy at surviving the treacherous river.

Daylight faded as they neared the thickening trees that framed the southern borders of Leddenwell. Black smoke beset them once again. Their time in the mountains almost made them forget about these suffocating clouds. They rode deeper into the reek of burning woods. Any invincibility Darrin might have felt from earlier vanished, just as the sun disappeared behind the murky breath of wildfire.

CHAPTER

RHEN

The Courseless Sea

RHEN AWOKE WITH a violent jerk. The huge cot he slept on, though soft and accommodating, slid over hard planks as the ship pulled from anchor and departed from the port of Towerglenn.

Two days had passed since Belo had brought him here, and now that Lord Byron Windsong's galley had finally undocked, any hope he'd held of the Graymeres rescuing him had vanished. Lord Byron spoke truth. The crown never intended to search for him.

The woody crash of the bow breaking against the waves sealed this fact.

He sat up and stared at his new home. The cage he'd spent his first night in remained opened. His previous bonds rested languidly against a slatted bulkhead and swayed ever so slightly as the ponderous ship sailed through choppy water. Other than those reminders of his unceremonious arrival, the vast hull was furnished for a king.

The long table where he ate his meals was of exquisite design. The area in which he received his lessons would not be out of place in the Hall of Glory. Though restricted from leaving, Lord Byron saw to every whim a nobleman might desire.

His captors had become his hosts.

Just as the two previous mornings had found him alone, so too did this new day.

Groggy as he was, he rose from bed and walked around the massive room. There on the table sat a large jack filled with mulled wine. He drank the warm beverage and sighed with pleasure. It was similar to the elixir Belo served him after their practices: an invigorating concoction of strange herbs, spices, and wine. Rhen gazed around, his tiredness dissipating. It was then he noticed that the sword he used in practice must have fallen to the floor when they'd set sail. Belo detested the idea of a weapon touching the ground. Rhen strode towards the blade and lifted it, staring at the polished steel. If he could no longer trust his family, he must place his faith in something, and this weapon proved a most fitting surrogate. He would protect this beautiful piece of craftsmanship in the same way his family had not protected him.

After caressing the steel with an oiled rag, he placed the sword back in its scabbard and rested it in its holder. Once he finished this ritual, he meandered to a basin in the corner of the room and splashed cold water against his face. Belo would be down soon, and once his instructor entered, his idle time would end.

His lessons consisted of three parts.

Defense for three hours, in which Belo explained new guards then ran drills over and over again.

Once his mastery of these were proven satisfactory, Belo might allow him a short break. During this time, they would keep light conversation, the topics ranging no further than the different makes of steel and their strengths and weaknesses. Belo, being a student of Rojiirin sword craft, scoffed at the primitive arts of Onyris blacksmiths.

"The children of Rojiir make stronger blades before they can walk!" Belo had said yesterday.

Rhen had laughed, but after hearing the detail he'd given between the difference in the two steels, he began to believe him.

Once they ate and drank, they would begin offensive training. This might last another three to four hours, and due to his incredible strength, Rhen excelled in this field.

Though yet to best Belo, this was the only part of the day where he might receive praise. This praise, given begrudgingly, filled him with the desire to prove himself even more.

After another break—that Belo typically filled by sharing philosophies of his people—they would revisit the new defenses, incorporating them into active strategies. This would go on for another few hours until Rhen grew too tired to continue. Belo would inevitably deride his lack of conditioning and demand he exercise more.

At the end of these lessons, Belo would serve him the elixir. He would not leave until he was certain Rhen had drank the last sip. According to his new instructor, the priests of Rojiir had developed this drink to aid in the recovery of soldiers after battle.

It tasted sweet, and each time Rhen drank it, his muscles would tense but then slowly relax. Whatever was in it surely worked. The wound on his arm had all but healed, and after only an hour, his body would no longer ache from their sparring.

By this time, Lord Byron would appear with wine and food—this had become Rhen's favorite part of the day. Often, their conversations would last near as long as his training, but the education he would receive at these dinners was more informative than anything he'd learned while sitting through one of Laustair's lectures.

Today would prove to be no different. Nor the five that followed after the ship set sail.

"**Better!**" said Belo. "Much better."

The sword in Rhen's hand flashed through the air, a natural extension of his arm. He smiled, no longer considering his movements. His confidence had grown, his understanding of footwork now all but habit. There was not a feint nor slight Belo attempted that Rhen did not answer. In more than one match, he came close to besting his instructor.

This constant practice seemed worth it.

His feet danced across the wooden planks. There was nimbleness in his movements—no longer the lumbering strides he'd taken only a few days before.

"I almost took your arm off with that one!" he said with newfound pride.

"Boasting will get you killed, boy," Belo said. "The moment you underestimate your opponent is the moment you feel their steel." He gritted his teeth and pressed his blade against Rhen's. In a sudden flurry, he moved the tip of his sword against the brocken's neck.

"Yield," he demanded. "I have taken your head."

Rhen threw his blade to the floor in frustration. "Gods! I thought I had that one!"

"Pick it up!" Belo demanded.

Rhen knelt and pulled the sword from the ground. "I'm sorry. I just—"

"It is not your sword, boy!" Belo commanded, his voice

cold and unflinching. "Never disrespect your blade. If you are too daft to wield it properly, it is your fault...not the steel's."

"Yes, I just..." he tried to say.

"Just, nothing," Belo said.

He stepped closer to Rhen, holding his blade threateningly close to the giant's face.

"If you fail in the Shaded Realm, your head will not be the only one they take." Belo flicked his wrist imperceptibly, the tip of his sword slicing a thin line across the boy's cheek. Small drops of blood dotted the cut then dripped down to his chin.

"Let this be the last time your skin tastes steel. The kiss of Lord Nekkin's blade will not be so tender." His white eye gleamed in the torchlight.

"A NEW scratch?" Lord Byron asked, eyeing Rhen's wound. "Belo must be sore with you."

Rhen ran his finger against the cut. "I dropped my sword," he said, apologetically.

"Yes, yes," Byron said, handing a plate of suckling pig, sprouts, potatoes, and gravy to Rhen. "A man's steel must never be allowed to hit the floor, or so he says."

The loud pop of a bottle being uncorked rang in the hull.

"I have sat through his lectures on this topic many times." Windsong smiled while pouring wine.

"Is he from Rojiir?" Rhen asked. "I mean, well...he doesn't exactly look like one of them." He cut at his food and dredged the meat in brown gravy.

"No, he doesn't, does he?" laughed Byron. "He was born there—in some small village—but no, I do not believe he can trace his ancestry to that place."

Windsong sliced his food into small bites, picking at them delicately. "Met him…Gods!…twenty years ago, it is now. He sailed with a troupe of travelling oddities. *Belo the Big*, they called him." He laughed. "A terrible name, I know, but those folk weren't famed for their wit, were they?" He stabbed at a piece of pork and chewed before speaking again.

"I was taken by him, though. Never saw a man as large as him. Mind you, there are no brockens in the Vines, and at that time, I had not yet stepped foot in Rothspire."

Rhen flinched at the name of his old home.

"Pardon me," Byron said. "I did not mean to add salt to the wound."

"It is nothing," Rhen said, pushing back tears.

"You hoped I lied to you." Windsong stood from the table and walked over to Rhen, placing a hand on his shoulder. "I wish I could lie to you, my boy." He stared at Rhen, a sympathetic frown on his face. "But you will find a new family—this, I promise. You are under my protection…and I do not abandon my children."

The days since the tournament played out in his mind. The more he thought on them, the more the pain spread throughout his body.

They are my family…why would they leave me? Why would they let this happen?

He looked at Lord Byron. "They did abandon me, didn't they? My father has too."

Windsong leaned over and grabbed the wine. He handed it to Rhen and nodded.

After they drank from the bottle, he said, "The Wide-World is littered with the *rejected*, the *dismissed*, and the *orphaned*. It is but a cruel truth of the time we live in, my boy. But for every person who slips under the bow of cruelty and is dragged into its depths...another wades in this courseless sea. Some of these people tire and drown, but..." He clutched Rhen's arm.

"Those who fight against the thrashing waters, those who refuse to be swallowed by the black mouth of circumstance—well, they are the ones pulled up by the passing ship. They are the ones who are saved."

He grabbed Rhen's hand and tightened his grip.

"*I* am come to save *you*," he whispered. "I will pull you from *your* course-less sea." His lips spread into a placating smile. "*You* have arrived at the precise moment *I* need saving as well."

It was all true. What had his life been but a set course? He did not ask to be born a brocken. He did not ask to be the Shield of the Princess. But this is what the Graymeres groomed him for. He had no say in his life. He was but another in a line of servants, same as his father and all the brocken since the Sundering War.

Perhaps this was the best thing that could happen to him.

He was free. He no longer answered to the king. He no longer bent his knee to those who wished to *use* him.

Lord Byron spoke to him as an equal.

Yes, he would still have his duties...but who did not? Even a king had his duties.

But Ulisaren never sat with him. Ulisaren never shared his wine. Ulisaren never told him *he* was a king. Ulisaren, Odain, Aldir, Edlen...none of the Graymeres told him this. No! They only saw him as a tool, a weapon...a *thing* they might call on when needed.

Rhen did not make the ridiculous oath his great-great-great grandfather made, yet he was bound to it.

What have I done to them? Nothing. *Yes, I killed a knight. But what does that matter if the knight meant to kill me? Am I to stand trial for this?*

Was he to be held prisoner until the king pardoned him? This was not justice. He'd performed his duties. He'd done exactly as he was meant to. And how had he been repaid? Taken prisoner by the King's Blades. No...this would end now.

There will not be another Shield.

Chapter

ALDIR

The Third is for Truth

Lord Byron Windsong's private quarters smelled of polished pine and aged leather, each piece of furniture a treasure collected from his travels throughout the Wide-World. There was an attractive settee of elaborately carved teak adorned with plush, stitched seats purchased in Oakblade; a writing top personally commissioned by the famed carpenters of Dawnsun; and perhaps most impressive, a cellaret built from one piece of mahogany, inlaid with the ebony and gold scales of the Windsong family's sigil. This marvel was supposedly designed and constructed by Carn Homain himself.

It was from this magnificent cabinetwork that Lord Byron pulled a bottle of red wine and poured two glasses. As he finished, he handed one to Aldir and said, "It is unfortunate your first trip to the Vines is marred by the pall of such grievous events, my lord. Perhaps one day you will sail with me in happier times."

Aldir received the offered drink and took a sip. *Delicious,* he thought. *Must be from his own reserve.*

The adage was obviously true: the wines of the Vines surpassed anything available in Rothspire.

Aldir smiled. "My father offers his sincerest apologies for what took place the other day. Please do not let this tarnish your trust in the crown."

"Sir Hugh Castac was a miserable lout, but..." Windsong sat upon a finely made chair. "Donnel Baird *is* my son-in-law, and though I do not condone much of his behavior, the death of his knight is a grave insult." He gestured for Aldir to sit. "Your presence as my escort goes a long way in mending this slight. But it does not absolve the crown. Recompense will be required."

"I would expect nothing less," said Aldir. "The king empowered me with the means to set this insult to right." He glanced around the room, wondering what he might be able to offer a man who fitted a cabin in his galley with such extravagance. "We wish no ill between us and the Lord of Riverfront."

No smile appeared on Lord Byron's face. "I promised only to broker a peace with Baird. As for any ill—" He sipped his wine. "My son-in-law licks at wounds—real or perceived. I commit to nothing where his pride is concerned. Though your choice in companion does little to disavow the affront he surely feels from your family."

"I understand how his attendance might be misread, but believe me when I say that Sir Rhohl's attendance is meant only as a sign of goodwill from the crown. The Graymeres do not endorse Rhen's actions."

"It is not me you must resolve this issue with," said Byron. "I am but a voice in the chorus of Baird's conscience. Yes, my voice holds particular sway with him—but as you are aware, a man chooses their own path, regardless of advice."

"So, you believe Lord Baird will reject our attrition? He

will still hold us responsible for this—" Aldir searched for the word—"incident?"

A low laugh rolled from Byron's tongue. "Incident? Yes, how diplomatic."

He rapped his fingers against the rosewood table. "My dear Primacy, what is to be done with the boy?"

"The Shield of the Princess is to stand trial."

"Trial?" asked Byron. "And who is to oversee this?"

"As per law, the King's Cabinet, lord."

"Ha. Will my son-in-law be allowed to speak at this trial?"

"It would be highly irregular to entertain anyone but a member of the King's Cabinet as a juror."

Lord Byron shook his head. "Is this the message the king sends? A member of his own court *murders* a knight in the service of a lord of the realm, and the only justice he *might* receive is decided upon by the cronies of the crown?" He stared blankly at Aldir. "I am sorry, my lord, but this entire situation reeks of conspiracy."

Conspiracy? What are you suggesting? Rhen should have never been in that competition. You think we condone this?

"It is the law, Lord Byron," Aldir said. "If *we* do not uphold it...Onyris is left with nothing."

"The law?" Byron scoffed. "I do not claim to tell you your business, Primacy, but *the law* seemed quite flexible when it allowed a *brocken* to participate in a melee. And not a simple field melee either—but the King's Tournament. You do not need me to tell you how suspicious this sounds."

"I can swear to you, the crown knew nothing of this change in law before it was too late. Our adept brought this to my father's attention only moments before the melee began."

"And this fact brings Sir Hugh Castac back to life?"

"Well, no, b-but…" stammered Aldir.

"But you and the king thought I might agree to whatever you asked, because you offered to sail in my retinue?" Windsong's tone did not change; he maintained the same casual note, as though he said nothing more inflammatory than a comment on the weather.

"I suggest you and your father revisit *your* laws. Dalantis the Wise, though perceptive, was not prescient. We no longer live in the times of Dartsuil. Onyris grows, Aldir. It is time the crown grows as well."

Aldir wished again he'd never accepted the role of Primacy. He cared little for the game of politics. "I will advise my father on this."

Maybe if he just accepted Windsong's polite threats, he would be able to go back to his chamber and sleep. He no longer had energy for this bout of verbal fencing. "I do not disagree with you. The crown must mold to the kingdom it covers."

"You are no fool at least," said Byron. "But I question your power to change the king's mind." He opened a fresh bottle of red and poured a new round.

"Fate can be cruel. You would have been better suited to your brother's boots, but alas, second born is second considered." A rueful expression crossed his face.

What does that mean? "I prefer my own boots," said Aldir, as stoic as possible. The mention of his brother's boots, though—what was Windsong getting at?

"Ah," said Byron as he finished his wine. "The night grows late. Let us retire. If we are lucky, we might continue this conversation." He stood and shuffled over to the ornate cellaret, corking the bottle.

"I apologize in advance, but I will be rather indisposed for most of our journey," he said. "But please, four nights from now, I ask that you attend my final feast. It is a dismal affair for the most part; a groveling session for the gentry who sail with us, but...it would mean the world to me if you were to celebrate our arrival."

"How can I say no?" asked Aldir, finishing his drink. *If you mean for me to grovel...*

Aldir entered his quarters, overtaken by tiredness. These mental jousts did nothing but sap him of energy. The wine helped little. His eyes became heavy, and the silhouette of his bed drew him closer to a respite he desperately desired. With the last of his vigor, he stripped and fell into the warm, inviting comfort of his mattress. The moment his head hit soft pillows, he forgot about his conversation with Lord Byron Windsong. He had not realized how taxing the days since leaving Rothspire had been.

In a matter of moments, he drifted off to sleep.

He stood on the shore and smiled lovingly at Irymar as she bathed in soft waves.

She wore thin linens of green and red that clung to her wet body and beckoned him to follow her.

Her smile was a radiant glow in the moonlight.

The sound of the sea muted her calls, but Aldir guessed her desires.

"Not yet," he shouted, his voice silenced by the howl of crashing swells.

He wanted to stay in this moment—it was perfection; she was perfection.

Irymar crinkled her nose in mock anger and turned back to

her game. A large wave rolled in and she threw her body into it, letting it sweep her from the seafloor and carry her closer to him, only to be dragged back before reaching him. Each time this happened, she glanced over her shoulder, making certain he still laughed at her childish play. Then, once she caught his smile, she prepared herself for the next tug-of-war between the immeasurable power of the sea and her lover.

"*Irymar!*" *shouted Aldir, but the noise of the waves silenced his warning.* "*Irymar!*" *he tried again.*

Something was wrong… Gods no!

"*Irymar—*"

A wave of incredible size formed behind her. It rushed towards the shore and gathered in its immensity until it stood tall as a fortress.

She couldn't see it!

Aldir ran into the water, heedless of the sea's anger. The tide pulled at him, its icy slap causing him to lose his breath. His head dipped below the waterline. In an instant, his vision turned black.

Struggling against the might of this watery giant, he managed to lift his head for a moment. Cold air rushed into his lungs, and he choked, but Irymar had vanished.

No, not again.

With all his strength, he fought the incessant might of the waves, but they proved too strong.

I cannot help her if I drown.

He struggled back to shore.

Bent and gasping, he vomited seawater. His head raged in agony, his eyes—red with tears—stung as though he had been stabbed. He fell into the sand, his face bloodied by a million invisible knives.

He rolled over to his back, panting like a beast. The waves calmed themselves. He stared up into the black sky—empty but for six dark stars.

The sight of the ominous stars and the sudden chill that blanketed his body made him shiver. Sapped of energy, he slowly turned to his side and screamed. No sound came, but in his terror, he convulsed.

Beside him lay Irymar—pale and green. Her black hair was a tangle of blood and seaweed. The violence of the water had stripped her of her clothing, and the sand had stripped her of her flesh.

She lay face down, a mottled corruption of decrepit wonder. If not for the fact that he had just seen her, Aldir would never have believed this was his beloved; she was no more than a rotten carcass retched from the stomach of the sea.

He mustered what strength remained to him and pushed away from this drowned horror. Blood dripped from innumerable abrasions, but the pain compared little to the fear that engulfed him.

Irymar coughed and rolled over. She faced him—a black sludge spewed from lifeless blue lips. Her eyes, colorless, glowed with brilliant opacity. She fixed her gaze upon him. The greasy black substance that seeped from her mouth trickled down her chin.

She hissed.

"Malighaunt is coming..."

"My lord...my lord," said a faint voice.

Aldir awoke in panic. He swung his arm reflexively, warding off the dreadful creature of his dream. In his frenzy, he recognized the face of Worm, peering down like some flustered maiden.

"My lord?" asked Worm again. "Are you well?"

Gods! thought Aldir. *How long have you been here?*

He stared through half-open eyes and said, "I am well, Worm. I am well."

His body ached, but waking to the bright light that shone in through thin curtains helped wash away the fear of his nightmare.

Malighaunt. Where have I heard that name before?

The memory of his decaying wife receded, but he held onto the name like a starving man holding onto a scrap of moldy bread.

Malighaunt.

"Worm!" Aldir shouted. "Get me something to write with."

The young boy jumped at the request and busied himself with procuring his master's needs.

He asks no questions, thought Aldir. *He is my tractable dog.*

The more time he spent with Werman Gault, the more he understood his father's affinity for the boy. No one in the entire realm followed orders as diligently as Worm.

In only a matter of moments, Werman returned with a scroll of gilded parchment and a lovely, feathered dip pen.

Staying in the well-appointed quarters of Lord Byron Windsong had its benefits. There was nothing he might desire that was not already accounted for.

Without thanking his page, Aldir wet his dip pen and scribbled the word 'Malighaunt' on the parchment. He crumpled the paper and shoved it under his pillow, not allowing for the chance he might forget this name.

If Irymar's attempts to speak to him could be trusted, Malighaunt was sure to be a name he must not fail to remember.

Worm teetered nervously beside his bed. He asked, "Who is Irymar…my lord?"

He wouldn't know, would he? The Gaults were from Swordfish Bay, and though it was less than a hundred miles from Rothspire, a boy who was no more than 12 years old would have no reason to remember the name of a woman who had died six years before his birth. Not when the woman would never be a princess or queen. No. His wife's name was but a footnote in the history of Onyris.

"She was my…wife. Why do you ask?" He tried to sound nonplussed, but his red eyes and shaky voice belied his attempts.

"You called her name," said Worm. If he was pretending to sound unconcerned, he was a worse actor than Aldir. "Over and over…"

Aldir dragged himself from his bed. "She is of no importance, Werman. She is dead."

He bent down and grabbed the clothes he'd stripped off last night.

After he threw his trousers and tunic over himself, he mussed Worm's hair and said, "You will understand one day."

With that, he opened the door to his chamber and walked out into the halls of Lord Byron Windsong's galley.

The days of their journey passed with little significance. Aldir dreamt little, never again finding himself in the dark nightmare he'd had that first night.

His time was mostly spent holding council with Sir Rhohl, determining the best course of action upon their arrival in the Vines. If they were to find Odain, they must be sure to play the parts of Primacy and Shield to the best of their abilities. Never could they press their hidden agenda. After the tragedies that had befallen the kingdom, their presence would not be questioned; the prince must return to Rothspire.

Once they landed in Maresport, they would request transport to Whitecliff, the capital of the Vines. Lord Gambyn Halsted, the Lord of Whitecliff, would surely receive them and reunite the prince with his brother and his Shield.

"What if he is no longer there?" asked Rhohl, dipping his bread into thick, brown gravy. The mess hall was empty but for them. He bit into the soft loaf and said, "You have to think about these things."

Aldir thought on this for a long moment before he said, "I will demand we are brought to him."

I am the Primacy of the Realm.

He picked at his meal. Bits of tender chicken fell from his fork. "They cannot deny the courtesies of the crown." Grease dripped down his chin, and he wiped it away with a silk napkin.

"They do not hold to our courtesies, my lord."

"They are part of the realm, are they not?"

Rhohl lowered his head and stared at the roasted boar on his plate. "Yes," he said. "And no."

"How so?"

"Well," Rhohl said, "they are under the control of the crown, yes, but…the lords of the Seven Families are aware of their influence. The Vines provide the majority of coin for the banks of Rothspire, and they—" He closed his eyes as he drank wine from a crystal chalice. "They know that any threat we might impose is nothing but bluster. The crown cannot afford to lose their support."

"I am well aware of this," Aldir said. "But they are vassals of Rothspire! They hold no sovereignty. Their wealth is nothing more than succor of the king." He pushed his plate away.

"Gods! Al," Rhohl said. "You know how men are." He grabbed a leg of lamb from the table and tore at the perfectly crisped flesh. Pieces of burnt skin flew from his mouth as he spat out, "Give them the smallest amount of freedom and soon each of them become kings of their own lands."

And how many realms are in Onyris? Seven… Seven kings, eh? "What do you suggest?"

"Simple," said Rhohl, waving the bone. "We take back what is ours. We find Odain, put his stubborn ass on the throne, and reclaim the Vines. The king—no disrespect—has only a few more years at best. He will not deny this claim. Not if the prince and the Primacy both agree upon it. We have the might, Al. All we need to do is use it. If Rothspire musters its forces…there is not a realm in the Wide-World that might stand against it."

A̲ldir wandered the passageways under the deck of the galley.

Did he seriously suggest we go to war with the Vines?

This was a ridiculous proposition, but if Odain truly had come to harm, then… *We might have no choice. And Windsong's comment—a better fit for my brother's boots. What did that mean?*

That comment battered around his head as he turned a corner and mindlessly walked down a flight of stairs that led to a lower deck. The light dimmed and he realized he'd come across an area of the ship he was unfamiliar with.

How big is this bloody thing?

He made to turn around, but the slow groan of old hinges snapped him from his thoughts.

He blindly felt out for the bulkhead and noticed a gap in the walls. Without thinking, he squeezed into the dark gap and peered out, desirous of avoiding whatever came from beyond the creaking door.

The groan of metal rubbing against metal ended with a loud clang, as though something heavy had landed on the floor. Footsteps pounded against the decking and an extremely tall man plodded past where Aldir hid, panting.

Aldir watched while holding his breath. His heart raced and a searing pain exploded behind his eyes, but he would not take his gaze from the man's receding figure.

I am the Primacy of the bloody realm, he thought to himself, but the title was meaningless when he felt as afraid as a child who hid from invisible monsters. Why this man caused such fear in him, he did not know, but the idea of being found filled him with dread.

Though he saw only a glimpse of this man as he walked up the stairs, Aldir noticed his pale, deformed face.

It is a monster.

The man disappeared up the stairs into the upper passageway. Aldir waited a short time before he snuck out from his hiding place. He wanted to inspect the cause of the noise, but the possibility of the man returning was too much for him, and though his curiosity gnawed at him, the anxiety stirring in him told him to return to his cabin.

He dashed up the stairs and retraced his steps through the ship until he stood before the door to his quarters. His luck had held enough that he met no other soul on his way back. Sweat beaded on his brow as he entered his room.

Malighaunt...?

Aldir laid on his bed and pondered the name until he drifted into a dreamless sleep.

The last night of his journey found Aldir sitting behind a beautifully polished table in the mess hall. Drink flowed and the food seemed never-ending. Two hours of pleasant conversation had elapsed and Aldir had begun to believe that this invitation was no more than a social courtesy—a feast designed to impress a member of the royal family.

Byron Windsong sat at the head of a long table surrounded by a revolving cast of toadies and fawners; he spoke few words to this obsequious rabble, a pensive frown permanently carved into his face. Though he said little, his eyes darted around the room, studying each person intently.

Aldir noted this quiet inspection; he gave a gracious smile of acknowledgement each time Windsong fixed his gaze upon him.

Most of these guests were landowners or wealthy merchants who travelled to Rothspire for the King's Tournament—all of them indebted to Byron Windsong for various reasons.

If the flattery of those who called on the king irked Aldir, these unctuous lords and ladies must be insufferable to the Lord of Maresport. His conspicuous detachment from the affair was completely understandable.

As the evening wore on and more of these ephemerae excused themselves, Aldir wondered when he might be able to retire and return to his cabin—his longing for sleep grew cumbersome.

He placed his drink down and surveyed the hall, empty now, save for he, Rhohl, and Lord Byron. All other attendees had quit the feast in a courteous manner. A more appropriate time to thank his host and withdraw to his quarters might not present itself.

He stood and approached Lord Byron. "A glorious feast, Lord Byron! Again, my thanks for this invitation. I look forward to receiving you the next time you are in Rothspire. I only hope our cordialities will meet the measure of the Windsongs."

Lord Byron scrutinized Aldir. "Please, my lord, take a seat." His voice held no emotion, but he gestured to a chair beside him. "There is much to discuss."

Aldir bowed but politely declined the invitation. "We arrive tomorrow, and I have much to attend to before we disembark. Please accept my regrets, but the night grows late."

"I do not accept," said Windsong. He motioned to the chair once again. "Please, Aldir. I will not keep you over long." Cowed and uncertain of how to react to Windsong's refusal, Aldir smiled nervously and took the offered seat. He caught Rhohl's suspicious gaze but nodded in affirmation, expressing only the slightest hint of exasperation.

"Sir Rhohl, if you will excuse us, our host desires private words, and I am not one to deny such a distinguished friend. See to my page. Master Gault will need assistance with the readying of our things."

"Of course, my lord," said Rhohl, raising an eyebrow before bowing. He thanked Lord Byron and departed, ducking his head under the archway of the mess hall and closing the doors behind him.

Alone with Byron Windsong, Aldir dutifully praised his host again, hoping this might only be a brief matter of genial politics.

But hope more than often proved itself vain.

"You revel in queer company," said Byron.

"I have explained Sir Rhohl's presence, have I not?" *Why must we have this conversation again?*

"It is not the brocken I speak of." He poured wine into two ornate goblets. "I did not recognize him at first, but that is Damen Gault's boy, is it not?"

Worm? "Werman? Yes, he is Lord Gault's son," answered Aldir hesitantly. "Why is this queer?"

"How long has he been in your service?"

"He is my father's page and attends me at the king's request."

What does it matter?

"He has proven himself a more than adequate attendant," said Aldir.

"How long?" asked Windsong.

"Less than a year, I believe," answered Aldir, taken aback by the seriousness in the man's voice. "Do you find issue with him?"

"Interesting," said Byron. "He came into your father's service before the Iron Woman stepped down?"

"If memory serves."

"Perhaps the king would do well to vet his charges more vigorously." Windsong tilted his wine back and drank it all in one gulp. "We have a custom in my home; I would be most pleased if you indulge me."

He pushed Aldir's goblet towards him and said, "The first drink to be shared between friends is for pleasure."

Friends? Aldir thought. *If this will please you.* He followed his host's lead.

"And the second," said Byron, pouring another round, "is to savor."

Instead of downing the drink, he took a small sip and inhaled sharply. "Please, please." He smiled, his hands speaking the words his mouth did not.

I have been a part of worse customs.

Aldir took a moment to taste the wine. It was the most delicious thing he'd ever drank, its transcendent flavor so comforting it almost made him forget Windsong's strange question. His body relaxed; his tiredness receded.

They kept no conversation as they finished this second drink, but each time the grape met their lips, they nodded in silent agreement, as though they shared a long, unwritten history with one another.

Boldened by the intoxicating flavor, Aldir asked, "And what is the third for?"

Windsong sneered, "The truth, my lord." He emptied the bottle into their goblets. "For it is the truth you seek in the Vines, is it not?"

Aldir stared mistrustfully at Windsong and then searched the hall.

"You are in no danger here, my lord. Once you partake in the customs of the Vines, you are under my protection," said Lord Byron. "But I am quite concerned with young Master Gault."

"He is but a boy. Why would you find concern?"

"Did the king receive his father when the boy arrived?" Windsong's voice became hurried.

"I do not know," said Aldir. "Is this important?"

"I would not ask if it were not."

Stunned by the force of the statement, Aldir stammered, "I...I...do not remember us hosting Lord Damen, if that is what you mean?"

"Of course you did not host him, boy."

Byron Windsong slammed his drink on the table. "He has been missing for over a year." He glared at Aldir. "Odd that this is when his son arrived in Rothspire, is it not?"

"I was unaware Lord Damen is missing." *If you speak the truth.*

"You are unaware of too many things, Primacy," said Byron. The insult was not veiled.

"Mind your tongue, Windsong. I am the Primacy of the Realm. You dare not speak to the king in such a way; do not assume you may speak to me in any other manner."

A slow, languid laugh dripped from his mouth. "Perhaps I was wrong about you, Aldir. You and your father are fools."

Aldir stood in a rage. "The drink goes to your head. You forget yourself!"

"Sit, sit, sit," said Windsong, waving off his temper. "Your anger is childish. It does not frighten me."

"If you asked me to stay only to chastise me, I see no need to linger in your company." Aldir spun and stepped away from the table.

Unfazed by the Primacy's outburst, Byron remained seated and said, "Lord Damen is held by the Voress Ní. His son is not to be trusted. A boy will do many *unsavory* things in order to save his father." He sipped his wine casually. "I know what Kayvold Archwood brought to you, Aldir. Do you not wish to understand the danger you are in?"

Aldir staggered back to his seat and stared agape at Lord Byron. He wanted to ask…anything. But words would not reach his tongue.

"Do not be surprised, my lord. Your aunt is not the only one with their spies." He frowned. "The prince did not heed my warnings. I hoped his brother might be blessed with more sense. Or have I judged you incorrectly?"

"What happened to him?" asked Aldir, his voice a mixture of fear and anger.

"Happened?" asked Windsong. "I know as much as what happened to him as you, my lord…but *why* it happened—" He frowned then swirled his wine before taking a deliberate sip. "Well, that is something entirely different, isn't it?"

Gods! You could teach Laustair a lesson in riddles. "Are you saying those were his legs?"

"Yes," said Windsong with no hesitation. "Do you know the name Ichaem Leonardis?"

And there it is, Aldir thought.

His father had named the specter that haunted his family, and Windsong had just given life to the ghost. But he would be damned if he played along so easily. "No, I cannot say I do."

"That is unfortunate. Perhaps the Iron Woman and the King of Onyris wish they'd never heard the name either?" He sighed. "Dear boy, you are the Primacy, I should not have to tell you. But perhaps the Graymeres hope old promises die along with those who made them." Windsong smirked.

"Ichaem Leonardis and the Voress Ní do not forget promises so easily." He filled their goblets. "The years of peace the king so eagerly claims to have won are nothing more than a lease. When he and Teryse Killion signed their names on a silent contract with the Voress Ní, they only *rented* their time." Wine leaked from the side of his mouth, and he licked at the red liquid. "But now they refuse to pay what they promised, and…well…their time has expired."

"What are you saying?" asked Aldir. "What does Werman have to do with this?"

"A son will go to extraordinary measures to protect his

family, will he not?" He eyed Aldir. "You find yourself in the same situation, if I do say so."

"Are you telling me the Voress Ní have Odain?"

"There is the wisdom I knew you possessed!" Windsong pointed at Aldir and then pushed the goblet of wine closer to him.

"Your brother would not listen to me, though he claimed to know all about Ichaem Leonardis. Perhaps your father trusts him with secrets he wishes to hide from the Primacy. I do not judge." He winked. "The children of kings," said Windsong, almost as a judgement. "You have no idea of what goes on in the Wide-World. To you, Onyris is only as large as the walls of the castle. But it is not your fault. A king must shelter his children from the horrors of reality; if they do not, who would willingly take the crown?" He patted Aldir's knee.

"The Seven Families of the Vines are a fragile alliance held by mere threads of gossamer, but each of those threads can be traced back to a single point—a puppeteer's rod that hangs over our heads. The same rod that Rothspire is now attached to. When the prince decided to ignore my advice, he severed your family from this rod. The Voress Ní care for nothing but loyalty...and payment."

"Payment for what?" asked Aldir. "Ending Robart Moorcroft's rebellion surely cannot be worth my brother's life!"

He knew he'd shown his hand. Admitting to the knowledge of Ichaem Leonardis's involvement in the breaking of Moorcroft's insurrection proved he knew of the man. But he no longer cared for his game of secrecy. He must know why his brother had been attacked.

A short burst of laughter erupted from Lord Byron as he clapped his hands. "Well played, my lord...well played."

He smiled a grim smile. "I was wondering when you might break."

Frustrated, Aldir hissed, "No more games, Windsong! Tell me everything, or I will call Sir Rhohl."

"Everything?" asked Byron. "You are certain you want to know *everything*?"

The ship hit a large wave and rocked violently. Aldir grabbed onto the table while Windsong barely shifted his weight in his seat. He glared at the Lord of Maresport and seethed, "Where is my brother?"

The door of the hall opened, and a man entered.

He must have been over seven-feet tall, and his skin was as pale as a phantom.

The man from the lower deck. Aldir's skin tightened, gooseflesh covering him. An irrational terror crept across his body as the man lumbered past him. The terrible giant approached Lord Byron, paying no attention to Aldir. He leaned in close to Windsong's ear and whispered something.

Byron nodded in silent assent, but no change came over his face. He whispered something back then shooed the man off. He apologized to Aldir for the interruption and said, "The message is clear." His voice took on a mocking tone. "The prince's legs are but a symbol. Are you too daft to read it?"

He watched the man depart, strength returning to him the moment the doors closed behind the pale monster. "Perhaps I am too daft."

This had all become too much for him. Aldir glanced behind him, worried there might be another surprise. Not waiting for anything else to disrupt him, he shouted, "Just tell me! I am done with riddles."

"Two legs, in their boots." Windsong studied the door

and then calmly noted Aldir. "It is no more difficult to read than a child's tale. Your aunt, *the Iron Woman*, and your father have built their legacy on a myth, my lord. Robart Moorcroft was not defeated by the Graymeres. He was assassinated by Ichaem Leonardis, the ghost behind the Voress Ní. The prince's legs are but a symbol. What he could do to the Shaded Realm, he has done to Rothspire. The other boot has fallen, Aldir. War comes to the Graymeres."

Assured by the latching sound of the door, it was now time for Aldir to laugh. He remembered what Rhohl had said about the might of Rothspire. There was not a realm in all of the Wide-World that might stand against them. "War?" He clutched the polished table again as the boat shifted. "You must be jesting. No army in Onyris can hope to defeat us."

"The walls of Castle Dartsuil will not be assailed by men in armored plate," said Windsong. "No, that is not the way of the Voress Ní." He smiled again, a hopeful smile full of cunning. "Your family will suffer tragedy after tragedy, but you will not see your enemy. As you have not seen the young Gault boy for who he is. As your father has recklessly sent both his children to death."

Both his children? Aldir pushed away from the table and jumped to his feet. He reached for a sword that was not at his side. His body grew warm as terror gripped him. He tried to calm himself. "Why would you tell me this?"

"Because my lord, Malighaunt, requires it." Windsong's voice dropped to a whisper.

Malighaunt? How did he know the name?

"Malighaunt?" asked Aldir, his voice trembling by fear. "How...how do you...?"

The doors of the hall flew open, and a man of gargantuan

size entered, pushing a shrouded figure in a chair fixed to wheels.

The man was covered in steel plate—an enameled matte black—except for the glistening white mountain whose peak ended in the tip of a sword. The sigil of the Moorcrofts.

In the huge man's left hand was a sword twice the size of any Aldir had ever seen.

Rhen? What are you doing here?

"Rhen?" asked Aldir, paralyzed by confusion.

The brocken strode forward and lifted the shroud.

Gods!

Aldir gasped as he gazed in dismay at the horrific sight of the man lumped into the rolling seat.

Prince Odain's body sat tied to the chair. His legs were hewn just below the knees. His arms were severed at the elbows. His mouth hung open in a grisly frown from where tongue and jaw were removed. Where his eyes should have been were nothing but two black holes, as if scooped from their sockets. He did not move, save for the shallow rise of his chest. He was still alive.

"Odain!" screamed Aldir. He rushed to his brother's side but was stopped by the tip of Rhen's sword. He looked from Rhen to Lord Byron.

The memory of Rhen and Edlen darting through the halls of the keep as they battled with toy swords rushed to his mind. He had been there at Rhen's birth and had loved him as he did his own daughter. But now...

"Rhen," Aldir cried. "Rhen! Help me!"

There was no recognition in Rhen's eyes.

"Rhen!" pleaded Aldir again. But his words would not avail him. His voice quavered as he turned to Lord Byron and pitifully asked, "But your custom—I'm under your protection."

"I may have lied," said Lord Byron Windsong as he sipped at his wine.

The hilt of Rhen's sword crashed through the air and landed with an explosive thud as it smashed into the top of Aldir's head. A gout of blood sprayed over a finely polished table.

A quick sharp pain exploded behind Aldir's eyes before the room turned black.

CHAPTER 31

DARRIN

The Akkuladine

Less than a league from Leddenwell, Darrin slowed his horse and covered his face. The stifling heat of the massive fire washed over him. "We can go no further!" he said, his voice barely audible over the din of crackling wood and rushing wind. "It's too hot for the horses!"

The terrible blaze that ate away at the towering walls of the city filled the night with an unwholesome glow and vomited a foul smoke, which clouded the forest in smog and heat.

"You are an Eye, are you not?" asked Kayvold, coming to a stop beside him. "We have come this far. We do not falter before our mission is complete." A mad determination was upon him. "Ride until your mount drops, and then run." He laughed and galloped off.

I will drop before she does, thought Darrin, and he tightened his legs around his horse and quickened his pace. Hot wind whipped across his face as he attempted to overtake the Lord-Overseer.

The ground sloped gradually downwards as they raced from the high ridge, their hope of meeting Captain Hadley and the other rovers pushing them beyond care.

If luck held, they might reach Hadley and his men at the entrance of Leddenwell.

If not... Darrin would not allow himself to think about that.

Built in the earliest years of Dartsuil's rule, Leddenwell was one of the first outposts of Rothspire and the largest village in Nauringale Forest. Originally a small trading post between the capital and the eastern provinces of Onyris, Leddenwell had quickly grown in economic power.

Within a hundred years of its founding, the village had developed into a thriving city populated by the high merchant class. But as the wealth of Leddenwell had increased, so too did its worries.

After the sundering of the lands, Leddenwell had become a target of raiders from the Fyrelands, the now separated island beyond the Break. Realizing their city was defenseless to these brigands and marauders, the people of Leddenwell had raised a wall of trees to surround the land.

As they stood today, the close growth of hyperions towered nearly two-hundred feet tall and made entry into the city almost impossible from anywhere but the Wood Gate.

It was these enormous trees that now burned so hotly and lit the forest like gargantuan torches. And it was this dreadful pyre that Darrin and Kayvold rode towards at incredible speed.

Some hundred yards before reaching the fiery city, Kayvold's horse reared, almost throwing him from his saddle. Once he regained control, he motioned for Darrin to halt.

"Ho!" said Kayvold, though he did not take his eyes from

the thing that had frightened his charger. He dismounted and stalked forward, not saying a word.

"What is it?" Darrin asked.

Kayvold did not respond.

Is that...? Darrin stepped down from his horse and followed Kayvold. The heat was excruciating. He pulled up his hood and moved closer to the object that blocked the road.

Gods! It can't be...

In the center of the path that led to the city stood a giant pointed stake. A body dangled limply from the tip, the back of its head crushed by the force of whatever had the strength to run this great spear through armor and bone. The bottom half of the corpse was gone, eaten away.

Ragged flesh sagged from underneath the uniform of Captain Walker Hadley. Torn and gnawed, bits of ripped organs hung from his eviscerated carcass, still dripping black blood, which landed in a pool of bones and entrails.

Darrin bent over and retched.

"We are too late," said Kayvold before reaching for his sword. The sound of steel sliding from between leather and wood seemed unnaturally loud.

No, thought Darrin as he knelt, hunched in an obscene position, hot sick dribbling from his lips. *How is that possible? We should have been ahead of them!*

He gazed around, following the trails of blood set before him. His eyes darted from one direction to the other—he and Kayvold had ridden into a field of slaughter.

No matter where he looked, the mutilated corpses of his brothers lay strewn about, their bodies tossed aside in ruin, disemboweled remains littering the field like spoiled carrion.

Over the clamor of flame, the riotous noise of their horses sounded. The beasts, now released from the steady hands of their masters, neighed and bucked, the horrendous chorus of their screams filling the air. Darrin snapped from his shock and turned only in time to see his charger kick wildly and bolt, then both horses disappeared into the cloud of smoke obscuring the land.

Dismayed, he had not the will to chase after them. He merely groaned and fell to his knees.

Finally, Kayvold tore his gaze from the horror of Hadley's body and grunted. He grabbed Darrin, pulling him to his feet.

"Cantlay! Draw your sword!" His body stiffened into a statue of sinewy muscle and determination; he held his blade aloft, ready for battle.

Darrin—dazed and terrified—reached for the hilt of his sword, but the sweat on his hands made his grip clumsy and weak. His blade thudded against the ground, and he fumbled to pick it up. As he bent over, a small phial slipped from his pocket and landed in the dirt.

Gleaming in the brilliance of the fire, the phial shone like a star fallen from the sky. No longer thinking about his sword, Darrin knelt and lifted the sparkling glass vial from the blood-soaked ground. The Mermaid's Kiss. He remembered Laustair's words: "Keep to hope."

The light blue liquid inside the vial beamed against the blaze.

"Now, Cantlay!" commanded Kayvold. "Now!"

Without thinking, Darrin uncorked the vial and drank its contents. In an instant, every muscle in his body tensed and then relaxed, his mind cleared, and the heat of the fire receded. Swift and purposefully, he grabbed the hilt of his sword and lifted it from the ground. The weapon gave confidence to his clarity.

From beyond the shadows of fire, Darrin observed the distorted movements of some sort of animal, but the silted manner in which this thing crawled reminded him of nothing he'd ever studied. The creature stalked the gloom. It was a beast the size of a large person but twisted, contorted, and hulking. It kept itself hidden from the flames—a black presence that hunted its prey in darkness.

A Blood Drinker? They were real. Darrin slipped beside Kayvold and tapped him on the shoulder. "My lord," he whispered. "Do you see it?"

Kayvold shrugged and stepped to the side, placing his body in front of Darrin's like a father protecting their child. "I sense it," he said, his voice laced with fear.

There was the dry crack of trampled leaves, and Darrin spun around. He stared through a wall of black smoke to his left. A pale shape, similar to the one lurking in the shadows, appeared. Nearer now than the other, it drew close enough for Darrin to discern its features.

The face, though masked by shadow and flame, was manlike—except for a protruding snout that reminded Darrin of a wolf. The thing wore tattered clothes, its taut, white skin visible under befouled rags.

It paced, blocking their escape. At first walking on four legs, it then stood and seemed just as comfortable on two. Though it prowled only a short distance from them, it did not attack.

The other one closed in, but like its companion, it stayed far enough off that it posed no imminent threat.

Darrin's eyes darted between the two when a thunder of stamping feet exploded from the dark. He turned in time to note two more of these beasts approaching, running wildly towards them.

Kayvold moved swiftly and slashed through the smoke, but these new arrivals stopped short and slinked away.

Was that a feint? Darrin glanced back. The first of the creatures moved closer, tightening the ring that he and Kayvold found themselves within. *They have snared us.*

The four creatures circled, pressing nearer each time they passed. As they advanced, a low growl came from one of them. In answer to this, the other three snarled in the same deep-throated groan. They were speaking to one another.

Kayvold held his sword in front of him and whispered to Darrin, "Mark the one who spoke first. That is their leader."

How do you know? Darrin nodded and gripped the hilt of his blade tightly as he and Kayvold spun slowly around, never taking their eyes from these things.

The beast who'd issued the command raised itself to its full height and took a step closer, its lips pulled back, exposing a mouth filled with black fangs that looked like a hundred gnarled daggers. It was then that Darrin noticed the thing's hands—similar to his own, except that these creature's fingers were extraordinarily long and came to sharp points where bone extended from pale skin like some horrific claw.

"More Eyes," it said in the common tongue, though the words seemed to pain the beast as they dripped from its tongue.

Darrin recoiled at the thing's voice. His throat clenched, and he was bathed in cold sweat.

"Lay your weapons down, and we may spare you. We have already feasted this night." It laughed and pointed towards the mutilated corpse of Captain Hadley.

The thing's laugh was worse than its words.

"Who are you to treat with me?" asked Kayvold, his blade

still held in defense. "I am the Lord-Overseer of the Eyes of the Forest. You must answer for your crimes."

Darrin stared at Kayvold, his mouth agape. *These beasts have slaughtered all of Elmfort's strongest men and the Lord-Overseer hopes to threaten them?*

Again, the thing laughed. This time, though, it spat blood at Kayvold's feet. "I am well aware of who you are... Archwood. Do not fool yourself. Your titles mean nothing to the Akkuladine. If you wish to be killed for sport, then I will not deny you this desire." It snapped its jaws and dropped to all fours then leapt, its black fangs gleaming in the firelight.

Just as the creature sprang at Kayvold, the other three rushed forward. Darrin did not think; his sword flashed through the air and caught one of them in the neck as it bounded towards him. Cold blood splashed across his face, but he did not stop. If he killed the thing or not, it did not matter—there was no time to consider anything. He must fight.

But as Darrin swung his blade, thrashing at anything that approached, the other beasts halted.

Their leader, the moment it leapt forward, had been struck through its throat by an arrow and now lay dead at Kayvold's feet.

Thwap! Thwap! Thwap!

The dull thud of three more arrows finding their mark slapped against Darrin's ears. He stood dumbfounded, gazing madly through the dark clouds of smoke. His hands shook, and the sword he clutched weighed as if it had been forged from stone. He looked around, still in a daze, studying the four corpses of the Akkuladine. Each of them had been pierced by a single arrow.

"Aye, I owed ya that one, eh Cantlay?" Haron strode forward through the smoke, followed by four men. He ran up to Darrin and threw his arms around him. "Didn't expect ta find ya still alive, lad." He did not release him from his embrace.

"Haron?" said Darrin, almost in tears. "Thank the Gods!" He held his chief tightly. "You...you made it!"

"Aye, boy," said Haron. He squeezed Darrin once more then turned to Kayvold. "My lord, it is good to see you." He bowed.

"They killed Hadley," said Kayvold without emotion. He stared down at the beast and pushed at its face with his boot. "How long have you been here?"

"A few hours, my lord," he said. "And it ain't just Hadley they got." Haron lowered his head and told them of what he'd found when he and the men of Tarranfort had arrived. The Akkuladine had already massacred the men of Elmfort and raised their hideous totem.

"But I think we was too many for their scouts to handle. A battalion of Weyburn's men are hunting a detachment of the beasts as we speak, but there is more of these—" he glanced down at the carcasses—"things than we believed. Not sure we 'ave enough men to mount a proper fight."

"What are they?" asked Kayvold.

"Not sure o' that, my lord. They ain't beasts, but they ain't men either."

"You called them scouts?" asked Darrin. "The same as we might use?"

"Aye," said Haron. "Didn't realize it until they, well...until they came across you lot." He gazed off through the smoke and into the flames that engulfed Leddenwell. "Had to learn 'ow they thought, didn't we?"

"What have you learned?" asked Kayvold, eyeing the old chief.

"Pack hunters, like wolves. We was watching them from the trees." He pointed to the tall pines in the distance. "Those first two, well, they was sentries. Must've signaled to the others once they thought they had ya."

"I'm glad you were keeping an eye on us, Ridgefront," Kayvold said. "Next time, maybe don't wait until their fangs are at our throats, eh?"

"Sorry, my lord, but had we not waited, we wouldna seen that they can speak."

The memory of the creature's terrible voice growled in Darrin's head. *I am well aware of who you are, Archwood.* "How did they know your name, my lord?"

Kayvold turned to look at Darrin, frowning. "Not a clue, Cantlay. But these are no wild animals that hunt us. We must be prepared; these things are cunning and strategic. If those four were merely scouts, then we can be certain more will come when their messages do not reach their masters."

He sheathed his sword and spoke to Haron. "Do you have any idea of their numbers? Or where the bulk of their force is mustered?"

"Aye, my lord. We've no accurate count, but I'd guess somewhere near a thousand. They move from within Leddenwell, but the fire is too hot for us to follow. Ian, here—" he motioned to one of the men from Tarranfort—"he's got the eyes of a bloody hawk. Well, he climbed up to the top of one o' those giant oaks. Said he marked a mass of them behind the walls. Seems the damned fire ain't a thing to them."

"Master Ian," said Kayvold, addressing the rover. "What exactly did you see?"

The man came forward and bowed. Though it was dark

and he had his hood pulled up, Darrin noted the man must be somewhere in his late twenties. His skin was black, and his eyes gleamed blue in the firelight. He looked directly at Kayvold and said, "They move in formation, my lord. Clusters of thirty to forty each, but it seemed to me they await orders. I spent some time in the army of Rothspire, and these things act like soldiers preparing for battle."

"A battle?" asked Kayvold, almost to himself. He paused for a moment of reflection and then said, "If that bastard knew my name, then it is quite clear they're expecting another fight. They must have known Hadley as well. And if that is true, then they are aware of the numbers of the Eyes."

He scanned the forest floor and sighed. "Hadley walked directly into their assault and marched all of these men to their death. That is why they did this to him." A madness flared in his eyes as he pointed towards the mangled remains of the captain. "Take this abomination down. Haron, take me to Captain Weyburn."

They crept quietly through the forest for some time before reaching the captain of Tarranfort. Aware that more of these beasts might be tracking them as they moved, they kept their blades at the ready. The rovers who came with Haron fitted arrows to their bows as they peered through the smoke.

Captain Edwerd Weyburn was a stout man, and what he lacked in height, he more than made up for in muscle. He was bald and aged but hale and lively behind his wrinkled face. He greeted Kayvold. "My lord, I am pleased to find you here."

They stood under the outstretched limbs of gigantic oaks and eucalyptus at the top of a small hill. A ring of archers guarded the perimeter of this crude encampment where the smoke was less dense. From this spot, they were able to keep watch on any threat that might attempt to close in on them.

"I did not hope that I might find you, Edwerd," said Kayvold as he shook the man's hand.

"We are Eyes, are we not?" said Weyburn. "Besides, Chief Ridgefront can be rather persuasive." He glanced at Haron.

"Harry is a good man," agreed Kayvold, but wasted no more time with courtesies. "Do we have enough men to fight these things?"

Weyburn's eyes turned to slits. "Not unless they continue to attack piecemeal, my lord. My archers can pick a few off if they remain hidden, but… " He lowered his voice. "Well, you saw what they did to Hadley."

"Walker and his men were taken unawares. They did not know what waited for them."

"Regardless," said Captain Weyburn, "Hadley had near a hundred men with him. Aware or not, they should never have suffered those kinds of losses. You saw those boys." He made a fist. "Mauled—each and every one of them. What kind of a thing would do that?"

"The Akkuladine," hissed Kayvold. "And if we cannot stop them…" He looked at the ground. "I fear they will not stop."

Darrin watched this conversation in silence, but upon hearing the despair in these men's voices, he interrupted. "My lord, Laustair said we should keep to hope. Perhaps he rides towards us with the army of Rothspire?"

A sad grin appeared on Kayvold's face as he looked at Darrin. "Not even the fastest riders in Onyris could travel that distance in four days, Cantlay. I am sorry, but whatever Laustair meant by his riddle, it did not involve the army of

Rothspire. No. Unless we choose to hide from our enemy, attacking only when they are few, I fear it is our responsibility to do what we may to defeat them."

"I have told you, my lord," said Weyburn. "We do not have the numbers needed. If we attempt an assault, we will end up like Hadley's men."

Kayvold frowned. "And if we do nothing, we will end up like Hadley, and so will the rest of Onyris."

"What do you—" But Captain Weyburn's words were cut short.

The hollow cry of a hundred war horns bleating as one rent the air.

Darrin's blood ran cold and the hair on his neck stiffened. Something awful had been signaled. Death marched forward, their choice made for them.

One of the sentries called out from the top of a tree, "The gates of Leddenwell crumble! They are coming!"

"To arms!" shouted Kayvold. "To arms! We ride to slaughter!" He leapt atop a destrier and lifted his sword. "Ride now!"

DARRIN'S charger fell to the ground as one of the beasts lunged forward and tore his horse's throat open. He landed hard on the dirt and rolled away, managing to avoid the weight of the animal crashing on top of him. He jumped up and searched for his blade.

Not again.

The sword lay only a few feet from him, but the beast who'd killed his horse stood over it, its mouth awash with blood.

The thing snapped its jaws and roared. Darrin stared into the creature's eyes and saw nothing but black hatred.

The beast looked at Darrin's sword and howled in chilling laughter. Bits of gnarled flesh hung from its exposed fangs and long strands of blood dribbled down its chin. It kicked the blade towards Darrin and snarled again.

It is playing with me. He cared not for its reasons. Instead, he moved as quickly as he could and lifted the sword. But not quickly enough.

The thing raced forward and slammed into him. Before he knew it, they were rolling across the ground, the creature's teeth snapping at his throat. He let go of his sword and pushed with both hands against the thing's face, using all his strength to keep it from ripping him open. The beast was too strong. Darrin's muscles were already strained, and every moment they continued to wrestle, he could feel his resolve breaking.

It was too much. He could no longer fight. He released his grip on the thing's face and closed his eyes. *I am sorry, Laustair. I have failed.*

The beast reared its head back and bayed, the orange-red glow of firelight reflecting against its pale flesh. But as it plunged its bloody snout down, its cries were silenced.

Darrin opened his eyes as the headless body of the creature slumped to the ground beside him.

"Now ya owe me," said Haron from atop his brown destrier, his blade wet with the beast's blood. "Get up, lad. It ain't over." He rode off into the fray.

Darrin stared around the battlefield. There were hundreds of these things. At least two to every man. And though they attacked with a ferocity beyond anything he thought capable, they were not an unorganized mess of wild beasts. They moved in formation and kept their lines.

He got to his feet and lifted his sword. It would be foolish to stay in any one place too long. He looked for somewhere he might be useful and started to run. *If I can kill even one of them,* he thought, *perhaps that will be enough.*

Not far ahead, Haron thrust his blade into one of the things.

Thank the Gods, he hasn't gotten too far. "Harry!" shouted Darrin, but his voice was another muffled wail in the din. He ran forward, hoping that if he stayed near his chief, he might at least double his odds of survival.

Horses stamped past as he ran, and the horrible grunts and shrieks of the Akkuladine carried through the night.

Darrin slowed for a moment and glanced up to the sky. Far above the black smoke, the first rays of sun colored the tops of the trees. He tore his gaze from the sunrise and stared in front of him.

Two Akkuladine hunched over the place he had just seen Haron. They ripped at something, spitting bloody rags into the air.

No! Darrin rushed forward, his blade readied to kill whatever stood before him, no longer concerned with his own safety.

The moment he reached the two beasts, he slashed at the closest, getting his blade lodged halfway through the thing's hairless torso. It turned briefly to see the one who killed it before sagging over, wrenching the blade from Darrin's hand. The second pulled back from the body it feasted on and roared. But Darrin was no longer frightened by its sickening threats.

If they can think, they can feel fear.

Darrin roared back, pulling a dirk from his belt, and

leapt at the filthy creature. The small blade pierced the thing's neck and Darrin pushed all of his weight into the thrust. As soon as he felt the hard steel meet soft flesh, he did not stop. A madness was on him. Like one of these foul beasts, he continued to rip his dagger into the thing's throat until he was covered in its blood.

Once certain of the creature's death, Darrin released the handle of his dagger and gazed upon the mangled carcass. He felt nothing but anger. When he spun away from this carnage and looked down at the man the Akkuladine feasted on, he nearly collapsed.

Haron lay in a crumpled mess among the ruins of his horse. Both had been torn apart, their viscera intertwined in tattered ropes of half-eaten flesh. Neither moved in the slightest.

Darrin howled and grabbed at Haron, his eyes still opened in surprise. As he pawed at his friend, his hands smeared more blood over his chief's wrinkled face.

"Harry! Harry!" screamed Darrin. "Harry!"

Haron Ridgefront gave no answer.

"But I owe you! You cannot..." said Darrin, whimpering. "You old bastard, you cannot!"

Darrin leaned over and wept, but the battle had not ended. The awful cries of more Eyes meeting their vicious ends reminded him of this fact. He lifted his head and gazed through a blur of tears.

Everywhere he looked, he saw more of the same.

The Akkuladine washed over the men of Tarranfort. This was the end of the Eyes of the Forest. This was the end of Onyris.

He lowered his head and buried it into Haron's chest.

Above him, the sun rose and bathed the field in red light. A miasma of putrid smoke and death.

If this is the end, I will die a warrior.

Darrin stood. The thought of leaving Haron's side stung, but he would not let his friend's death be in vain. He grabbed the hilt of his sword and wrenched it from the corpse of the beast it was stuck in.

He raised his blade and shouted, "Haron!"

He bounded forward and raced towards the nearest creature.

As he ran screaming, his sword glinting in the morning sun, a blinding flash of white light filled the sky. Everything stopped.

Darrin gazed up. As though the sun itself burst forth from the sky, a brilliant radiance entered the battle. From inside this burning star, an enormous bear bolted across the field. This bear towered over all others—even on all fours, it stood nearly twenty-feet tall.

The massive animal tore through the remnants of the Akkuladine; those who did not flee at the sight of it soon found themselves nothing more than dead branches in a storm.

Darrin stood frozen, mouth agape.

The bright star, which heralded the end of the battle, floated forward, dimming slightly. Once it reached the middle of the field, it no longer shone with such terrible brightness. A great white fire glowed in the center of the flame. Inside was a man, but a man of incredible size and a beauty beyond imagining. He spoke without words, his voice entering the thoughts of all on the battlefield.

"Return to your master, foul beasts. You are no longer permitted to plague the lands of man."

Darrin fell to the ground and clutched his ears, but the voice pierced his mind. He felt as though his head might shatter. Through squinted eyes, he watched as man and beast dropped at these words.

Another voice entered his mind. From where, Darrin could not see.

"You arrive too late, Somath," it said.

Whereas the first voice rang so clearly in Darrin's mind, almost to the point of pain, the words that came from the second were a bitter dagger in his heart. Dread and despair filled him, as though he may never know anything but fear and horror.

It continued, this time almost laughing. "Malighaunt will be pleased to know you have revealed yourself."

From beyond the walls of Leddenwell, a figure appeared, striding forward past the retreating forces of the Akkuladine. The figure stood near in size to the man wreathed in white fire, but in place of bright-white flame, this being was encased in an inferno of yellow-orange. It too held a beauty that inspired awe. Flaxen hair flowed wildly around it and mingled with the strands of delicate golden robes.

It stepped from beyond the flames and raised its hand. "Call our brother back, Somath. Dalnor need not hide behind his costumes. We are brothers, are we not?"

"I see you remain his shadow, Inganar," the man encased in white fire said. "I will call you brother again when you rid yourself of Malighaunt's darkness." He walked forward, casting the flame away. His voice was no longer filling men's minds; instead, Laustair spoke aloud. "The path of Clear Wisdom is still yours to choose, Inganar. Forsake your master and walk amongst your brothers. We shall forgive your trespasses."

"So speaks the one who wishes his trespasses forgiven," laughed Inganar. "No, Somath. The dam is burst, and there is no ground high enough to escape the flood. The time is come to answer for your misdeeds. What secrecy you once held is laid bare. The girl is found and now resides with Malighaunt." Inganar glided over the corpses of the fallen.

Laustair winced but regained himself. "What girl?"

"Your deceits are no longer looked upon as honorable, Somath. You and our brothers have failed. We have seen to the others in Allevghaunt—those who believed your actions admirable. There are none left who support you. She told Malighaunt everything..."

"Who?" Laustair asked.

With slight irritation in his voice, Inganar rasped, "Your *daughter*." The word slid from his tongue as if it pained him. "Irymar. The abomination." Each syllable uttered in disgust.

"It seems I am not the only one who deceives," Laustair said. "Irymar is dead."

Inganar neared closer to Laustair and Dalnor, his yellow robes flowing across the blood-soaked ground before him. "Oh! But I do not deceive, Somath." His eyes flamed. "She is Valdryz...and so is her daughter." A breath away from them now, he lowered his voice and said, "Edlen Graymere." With that, he turned, his robes swirling around him, and vanished.

The towering walls of Leddenwell crashed to the ground. Smoke and ash erupted, covering the sky in billowing clouds of soot. None of the Akkuladine remained. Their master had called them back to some dark void from which they might again emerge to haunt the steps of man.

Darrin raised his head and gazed upon Laustair. But this was not the old man he'd traveled with. Gone were his gray robes and bent frame. The being who stood in the center of the field was a thing of extraordinary light and fairness. A thing that existed beyond thought and time, a vision man had no right to gaze upon.

Darrin looked at a God.

But though he knew he could not comprehend what he saw, a brief flash of understanding sprang to his mind, and he thought, if only for moment, that he recognized something in Somath's eyes as they stared at one another... Fear.

Twenty Years Prior

A THIN ARM ROBED in black silk stretched across the game board. Slender fingers lifted one of the pieces and moved it to an adjacent square. Once it had placed the expertly crafted figurine in the correct position, his deep voice said, "You failed to stop my soldier. Are you feeling well, my lord?"

Prince Nekkin Moorcroft, the eldest son of Lord Dysternis Moorcroft, scanned the game board. Of one-hundred-and-sixty pieces, only thirty remained. From where he sat in the center of the circular board, he had the perfect view of his movements.

How is this possible? He surveyed the board, marking each of his figurines.

The king sat exactly where he wished, guarded by four towers. His two remaining clerics patrolled the borders of his realms, and the queen moved comfortably between his remaining regiment of soldiers.

He glared up at Malighaunt. "You cheat!"

Malighaunt, his black robes draped over his lithe frame, smiled warmly. His dark eyes radiated like jet glinting in the sun. Long, black hair was tied into a braid that hung down his back and pulled slightly at the pale skin of his forehead. His smile lit a beautiful face that seemed to have seen only a few more summers than Nekkin. He seemed stunned by the accusation. "I do not cheat, my lord. You never garrisoned your eastern territories."

He pointed his finger to the left of where Prince Nekkin sat. "Your defenses are lacking there—my soldiers have merely exploited your neglect." His sneering grin split his face. "Perhaps you have dozed during my lectures on strategy?"

Nekkin slammed his king over and said, "The bloody east!"

He separated the table and stepped from within the ring of squares. Though nearing the age of twenty-three, he maintained the youthful appearance of his teenage years. His long, blonde hair cascaded over muscled shoulders, and his purple-yellow eyes flared in anger. "It is always the bloody east!"

His frustration turned to laughter. "I do not doze during your lectures, Malighaunt. But dear Gods! If you expect me to learn a thing, you might reconsider your lessons." He slapped his tutor on the back and smiled. His comely face was warm with reverence. "Who is it we are receiving today? A man from the Vines, is it not?"

Malighaunt lurched forward as the prince's hand slammed into his back. He straightened himself and glided across the icy floor. When he turned to answer Nekkin, his black robes slithered in clawing tendrils at his feet.

"He is a rather important man, my lord. It would be well that you treat him accordingly."

"They are all important men," said Nekkin. He grew tired of entertaining the various lords and ladies of the Shaded Realm, and though this man had sailed from the Vines, what was another groveler in a litany of flatterers?

"Is my father too busy to treat with this one as well?"

"On the contrary, my lord. Ichaem Leonardis does not wish to speak with King Dysternis." Malighaunt neared Nekkin, his robes reaching out, only barely avoiding contact with the prince's legs. "He comes a far distance to discuss a matter on which your insight is desired."

Leonardis? The name rang familiar, but he could not place it. "Where have I heard his name before, Malighaunt?"

A dark grin appeared on Malighaunt's face. "He killed your grandfather, my lord."

"I promise to deliver all of Onyris to you, my lord," said Ichaem Leonardis. He steepled his fingers under his fat chin, thin strands of gray hair slicked back over a head of near-complete baldness. But his face was stern, and his eyes keen.

"If only you would foster my dear son." His voice was honey poured over ice.

Nekkin glanced over at the boy and studied the child's face. A mop of red hair hung lazily over his eyes. The boy was thin and young, maybe ten years old. He watched him as he stared at the game board. The child did not take his eyes from it. "And why do you ask that my family foster your son?"

"He is not my blood, my lord, but yes, he is my son." Ichaem Leonardis turned his head and stared at the boy. "He is gifted, and I hope to one day see him a pedagogue."

"A pedagogue?" asked Nekkin, sneering. "This is a tall order, Master Leonardis. Am I to accept your offer of Onyris as payment alone?"

"It is not an offer, my lord. It is a promise." Ichaem Leonardis stood and walked over to his adopted son. He ruffled the boy's hair. "If you give me what I ask—" his voice lowered to a whisper—"I will hand you the throne of Rothspire."

"And how do you propose to do this?" Nekkin asked. "With this child?" He stepped from his chair and approached the boy. Kneeling, he looked him in the eyes. "What is your name?"

The boy took his gaze from the game board and stared up at Nekkin. "My name is Tomm, my lord. Tomm Harken." He glanced back at the game. "If the white king only moved his horse from the western province and placed it three squares down from his eastern tower then positioned a soldier at the southernmost spot here—" he pointed to a section of the board unmanned by any of Nekkin's pieces—"he might have forced the black king to send his troops over here."

Again, he motioned to an area of the game board that neither Nekkin nor Malighaunt occupied. "After that, the white king need only bring his tower to the black king's castle. It would not have been difficult." He looked up at Nekkin. "People rarely look within their own fortresses, but that is where the most damage often comes."

Author Biography

Daniel Thomas Valente was born into a family whose sense of humor and love for learning was only exceeded by their unceasing amount of patience. Growing up in Canoga Park, California in the 1980's, he fell in love with all the quintessential pop-culture of his time. As well versed in He-Man, Transformers, and Ghostbusters as he was with Mr. Belvedere, and Saved by the Bell, he soon found an almost infinite realm of worlds within the books that sat dog-eared on his father's bookshelf. Avoiding college after graduating from Canoga Park High School in the year 2000, he attempted to become a rock star. As a drummer in a band most famous for their use of Twinkies, he soon laid his drumsticks down and picked up a pen. Hundreds of thousands of words later, *The Sins of Kings* was written. Daniel enjoys cheap beer, classic rock, and warm summers. He currently lives in Frazier Park, California with his exceedingly patient wife, two amazing daughters, a German Shepherd, and two cats. You can most likely find him out in the garage working on his next masterpiece.

Printed in the USA
CPSIA information can be obtained
at www.ICGtesting.com
LVHW040420101023
760559LV00023B/89

9 798988 647515